The Distant Legacy

Legacy

BOOK 3 THE DISTANT SERIES

ANNEMARIE BREAR

ANNEMARIE BREAR

Contents

Chapter One

Berrima, NSW, Australia

February 1866

In the morning sun, Bridget Kittrick galloped through the brown grass edging the river, laughing. She looked back at her stepfather, Rafe Hamilton, and grinned before slowing down her horse, Ace, and whirling him round to wait for the man she called Papa.

Puffing, Rafe reined in his horse beside her. 'A fair win.'

'Ace will do it every time, Papa. I don't know why you dare to race me,' she said cheekily.

'Because I am a fool,' he replied, amusement in his eyes. 'Come along, we should be getting back. It's going to be another hot day. Besides, your mama will have the servants scurrying about, making everything perfect for your birthday.'

'I told her I didn't want a fuss.' Bridget shook her head wryly. 'I am twenty-one now, not ten. I do not need a birthday party every year. We can leave that to my younger siblings.'

'And you know she cannot help herself.' Rafe relaxed in the saddle as they rode side by side. 'Poverty in Ireland will forever haunt your mother. Ellen still believes she has to make it up to you older children for all you missed out on when you were younger.'

'County Mayo and the Great Hunger in Ireland was years ago. Mama needs to let it rest.'

'Easier said than done, dearest.' Rafe reached over and patted her arm. 'Let your mama have today. Both she and your aunt Riona enjoy their celebrations.'

'I will. After all, it is all for me!' She laughed. Despite her protest that she was too old to have birthday parties, Bridget enjoyed a good get-together. Mama said it was the Irish blood in her, for her ancestors had loved to sing and dance.

As they took a gentle walk away from the river and up the hill towards the homestead, Bridget reflected on the beauty of the house, which was situated on a flat-topped ridge overlooking the Wingecarribee River and hundreds of acres of prime grazing. She understood how privileged she was now, and how it was a world away from Ireland and their life there.

Her memories of their little cottage in Ireland were growing hazy now. She had no clear recollection of her birth father, Malachy Kittrick, who died in a drunken fight when she was six years old, leaving them even more destitute than they already were. Her mother couldn't pay the rent and the English landlord had their cottage burnt to the ground. They had been desperately poor, homeless and only through the aid of two decent Englishmen, Mr Wilton and Rafe Hamilton, had they managed to come to this new country and begin again.

Bridget was intensely proud of her mother, Ellen Kittrick-Emmerson-Hamilton. Three times married and mother to eight children, Ellen was a force to be reckoned with, and her fighting spirit ran through Bridget's veins. She knew her mother suffered greatly in Ireland, burying numerous family members, including Thomas, Bridget's brother. It was another tragic accident to persuade her mother to emigrate to the other side of the world, a decision which Ellen's sister Riona didn't agree with but who came with her anyway to help look after the children and escape a life of drudgery. Bridget's grandmother also made the journey, but she died on the ship. Such sadness, such hardship, yet Ellen Kittrick made it through, determined as ever to give her children a better life.

'Here come your brothers.' Papa pointed to the twin boys running down the hill to meet them. At nearly eleven years old, they were the double of each other and Rafe.

Panting, the boys ran up to them. 'You're to come home and change, Mama says,' Ronan told them.

'Mama is hopping mad that you're late,' Aidan added.

'Then we best hurry!' Bridget, loving her twin brothers fiercely, urged Ace on as the boys whooped and hollered back up the hill.

At the stables, she sent the boys inside the house to tell Mama she'd be quick.

'Leave that, miss,' said Douglas, the groom, coming to take Ace's bridle.

'Thank you, Douglas. Papa is not far behind.'

'And happy birthday, miss.' He gave her a cheeky grin, allowed from a servant who'd been with the family for fifteen years.

She smiled warmly at the man who'd been her friend since she was a child, the man who had expanded on her training to ride as though she was one with the horse and how to drive a horse and buggy. 'There will be food and drink for the staff. Make sure you get some.'

'As if I'd ever miss out? Moira sees that I never starve,' he joked.

Hurrying across the service areas, past the outbuildings containing the laundry, dairy, stores, Bridget entered the largest service area, the kitchen, which was attached to the main house via a covered corridor. The kitchen was Moira's domain, a fellow Irish woman who'd they'd met on the ship. Moira had married Ellen's overseer, Mr Thwaite, and Bridget loved her like an aunty.

'There you are, girl.' Moira tutted, spooning dollops of cream into glass bowls. 'Ellen has been in and out of here looking for you and getting in my way, so she does.' Her lilting words had no sting in them for she loved the family, especially Ellen, fiercely. 'The guests will be arriving in a couple of hours, so they will, and look at you, not even bathed and dressed.'

'I have time.' Bridget selected a date scone and quickly stuck it under the dollop of cream Moira was about to spoon into a bowl. 'I'm so hungry.'

'Whist, girl. You're always hungry,' Moira said, but laughter lurked in her eyes, for she was never happier than when feeding the family.

Bridget propped her bottom on the edge of the large table, eyeing the legs of lamb basting on the spit over the fire, the trays of potatoes and other vegetables the kitchen maids were peeling ready to be roasted later. The kitchen smelled divine. Two maids from the village were arranging salads onto platters. 'Where's Mrs Duffy?'

'She has one of her headaches,' Moira puffed. 'She usually does when there is work to be done.'

Bridget grinned and poured herself a glass of lemon cordial. The Duffy family had also been fellow travellers with them on the ship. Mrs Duffy, a strict Catholic, ruled her husband, Seamus, and two daughters, Caroline and Aisling, with an iron rod. She'd not wanted to leave Ireland, but again, poverty sent them seeking a new life. Mrs Duffy found it difficult to work for a family who were once as poor as she was, but Seamus enjoyed being a labourer on the estate. Caroline had become a companion for Mrs

Ratcliffe, while Aisling had married young, to another Irish Catholic, and moved away. Many said to escape her mother.

'You'll be dancing tonight?' Bridget asked Moira.

'I'm too old for dancing.'

'Nonsense. You don't stop dancing until you're in your coffin.'

Moira quickly made a sign of the cross. 'Mother Mary, get away to your room before your mammy comes.'

At that moment the door opened, and Ellen sailed into the kitchen wearing a magnificent dress of silver with white lace edging. Last month Ellen had celebrated her forty-third birthday, and despite everything she'd been through, she still looked half her age, with sharp blue eyes like Bridget and flawless skin.

'Sweet Jesus, Bridget. Have you seen the time? Go and bathe!' Ellen said, observing the kitchen maids as they performed their tasks.

Popping down from the table, she stepped to her mother and kissed her cheek. 'You look splendid, Mama.'

Love entered Ellen's eyes. 'Yes?'

Bridget nodded. 'You always do.' She enjoyed the fact that out of her and her two sisters, Lily and Ava, she resembled her beautiful mother the most. Lily was dainty like their mother, but she had the look of Rafe, whereas Ava was blonde and the image of her late father, Alistair Emmerson, Mama's second husband.

Although Lily had been born while Mama was married to Alistair, Mama had confessed to the family a few years ago that Lily was, in fact, Rafe's daughter. Thankfully, Lily had taken it in her stride since she'd only been a baby when Alistair died and knew only Rafe as a father. Mama had loved Rafe since first meeting him in Ireland before she emigrated, but on arriving in Sydney she had married the wealthy Alistair Emmerson to give her family stability and security. Ellen's need to escape the clutches of poverty influenced her decision to marry a man she didn't love, but who she admired and who would give her protection from poverty.

Entering her bedroom, Bridget began unbuttoning her blue riding habit bodice as the lady's maid, Una, who she shared with her sisters, added another jug of hot water to the bath.

'It's ready for you, miss.'

Bridget eyed the cloudy water. 'Have my sisters bathed before me?'

'Aye, miss. The mistress said they must not wait as you were late returning from your ride.'

'Did they use my soap? My special soap Austin bought me?'

'No, miss. I hid that in your top drawer.'

'You are good, Una. I would be unhappy if they had used it. My brother's Christmas present was the best he's ever bought me.' Naked, Bridget stepped into the bath and relaxed in the warm, scented water.

Una brought the rose-scented soap from the drawer and gave it to her. 'You've still got plenty left. The second cake is hidden at the back of the drawer, too.'

'With my sisters around, I have to hide everything. Ava was wearing my straw bonnet yesterday, the one with the red flowers. She knows it's my favourite and when I got it back, a flower had fallen off.'

'I'll sew it back on this evening, miss,' Una soothed. 'Your dress is pressed and ready.' Una admired the gown hanging on the outside of the wardrobe.

Bridget gazed at the rose-coloured silk gown with its inches of white embroidery and small white bows at the sleeves. 'It's the finest dress I've owned, aside from my coming out dress. Papa spotted the bolt of silk in one of his shipments from China and knew I'd like to have a dress made from it for my special birthday.'

'It's very pretty,' Una agreed, looking doubtful.

'What is it?'

'Well, you have a tendency to ruin your dresses. You go to the stables wearing them, or suddenly decide to collect vegetables, or walk through the mud with your brothers, or help one of the cows give birth...'

Bridget laughed loudly. 'You must despair of me!' For it was all true, as much as she liked pretty dresses, she was also very much one of the boys sometimes and didn't mind getting dirty.

'You'll have to stop all that when you're married, miss.'

'Married?' She jerked around to stare at her maid. 'I have no wish to marry for years yet. I'll not be stuck with having a baby every year while my husband does as he pleases! That's not for me. I intend to have some fun before that happens.'

'What of all the beaus who are coming to your party? Mr Porter thinks highly of you and then there are the Throsby gentlemen, the Atkinsons, and Samuel Smith, who sent you flowers last week.'

'None of them are enough to make me give up my freedom for.' Bridget leaned forward as Una poured another jug of warm water over her. 'The man I marry will be brilliant at everything.'

Una giggled. 'There's no such man, miss.'

'Well, at least he has to adore me but also realise I have a brain, like Papa does with Mama. They are partners in everything.'

'Aye, but men like Mr Hamilton are few and far between, miss.'

A sharp knock and then the door opened, and Mama walked in. 'Oh good, you're bathing. I have your father getting ready and then we can all gather in the drawing room before the guests arrive.'

'Is Austin here yet?'

Mama inspected Bridget's dress. 'No. Let us hope he hasn't been held up on the road. Higgins has taken the carriage to meet him at the train station at Picton.'

'They still have to travel by road through the Bargo Brush. Reports of bushrangers holding up carriages have been rampant lately,' Bridget said as Una washed her hair.

Una shivered and gulped loudly.

'We shan't think of that,' Mama said tersely.

'It's all anyone can think about,' Bridget murmured. The daring escapades of bushrangers were regular newspaper fodder. It seemed every month there was another outlaw holding up innocent people, demanding their money and goods. Only in recent years, the number of robberies were escalating and happening in areas previously untouched by the villains.

The door burst open, and her two younger sisters clambered into the room. Lily aged thirteen and Ava aged twelve were a pair of giggling girls, with heads full of silly secrets and ringlets, opposite in looks but so alike in mannerisms they could be twins like Ronan and Aidan.

'Can I not have privacy in my own room?' Bridget demanded, reaching for a towel as she stepped from the bath. 'Why are you not with Miss Lewis?' She spoke of the girls' governess, who used to be her own.

'Miss Lewis is getting dressed for the party,' Lily said.

'Out girls, leave Bridget in peace. Go and play the piano until our guests arrive.' Mama ushered them out and followed them, pausing at the door. 'Come into the drawing room when you're ready. Your papa has a gift for you.'

'But I opened my presents this morning at breakfast.'

'Indeed, but Rafe spoils you, and has one more.' Mama rolled her eyes, but everyone knew how much she adored her husband and would never accept he did anything wrong.

By the time Bridget entered the drawing room, the whole family were waiting, except Austin, who'd still not arrived from Sydney where he lived in the family's grand house on the harbour that Mama and Papa bought when they married.

Patrick, her second oldest brother, the quiet one in the family, sidled up to her and handed her a glass of fruit punch. 'Are you ready for this evening?'

'I am looking forward to it. Are you?'

He grunted. Tall and auburn-haired, which he'd inherited from Mama's side of the family, Patrick was the least demanding out of them all. 'A night of dodging hopeful girls wanting to dance, making polite talk, and trying to be interested in other people's boring stories? What do you think?'

Bridget laughed. 'One day you will actually talk to a girl and fall deep in love with her.'

'I very much doubt it. None I have met in our social circle have a sensible thought in their heads.'

'Because they are not interested in sheep or cattle?'

'What is wrong with that?' Patrick scowled. '*You* understand about those things.'

Bridget shook her head at him. 'That is because I am interested in farming but look at Lily and Ava, neither of them care a jot about the estates.'

'They are only young girls. They will in time.'

'I doubt it.' Bridget was sceptical. Her sisters weren't great riders, no matter how hard she tried to teach them, and that alone was a failing in her eyes. She loved them dearly, but they didn't seem to have her strength of will, or her boldness, as Aunt Riona often said, and Mama would add that having one Bridget in the family was more than enough.

Inwardly, this made Bridget smile. She was glad she made people sit up and notice. She never would be considered a wall flower.

'There is a carriage coming,' Lily announced, looking through the French doors.

Rafe sighed. 'I had wanted to give a little speech before everyone arrived. Is it Austin?'

'No, it's Mrs Ratcliffe,' Patrick said as they all glanced at the older woman descending the carriage and after her came Caroline Duffy.

Bridget watched Patrick, who stared at Caroline Duffy. She felt sorry for Patrick for he'd always had a soft spot in his heart for Caroline, but sadly the eldest Duffy girl only had eyes for Austin, not that Austin realised. Bridget sometimes wondered if she was the only one who knew.

Greetings were made and a comfortable chair found for Mrs Harriet Ratcliffe, who was getting on in age and wasn't the smallest of women. Her heavy weight often left her short of breath. 'I realise I am early, but I also know you would not mind,' Mrs Ratcliffe panted, accepting a kiss of greeting from Ellen. 'I felt there was no need sitting around once Caroline and I were ready.'

'Of course, we don't mind,' Ellen replied. 'We've been friends for so long, you're a member of this family.'

Caroline Duffy, pretty and slender, stood behind her employer, smiling at the family she'd known for years. Her dress, simply made of white and blue blossom with a matching dainty hat, suited her.

'Do you wish to go and see your mother, Caroline?' Mrs Ratcliffe asked, taking a seat on the sofa.

'I will soon, yes.' Caroline looked about the room. 'Is Austin not here?'

'Hopefully, he will arrive shortly,' Aunt Riona told her.

Rafe held up his hands. 'Now, if I can have your attention. I will make my announcement as Austin is already aware of it, and Mrs Ratcliffe is a long-standing friend who already knows all this family's business!' Rafe laughed as did everyone else.

'Indeed, it is true,' Mrs Ratcliffe admitted, smiling fondly at Ellen, who, in respect of their friendship, had asked Mrs Ratcliffe to be the twins' sponsor when they were born, an honour she gladly accepted.

Rafe continued. 'Today, on Bridget's special birthday, I have some news that affects her and also Patrick. I have recently received some information which, although is sad and tragic, it comes with a token of good fortune.'

Surprised, Bridget glanced at Patrick, but he shrugged his shoulders equally in the dark about it.

Rafe took Ellen's hand. 'My old friend and business associate, Mr Wilton of Louisburgh, County Mayo, died recently.'

'I remember him.' Patrick nodded. 'Mam worked at his manor before we left Ireland.' Patrick was the only one who still called Ellen the Irish Mammy, instead of Mama as Alistair Emmerson had taught them to do on his marriage to their mother. Patrick had flatly refused. Mammy would always be Mammy to him, for he wasn't ashamed of being Irish even if Austin was. Bridget, being so much younger when Alistair was her stepfather, had simply followed his instruction to speak properly.

'That's true,' Mama agreed. 'He was a good and kind man who helped us flee to England, and then to Australia, with Rafe's help.'

'He was indeed a very good man, and a valued friend,' Rafe said softly. 'He felt the same in regards to me, for in his will he left his manor and estate to me. He had no family.'

'Wilton Manor is yours, Rafe?' Patrick asked incredibly.

'It is, and as such, we, your mama and I, have decided to give it to you, Patrick, and you, Bridget. It is Irish property, and you are Irish born from the same area. The manor and the estate are yours to do with as you wish.'

Bridget's mouth gaped open. 'Really, Papa?'

Rafe smiled. 'Yes, really. You and Patrick can discuss what you wish to do with it.'

'I don't know what to say.'

'That will be a first,' Aunt Riona joked.

Patrick crossed the room and shook his stepfather's hand. 'Thank you, Rafe. That is kind and generous.'

Rafe grinned. 'As your stepfather, it is my duty to help provide for you, but it has always been my pleasure, too.'

'All of us are very fortunate to have you as our father.'

'I believed it only right,' Rafe answered. 'Though your mama took some convincing.'

'Only because I do not want Patrick and Bridget to leave for Ireland to claim this property,' Ellen said stubbornly. 'Australia is our home.'

Patrick kissed his mother's cheek. 'I'm honoured you would do such a thing for me. But return to Ireland?' Patrick rubbed his chin in thought. 'I never considered it.'

Bridget saw the worry in her mother's eyes and knew how devastated she would be if two of her children went to live on the other side of the world. It was bad enough when Austin spent years in England being educated. 'Do not stress yourself, Mama. This is our home, not Ireland. We have no wish to leave, do we, Patrick?'

'No, this country is home.'

'Are we all going to Ireland?' Ronan asked, confused.

'No.' Ellen embraced him. 'You two are heading for boarding school next year in Parramatta.'

'Carriages are arriving, Mama,' Ava said excitedly.

Aunt Riona stood and gazed out of the open French doors. 'It's Father Lanigan. I am so happy he came. He's such a busy man.'

Mrs Ratcliffe sniffed at the mention of the Irish priest. 'Probably he felt he should, after all the money you donate to his church, Riona.'

'He is a well-respected man of the cloth, Mrs Ratcliffe,' Aunt Riona defended. 'He brings such comfort to those of the true faith.'

'Riona,' Ellen warned. 'Not today, please.' The whole family knew of Aunt Riona's strong Catholic views, which grew more intense the older she became, unlike Ellen, who'd denounced her Catholic religion on marrying Alistair Emmerson, much to her sister's horror.

Bridget smoothed her skirts, trying to gather her thoughts before their guests descended on them. She owned property. She would have money in her own right. The thought was exceedingly heady.

Papa frowned slightly. 'We shall continue the discussion on the Wilton estate tomorrow.'

'Yes.' Ellen looked with relief at Bridget. 'Shall we go out and welcome our guests, Bridget?'

'Coming, Mama.'

Hours later, strolling through the beautiful gardens her mother had established over the last twelve years, Bridget gazed at the golden sunset. The party was in full flow. Music played from the quartet, platters of food were spread over the tables and drink flowed from the barrels and jugs. Guests mingled, children ran about playing, and the delicious smell of a roasting pig on the spit near the kitchen filled the air, but the last few hours had been difficult for Bridget to enjoy as the news whirled in her head that she was part owner of Wilton Manor. She had never expected such a thing to happen.

'There you are.' Mama rounded the path through the rose garden, the flowers of which splashed a kaleidoscope of colour as pretty as the summer dresses the women wore.

'Were you looking for me?'

'Yes, I couldn't find you. I noticed you've been rather quiet during the party and was worried because you enjoy a good gathering, especially when it's a celebration for you.'

'I have been mixing with our friends and making sure they had enough to eat and drink. But I just needed a moment to be alone. Talking for hours is exhausting.'

'It's never bothered you before.' Mama peered at her, then took her arm and they continued to stroll. 'I feel the news of the manor has shocked you.'

'How could it not?'

'Patrick told me a few moments ago that he definitely has no wish to live in Ireland. Do you?'

'None at all.' Her memories of Ireland were of being hungry, cold and then frightened as they fled their burning cottage in the middle of the night. She remembered a few good times, of running on the beach chasing after her brothers, collecting seaweed to boil up and eat and of sitting on her grandmother's lap, listening to her sing.

'I am relieved to hear it.' Mama's shoulders relaxed.

'This country is where we belong,' Bridget repeated her words from earlier.

'Then you are happy for Rafe to sell the estate on your behalf and you, and Patrick, will share in the profit?'

'Of course. However, why is Austin not included? He was born in Ireland, too, and would probably remember Mr Wilton better than either me or Patrick.'

'Austin is set to receive some inheritance from Alistair's parents when they die. He stayed with the Emmersons a great deal while he lived in England, as well as Rafe's family. Both treated him like a grandson, and he split his holidays between the two families, as you know. The Emmersons have already written to me and stated that Austin, Lily and Ava will share in their will. So, we felt that it was only right you and Patrick have this good fortune.'

'But Lily isn't an Emmerson.'

'They were never told that, and they love her as a granddaughter,' Mama admitted. 'Alistair died before any damage could be done in that regard. Lily knows the truth, the immediate family knows the truth about her true parentage and that is enough.' Mama walked on for a moment, lost in her own memories. 'Rafe and I have been discussing at length about the future, once we have gone, that is.'

Bridget lifted her eyebrows. 'Mama, this is a morbid subject to talk about at my birthday party.'

'It is, but nevertheless, I feel it is important to speak of it now. Rafe and I have built up a large portfolio of properties, and we aren't stopping yet. You all will be taken care of handsomely.'

'We know that.'

Mama stopped to sniff a rose as laughter and chatter carried across the lawns to them. 'You know my heart is at Louisburgh?' She spoke of the country estate near Goulburn, forty-five miles south of Berrima, that she had bought after marrying Alistair. It was the one place Mama felt was fully her home. She had bought the sheep farm when it was nothing more than a hut and fields of dirt. Over the years she had improved the soil, grown imported English grass seed for the flocks to graze on, expanded the flow of the creek bed, and built a good size house. Ellen had also named the property after her birthplace in Ireland.

'Yes, we all know Louisburgh is your favourite home.'

'Eventually, the railway will reach Goulburn, but it is bypassing Berrima. Already the workers are creating the railroad towards Mittagong, Bong Bong and Moss Vale. Berrima will be left behind and without a railway, it won't be the central place of business.'

'Yes, Papa mentioned it before.'

'Which is why I want to buy more land around Goulburn, sheep grazing land. This country's population will only keep growing, and they need food.' Mama paused. 'You need to be hungry, too, Bridget, hungry for land. You will have the money to purchase. Don't waste it on harbourside mansions, not yet. I want you to stand on land that is yours as far as the eye can see.'

Bridget had grown up aware of her Mama's passion for land, which for her meant security. 'I want land, too.' She heard their names being called, but Mama held her back, an intense expression on her face.

'You understand this estate by rights belongs to Ava. It was her father's country residence, and she will inherit it.'

'We all know that.' As much as Bridget loved Emmerson Park, the whole family knew it would belong to Ava one day.

'Austin has his sights set on the harbour house,' Mama continued. 'He prefers being in Sydney than out in the country. We feel that Austin should inherit the Sydney house, and our other properties will go to Lily and the twins.'

'And now Patrick and I have the estate in Ireland,' she finished for her. 'Or the money from it.'

'Plus, other things as time goes on.' Mama took a deep breath. 'But I want *you* to have Louisburgh and we will leave another property to Patrick, probably the farm in Kangaroo Valley.'

'Louisburgh?' Bridget gaped at her mother. 'I am to *inherit* Louisburgh?'

'You know it is the one place I adore above all the others, and I see you love the place as much as I do.' In truth, her mother spent all her time at Louisburgh, only coming to Berrima occasionally, and Sydney even less.

Mama glanced at Rafe, who was making his way towards them. 'I will have a document drawn up stating that Louisburgh is in trust for you and your children, *not* your husband. Do you understand? Whomever you marry will not own Louisburgh.'

Bridget nodded, aware of her mother's steely tone. Ellen Kittrick-Emmerson-Hamilton was a strong woman of strong convictions, who believed in working hard and buying land for security. Her years of suffering poverty in Ireland and being thrown off the little farm she tried so hard to save had changed her. Her main goal in life was to see that her children would never suffer the same fate, that they would stay in control of their futures.

Taking a deep breath, Mama took Bridget's hand. 'The money from the Wilton estate sale will make you a wealthy woman, my darling, and many a man will come sniffing around you, declaring his love. Some will be true, while others will only want your money. You must let them know at once that Louisburgh is held in trust for your children and will not become your husband's property on your marriage. Any other property you purchase is yours to do with as you wish, but I beg of you to never rely on a man.'

Bridget bristled slightly. 'Do you believe I cannot make a decent choice of husband?'

'Dearest, we can all be fools when it comes to the opposite sex. Remember that. I married your father when I was a silly girl of sixteen, then I married Alistair for security, only to find on his death we were nearly bankrupt. Rafe is the only man I have been able to trust. With him I have I found a deep and satisfying love. There is so much pressure on women to marry and produce children, to run a home and be a good wife. That pressure can sometimes lead to bad choices.'

'When I marry, the gentleman I choose will be good and decent,' Bridget declared.

Mama smiled. 'I have no doubt about it, my darling. I simply ask that you take your time and choose wisely. Marry a man who will understand your character and who loves you not for what you bring to the marriage in regards to money and property, but who *you* are. Take the time to learn about each other before you make a lifelong decision.'

'You make it sound such a difficult task, Mama.' Bridget laughed. She fully believed that Mama was being over-protective for no reason. Bridget knew her own mind, and no man would play her for a fool.

'Oh, my sweet girl, it is!' Mama turned as their own carriage came down the drive and Rafe stopped to welcome it. 'Ah, Austin, finally. We will talk more about this later.'

Bridget followed her back towards the house, her mind filling with ideas about the future now she would have money of her own, and none of them included getting married just yet.

They stood by the drive as others gathered to welcome Austin home. He'd not seen most of his family since Christmas. Only Rafe went to Sydney regularly for business.

'Mama!' Austin hugged his mother warmly and shook hands with Rafe, 'Papa,' before being surrounded by his brothers and sisters. Finally, he turned back to the carriage and held out his hand to assist a young woman down.

Bridget frowned, wondering who the well-dressed and pretty woman was, then she noticed Caroline Duffy's face alter from happiness to wariness.

'Mama, Papa, everyone,' Austin said, his handsome face breaking into a wide grin. 'This is Miss Marina Norton and her companion, Mrs Sybil Warren.' He paused as a tall gentleman dressed in dark grey exited the carriage last. 'And this is my friend, Mr Lincoln Huntley. They are my guests. Forgive me for not sending word ahead, Mama, but it was all very suddenly done.'

'Pleased to meet you, Miss Norton, Mrs Warren and Mr Huntley.' Mama shook their hands. 'Come inside. You must be weary after a long journey.'

Much fuss was made of Austin by the family's friends, and the party continued, though Bridget sensed Mama's unease. For Austin to bring strangers to a family celebration without any warning was highly irregular.

'Who is she?' Caroline asked Bridget, with a nod to Miss Norton. They were in the drawing room, drinking rum punch in small glasses.

'I have no idea. None of us have heard of her before.' Bridget didn't have much interest in Miss Norton, for she found it difficult to drag her gaze from Mr Huntley. He was older than Austin and carried an air about him of an easy manner and a quick smile, but she noticed he was taking everything in and spoke only when spoken to. Mr Huntley wasn't a classically handsome man. His nose had a small bump on it as though it had been broken at some stage, but he had something about him, an intriguing presence that captivated Bridget.

'Then why would Austin invite Miss Norton and the others here for your birthday?' Caroline muttered.

'Everyone is welcome, you know that. Mama never turns anyone away.' Bridget glanced at Caroline, seeing the dejection in her friend's manner. 'I am sure we will soon find out.'

'Heavens, he is bringing them over.' Caroline stepped behind Bridget as though to hide.

'Sister, happy birthday.' Austin embraced Bridget warmly. 'I have brought you a present. It's in my trunk.'

'That is kind of you, brother.'

'And these are my friends, Miss Norton and Mr Huntley.'

Bridget shook hands with them both, but it was Mr Huntley who drew her gaze. His eyes were the blue of the cornflowers in her mama's garden, and they were smiling at her as though they were already the best of friends. A fizz of awareness bubbled through her body, and she raised her chin, instinctively knowing this man would affect her life.

Chapter Two

'I am very pleased to meet you, Miss Kittrick,' Miss Norton gushed. 'Your brother speaks so highly of you.'

'Does he?' She raised her eyebrows at Austin, though completely aware of Mr Huntley watching her. It didn't go unnoticed by her that Miss Norton hardly took her eyes off Austin. They were clearly well acquainted. Bridget grabbed Caroline's hand and thrust her forward. 'Caroline is here.'

'Indeed, why would she not be?' Austin said with kindness, gently taking Caroline's hand and kissing her cheek. 'You are like another sister, are you not?'

'How are you, Austin?' Caroline asked, her smile strained.

'Very well. No doubt your parents are nearby, and I shall speak with them shortly, but what of Aisling? Is she well? And still in Braidwood?'

'Yes, and about to have her second baby.'

'Dear Lord. Amazing. We are not children any longer, are we?'

'No.' Caroline lowered her gaze. 'Time goes by so quickly, yet sometimes so very slowly.'

'And how did you and Miss Norton meet, Austin, and Mr Huntley, of course?' Bridget asked brightly, aware of Caroline's discomfort.

'Sydney society can be rather small sometimes.' Austin chuckled. 'Miss Norton's father and I have done business together, and I have dined at your family home several times, have I not, Miss Norton?'

'Yes, several times,' Miss Norton repeated. 'And Mr Huntley was there one time, and everyone was introduced. We have all become great friends since then.' She laughed delicately.

'Sadly, Miss Norton's mother passed away last year, and her father is at a loss about how to keep his daughter entertained,' Austin added.

'He is not one for society, you see,' Miss Norton said quietly.

'When I mentioned I was coming home to the country for a party, he begged me to invite Miss Norton along and show her some of this part of the country.'

Miss Norton looked with adoration at Austin. 'Mr Kittrick was so very kind. I have not been out this far, you see. In fact, I have not been past Campbelltown!'

'You will find this area very different to Sydney, Miss Norton,' Bridget told her. 'We are of a higher altitude, giving us four perfectly good seasons, which is excellent for farming.'

'I heard it can snow here?' Mr Huntley enquired, his focus on Bridget. 'As it does in Tasmania.'

'Yes, that is true,' she answered him. 'Not every year, but it can be cold enough to freeze the water in the troughs.'

'Are you from Tasmania, sir?' Caroline asked.

'I am. I was born in Hobart. My father was in a Scottish Highland regiment serving there and when they recalled the regiment home to Scotland, he resigned and he and mother stayed, having settled in Hobart.'

'So, you are Scottish?' Bridget asked him.

'It would seem I am Tasmanian. My father was Scottish, my mother English.'

Austin held out his elbow for Miss Norton. 'Shall I introduce you to more people? Lincoln?' He led Miss Norton away.

Mr Huntley lingered a moment. 'Perhaps we can discuss this area later, Miss Kittrick? I am most interested to explore it. Austin says it is quite beautiful.'

'Absolutely, Mr Huntley. I would like that, and for once Austin is correct. We live in a beautiful part of the country.'

'Perhaps you will be my guide while I'm here?' His blue eyes darkened to violet. 'If that is convenient?'

A shiver ran over Bridget's skin as she gazed at him. 'I am certain I can show you some of the district's attractions. Can you ride?'

'I can.'

'Then you must borrow a mount from our stables, and we shall visit a great many places.'

'I look forward to it. And maybe a dance this evening? Austin tells me your family parties go on into the small hours.' His low voice was soft as velvet.

'They do indeed,' she said proudly. 'We are Irish, after all.'

He gave a wry grin and then a small bow before walking away.

Bridget took a steadying breath.

'Gracious, he is... impressive,' Caroline whispered. 'His eyes... Beautiful for a man.'

'How pleasant it is to meet someone new,' Bridget murmured, excited for the evening to come and the promised dance, but also for the upcoming rides with Mr Huntley.

'True, though Miss Norton seems a little nervy, don't you agree? Not someone I would have thought Austin would be attracted to.' Caroline watched Austin and Miss Norton where they stood on the far side of the room chatting to Aunt Riona and Mrs Riddle, and other guests.

Grasping Caroline's hand, Bridget gave it a gentle squeeze. 'Over the last couple of years since Austin returned from England, he's been so busy learning the ways of Papa's businesses that he's not been interested in finding a wife, but now he is settled into the running of the companies, perhaps he senses the time has come to start looking.' She brought Caroline's hand up to hold it with both hands. 'Dearest, don't let him overlook you!'

Caroline blushed. 'I'm not worthy of Austin. He's educated, worldly now. One time it might have been something I could expect, but not since he was sent to England to be educated. Austin is no longer in the same class as me. He has risen above me. Who am I but an Irish labourer's daughter?'

'Don't forget Austin, Patrick and I are Kittricks. Children of an Irish labourer, too. We are the same as you.'

'Once, maybe, but not any longer. The moment your mammy married Mr Emmerson, you all grew in stature and importance. Your mammy, for instance, single-handedly took over running Mr Emmerson's business interests when he died. She drove her family from poverty to wealth. Then when she married Mr Hamilton, your family grew even wealthier. You are a prominent family, not only in this area but in Sydney as well.' Caroline shook her head. 'We Duffys will never rise. My da is a labourer on this property, my mammy works in the kitchen. Why would Austin ever look at me? Excuse me.' She gave a small smile and quickly walked back to stand with Mrs Ratcliffe.

Poor Caroline. Nothing Bridget said would ease her sadness of loving a man who didn't love her in return.

Bridget turned as Patrick came to stand beside her, eating cake. Suddenly hungry, she stole the rest that was on his plate.

'You are a nuisance.' He shook his head. 'I was enjoying that.'

'What do you assume of Austin's lady?'

'Is she, his lady?' Patrick shrugged. 'And does it matter?'

'It does if he marries her, and she becomes a member of this family.'

'Then perhaps we should get to know her?' He dabbed his mouth with a napkin.

'Do you consider that she suits him?'

'How should I know? I have barely said two words to her. Austin doesn't confide in me. I'm as surprised as you that he brought guests, but our brother mixes in different circles to us, doesn't he? He is a city man, and I am a country man.' Patrick glanced at her. 'What's wrong?'

'I just have the sense of everything is changing or going to change.'

'What's wrong with that?'

'Because we are all so happy right at this moment.'

'Change doesn't have to be a bad thing.'

'Papa will go to Ireland to sort out Mr Wilton's estate for us, you understand that, don't you?'

Patrick frowned in thought. 'Yes, and I feel guilty for not wanting to go with Rafe when he has been so generous.'

'If Papa goes to Ireland, Mama will go with him. She will not want him to be away from her for a year, for that's how long it will take with all the travelling.'

'I hadn't thought of that.'

'And if Mama goes, she will take Lily, Ava and the boys with her.'

'You suppose so?'

Bridget nodded. 'Without a doubt. Mama won't spend a year away from them either.'

'So, it would be just us two left here?'

'With Aunt Riona.' She glanced at him, making a decision. 'I will go to Louisburgh.'

'Oh charming, you're abandoning me too?' He grinned.

'You'll have Aunt Riona. Someone will need to look after this place.'

Patrick gazed down at his feet. 'I have plans of my own you know.'

'You do?' Intrigued, Bridget was all ears.

'The opening up of the Yarrawa Brush, east of Bong Bong, is gathering pace. Land lots are selling, the wilderness is being tamed. The government wants people to cultivate the area.'

'It's nothing but swamp and thick bush. No one will want to live there. There are no roads or shops. The minute it rains the track to Yarrawa is unpassable. Why would anyone want to have land there?'

'Because it does have good rainfall being on the edge of the mountain escarpment. Just about anything grows there, potatoes, turnips and so forth. The government is improving the track down to the coast all the time. From the coast it's only a day's boat ride up to Sydney and the markets there.'

'Are you saying the land there is worth buying, despite it being all swamp?'

'It's not all swamp.' His tone held a frustrated note. 'Last week I rode over a good part of it with Ogilvy.' He spoke of his good friend, George Ogilvy. 'Now I will have some money of my own, I want to buy land, run a farm, build a house.'

'Mama says you'll inherit the Kangaroo Valley farm.'

'And that is generous, but I don't want to wait for an inheritance. I want to begin building my own property.'

'As I do.'

He stared at her in surprise. 'Really?'

'I'll not wait for a husband to have a home of my own. There is land for sale south of Goulburn, Mama mentioned it last week. I want it... The idea of having my own estate is very appealing.' Since her conversation with Mama, the notion of being her own woman, just as Mama had been, grew more attractive.

'You are much like Mammy,' Patrick murmured. 'Independent.'

'What is wrong with that?'

'Because you'll not be satisfied to simply be a wife and mother. You'll want it all, as Mammy does.' He took two glasses of wine from a passing maid and gave one to her.

Bridget frowned. 'And why shouldn't I?'

'Because it's not normal.'

A wave of anger flowed over her at his words. 'Not normal?'

'Don't be getting all irate at me.' Patrick raised his hands in surrender. 'I simply meant that most women are happy to be a wife and mother and let their husbands see to the money side of things. A man should be the boss of his own household.'

'You should know by now, brother dear, that like Mama, I am not like most women.'

'True. Well, anyway, whatever the future brings, we should raise a toast to good old Mr Wilton. He has changed our lives.' Patrick held up his glass. 'To Mr Wilton.'

'To Mr Wilton.' Bridget raised her glass as well. 'How amazing it must be to know you have changed someone's life.'

'He's dead. He has no notion you and I will benefit from his estate,' Patrick said.

'True, but *we* know it. I would like to help others.'

'Aren't you on different charity committees in the village with Mama and Aunt Riona?'

'Yes, but that's not enough.'

'You want to change lives?' Patrick looked doubtful. 'How will you do that?'

Her thoughts began to swirl, and excitement grew. 'I'm not sure, open a school, employ people on my estate, make their lives better... I don't have the answers yet, but I will, somehow. However, first, I shall enjoy this party.'

'I'm not dancing with you,' he warned as though reading her mind.

'Yes, you are!' She grinned and took his glass and placed it and hers on the little table behind them. She grabbed his arms and dragged him outside where on the lawn lanterns were being lit as the sun slid behind the trees. The quartet who'd played gentle music all afternoon were replaced with an Irish folk band made up of men from the village and some of the estate's workers. The air filled with the sounds of two fiddlers, a man playing the bagpipes, another with a tin whistle and an older man who played a bodhran, a handheld drum. Their enthusiasm brought a smile to everyone's face.

Patrick laughed, swirling Bridget around on the temporary wooden dance floor. She let go of him to clap as others joined them, and then she was swung around by Patrick again. Rafe took over next, dancing and turning her around in time to the music. She grinned as Patrick whirled Mama past with a shout.

Soon the whole dance area was filled with guests dancing. The band played faster, Bridget's feet moved quicker, her skirts flew out behind her, and she threw her head back, laughing at the sheer joy of dancing.

To give the guests a chance to catch their breath. The estate's labourers' children lined up and performed an Irish dance. The guests clapped as the children weaved in and out of each other, their bodies straight, their feet tapping rhythmically.

'You always cry, Aunt,' Bridget soothed Aunt Riona who cried at the sight.

'It just reminds me of when Ellen and I used to dance like this as children. Mammy taught us, and Da would sing... He had such a brilliant voice did Da.' She wiped her eyes.

Bridget embraced her, knowing how much her grandparents were missed by her aunt and mother.

Wine, rum and beer flowed as the night grew long. Millions of stars twinkled in the vast blackness above their heads, but the guests were too busy enjoying themselves to stop and gaze upwards.

'A dance, Miss Kittrick?' Mr Huntley asked, coming beside Bridget as she stood with friends, catching her breath.

With a grin, she held out her hand. A shiver of excitement heightened her senses as he led her onto the wooden floor. The band paused then began to play a softer melody. Unprepared for a gentler dance, Bridget stared at Mr Huntley as he gathered her in closer. The material of his jacket was soft under her left hand while her other hand was clasped in his. She'd danced this way many times but tonight, with Mr Huntley, it all seemed different, more intimate.

A wry smile lifted his lips. 'Did you think I'd want to dance one of those mad dashes that have been the entertainment?'

She stared into his cornflower-blue eyes. 'You asked for this slower music?'

'Of course. How else was I to hold you properly?'

His frank admission gave her pause for thought, though her feet kept in time as he guided her around the floor. 'You are bold, Mr Huntley.'

'Sometimes. When there is something I want.'

Bridget swallowed unable to take her eyes from his. 'Do you often get what you want?'

'Not all the time. Do you?'

She frowned. 'No.'

'What is it that you want but can't have, Miss Kittrick?'

'I haven't yet decided.'

'Spoken by a true innocent.'

She stiffened slightly. 'What do *you* want, Mr Huntley?'

For several turns he didn't answer. 'What I want and what I can have are two different things.'

She felt his hand move slightly on her back and her skin goosebumped in response. Her pulse quickened. She had to act rationally. 'Are you staying in this part of the country long?'

'That depends. I am looking for a property to purchase and if I find one in this area that suits, then yes, I shall stay.'

'Do you have property in Tasmania?'

'I sold my family home in Hobart. I shan't be returning there.' Immediately his manner changed, his tone hard. He gave her a sour look. 'Am I being prized up for my worth, Miss Kittrick?'

She stopped mid-step, insulted. 'Indeed not, Mr Huntley. I simply was inquiring if you had a home in Tasmania.'

He sighed and took her in his arms again, and they continued to dance. 'Forgive me.'

'What you are worth, Mr Huntley, is of no consequence to me, I can assure you of that,' she rebuked him.

'Really? Isn't that the aim of every young woman to find out a man's worth?'

She laughed. 'No, that is every parents' aim to find out.'

He relaxed. 'You have a wonderful laugh. I feel you do it a lot.'

'Laugh? Oh yes. How could I not? I've brothers and sisters who make me laugh, the grooms in the stables make me laugh, so many things make me chuckle.'

'You are fortunate,' he murmured, his expression closed.

She suddenly felt aware of his unhappiness, that is all she could call it. She realised he carried a burden about him as though he was constantly aware of who was around him, what they were saying and doing. Every time she'd glanced at him this evening, he seemed to be watching the scene, not being a part of it. Sizing up the situation. He did not seem a happy man, and that affected her for some reason. 'Maybe you will laugh while you are here, Mr Huntley.'

'I hope I do, Miss Kittrick, I really do.'

'Being with our family, it's difficult not to find things funny. The twins say the most outrageous comments.'

'How lucky you are to have such a wonderful, loving family.'

She sensed that perhaps he didn't have that. 'Do you enjoy being in Sydney? Austin prefers it so much more than out here.'

'I do like Sydney for certain reasons, mainly I can conduct my business with ease there. However, the city, like all cities, is overcrowded and dirty and society can be fickle.'

'I agree. I much prefer to be on our estates, either here or at Louisburgh.'

'I thought young ladies enjoyed the delights of the city?'

'Oh, don't get me wrong. When the family does go to Sydney, I find it very entertaining. We have so much to do with parties and dinners, days at the beach and shopping. Only, after a few weeks, I find myself longing for home and to ride my horse.'

Mr Huntley stared down at her for a long moment, his expression unreadable. 'Will you ride with me tomorrow?'

Her stomach swooped. 'We could ride down by the river.'

'Wherever you wish.' His thumb moved gently on her back. Then he suddenly stopped as though he'd realised what he'd been doing.

The music stopped and he bowed to her. 'Thank you for the dance.' He spun on his heel and left her.

Stunned by his abrupt departure, Bridget escaped the dance area, trying to make sense of the man.

'Bridget?' Austin grabbed her arm as she hurried past him. 'Is everything all right?'

'Who is that Mr Huntley?'

He raised his eyebrows at the question. 'Lincoln is a good man. A little prickly at times, and quiet, but decent.'

'Why are you friends? He is older than you.'

'Not by a great deal, maybe seven years or so. What does age have to do with it? We are shareholders of a manufacturing company in Sydney. I would not do business with a man I did not trust or respect.'

She glanced over her shoulder to find Mr Huntley standing with Miss Norton, but his gaze was on her. 'He seems rather intense.'

'He's a self-made man and rather private. His father was a soldier and then he owned an inn. That's all I know. I'm not aware of his entire history.'

'Perhaps you should before you bring him home to your family?'

Austin frowned. 'Has he upset you?'

'No...'

'Lincoln has been a good friend since we met last year. I like him,' Austin defended. 'In all the time I've known him, he's never once given me reason to dislike him. He's quiet, sure, a deep thinker, and he refuses to touch a drop of alcohol, which is odd, but he's clever and I admire that.'

'Interesting.'

'Give him a chance. You will like him as much as I do, I'm sure of it.'

Bridget wasn't entirely certain about that. True, she felt a flicker of attraction towards him, but Mr Huntley was unlike any other man she'd known, and she couldn't understand why.

Chapter Three

The thunder of the waterfall could be heard before it was seen. Bridget dismounted Ace alongside Mr Huntley who rode Blaze, a horse he'd borrowed from their stables. The thick bushland mixed with some rainforest trees and ferns hid the valley where the FitzRoy Falls fell. Behind them came the carriages with the family and guests and the farm cart carrying all the picnic paraphernalia. The party had set off at dawn, riding the sixteen miles to the falls.

'Is everyone ready to view the falls?' Austin said to the group.

'I'll stay and supervise the picnic set up,' Aunt Riona replied. 'I've seen them several times already.'

'I shall help you,' Mrs Warren said. 'I have no wish to walk through the forest to see water. I'd likely turn an ankle.'

'And I've seen it before, so I'll stay too,' announced Mrs Ratcliffe. 'You go Caroline. I'm quite all right with Riona.'

Aunt Riona smiled. 'Then we shall have everything ready for their return.'

Bridget walked with Patrick and Mr Huntley and in front of them were Mama, Papa, Austin and Miss Norton, with the twins running on ahead and behind dawdled Lily and Ava, with Caroline bringing up the rear.

'Have you been to the falls many times, Miss Kittrick?' Mr Huntley asked.

'Several times. Patrick and I often ride out here in the summer, don't we?'

Patrick nodded. 'Although we did come in winter one year when we'd had a heavy downpour for days. The waterfall was thunderous. An impressive sight.'

'The power of the water was astonishing but wonderful to see,' Bridget added. 'The spray rose up like a fog.'

'We won't get that today,' Patrick said, stepping over a fallen tree branch. 'We've not had rain for some weeks.'

Mr Huntley took Bridget's elbow to help her over the trunk. 'Will the waterfall be flowing at all then?'

'Yes, it will. Only in drought does it lessen to a trickle,' Patrick said before turning to help Caroline, Ava and Lily over the branch.

Bridget smiled as Patrick stayed with Caroline and the girls. Her poor brother loved a woman who saw no one but Austin.

Alone with Mr Huntley, Bridget continued through the bush, the sound of rushing water growing louder with every step. Aware of his presence, she kept her gaze down on the path, not wanting to trip over a rock or a stick. Since their ride three days ago, Mr Huntley had been touring the area with Austin looking for a suitable property and she had not seen him.

'I did enjoy our ride together the other day,' he said suddenly. 'Your brothers are quite the diversion, aren't they?'

'The twins are characters, for sure,' she answered.

When Mr Huntley arrived for their ride, the twins had implored her to join them. She could never say no to them and so the four of them set out to ride along the riverbank. Ronan and Aidan chatted continuously, giving Mr Huntley their opinions and knowledge on everything they saw, from a kingfisher diving into the water, to cockatoos in the trees and everything in between.

To his credit, Mr Huntley took their constant conversation in his stride, yet Bridget wondered if he'd wanted her company to himself. Listening to him talk to her brothers revealed another side to him. He was patient with their questions and encouraged them to tell their own stories.

Only on the ride home, when the boys raced on ahead, did Bridget have a chance to talk to Mr Huntley alone. They had spoken of the estate, of buying land, of his desire to breed Angus cattle and before they were aware, they were back at the stables and the ride over. Although she had learned a little more about him, Bridget felt unsatisfied when he declined the offer to stay for dinner and returned to the village inn.

In a break in the trees, the forest covered valley opened up before them. The family slowed and spread out to take in the view.

'It's impressive.' Mr Huntley smiled at her.

'Ronan! Aidan!' Mama called to the twins. 'You're too close to the edge.'

While the twins gave excuses to why they were perfectly safe near the cliff edge, Bridget pointed to the roaring waterfall. 'Isn't it beautiful?'

'Stunning,' Mr Huntley agreed.

'You can go closer. There's a track down to the bottom but it's rather steep and on the other side of the creek.' Bridget glanced up at Mr Huntley. 'Shall we?'

'I will if you will.' His grin was full of mischief.

'Mama, we're venturing down,' Bridget said.

'We want to go to!' Ronan asked.

'Rafe?' Ellen left the decision to her husband.

'I'll take them down, or we'll get no peace otherwise.' Rafe turned to his younger daughters. 'Lily? Ava? Do you want to come down to the bottom?'

'No, thank you, Papa.' Ava looked horrified at the idea.

'We'll stay here with Mama,' Lily told him.

Austin held out his arm for Miss Norton. 'Do you wish to go down to the bottom of the waterfall?'

Miss Norton's expression clearly showed she did. 'I will only if you stay with me?'

'Of course.' Austin near swelled with pride.

No one saw Caroline's unhappy expression except Bridget.

'Be careful all of you!' Ellen warned.

Bridget smiled at Mr Huntley. 'Shall we show them the way?' she asked, venturing over to the creek that fed the waterfall.

Rocks had been placed across the creek as stepping-stones. Balancing carefully, Bridget lightly tripped across them. She waited for Mr Huntley and then continued on, not wanting to be with the others.

'It's steep,' Bridget warned him. 'I hold on to the trees to help me.'

'Or you can hold on to me.' Mr Huntley's eyes held hers.

Grinning at the excited sensation he created in her, she boldly took his hand and started down the incline. The cliff dropped away sharply, but a path had been roughly cut out of the side in places, and elsewhere large boulders helped to break up the near vertical descent.

Gripping Mr Huntley's hand gave her a thrill as she skidded and slipped down the narrow path through the trees. At one point she heard Miss Norton squeal as she descended, but Bridget kept her focus on each foot she placed and her hand clasped in Mr Huntley's warm hand.

'Does nothing scare you?' he asked halfway down.

'Not really, no.' She took a step only for a stone to shift under her boot and knock her off balance. She jerked and swayed, trying to keep upright. Mr Huntley grabbed her arms, but Bridget's unsteadiness caused him to tilt forward. He jerked backwards to counteract the movement and suddenly both of them were on their buttocks.

Bridget gasped as she slid down, clutching Mr Huntley's forearms and he held her to him, but the momentum took them several yards down the cliff just a yard from the waterfall itself.

Abruptly, Bridget's feet skidded into a rock, halting them to a shuddering stop.

For a moment Bridget stayed quiet. Her heartbeat thumped in her chest like a hammer.

'Good God!' Mr Huntley breathed. 'Are you hurt?'

'No. I don't believe so.' Bridget chanced a glance at him, then burst out laughing. 'That's one way to get down!'

Mr Huntley grinned and then chuckled. 'You're crazy!'

That made her laugh even more.

'Bridget!' Papa and the twins came crashing down beside them. 'Are you injured, sweetheart?'

'No, Papa. We're both fine. I slipped and brought Mr Huntley down with me.'

'I know,' Rafe panted, relieved. 'I saw you one minute and then the next you were both gone.'

'Was it fun?' Ronan asked, full of excitement.

Mr Huntley helped Bridget to her feet, and she rubbed her backside. Dirt coated her green riding habit. 'It's not a way I would recommend...'

'Let us not have any accidents, please.' Rafe wiped a hand over his face. 'Your mama would never forgive me.'

'I'll not let her go, Mr Hamilton,' Mr Huntley said with a wry smile.

'Good. Please don't.' Rafe walked away with the twins, who were excited to explore close to the pool that the waterfall crashed into.

Mr Huntley took Bridget's gloved hands in his. 'Are you unhurt?'

'I'm completely fine.' She stared into his eyes, such a beautiful cornflower colour. 'And thank you for holding on to me, even if it meant I brought you down with me.'

A look of something tense yet soft entered his eyes, but he quickly turned away. 'Hopefully the climb back up is safer,' he joked.

They were soon joined by the others and although Mr Huntley stayed by Bridget's side, she felt a closure in his manner, and he rarely spoke again. The change in him fascinated her. He seemed afraid to be happy and carefree, which saddened her. How could she make him more open with her? There was an attraction between them. She felt it and knew he felt it, too. Only, he withdrew every time they grew close. Why? She didn't understand. Surely if he felt a friendship could develop between them into something more, he'd want to pursue it? Or did he? Perhaps she was reading more into this than was there?

As the light mist of spray touched her face, she gazed at the dancing rainbows the sun caused. The rush and roar of the crashing waterfall gave her such a sense of awareness. Her spirit soared when she caught Mr Huntley's stare. Instantly, she knew that he was as confused by her as she was about him.

What did he want?

Usually, she could read the signals men gave her. She was used to flirtations with gentlemen at social gatherings and was never without a dance partner for long at parties. She knew she was pretty enough to be considered by many a young man. She also knew that for some she was a little too outspoken, could be loud at times, and rode too fast to be ladylike. Before she had always dismissed those men who frowned at her behaviour. One gentleman had said that if she was his wife, he'd rein her in. She'd replied that he should probably marry one of his horses then!

But was her behaviour too much for Mr Huntley to handle? Could he not understand her ways, the way her mind worked? Did he consider her too adventurous, too opinionated? Did he want a woman who was demure, quiet and biddable? If he did, then she wasn't the woman for him. Was she the right woman for any man?

Yet, there was a subtle tension between them. She knew where he was in a room, her ears were attuned to his gentle voice. Lincoln Huntley had started to invade her dreams and gave her pause for thought during the day.

Did she want Mr Lincoln Huntley to feel emotions about her? Yes, she did. She wanted him to desire her just as much as she desired him.

—ele—

Walking past the library, Bridget heard a muffled curse and a thump. She took a step back and peeked into the room to see her mama pacing, a letter in her hand. 'Mama? What is it?'

'This!' Mama waved the letter in the air. 'The hide of the man!'

'Who?'

'Mr Roache, the good-for-nothing scoundrel,' Mama fumed, slapping the letter on the desk.

Bridget picked it up. 'It's from Mrs Barnstaple.' She spoke of a widow who lived in Goulburn and who had become a friend of Mama's some years ago.

'Yes, thankfully, my dear friend has written to tell me that Mr Roache has put Northville up for auction.' Mama's furious face matched her tone. 'If Mrs Barnstaple hadn't written to me, I'd never have known until it was too late.'

Rafe and Patrick came in. Rafe held mail in his hands. 'My darling, I—'

'Mr Roache is selling up!' Mama cut him off. 'At an auction next week!'

Rafe frowned. 'He's selling Northville? I am surprised.'

'And he'd not want me to find out, of course. Mrs Barnstaple writes that she only found out by mistake, a friend of hers let it slip when they met for tea yesterday. She wrote to me immediately. The sale is not being advertised, and we know why, don't we?' Mama paced once more. 'That man will do everything he can to prevent me from buying his property.'

'You should never have quarrelled with him, Mama,' Patrick mumbled.

Mama glared at him. 'We quarrelled because the man is a thief. He was trying to steal Louisburgh land and then divert the creek to his own farm to leave us without water. Should I have ignored that?'

'No, but it could have been dealt with differently.' Patrick shrugged.

Bridget shook her head slightly at him to warn him now wasn't the time to remind Mama of the time she had a fiery confrontation with Mr Roache over a boundary dispute and the creek.

Rafe took Ellen's hands. 'Darling, calm down. Roache will never sell the property to you. He knows you want it too much.'

'Naturally, I do. We share a boundary. I could annex Northville to Louisburgh and extend our holding by another six thousand acres.'

'Exactly.' Rafe sighed. 'Sweetheart, he doesn't like you because you stood up to him. He doesn't like the Irish and women who have minds, especially Irish women. We know this. He will never sell to you.'

'So, we must accept it without even trying?'

Bridget looked at the letter. 'The auction is next week in Goulburn. You will have sailed to England by then.'

Rafe stiffened. 'I am not going to sail without you, Ellen. You have promised the children. They've talked of nothing else since the day after the party when we told them we were all going.'

Hanging her head, Mama plopped onto the chair behind the desk. 'This could not have come at a worse time. I want that land.'

'Shall we just not be grateful that Roache is leaving, and we'll never have to see him again?' Rafe said.

'And we could have a worse neighbour move in,' Patrick muttered.

'No one could be worse than Roache,' Mama snapped. 'The man threatened to shoot me!'

'Well, you did threaten to have him hanged,' Patrick replied.

'Patrick!' Bridget nudged his arm, a warning look in her eyes.

'Northville must be ours.' Mama tapped her fingers on the desk, a thoughtful expression on her face. 'We just have to work out how we can achieve it.'

'What if we get someone else to bid on our behalf?' Bridget suggested.

'Who?' Mama asked. 'Mr Roache knows everyone in our family.'

'Does he know Mrs Ratcliffe?'

Mama rubbed a hand over her face. 'I don't know and I'm not sure if Harriet is strong enough to make the trip to Goulburn, her chest has been giving her problems in the last couple of weeks.'

Bridget nodded. 'At the party Caroline said she was worried about her health.'

'Yes, and she had a bad turn after our trip to Fitzroy Falls. So, I wouldn't like to trouble Harriet with this business.' Mama walked to the window to stare out of it. 'I could ask Gil Ashford.'

'He and Pippa are in Melbourne until April,' Rafe reminded her.

'Augusta then?' Mama spoke of Gil's sister and another dear friend.

Rafe gave his wife a meaningful look. 'Even if we found someone, we would have to limit the price paid.'

'What do you mean?' Mama scowled at Rafe, sitting back at her desk.

'You know you would keep bidding just to get the land and pay more than what it is worth.'

Mama jerked to her feet. 'And are we suddenly too poor for me to bid?'

'No, my love, but the land is inferior to Louisburgh, which is why I imagine Mr Roache is selling. He will make you pay top price.'

'The land can be made good. He has done nothing with it for five years since taking ownership. He runs sheep on it until the grass has turned to dust. Not once has he ploughed and reseeded. He refuses to spend money on ointments to cure the scabs his flocks always get. The creeks are not maintained and cleared to improve water flow. The man has no idea how to farm.'

Bridget stepped forward and placed a hand on her mama's shoulder. 'Let Patrick and I see to this issue. Trust us to do our best to secure the land. Don't spoil your last night with us fretting over Mr Roache.'

'I agree.' Rafe took Mama's hand. 'Come into my study and we shall work out a price for the land. Bridget can take that with her to the auction.'

'Bridget nor Patrick can go to the auction. Roache will never sell to them. Perhaps Austin will know of someone to bid for us?' Mama said hopefully. 'He has a great many friends in Sydney.'

'True, that might be worth considering,' Rafe agreed. 'We shall talk to him when he returns from his excursion with Miss Norton and Mr Huntley.'

'Mama, Patrick and I can sort this problem out. Austin has enough to keep him busy,' Bridget told them, desperate to show her that she was responsible enough to deal with this.

'Yes, but Austin knows a good many businessmen who Mr Roache will not realise are linked to us.'

'I will leave for Louisburgh tomorrow,' Bridget said, focusing on her mama. 'You said Louisburgh was to be mine, so let me start taking responsibility.'

For a long moment, Mama looked at her, then smiled. 'You have full responsibility for Louisburgh while we are away, I trust you, of course I do, but would it hurt to have someone else helping you fight for Northville? To gain that property will only benefit your future children.'

'What of Mr Huntley?' Patrick asked suddenly. 'He seems a good chap and last night at dinner he was speaking of wanting to venture further south to look for a property.'

Bridget stiffened slightly at the mention of Mr Huntley. Although, he was lodging at an inn in the village, he was often at the house as Austin invited him and Miss Norton to dinner each night and they went on excursions each day. Sometimes she and Patrick joined them, but since the trip to Fitzroy Falls, Mr Huntley had kept his distance. Had she offended him somehow? She didn't understand why, and his behaviour confused her. Especially, when each time she saw Mr Huntley, she felt a pull of attraction and the need to find out more about him.

'That is an excellent suggestion, darling. Mr Huntley is Austin's good friend, and he seems an intelligent man who we can trust. We can ask him at dinner this evening,' Mama said, gathering up her correspondence. 'If he says no, then I will have to find someone else.'

When Mama and Rafe had left the room, Patrick stayed behind. 'I could do without going to Louisburgh. There's new land for sale in the Yarrawa Brush area that I want to purchase, and I don't want to miss out on it.'

'Can it not wait a week or two?'

'The new village of Burrawang has land lots that are selling quickly by all accounts.'

'A village? Why do you want land in a village and not a farm?'

'I intend to have both.' Patrick grinned. 'In the new village I will build shops, and I'll sell the produce in them from my farm.'

'You have it all worked out.'

'I do and I want to get started.'

'Fine. I'll go to Louisburgh by myself.'

'Mama won't allow that.'

'Yes, she will.'

'Mr Huntley might agree to bid on our behalf on the Northville property. You and he can't be alone together at Louisburgh.'

Bridget grinned at him. 'Then you will have to come with us, won't you, to save my reputation?'

'Damn it,' he mumbled.

'Unless Mama speaks with Austin and convinces him to go south, too, then you're off the hook.'

Patrick stretched and yawned. 'Let's hope so, but Austin wants to get back to Sydney. He and Miss Norton, and her companion, are meant to be travelling with Mama and everyone when they leave in the morning.' Patrick headed for the door. 'I promised the twins I'd help them pack. You know what they are like, they'll take everything but clothes.'

'Are you regretting not going to England and Ireland?' Bridget asked.

Patrick shrugged, as he always did. 'Not really. I'll miss the family while they are gone but I've too much to do and keeping busy will make the time go by fast.' He paused. 'Do you wish you had decided to return to Ireland?'

'Oh, no, not at all. You know I'm not a very good sailor. I get sick just being on a boat on the harbour. The thought of months at sea gives me the chills. I shall be quite happy at Louisburgh.'

Patrick sauntered to the door, smiling happily. 'And I at Burrawang.'

Left alone, Bridget wondered if Mr Huntley would stay on and travel to Goulburn to bid on their behalf. More time spent in his company gave her a secret thrill. In Goulburn she might find the opportunity to learn more about the man, if he agreed to attend the auction. The thought excited her. Tonight, she would see him again at dinner. She would wear her pink gown with the silver lace.

That evening after dinner, the family sat in the drawing room, the French doors open to catch the breeze coming up the hill from the river. February had disappeared into March without Bridget been too aware of it. Having guests for an extended stay and the days of entertaining them had started to blur. But even though summer had finished and now autumn would change the leaves in the park, the weather remained warm and dry as though summer was loathed to give up its dominance just yet.

Lily and Ava twittered with nervous excitement about leaving tomorrow for Sydney and the ship which would take them to the other side of the world. The twins were restless, eager to ask questions about the journey to anyone who'd listen.

Eventually, Mama raised her hand. 'We have an early start tomorrow. It is time for the children to go to bed.'

'Let me say good night to them,' Aunt Riona said rising. 'It will be awhile until I can do it again.' She ushered the girls and the twins out of the room.

'Mr Huntley, there is some business we would like to discuss with you, if we may?' Rafe asked him.

Surprised, Mr Huntley put down his cup of tea. 'Absolutely.'

Mama glanced at Patrick. 'Dearest, perhaps you can take Miss Norton and Mrs Warren into the parlour for a game of cards? I'm sure they do not want to listen to us talk business. Forgive us, Miss Norton.'

'Of course.' Miss Norton rose with a smile to Austin and left the room with Mrs Warren and Patrick.

Briefly, Mama spoke of the auction and Mr Roache, explaining the need to have someone outside of the family to bid on their behalf. 'Naturally, you must say no, Mr Huntley, if this doesn't sit well with you, or if you have plans which you do not wish to alter,' Mama finished.

'Bridget and Patrick will have the money with them, so you can be assured the sale price is covered as you bid,' Rafe added.

'And we will pay for your expenses in Goulburn, Mr Huntley,' Mama said.

Mr Huntley gave her a small smile. 'No need, Mrs Hamilton. I can cover my own expenses, and yes, I'd be happy to bid on your behalf.'

Mama sagged with relief. 'I cannot thank you enough.'

'I have wanted to visit Goulburn and the country beyond it, so this is a perfect opportunity.'

'Do I need to go, Mama?' Austin asked. 'I had planned to return to Sydney with Miss Norton and you all in the morning. I have meetings at the end of the week.'

'Let Austin return to Sydney,' Bridget answered quickly. 'I'm sure Patrick and I can assist Mr Huntley on this occasion.'

'That's settled then.' Rafe shook Mr Huntley's hand. 'We are much obliged, Mr Huntley. I will write letters of authority for you to show the auctioneer and to meet with our solicitor in Goulburn that we use for Louisburgh dealings.'

While her parents and Mr Huntley talked business, Bridget kept a tight control on her emotions. The sense of freedom filled her veins and also the exciting prospect that Mr Huntley would be travelling south with her and Patrick.

Chapter Four

Early the following morning, the family gathered on the drive as the pink light of dawn broke over the trees. Grooms added the last pieces of luggage to the two carts that were packed with trunks the day before. Mr Higgins sat high on the seat of the front carriage, while Douglas sat waiting to drive the second carriage, and a third they'd borrowed from Mrs Ratcliffe.

Varying emotions coursed through Bridget as she stood watching the family prepare to depart. She'd not see them again for over a year, which squeezed her heart sorely, but to contradict that sadness was the sense of independence. She'd be at Louisburgh, in charge of the property for the first time, and also in charge of her own life without parental supervision. The notion was heady.

'Goodbye, Miss Kittrick.' Miss Norton came to her and shook Bridget's hand. 'Thank you so much for your friendship.'

'I'm sure we will meet again, Miss Norton,' Bridget said, knowing Austin was smitten with the young woman. 'Safe travels.'

Bridget gave Austin a kiss. 'I'll write to you about how we do at the auction.'

'Huntley will do his best, I know it.' Austin smiled before he walked Miss Norton to the second carriage that she was to share with him and Mrs Warren.

Aunt Riona, crying silently, hugged the twins to her tightly. 'You must be on your very best behaviour, my darlings.'

Bridget, her own eyes welling, embraced Lily and then Ava. 'Have a wonderful time. Send lots of long letters and bring back as much gossip as you can remember.' She kissed them both. 'I will miss the pair of you.'

'Look after Aunt Riona for us,' Lily said, excited yet sad. 'I wish you were coming with us.'

'And take care of Moira,' Ava added, having a soft spot for the family's cook. 'I hated saying goodbye to her just now.'

'Make sure you write to her, she'll be made up about it.' Turning, Bridget shook both hands with Miss Lewis, the girls' governess who was accompanying her sisters. 'Enjoy yourself, Miss Lewis.'

'I sense I will, Bridget dear.'

Next, Bridget gathered her brothers into her arms and held them. 'I hope the time goes quickly,' she whispered, knowing she will miss them dreadfully. They were the ones who went riding with her, or fishing, or on long walks. Unlike her sisters, she was close to the twins in sharing their activities, wanting to hunt with them, find frogs, jump in muddy puddles. 'Have fun! Don't forget me,' she warned, kissing them fiercely on the cheek.

'As if we ever could?' Ronan laughed but his eyes glistened. 'You'll visit our ponies, won't you? They will miss us.'

'I'll take them carrots the minute I return from Louisburgh.'

'But that will be months!' Aidan protested.

'I'm sure Douglas will look after them very well, hasn't he always?' Bridget soothed. 'And I'll be coming back here from time to time to visit Aunt Riona.'

'Can you not take our ponies to Louisburgh?' Ronan asked.

'No. They will be fine here, I promise you.' Bridget embraced them again.

'Into the carriage, boys,' Papa ordered before pulling Bridget into his arms. 'Now, we shall send letters the day we arrive in Liverpool, so you know we have arrived safely.'

She nodded, her throat too tight to speak.

Mama hugged her close. 'Stay safe. We'll be back before you know it. You have all the instructions for Louisburgh but make sure you return often to Emmerson Park and Aunt Riona. She will be lonely with us gone.'

'Whist, sister,' Aunt Riona said from behind. 'I will be fine, so I will. Get going or you'll be late.'

With final waves and blown kisses, the family carriages and carts drove away.

'And you both leave today?' Aunt Riona asked Bridget and Patrick.

'Yes. Unless you want us to stay another day?' Bridget felt sorry to leave her aunt alone.

'No. You must live your lives. I shall be busy enough.' Aunt Riona smiled. 'I'm having Father Lanigan for dinner this evening and Mrs Ratcliffe for luncheon tomorrow. I'm to attend the Riddles' dinner party next week and I have all my other charitable responsibilities and now running this estate. I shall be busy enough.' She turned to walk indoors. 'I have to make a life for myself for the next year or so, but the peace might be rather nice, too.'

Bridget laughed. 'You'll hate the quiet.'

Aunt Riona pulled a face. 'I probably shall. Now do you need help packing or has Una finished the task?'

'It's all done. We are riding, so only taking saddlebags. I have clothes enough already at Louisburgh.'

'Why not go by the mail coach?'

'Because they get held up at gun point far too often,' Bridget answered. 'I'd rather try to out ride a bushranger than be stuck in a carriage at their mercy.'

'Holy Virgin.' Aunt Riona shivered and made a sign of the cross. 'And Mr Huntley?'

Patrick paused in the doorway. 'We are meeting him in the village, at Victoria's Inn where he's been lodging. He still has one of our horses, Blaze, and will ride him. We'll stay overnight at Marulan. I just need to gather a few things and then we can go. Abel is bringing the horses around.'

Aunt Riona held Bridget's hands. 'Your mother has given you a large responsibility. You know how blinded she gets about buying land, and especially her feud with Mr Roache about Northville. Do what you can to secure it, but do not antagonise the man any more, I beg you. He hates this family enough.'

'Hopefully, I won't even have to speak with him. Patrick doesn't think we should attend the auction.'

'It's probably best.'

'I'd still like to see it for myself. Mr Huntley will do all the bidding so I don't see why we can't attend. We can simply watch the proceedings.'

'Any member of this family attending will infuriate Mr Roache. You know what a terrible fellow he is with that wicked temper he has. If he saw you, he'd likely stop the auction and then sell privately or not at all, and how will your mother feel then?'

'I know we must play the game.' Bridget sighed, annoyed.

Aunt Riona cupped Bridget's cheek. 'Just be careful. You'll be playing in a game where men always win.'

'Mama has done it and won, and so will I. Don't worry.' Bridget kissed her aunt, eager to begin her adventure.

ele

The following day, Bridget sat astride Ace, her thoughts on Mr Huntley who rode on one side of her, with Patrick on the other side. Behind them, road dust drifted on the still air from the horses' hooves. The night before they'd slept at an inn at Marulan after eating a plain meat stew and thick damper bread. Black tea had washed it down before they retired to their rooms and slept, waking before dawn to saddle up. Although the accommodation had been sparse, she'd enjoyed an evening chatting to Mr Huntley, even if they were joined by the landlord and his wife for most of it and so she couldn't ask him the personal questions she longed to do.

The heat of the sun burned down, boiling them in their clothes. The sizzling air made them sweat, even the birds stayed quiet in the trees. March was proving as hot as the summer months.

Ahead the dirt road stretched for miles through a parched country of knee-high dry grass. In the distance sheep could be seen, but only just. Their wool the same colour as the paddocks they grazed. On the right the blue haze of the Cookbundoon Ranges spilt the landscape. On the other side of the ranges was Louisburgh, but they had to travel south of the ranges to near Goulburn before they could split off from the main road and onto the rutted track towards the property.

They shared the road to Goulburn with many others. Often a trundling coach would pass them, washing them in a cloud of dust. In turn they overtook slow, lumbering bullock wagons, heavily loaded with bales of wool, sacks of grain, or the contents of someone's house.

Bridget unlatched her water container and drank deeply, thankful that just after midday they will have reached Goulburn.

'We should have caught the mail coach,' Patrick murmured, swiping sweat from his brow.

'I wanted to bring Ace to Louisburgh. If I am to be there for some considerable time, I don't wish to be without him. Besides, we are safer from bushrangers this way. They pick off coaches too often.'

'Yet you allow your maid to ride on the mail coach,' Patrick teased.

'Una had no choice. She cannot ride.'

Patrick scanned the horizon. 'It's been quiet around here lately. The bushrangers are further out west, mostly. Douglas could have ridden Ace over to Louisburgh when he returned from Sydney and the three of us could have travelled in the mail coach.'

'Will you stop going on about it? I could have done this ride without you, Patrick,' Bridget snapped. 'If you wanted to travel in the mail coach, then you should have said.'

'I did, and you wanted to ride.'

'Because of Ace!'

'And because of that Papa said I wasn't to let you ride alone all the way to Goulburn. I'm sure Mr Huntley would have preferred the coach, too.'

'Would you, Mr Huntley?' She swung in her saddle to ask him, aghast she'd been rude to the man for making him ride.

'I am happy to ride. I must admit that riding allows me to see the countryside better than it whizzing past a coach window.'

'Mr Huntley is well pleased to be riding,' Bridget gloated to Patrick.

'And you say the railway will reach Goulburn in a few years?' Mr Huntley asked, drinking from his own canteen, seeming amused at the squabbling siblings.

Patrick reached for his water and drank as well. 'Yes, it will. They predict it to be eighteen sixty-nine, if all goes well. You saw the surveyors working at Marulan yesterday? They are the busiest men in the country. Soon the railroads will criss-cross all over the country.'

'Yes. Busy times. The railways will change the fortunes of many people. The Sydney markets will be more easily reached for the farmers of this area.'

'A prosperous area to buy land, Mr Huntley,' Bridget suggested.

'Indeed, and I have read in the newspaper that further south is ideal farming land.'

'And farming is what you want to do?' she asked.

Before he could answer, they moved to the side of the road to allow a carriage to go by.

'Yes, mostly cattle and some sheep, but also grain could work if there is enough rainfall in these parts.'

She glanced at him under the brim of her wide straw hat. 'Is farming what you did in Tasmania?'

A muscle ticked in his jaw as it seemed to do when anyone asked him about Tasmania. 'I did some farming, yes.'

She sensed he didn't want to reveal any more information and stared ahead at the hills they would soon be riding over and which on the other side would reveal the spread of the emerging town of Goulburn.

'We shall soon have to split from Mr Huntley,' Patrick said. 'We do not want to encounter anyone from the auction seeing us arrive together.'

Bridget reined in Ace, and they all stopped. 'Yes, even though we would split on entering the town to turn north for Louisburgh, it might be wise for Mr Huntley to ride on ahead.'

Mr Huntley's gaze lingered on her face. 'It makes sense to be careful.'

She smiled, wishing he could stay with them longer. 'We'll meet for supper at Mandelson's Goulburn Hotel on Wednesday evening after the auction.'

'With good news I hope,' Patrick added.

'I thought to attend the auction,' she said. 'I could wear a low hat and a veil.'

'No, Bridget,' Patrick warned. 'It's too much of a risk. If Roache thinks we are linked in any way to Mr Huntley, the game is up. We stay at Louisburgh until Wednesday afternoon once the auction is completed.'

Frustrated, she nodded and looked at Mr Huntley. 'We recommend that you stay at Mandelson's, too. It's the best in the town. I'm sorry you will be on your own for a few days.'

He gave a wry smile that she was beginning to know well. 'Rest assured, Miss Kittrick, I will find things to keep myself occupied.' He shook Patrick's hand and then Bridget's.

'Just watch out for bushrangers,' Patrick snickered. 'There was a shootout only three years ago in one of the hotels.'

'Patrick!' Bridget tutted. 'Don't put Mr Huntley off.'

Huntley chuckled. 'I can handle myself well enough, Miss Kittrick.' With a touch of his finger to his hat in farewell, he clicked his heels and his horse trotted off.

Bridget stared after him, acknowledging his broad back, the easy way he sat in the saddle. For all his quietness, he was fast growing on her, and she was keen to see him again at the auction. What did that mean? Did she only want his attention because he was so different to the other young men she knew who flirted and teased her? Did Mr Huntley, an older man, fascinate her because he wasn't obvious? She saw the looks he gave her, but he remained aloof. She didn't understand any of it and that frustrated her no end.

'Come on then, let's go to our second home,' Patrick urged when Mr Huntley was some distance away.

By mid-afternoon they were riding down the long dirt track leading to Louisburgh. From the open gates, a mile back, parallel rows of English Plane trees bordered the track, planted under instruction by Ellen ten years ago. The trees, now strong saplings, were always a welcome sight to Bridget, for at the end of the long track, the welcoming homestead greeted them.

Over the last five years, her mama had spent a great deal of money to enhance the property, especially the house, which when she bought it was only a bark hut. Now, a solid sandstone two-storey structure dominated the landscape with sweeping verandahs on both levels. The grounds were still rather bare, not as lush as Emmerson Park, but a young orchard was doing its best to cope with the hot dry winds that tormented the landscape in summer. Numerous outbuildings were scattered beyond the stables, plus a small cottage for the estate's overseer, Mr Denby.

They rode to the timber-built stables with its paved yard and dismounted.

'Ah, O'Neil.' Bridget smiled at the young groom who came out to take the horses. 'How are you?'

'Fine, miss. We weren't expecting you.' He glanced nervously at the house.

'Is that a problem?' Patrick asked, taking the saddlebags.

'Only that nothing will be ready, sir.'

'I'm sure Mrs Palmer will soon sort us out,' Bridget said happily. Like her mother, she felt a sense of home at Louisburgh. Here, they were far enough away from Goulburn to not have constant visitors, unlike in Berrima where they were constantly entertaining. 'Can you take the cart into Goulburn and collect Una from the Royal Hotel, the coach will be arriving at four o'clock.'

'Yes, miss.'

'Where's Mr Denby?' Patrick asked.

The youth's Adam's apple bobbed in his throat. 'He rode into Goulburn this morning to report to the police.'

'The police?' Bridget and Patrick spoke together.

'What has happened?' Bridget demanded.

'There's been trouble over at Northville, miss,' O'Neil said defiantly. 'Mr Denby wasn't having any of it, not after what Mr Roache did.'

'What did he do?' Patrick asked, suddenly on alert.

'He shot at his housekeeper, Mrs Webber. She had to flee and came here to hide.'

'Shot at her?' Patrick fumed. 'The man is insane.'

Bridget tried to keep her temper. Roache was a blackguard. 'Is Mrs Webber still here?'

'Yes, she's been hiding here for two days, and Mr Roache and his men have come every few hours to harass us, saying they know she's here and they want her back. Mr Denby has gone to speak to the police about it.'

'Take care of the horses, lad,' Patrick said and taking Bridget's arm they marched towards the house. 'This is all we need. Roache is a madman.'

'How dare he come here and harass our staff?' she flared.

'You might be better staying in Goulburn.'

Bridget glared at him. 'I'll not be run off my own home by that man!'

'Us being here will only antagonise the fool.'

'This is our home, Patrick. I shan't run from it because of that horrid rat! If he comes onto our property again, it'll be me who will be doing the shooting.' She stormed ahead into the house.

An older woman with grey hair tied into a neat roll at the back of her head came hurrying down the hallway beside the staircase. 'Miss Kittrick, and Mr Patrick!'

'We have come unannounced, Mrs Palmer, we're sorry,' Patrick said.

'No, no, come in and let me take your things.' Mrs Palmer flustered around them, a widow their mother had hired some years ago after finding her in the Goulburn shelter for homeless women.

'What is this business with Roache, that O'Neil has just informed us about?' Patrick asked her as they stepped into the square parlour decorated in wood panelling and pale floral wallpaper and furnished with pieces of cedar.

'Oh, Mr Patrick, the man is fit to be tied.' Mrs Palmer put her hand to her throat in dismay. 'His housekeeper, Mrs Webber, came running here late one night, frightening us all to death with her tale of being shot at by Mr Roache. The bullet grazed her upper arm and I have bandaged it, but she refuses to leave my bedroom to report it to the police. We, Mr Denby and I, thought to leave it, as it was her decision, but the following day, which was the day before yesterday, Mr Roache and his men rode up and banged on the door demanding we release Mrs Webber to them. I refused. He became so angry, shouting and abusing me. Mr Denby saw him off with a rifle blast, and for a moment I thought there would be a shootout, honest I did. Only that simply enraged Roache more and all day yesterday and last night he sent his men here to ride about the house, shooting their guns and hollering. Mr Denby tried his best to see them off, but he was outnumbered, and they said they'd kill him and take his daughter if he stepped out of the house. Mr Denby brought all the staff into the kitchen to keep them safe.'

'Roache is unhinged.' Patrick paced the floor, reminding Bridget of their mama.

Mrs Palmer twisted her hands. 'He's a nasty piece of work, for sure, and hates us all. He's threatened to burn the house down if we don't release Mrs Webber.'

Bridget turned to Patrick. 'The police need to be involved.'

'I agree. Mr Denby has gone there now you said?' he asked Mrs Palmer.

'He left at first light while Roache's men were sleeping off their drink down by the creek.'

'Let us see what Mr Denby has to report. If he has not received any satisfaction, then I shall go into town and demand action.' Patrick walked to the drinks' table and poured himself a small brandy.

'I shall go and speak with Mrs Webber before I wash,' Bridget said.

'And I shall serve some tea.' Mrs Palmer followed her.

'Should we both speak to her,' Patrick forestalled them.

Mrs Palmer's face paled. 'Oh dear... Er... Mr Patrick, may I suggest that just Miss Kittrick speak with the poor woman? She is rather delicate at the moment.'

Patrick nodded. 'Of course.'

'Go and wash, brother, while you wait.' Bridget headed down the hallway, turning slightly at the end of it to open the door leading into the long kitchen, which ran the length of the house. From the kitchen were several doors, one to the cellar, one to the scullery, one to outside, and then lastly a door leading to a small box room that was Mrs Palmer's bedroom.

Bridget knocked gently and opened the door. A woman on the bed scrambled up in fear.

'Forgive me, Mrs Webber,' Bridget said softly. 'I'm Miss Kittrick, my mother owns Louisburgh.' Bridget expected an older woman, but Mrs Webber seemed to be aged in her late twenties.

The frightened woman eyed Bridget, scrunching the bed sheets up to her chin, her long hair loose and knotted about her head.

'May I talk to you for a moment?' Bridget eased slowly onto the wooden chair by the door. Having spent all her life with horses and animals, she knew how to behave with a terrified creature, and Mrs Webber was certainly that.

'You won't send me back?' the voice croaked from the bed.

'No, not at all. You are safe, I promise.'

The woman sagged. 'I'll kill myself if I have to go back, I will!'

'Please, calm yourself, I promise you are free of that man.'

Tears fell over her cheeks, but she didn't wipe them away and Bridget noticed bruises around her eyes, her nails torn and bloodied beneath.

'Are you hungry, or thirsty?'

'No. Mrs Palmer has been kind.'

'Can you tell me what happened?'

There was a long silence. So long Bridget thought the woman wouldn't answer her.

Then she murmured. 'I started working for Mr Roache two months ago. At first, I thought it a decent place, a little rough being a bachelor's house, but good enough. Only, *he* soon changed my thoughts on that. Within a few weeks of living there, he started coming into my room. I screamed and fought him, but he's stronger...'

Bridget gaped. 'He attacked you?'

'Every night. I tried to run away, but I was watched constantly. I had no money, and the other staff were threatened if they helped me. Then, three days ago, he had friends staying, they rounded up all us women working there, the housemaid, the kitchen maid, me, even the stockman's daughter who is barely fifteen. I tried to protect them, but I was beaten when I did. The men took it in turns to have us...' Mrs Webber shivered, her voice fading.

Stunned, Bridget couldn't think straight. She hadn't been expecting such an admission. She'd never been faced with such brutality, never had to deal with such evilness.

'I managed to escape because the men fell asleep drunk. I took the stockman's girl back to her hut and her parents... The other girls were too frightened to run, though I sense one girl enjoyed it, liked being the centre of attention... As I was running into the trees, I heard a shout. I looked back and Roache stood with his gun. He shot at me. The bullet skimmed my arm.' She gently touched the bandage.

'I can't believe this.' Bridget paced the room.

Mrs Webber's head shot up, her eyes wide. 'I speak the truth!'

'Yes, yes, of course. I believe you,' Bridget quickly assured her. 'I simply mean I can't believe this would happen here, not five miles from this house, my home.'

Mrs Webber slumped back against the pillows. 'Mrs Palmer wants me to tell the police, but Roache said if I did, he'd find me and kill me.'

'He must be charged, locked up. You must speak up.'

Mrs Webber snorted. 'Who will believe me against someone like him? He has most of the town as his friends and the rest he bribes, including the police.'

'That doesn't make it right. We will help you.'

'No. I want nothing to do with the police or going to court.'

'He will get away with it!' Bridget protested.

'He will anyway.'

'Not if we—'

'Please, Miss Kittrick.' Mrs Webber shook her head. 'I won't say a word to the police. I can't risk it.'

Frustrated, Bridget tried to think in the tiny room. 'Is there family we can write to?'

'No. My husband died six months ago. My parents died on the ship coming over ten years ago. I'm alone.'

'Not any longer. I will help you.' Bridget opened the door. 'Rest now. We'll speak later.'

In the kitchen, she held onto the edge of the table, reeling from shock. Mama had been right all along, Mr Roache was a scoundrel and should be horsewhipped and more.

'Miss?' A young woman came in from outside, holding a box of vegetables.

'Ruth,' she acknowledged the kitchen maid, another young woman her mother had employed.

'You've heard then, miss?'

'I have.' Bridget straightened, suddenly feeling older than her years. 'I want you all to stay close to the house until this business is dealt with.'

'Yes, miss. I've told Jilly to not go beyond the well and the stables. You know how she is, always wandering.'

'Good.' Bridget knew of Jilly's habits. The girl was barely twelve, and Mr Denby's daughter. She worked in the house, training under Mrs Palmer and Ruth.

Entering the parlour, she found Mrs Palmer pouring tea for Patrick, who'd washed and changed. Bridget sat on the red sofa with a tired sigh.

'How is she?' Patrick asked.

Bridget caught Mrs Palmer's eye. 'She refuses to speak to the police.'

Mrs Palmer nodded and poured a cup for her.

'We can't force her,' Patrick said, sipping his tea. 'Mr Denby has returned from Goulburn and informed me that the police troopers will visit Roache and warn him to keep his men off our land.'

'No, that's not enough. The incident should be reported, Patrick, and you will agree when I've told you what's happened.'

After telling Patrick what had occurred to Mrs Webber, Bridget went upstairs to her bedroom and washed off the road dust. She lay on her bed for some time, absorbing the shocking story, while fighting the surge of anger that flared in her chest. Roache could not get away with what he'd done, but what could she do? Fleetingly, she wished her mama was there to help. Mama would know what to do, but Mama and the family would now be sailing out of Sydney Harbour and not be seen for over a year.

Una arrived full of gossip about her fellow coach passengers and helped her change into a plain chocolate-coloured dress for the evening. Normally, Bridget would laugh at her tales, but she didn't feel like laughing when downstairs a woman lay scared and alone after enduring a nightmare ordeal.

'Shall we take a stroll before dinner?' Patrick asked her as she joined him downstairs.

She nodded, and they silently stepped outside to a beautiful sky streaked with pink and gold as the sun descended. The warm air provided some comfort as did the birds twittering in the trees edging the creek bank.

'Mrs Webber can't stay here, Brid,' Patrick said softly, using his pet name for her. 'It will give Roache reason to come here. Mrs Webber signed an employment contract, Mrs Palmer told me.'

'No contract can give him the right to do what he did to her!' she muttered harshly. 'She has nowhere to go.'

'Then we'll send her to Emmerson Park. Aunt Riona will know how to help and keep her safe.'

Bridget sighed. 'That is the best solution, yes. Well done for thinking of it. I've just been consumed with wanting to deal with Roache.'

He rolled his eyes. 'There is nothing you can do.'

'We have to do something! Surely you want to see him punished as much as I do?'

'Of course. But we aren't the law and Roache will be gone as soon as Northville is sold.'

'We must buy it, and when we do, I shall crow loudly in Roache's face.'

'No, you won't. We don't want any more dealings with the man.'

'Don't you dare try and stop me!' she flared. 'If Mr Huntley is successful, the minute those papers are signed and we own Northville, I will seek Roache out and confront him.'

'I forbid it!'

Bridget glared at him. 'You forbid me? You are not my father.'

'No, but I'm your older brother and you'll do as I say.' Patrick ran a hand through his hair in exasperation. 'Do you suppose I need this extra worry about you when I return to Berrima?'

'And do you honestly think I'll allow Roache to get away with the pain he's caused? He's not only terrorised his own staff but ours as well. Are you willing to stand by and do nothing about that? Are you a coward?'

'I'll pretend you never said that.' Patrick glowered.

'I refuse to allow Roache to bully us all. Once Northville is ours, he will know we bought it and I will speak with the police about his abuse.'

'Jesus, Mary and Joseph!' Patrick suddenly sounded very Irish, something she'd not heard from him since they were children.

Feeling calmer, she couldn't help but grin. 'You can't stop me, so you can't,' she said in an Irish accent, one she had long lost.

Patrick rubbed his eyes. 'I can't wait for Wednesday to be over, then I'm heading back to Berrima. I'll deposit Mrs Webber with Aunt Riona and then I'm off to Burrawang to buy my land.'

'And I shall spend my days riding the ranges.' She wondered if she'd meet up with Eddie Patterson, the man who'd saved her from kidnap by her Irish uncle, Colm Kittrick when she was a child. Eddie Patterson, an outlaw, but only ever kind to her and her mother, lived in the ranges, hidden in the gullies, safe on Louisburgh land. Over the years she had seen him maybe three times, but she knew her mama had seen him more than that. Often giving him new blankets and food staples such as flour and oats, tea and sugar.

The sound of thundering hoofbeats made them turn in surprise. On the other side of the creek, Mr Roache, flanked by three men, came riding down the hill towards them.

'Get to the house!' Patrick pushed her behind him.

'The hell I will!' Furious, Bridget squared up to the man who'd plagued her thoughts all afternoon.

'I don't have a gun with me,' Patrick snapped. 'Christ! Stay calm, Bridget, I beg you.'

Roache splashed across the narrow creek, his manner unfriendly. 'Ah, I see the sprogs of the witch are visiting. Tell me, how is your dear mother?'

Patrick tensed. 'Is there a reason for your visit, Roache?'

'There is, young Kittrick, there is,' Roache declared, sitting back in the saddle, his extended stomach straining his waistcoat buttons. In his sixties, Roache was overweight with a florid face and thinning hair under his wide hat. He had a disgusting habit of spitting tobacco wherever he pleased.

'I fail to see why you would have any reason to visit us.' Bridget barely kept her temper.

'I wasn't talking to you, wench. My business is with your brother. I don't deal with women.'

'Only if it's to deal out abuse, apparently,' Bridget taunted.

Patrick gripped her arm.

Roache gave her a sneer then ignored her. 'A couple of days ago, one of my servants ran away. We believe she has run here and is in hiding.'

'We only arrived a few hours ago,' Patrick told him. 'We have not been made aware of any runaway servant.'

'Then *your* servants are lying to you.'

'Or perhaps your servant has fled the area? Maybe the person is in Goulburn, or further?'

'They were bleeding. My dogs found drops of blood in the bush. I've a black tracker, too, who said she came this way right to your kitchen door. So, don't lie to me.'

'Then we shall look into it and let you know.' Patrick took Bridget's elbow. 'Good evening, Mr Roache.'

'I want her back! She's under contract!' he roared.

Bridget itched to slap his fat face. 'Why was she shot at?'

'For fleeing!'

'What reason did she have to flee?' Hatred filled her voice.

'That is my business, not yours,' Roache jeered.

'And police business?' Bridget threatened.

'Bridget,' Patrick hissed, tugging her arm.

Roache gave her a filthy look. 'Keep your nose out of my affairs, witch's spawn, or you'll be sorry.'

Bridget jerked forward, incensed. 'Get off my land, you degenerate! You don't deserve the air you breathe!'

Digging his heels into his horse's sides to force it to lunge forward close to Bridget, Roache leaned down in the saddle. 'Just like your mother you consider you are better than me. You'll rue the day you argued with me, bitch!' He spat at her feet and yanked his horse's head around and thundered away.

'What did I tell you!' Patrick yelled at her, stomping away. 'I was one man against four should he have given a signal to do you harm.'

She stormed past him. 'Then start carrying a gun!'

'Don't be stupid, for God's sake. If I shoot him, I hang, is that what you want? You have to control your temper, Bridget. It's always getting you into trouble ever since you were a girl in braids.'

She was about to give him another tongue lashing when she noticed his worried expression. Taking a deep breath, she tried to calm down. 'I'm sorry, but he infuriates me. Ever since he had that confrontation with Mama, called her nasty names and embarrassed her in the town council meeting, all I've wanted to do is slap him silly!'

Patrick slowed his steps. 'Do you not think any of us don't want to do that, too? Do you not deem that Rafe and Austin have tried to get something on the man to have him arrested? The man is a villain, but I alone can't take him on, and nor can you. I promised Mammy I would look after you.'

Bridget relented as soon as she heard him say mammy. She knew Patrick would carry the heavy weight of responsibility until Mama returned home. 'I will try to behave.'

'Again, I judge it's wise for you *not* to go to Goulburn on Wednesday.'

But her rebellious streak refused to die. 'Not on your life, Patrick Kittrick, will I stay home!'

Chapter Five

In the crowded, smoky haze of the London Tavern's back tap room, Lincoln Huntley stood near the wall and an open window. The noise of jovial men thrummed and in the centre of it was the man selling his property, Mr Roache. He had shaken Lincoln's hand when he arrived and as Lincoln signed the register to bid, Roache had sidled up to him, asking where he was from.

'Tasmania, originally,' he answered truthfully. 'I moved to Sydney just recently, but I'm after some land.' Lincoln held out his hand. 'I'm Lincoln Huntley, Mr Roache.'

Roache shook his hand. 'You knew who I was?'

'Doesn't everyone in this town?'

Smirking, Roache scratched his chin. 'Where did you hear about this auction?' he quizzed. 'It has not been advertised.'

'Yesterday, I overheard someone mention it in Mandelson's at dinner,' Lincoln lied.

Roache frowned and scratched his long whiskers. 'Nothing is kept a secret in this town.'

'Well, I thought it worth further investigation.'

'Wise man.' Roache instantly cheered up.

Lincoln held up the pamphlet he'd been given at the door. 'Tell me, is there sufficient water for stock?'

'Plenty, my good sir. I have a creek flowing through the property which in the five years of ownership I've never seen dry up.' He pointed to the map on the pamphlet. 'An excellent watercourse.'

'May I ask why you are selling up?'

Roache instantly looked shifty. 'I'm heading north to try my hand at a larger sheep run. My property is hemmed in by neighbours,' he leaned closer to whisper, 'some of which claim to be more superior than what they are, and I'm eager to expand.'

Lincoln blinked and leaned away from the waft of stale onion breath that washed over him. 'Indeed?'

'Oh, yes, but don't let the neighbours put you off. No, pray not. On the northern border the landlord is never there, just grazes his flocks and leaves it to his shepherds.' Roache lowered his voice again. 'An absentee landlord is a godsend, for if your flocks happen to stray and eat his grass while his useless shepherds lie drunk all day, then what's the harm of it?' Roache smirked, his small eyes darting around the room. 'Ah, Floyd is here. Forgive me, Mr Huntley I must speak with him. Good luck and bid well!'

Lincoln watched the odious man cross the room to shake hands with the new arrival and fawn over him.

'Excuse me, may I stand here?' asked a thin young man dressed in a coarse suit.

Lincoln nodded.

'You are bidding, sir?'

'Perhaps, yes.' Lincoln gave nothing away.

'It's too rich for my blood, but I wanted to see the auction.'

'Why?'

'Are you his friend?' The young man's loathing glare rested on Roache.

'Not at all. I don't know the man.'

'I want to witness the sale in the hopes the rotten fellow actually does leave town.'

'Not a friend then?' Lincoln murmured.

'I'd see him hang if I could,' the young man whispered, never taking his eyes off Roache. The cabbage-tree hat he held was twisted in his roughened hands.

'That is a serious statement.'

'And not made in jest either.'

Lincoln held out his hand. 'Lincoln Huntley.'

'Silas Pegg,' he answered, shaking Lincoln's hand. 'I hope you buy the place, Mr Huntley, but if you do, don't expect any black fellows to work for you. They say it has bad spirits there. Roache has an old black tracker who is too old to work anywhere else, but the younger ones, they won't come on the land.'

Lincoln stared at him before schooling his features. 'Any reasons why that is?'

Silas grunted. 'He's standing over there.' He nodded to Roache. 'You know he is nearly bankrupt?'

'No, I did not. As I say I do not know the man.'

'He's not been paying his taxes on his stock, and he gambles unwisely, and drinks heavily. He's a mean bastard when drunk. Forgive my language, sir.'

Lincoln's blood ran cold at the mention of drink.

The auctioneer brought the room to order and began his spiel about Northville and the advantages of buying such a fine property. Lincoln listened, but his gaze was on Roache who stood a little to the right of the auctioneer, grinning like a fat toad, his waistcoat straining its buttons and his thick hands fondling his pocket watch. He could easily believe that the odious man had made enemies, including Ellen Hamilton, a clever woman who didn't suffer fools.

His thoughts drifted to Bridget. There was something about her that caught his attention. In her company he was intrigued by her bold manner. She talked and laughed and found fun in all that she did. She was no shy, demure young lady, hiding behind her mother's skirts. When someone spoke to her, she looked them in the eyes with an open and honest gaze, ready to discuss any subject. Nothing seemed to phase her. She rode fast like a man, hunted, fished, could saddle her own horse, yet she was the epitome of a woman. Her curves, her beauty, the softness of devotion towards her family. When he held her in his arms while dancing at her birthday party, he felt the primeval urge to want more of her. To kiss her lips, feel her delicate skin...

What a wife she would make.

But not for him.

The crowd of men around him grew animated, bringing him out of his thoughts and he concentrated on his task. Austin Kittrick had become a good friend, despite the difference in their ages, and he'd liked the whole family and that was the reason why he stood in this back room today. He would do his best to secure the sale and then he would leave for Sydney, and perhaps sail to New Zealand or Fremantle. He didn't have to buy land in this area. In fact, it would be prudent to place himself as far away from Miss Kittrick as possible.

The bidding began at four and a half thousand pounds. Lincoln stayed quiet while a war of bids played out in front of him. He was conscious of Silas Pegg standing beside him, the fellow could not take his eyes off Roache, who pushed out his chest triumphantly as the two men shouted out their bids. The tallest of the two men called out seven thousand and six hundred pounds, which slumped the shoulders of his opponent, who shook his head and told the room he was out.

'Any other bids, gentlemen?' The auctioneer held up his hand, eyeing the men.

'Eight thousand pounds,' Lincoln said, loud enough to be heard, but no more than that.

'A new bidder!' the auctioneer announced.

The other bidder scowled at Lincoln. 'Eight thousand and fifty pounds.' He was sweating and kept wiping a handkerchief over his face.

Lincoln believed the other bidder was close to the end of his limit. Lincoln had no wish to stand here for another hour and bid in small amounts. 'Eight thousand one hundred pounds.'

A gasp echoed around the room. Roache stared at Lincoln before grinning like a fool.

'Do we have more bids?' the auctioneer called.

'Surely, we do!' Roache encouraged. 'Mr Reading did you not want to bid?'

Lincoln waited for a counteroffer. Murmurs erupted, the auctioneer called again. Expectations mounted. Roache strutted before them, whispering to gentlemen nearby, pushing them to commit.

'I will be calling this to an end if there are no more bids,' the auctioneer warned.

Lincoln just wanted him to get on with it.

The auctioneer glanced at Roache who frowning nodded and waved his hand to complete the task. After two calls to offer above Lincoln's bid, and when no one made an offer, the auctioneer called for a third time, and then slapped his hand and declared the auction over and Lincoln the winning bidder.

Silas Pegg shook Lincoln's hand. 'Well done, sir, well done indeed.'

Relieved it was over and he'd made Mrs Hamilton proud, Lincoln stepped forward to shake hands with the auctioneer and Roache.

'Excellent, sir, excellent. Your name again?' Roache asked, observing the paperwork that a clerk was writing out.

'Lincoln Huntley.' He signed several papers presented to him by the clerk.

'And the payment?' Roache demanded, rubbing his hands happily.

'I will leave a deposit now of one hundred pounds.' He gave the money to the clerk. 'A receipt, please.' He looked at Roache. 'The full payment will be handed to you once I have inspected the property and it is as you have claimed it to be. I shall bring my own solicitor, plus the town surveyor who has history with measuring the property's boundaries and also an overseer to count the flocks and all beasts listed in the deeds of sale.'

'That is hardly necessary,' Roache blundered.

'But in business, as you must be aware, Mr Roache, it is better to be safe than sorry. I shall meet you at your property tomorrow at nine o'clock. Please have a witness to attend on your behalf.' Lincoln smiled, knowing he'd taken the wind out of Roache's sails. 'Good day, gentlemen.'

Leaving the tavern and stepping out into the sunshine, he was surprised when Silas Pegg joined him as he walked down the dirt street.

'I don't wish to delay you, sir, as you must have important things to do but I was wondering if you're keeping on Roache's men at Northville?'

'I hadn't thought that far.'

'Roache's men are a bunch of swine, sir, if you don't mind me saying so. Drunks and brigands, the lot of them.'

With Pegg beside him, Lincoln crossed the road and turned the corner, thinking over Pegg's comments. Drink would always be the devil in his mind. He didn't want Bridget's family tormented by men who couldn't hold their liquor. 'I would never have such men work for me.'

'If you need a stockman, Mr Huntley, I have references.'

'You are out of work?'

'No, I have a position in the stables on Clifton Street, but I'm a stockman, and a good one. I'd be happy to build my own hut and my wife would take care of it and work in the house if needed.'

'You're married?'

'Yes, just six months ago.'

Lincoln paused. 'Why do you dislike Roache?'

'He abused my sister, Jinny, when she was working for him at Northville.' Silas fists clenched by his side. 'There was nothing I could do about it as it would have been her word against his, and most of the local police are hand in hand with him. Then Jinny found out she was pregnant by the filthy bastard.' Silas glanced at his feet, his cheeks red. 'She came home to me and Ma, but hanged herself from a tree behind our cottage.' He looked up at Lincoln with such a haunted expression.

'I am sorry to hear that. The whole episode must have been very painful for you.' Lincoln felt the other man's anguish.

'It was, still is, even though it's been three years.'

'And you would want to work on a place that has such memories of your sister's attack?'

'My wife's father works there. He's a shepherd out in the hills. My wife was born there, before Roache bought the place, and would like to be closer to her father, for he's getting older. Besides, the cottage we rent is falling down and the landlord won't repair it. We don't like living in town and now my ma is dead, we have no need to stay here.'

'I shall tell you something in confidence, for I believe I can trust you.'

'You can, Mr Huntley.' The sincere look on Pegg's face made Lincoln feel more comfortable about revealing the truth.

'I have bought Northville on behalf of someone else. It is up to them what they decide to do with it, but I will let them know about you should they need another stockman.'

Silas shook his hand. 'Thank you, Mr Huntley. That is kind. Your secret is safe with me. Good day to you.'

Lincoln walked on to Sloane Street and entered Mandelson's Hotel. He was heading for the grand staircase when he noticed Bridget and Patrick seated in the sitting room on his right. He was aware of his pulse speeding up at the sight of Miss Kittrick dressed in light-blue cotton with a pale-yellow pattern on it. Her dark hair was twisted and pulled under her jaunty little hat pinned to the side of her head. She looked ravishing.

'Mr Huntley!' Bridget stood quickly, Patrick following her and came to shake his hand.

'How was it?' Patrick asked, a little nervously. 'I have been battling my sister to stop her from marching over to the London Tavern to see what was happening.'

Lincoln admired Bridget's spirit. 'Wouldn't that have defeated the purpose?'

'Exactly!' Patrick glared at his sister.

'Come sit down, Mr Huntley, and tell us all about it,' Bridget invited him, eagerness in her voice. 'Were you successful?'

A maid entered and spoke to Patrick. 'Excuse me, Mr Kittrick, your table is ready.'

'Thank you.' Patrick rose from his chair again. 'We were about to eat, Mr Huntley, or try to for our stomachs are in knots. You must join us.'

'We have asked for a third place to be set at the table,' Bridget told him, leading the way across the hall into the dining room. 'We assumed you'd be ravenous if successful.'

'And what if I failed, Miss Kittrick?' Lincoln asked helping her to her chair and smelling her faint fragrance of roses.

'Goodness, it never crossed my mind you would fail, Mr Huntley.' She gave him an odd look as though such an idea was preposterous.

'Shall we order?' Lincoln teased, feigning sombreness.

Bridget and Patrick stared at him.

Lincoln grinned ever so slightly. 'To celebrate the success of owning Northville?'

'Oh!' Bridget breathed, sagging against the chair.

'Very well done, Mr Huntley.' Patrick left his chair to shake his hand vigorously.

'I never doubted it,' Bridget declared, laughing. 'I could kiss you, Mr Huntley, really I could.' Then realising what she'd said she spun to the hovering maid. 'Your best bottle of wine, please.'

'None for me,' Lincoln instantly said, inwardly wishing he could kiss Bridget for the rest of his life, but of course he couldn't. 'I can toast with a cordial, if I may?'

'Absolutely.' Patrick patted his arm. 'You can have whatever you wish for!'

'And your finest steaks, too,' Bridget told the maid. 'No mutton for us today.'

The maid blinked rapidly. 'There is only pork chops or beef stew on the menu today, miss, I'm ever so sorry.'

Bridget waved her hand. 'Pork chops will do, won't it?' she asked the table.

'Fine by me,' Lincoln answered, amazed at her confidence in everything she did.

'And what dessert do you have?'

'Apple pie or peaches and cream.'

'We will have both and share, thank you,' Bridget ordered, before turning back to Lincoln beaming. 'I am so happy, Mr Huntley. I shall write to Mama this very evening with the joyful news. What a shame she won't know of it for months yet, but I know she will be thrilled. Tell us everything.'

'Your parents placed their trust in me, and I am pleased to have helped them. From everything I've heard about Roache, he isn't a man you want living close to you.' Relaxing back in the chair Lincoln waited while wine was poured for Bridget and Patrick, and he enjoyed a refreshing raspberry and mint cordial.

'No one could have done as well as you,' Patrick told him.

'I wish I had been there.' Bridget raised one eyebrow at her brother.

'I'm glad you were not,' Lincoln said truthfully. 'You would have been a distraction being the only woman in attendance.' And for him personally.

'Well, I cannot wait to see the smug smile wiped off Mr Roache's face when he does find out.'

Lincoln told them every detail of the auction as they ate and answered all their questions.

'Eight thousand one hundred pounds.' Bridget breathed in relief. 'Mama would have paid ten thousand at least.'

'Yes.' Lincoln put his knife and fork together on the empty plate, amazed to be so hungry. 'So, tomorrow I go to Northville with Mr Allen, the town's surveyor, who I have paid handsomely to accompany me and check the boundary surveys, which he originally surveyed in the past. I knew your mother would want that done properly and I will use some of the sundry money Mr Hamilton gave me for that expense and to pay Mr Stone the solicitor to transfer the deeds from my name into Mrs Hamilton's. I understand your overseer will check the beasts?'

Before Patrick could answer a voice boomed across the room.

'Ah, Huntley. Let us have a drink to celebrate!' Roache sauntered into the room, only to falter on seeing Bridget and Patrick. 'You know the Kittricks?'

'We have just been introduced. Apparently, they are my new neighbours.' Lincoln stood, fleetingly astonished at his ability to lie with ease. 'They saw me alone and invited me to their table,' he said smoothly.

'Do not befriend them, Mr Huntley,' Roache spat, looking at Bridget with distaste. 'They are unworthy of a decent gentleman such as yourself. Come with me and separate yourself from such poor company.'

Patrick jerked to his feet, offended, and Lincoln stepped away from the table to face Roache. 'Please allow me to make judgements for myself on who I dine with, Mr Roache. One cannot have too many friends, do you not agree?'

'You don't want to be friends with them, Huntley,' Roache sneered. 'Their mother was an Irish peasant living with pigs. She married up the minute she stepped off the ship, likely opening her legs to the first man who looked at her.'

Patrick twisted so fast and punched Roache in the mouth before Lincoln could stop him, but he quickly grabbed him before he followed with another punch. 'No, Patrick!' he whispered in his ear. 'He'll have you on a charge. He has friends everywhere I've been told.'

Bridget marched over to where Roache leaned against the fireplace mantle, a hand to his bleeding lip. 'You dare to speak of my mother in such a way, you grubby, disgusting excuse of a man?'

'I dare to speak the truth!' Roache chuckled and spat blood at her feet. 'Thank God I've sold my farm and never do I have to see any of you Irish scum again!' He glared at Patrick. 'I'll have you charged. I will. Your mother won't be able to save you from prison, lad. There are witnesses.'

'I saw nothing,' Bridget declared. 'I'll swear under oath that you tripped and fell.'

'You bitch,' Roache swore under his breath. 'You deserve a good thrashing.'

'There is no need for that, Roache. Everyone needs to calm down.' Lincoln tried to soothe the situation, releasing Patrick slowly. 'It was all a heated exchange, tempers ran high, things were said. Let us shake hands now.' He felt a muscle twitch in his jaw, something that happened when faced with violence.

'I'd rather eat dirt than shake a paddy's hand.' Roache's expression was full of hatred.

Bridget, high spots of colour on her cheeks, glared at Roache. 'If you have a charge put against my brother, I will speak to the police about what you did to Mrs Webber, and all the other girls at your property.'

Roache paled, but anger flared in his small eyes. 'You dare to threaten me!'

'Enough!' Lincoln strode forward in front of Bridget. 'Mr Roache, we are causing entertainment for fellow guests.' He nodded to the collection of people gawping at them from the hall. 'Shall you and I go for a drink somewhere else? It is a night of celebration, is it not?'

Reluctantly, Roache took a few steps back, straightening his coat. 'As you say, Mr Huntley, it is a night of celebration. I shouldn't allow it to be spoilt by those who are unworthy of air. Shall we go?'

'I shall fetch my coat and meet you outside.' Lincoln remained where he was until Roache had gone from the room and the other guests drifted away. He quickly spoke to Patrick and Bridget. 'I shall call on you at Louisburgh after the meeting tomorrow.'

'You don't have to drink with the man,' Patrick said, rubbing his knuckles.

'I can spare an hour to pamper the man into a good mood, so he doesn't become suspicious, or go to the police about you. We need to play this correctly until the final papers are signed tomorrow.' He looked at Bridget and gave her a smile. She was so brave yet foolhardy, daring to stand up to a man like Roache.

'Thank you again, Mr Huntley.' Bridget wiped a tired hand over her eyes. 'It seems we shall be in your debt even more deeply if you can persuade Roache from reporting Patrick's attack on him.'

'I'll talk Roache out of such a move, don't fret. Good night, Patrick, Miss Kittrick.'

He spoke to the wardrobe attendant and reclaimed his coat. Although the night air wasn't cold, Lincoln knew he'd walk for hours to clear his head. First, he needed to pacify Mr Roache, a task he wished he could forgo. His hands shook slightly as he walked out of the hotel. Fighting caused recollections to invade his head, even when he wasn't the one in combat. Flashes of dark memories, ones that woke him up in the middle of the night in a sweat, were pushed away as Roache signalled to him from further up the street.

Now all he had to do was spend an hour in that odious man's company, drinking more cordial. God help him.

Chapter Six

Bridget leaned against the verandah rail, watching the track which crossed the open paddocks between the boundary of Louisburgh and Northville. It had gone past six o'clock and the sun was on its descent beyond the hills in the distance.

'Will you sit down? You're making me nervous.' Patrick leaned forward in the sling chair made of hide.

'Why is it taking so long?'

'I don't know. Perhaps Mr Huntley has found some problems?'

Bridget began pacing the verandah while watching the track that she had a clear view of for no fancy gardens disrupted the view across the wide brown fields.

Although their mother had made vast improvements on Louisburgh, including building the two-storey house to replace the original bark hut, the house wasn't as decadently furnished as at Emmerson Park. Louisburgh was a large sheep and cattle farm over thousands of acres, a serious income provider for the family, and grew larger by constant additions to it, by

Mama purchasing adjoining farmland. Emmerson Park ran a few cattle, but was, at heart, an entertaining estate with its lush gardens, orchards, a river full of fish and stables full of horses to ride for pleasure. Everything at the Berrima house was to cater for guests and comfort for the family.

Louisburgh was the harder, harsher sister. Here, the way of life revolved around the farm. The animals were the main priority, and it showed, for their mother hadn't built pretty gardens to stroll amongst, here to walk a person would wander through the native trees or along the creek. Although guests were welcomed, no extravagant parties were held here.

Despite the differences between the two estates, Bridget loved them both, though Louisburgh held her heart a little more as it did with her mother. She enjoyed the comradery of the workers, knowing about their families, celebrating the marriages and births and commiserating the deaths. Mama, naturally, took everyone under her wing who worked on Louisburgh. The staffs' stores were constantly stocked with essential goods for them to purchase like flour, tea, sugar, but also extra ingredients to make their lives happier - currants, dates, jams as well as an assortment of clothes and household goods for their cottages or living quarters.

Bridget wanted to do the same at Northville. She wanted to create a station equal to Louisburgh where those they employed were good trustworthy people, happy with their lot. Her thoughts ran to building a school for the workers' children on the two properties, maybe a small church for them to worship in...

'A nice cup of tea,' Mrs Palmer announced coming out on to the verandah with a tea tray.

'How is Mrs Webber?' Patrick asked.

'A little better.' Mrs Palmer poured out the tea. 'She feels safer now you both are here. Perhaps she believes Mr Roache won't come here now he knows the family have arrived.'

'He'll see the wrong end of a rifle if he does,' Bridget smarted.

'And Mrs Webber is happy to travel with me to Berrima when I leave?' Patrick asked, taking a cup and saucer.

'She is, Mr Patrick. She wants to be gone from this area, and that's understandable.' Mrs Palmer squinted into the distance. 'Riders.'

Bridget spun to see movement on the open grassland. 'Is it Mr Huntley?'

'I think it would be.' Patrick rose and joined her at the rail. 'Let us pray it all went well.'

Bridget held her breath the whole time the riders came closer and only let it out when she saw Mr Huntley raise his hand to them. She and Patrick waited on the verandah as Mr Huntley, Mr Allen and another man dismounted and walked up the four steps to join them.

'Well.' Mr Huntley gave a half smile, slipping off his leather gloves. 'It is done.' He handed the signed papers to Patrick. 'We must meet with Roache in the morning at the bank to transfer the money to him and then I shall meet you both at the solicitors to sign the deeds over into your mother's name.'

'Thank you.' Patrick shook his hand. 'Excellent work. We are deeply grateful.'

Bridget could have kissed him and instead shook his hand, enjoying the feel of his skin against hers. Mr Huntley's tender gaze warmed her soul.

'And Roache won't be going to the police about the assault last night.'

Patrick sagged with relief. 'I was worried he might.'

'I managed to talk him out of it.' Huntley turned to Mr Allen. 'Mr Allen has done a stellar job today.'

'Thank you, Mr Allen.' Patrick shook his hand.

'Everything is as it should be, Mr Kittrick. All buildings are as listed on the deeds. Tell your mother that the boundaries of the six thousand acres are clear and defined. Mr Roache obviously has been grazing his animals on crown land to the northeast of his boundary, but that is not for me to judge.'

'I wouldn't be surprised,' Patrick replied. 'Crown land grazing has always been done.'

'He also let his flocks stray to the north onto his neighbour's land. That may be a problem you have to deal with in the future.'

'Patrick, Miss Kittrick.' Mr Huntley motioned to the other man with them. 'This is Mr Silas Pegg. A stockman living in town but looking for a situation. I brought him with me today to judge the state of Roache's flocks.'

Bridget nodded to him. 'And how did you find them, Mr Pegg?'

'A little poor in condition, to be honest with you, miss. No foot rot that I could see, or scab, but underfed.'

'We've had problems in the past with Mr Roache's flocks getting scab and infecting our flocks. I'm pleased to hear they are free of it.'

'Are they worth keeping, or sending to market, Mr Pegg?' Patrick asked. 'I will naturally be checking them myself, but I value your opinion.'

'Without a too close look at them,' Silas replied, holding his hand in his hands, 'some of the older ewes could be sent for tallow. The two rams I saw were underweight for my liking. Introducing another ram or two wouldn't be a bad idea.'

'Please, gentlemen, sit down.' Bridget waved them to the assorted chairs around the verandah. 'I shall send for fresh tea. You will all stay the night and join us for supper? I'm sure you do not fancy riding back to Goulburn in the dark?'

They all agreed to stay the night and Bridget was secretly pleased Mr Huntley would be spending more time in her company. She went into the kitchen to speak to Mrs Palmer about the meal and to Ruth regarding making up the spare beds. Mrs Webber, sitting at the kitchen table, covered her bruised face with her shawl.

'You must not fret, Mrs Webber,' Bridget told her. 'Our friends are perfect gentlemen in every respect, nothing like Mr Roache's friends. You will not see them.'

'Thank you, Miss Kittrick.' Relaxing, Mrs Webber allowed her shawl to slip back onto her shoulders. 'Perhaps I can help in the kitchen with the meal? To thank you for taking care of me.'

'If that is what you wish, but don't feel you must if you are unable.'

Mrs Webber smiled, looking fresher now she'd washed and changed into a clean dress borrowed from Mrs Palmer. 'I can be of use to Mrs Palmer and to Ruth.'

'Mr Huntley has just purchased Northville,' Bridget told them as Nellie, a young daughter of one of the stockmen came into the kitchen. 'He, Mr Allen and Mr Pegg will be staying the night instead of returning to Goulburn in the dark.'

'Mr Pegg?' Mrs Palmer asked. 'He's a workman, he should sleep in the men's quarters, not in the house.'

'He has done us a service today at Mr Huntley's invitation. I cannot be so rude as to ask him to leave the house. Mama would have insisted that he stayed, too.'

'He should have the sense to make the decision for you.'

'I don't mind him sleeping one night under our roof.' She turned to Nellie, a young girl who often worked in the house. 'How is your mother, Nellie?'

'Well enough, miss, still a bit weak.'

'And the new baby?'

Nellie shrugged. 'Another boy. That's four brothers I've got now. I could have done with a sister.'

Bridget caught Mrs Palmer's eye and they shared a grin. 'As long as your mother and the baby are healthy, that's all that matters.'

'Does your mother not need you tonight, Nellie?' Mrs Palmer asked.

'No, she said to come here and work. Me pa has come in from the out station. He swapped with Old Sammy for a few days. Pa can get the boys to bed for Ma.'

'Tell your mother I'll come and visit her tomorrow.' Bridget left the kitchen, eager to return to Mr Huntley, but her thoughts strayed to Nellie's mother, who'd given birth only hours ago in the tiny one-roomed hut on the other side of the stables. Unlike Emmerson Park, which had comfortable cottages for the married workers, Louisburgh had mainly single men working here and who slept in one long hut near the stables. Nellie's family had the only other hut aside from Mr Denby's. It didn't sit well with her that their workers' living accommodation was not as good as it could be. Mama always mentioned building more cottages for families, but as yet the extra ones hadn't been built. Perhaps she could organise that while Mama was away?

'Is everything all right?' Patrick asked as she joined them.

Bridget nodded. 'Yes. I was simply thinking about the workers' quarters. They need improving. Also, we need a school here for the workers' children.'

'They can't be worse than Northville,' Mr Huntley said. 'I wouldn't house pigs in some of their huts.'

'We'll change that.' She turned to Patrick. 'We need more families. Northville needs civilising. I know Mama says families cost more to have on a property than single men because of the need for more housing and food supplies, but I reason a balance can be sort.'

'You could turn Northville into a village,' Mr Huntley suggested.

'A village?' Bridget was surprised by such an idea.

'It is done all over the country,' Mr Allen added. 'The government wants settlements.'

'Mama wouldn't want a village so close to here.'

'Surely a few miles away is not that close?' Mr Allen asked.

'Have you *met* our mother, Mr Allen?' Patrick laughed.

'I have and, yes, she would be appalled.' Mr Allen chuckled.

Bridget gave the idea some thought. 'Unless it's a village done tastefully. Tree-lined streets, a school, a doctor's house, a church.'

'Sounds promising,' Mr Huntley agreed, his eyes upon her and a small smile playing about his lips.

She leaned closer to him, suddenly wanting his opinion on everything. 'Your thoughts on Mr Pegg?' she whispered, so that Silas couldn't hear them talking about him.

'He seems a good man and knows his stuff about stock. He is wasted at the stables where he works in Goulburn,' he murmured in reply.

'Should I hire him? I want to rid Northville of Roache's men. They all seem to be scoundrels.'

Huntley sat back and crossed his legs. 'Silas would be an excellent addition to your workforce from what I have seen of the man. Decent young men are hard to come by.'

'Especially out here. They turn to drink or crime so easily.' She looked at Silas Pegg, who seemed a little out of place in his work clothes and made a decision. 'Mr Pegg,' she spoke loud enough for him to hear and turn his attention to her.

'Yes, Miss Kittrick?'

'If you are looking for work, we can offer you a position at Northville as a stockman.'

Surprised, Silas sat straighter. 'I'd be grateful for it, Miss Kittrick, but I'm married.'

'We'll find you and your wife some accommodation, do not fear. Even if we have to build you a hut.'

'Then I'd be grateful, miss, and work hard for your family.' His grin and grateful expression was lovely to see.

'That's settled then.' She glanced at Huntley and was pleased when he smiled at her. How amazing was it to covet a certain man's smile? One look from him and she felt empowered and desirable.

While the men talked Bridget thought of making her own improvements to not only Louisburgh but Northville, and the first thing she'd do would be to change the name of Northville to something else entirely and rid the stain of Roache.

After supper, the men joined Bridget in the parlour for drinks, though she again noted Mr Huntley asked for tea or cordial, as he had at the dining table. He was the only man she knew who didn't drink alcohol and it fascinated her.

'You seem deep in thought?' Mr Huntley asked her quietly, as he came to stand beside her chair as the others spoke of local news.

'I am thinking of the name to call Northville. Can you suggest anything?' She gazed up at him, wondering what it would be like to be kissed by him, and the thought gave her a small shiver of pleasure. To calm her thoughts, she held up her pencil and paper. 'As you see my efforts so far have drawn a blank.'

'Changing the name would be wise.' He continued to watch her, as if doing so gave him enjoyment.

Bridget's pulse quickened. 'We should name it after you. After all, you were the one to help us buy the property.'

His eyes widened in astonishment. 'Perhaps you should write to your mother about such an important decision?'

She paused for a moment. 'Huntley Vale.' The name came to her easily and she instantly liked it. 'Mama would approve.'

'Huntley Vale?' He tapped a finger against his mouth in thought. 'It does sound rather grand, doesn't it? But I do not deserve it.' The light died from his eyes.

'You do, absolutely you do.'

'No, I do not. You do not know me well enough to make such a statement.'

'I know you have been good and kind towards my family. Austin calls you a friend and you have secured Roache's property for us when it might have been nearly impossible for us to have it otherwise. That is all the proof I need to declare you a friend to this family, to me...' she added softly.

His expression seemed haunted for a moment, then he gave a slight nod. 'As you wish.'

'Patrick.' Bridget swung around to her brother. 'Northville will be now known as Huntley Vale. I've decided.'

'Really?' Patrick shrugged. 'I suppose it's a suitable name after everything Mr Huntley has done for us.'

'Your mother may not wish it,' Mr Huntley said.

Patrick shook his head. 'Mama won't mind in the least and besides she will consider it fitting, too.' He raised his glass. 'A toast to Huntley Vale, may the property long be successful.'

'Cheers!' They all toasted.

'Well,' Mr Huntley said more quietly to Bridget, 'if I achieve nothing else in this life, I will have a small piece of this country named in my honour.'

'I am sure you will achieve many more things.'

'How confident you sound,' he mused.

'And you aren't? Confident?'

'Sometimes, yet I know how quickly life can change and the path you want to take is suddenly diverted to another.'

'You don't like change? Would you prefer a dull life with no surprises along the way?'

He sipped his cordial. 'Actually, I would. Would you think less of me because of that?'

She tilted her head to study him. 'For some reason I expected you to be the type who wasn't afraid of anything.'

His wry smile returned. 'I never said I was afraid. I just would prefer a quiet life.' He paused. 'And I assume you are the opposite.'

She chuckled. 'You are getting to know me too well, Mr Huntley.'

Patrick came to them. 'More wine, sister?'

She raised her glass for it to be refilled. 'Thank you.' When Patrick had walked away, Bridget turned back to Mr Huntley. 'Will you stay in Goulburn many more days?' She didn't want to think of him leaving.

'I may travel south to Yass, and maybe beyond that for a while. While staying in Goulburn I've spoken to a good many people about lands to the south.'

'To find a property of your own,' she stated, sipping her wine. He would be days' ride from here if he bought in the southern counties. She would miss him.

'Yes. I wish to breed cattle, black Angus. I have given it much thought and decided that is the path I wish to take.'

'Do you have the cattle already?'

'No, not yet. The minute I find a suitable property I shall write to a cousin in Scotland to purchase a few beasts, a bull and some cows and ship them over to me. I'm told that the land in the far north is also good for pasture, but there aren't many towns yet established up there in the Queensland colony, not inland at least. I'd rather not be too far from the markets. I want my cattle to be known for its breeding. There are some beautiful herds of them in Tasmania. As a young man I worked for a gentleman who had a small herd of Angus. He taught me a lot. That is the breed that I know and have studied, and I believe they are my future.'

She heard the passion in his voice. 'Cattle are bred in these parts quite successfully.'

'So, I am told. I do like the region. From Berrima to Goulburn, the countryside is beautiful, lush. Perfect grazing.'

'Then perhaps you'll stay close?' she asked hopefully.

His eyes never left hers. 'Who knows, Miss Kittrick? Perhaps something or someone will convince me that I should put down my roots here.'

She smiled, full of joy at meeting this fine man. With every conversation, she felt more drawn to Lincoln Huntley. A smart and good-looking gentleman such as he was not easily found. What is more, he seemed to regard her highly in return. Her mind raced. Might he be someone she could marry? The notion astonished her because up until now, she'd not considered marriage as something important or needed. She'd been content to remain unattached, to set her own pace and do as she pleased. As yet no other man in her acquaintance had come close to catching her attention for more than an hour or so.

Was she ready to give up the freedom she enjoyed? Mama spoke of her being financially secure. Unlike other young women her age she didn't need to marry a man for money, for what he may possibly provide for her. She was in a very small minority where she could take care of herself. So, she could marry for love not protection. Did she want to be shackled to a man or was it wise to wait a few more years? Was Mr Huntley ready for a wife?

'I have lost you again, Miss Kittrick,' said Mr Huntley, amused instead of offended. 'I am in fear of believing myself to be as boring as an old man napping in his chair.'

'Oh no.' Bridget laughed. 'Not at all. My mind has a tendency to run away with me.'

Mr Huntley raised his dark eyebrows, considering her words. 'May I ask what you were thinking?'

'I would shock you if I told you.' She bit her lip to stop from grinning like a fool.

'I am not easily shocked, Miss Kittrick,' he spoke softly.

She sensed a change in him. Was it desire that darkened his eyes? Her heart thumped like a hammer in her chest. Her corset seemed too tight. 'One day I shall tell you, but not tonight.'

'One day... Are you saying we shall stay friends?'

'I would like to imagine so.'

'As would I.' He reached for his glass which was close to her own on the small table beside her chair. His fingers lightly touched the back of her hand and Bridget's stomach swooped in response.

Muttering a soft groan, Mr Huntley stood abruptly. 'I should call it a night. It's been a long day and we have another important one tomorrow.' He bowed to Bridget. 'Good night, Miss Kittrick.'

'Good night, Mr Huntley.' His sudden departure gave her a sense of loss. Had she said or done something wrong?

Huntley's leaving broke up the party and Bridget rose to go upstairs herself.

Patrick held her back a moment. 'One more day and then it is all finalised. Mammy would be proud.'

'I feel we have done very little. It has all been Mr Huntley's doing.'

'But we are here, overseeing it all. How happy she will be when she receives our letters that Northville is ours.' Patrick locked the front door.

'It will make her visit to England all the more enjoyable,' Bridget said as she closed the window shutters.

Patrick sighed. 'I miss them already.'

'Me, too. At least we have each other.' Taking a lamp, she lit the way for them up the stairs. 'Good night.'

Going into her room, she thought of Mr Huntley in the bedroom on the other side of the wall and her skin tingled at the image of him lying in bed. Was he naked? Her blood ran hot at the thought. She hoped he was thinking of her, too. Did he imagine her without clothes? Her skin goosebumped.

Una came in to help her undress, dispelling her wild thoughts of Mr Huntley.

'Was it a nice evening, miss?' Una asked, untying Bridget's corset.

'Very much so.'

'Mr Huntley is lovely. Earlier, he stepped aside on the stairs while I came down carrying a basket of washing. Not many gentlemen would do that for a servant. Usually, they'd make the servant move out of the way.'

'True,' Bridget murmured as Una brushed out her hair. 'Mr Huntley is indeed a fine gentleman.'

Along the busy thoroughfare of Goulburn's Auburn Street, Bridget rode in the horse and buggy with Patrick driving. Their gentlemen guests had ridden off to Goulburn straight after breakfast, but Bridget had finished another letter to Mama before she and Patrick drove into town.

She thought of the letter, hoping Mama would receive it and that it wouldn't be on a ship that is lost at sea, as so many were.

Dearest Mama,

You will be pleased to know that Northville is, as of today, to be signed over to you. I thought to get the most important piece of news written to you first as I know you'd want it.

Mr Huntley did a splendid job of winning the auction as I wrote to you in my letter on the night of the auction, and yesterday he and Mr Allen, the surveyor, had a meeting with Mr Roache and everything was considered accounted for and correct. The gentlemen, along with Mr Silas Pegg, an overseer, stayed at Louisburgh as our guests and this morning rode to Goulburn to finalise all documents.

Patrick and I will also journey into Goulburn to witness the signatures and act as your proxy. Mr Roache is not aware of our involvement yet, but I feel it will only be a matter of time until he does. By then it will be too late!

Mr Huntley has proven a good and honest friend, Mama. It was a fine day when Austin brought him to meet us at Emmerson Park on my birthday. Mr Huntley has been the most sincere friend we could have wished for. The entire episode could have been much harder fought without Mr Huntley as our champion. In his honour, I have renamed Northville, Huntley Vale. I do believe you would approve for without Mr Huntley none of this would have been achievable.

The livestock on the newly acquired land is in poor condition, as you would remember. I have employed Mr Silas Pegg to the role of overseer — he comes with prior knowledge of Northville and an equal distaste of Mr Roache. He and his wife will have a hut, and Mr Pegg will work alongside Mr Denby to improve Huntley Vale to the standard we have at Louisburgh. It will take time and money, Mama. However, I am equal to the task of establishing Huntley Vale as a property to be proud of.

I have sent a letter to Aunt Riona and Austin with the news. Austin wrote only yesterday that he was looking at purchasing more warehouses in Sydney. Aunt Riona wrote saying Miss Norton sent her a thank you note for the kindness Aunt Riona had shown her while she visited Emmerson Park. I received no such note, which is a little vexing. I accompanied her on many rides about the district!

Patrick and I are in good health. The weather is beginning to change. Summer is behind us. The heat not so torturous, the days not so long.

I will write again in a few days. I have enclosed a stock report from Mr Denby.

My love as always to Papa, my sisters and brothers, and to you, dearest Mama.

Your loving daughter,

Bridget.

Bridget still smarted at Miss Norton's lack of manners. No thank you note after all their rides? Rides that Miss Norton had enjoyed and been able to be with Austin without her old chaperone Mrs Warren, who had been left behind in Berrima. Bridget wasn't sure she wanted Austin to spend any more time with the woman. There was something about her that Bridget didn't like.

The buggy's wheel bumped over a hole jerking her back to the present. They were entering the wide dirt streets of Goulburn. The smell of manure and cattle filled the air as they passed the cattle market. Town noise replaced the quiet hush of the bush they'd just driven through.

'After meeting Mr Huntley at Mr Stone's, I need to visit the cobbler on Sloane Street,' Patrick told her as he halted the horse outside of the post office. A bullock wagon trundled past piled high with furniture.

'And I to post our letters.' She gathered her bag and smiled in surprise as Mr Huntley stepped out of the shade of a shop's awning to help her down from the buggy. 'Good day, Mr Huntley.'

He bowed slightly as she faced him. 'Miss Kittrick.'

'All set, Mr Huntley?' Patrick asked as they walked along to Mr Stone's office.

'Indeed. I met with Roache at the bank twenty minutes ago and the money was transferred into his account, and I have the deeds right here from Roache's solicitor, Mr Renney, as well as the auction note and a letter from the bank stating the property is unencumbered by debts.' He held up a small leather satchel. 'Roache asks for two days to collect his belongings and vacate the property. I agreed.'

'I'd have given him two hours,' Bridget muttered.

Mr Huntley's stride faltered. 'I did wrong?'

'No, not at all,' Patrick soothed, giving Bridget a scowl.

Bridget carried on. 'Forgive me, Mr Huntley. I was being ridiculous. I simply want the man gone.'

In the solicitor's wood-panelled office, Mr Stone greeted them warmly. He was Mama's solicitor for all her properties in the country, while Papa used a man in Sydney for the businesses. Grey-haired with steel-rimmed glasses, Mr Stone was a small, wiry man with intelligent eyes.

After general chatter for a few minutes, they sat down, and Mr Stone set to work. He'd received the letter from Mama granting Patrick power to oversee the transaction and act on her behalf.

'It is all rather straightforward. Mr Huntley signs over the deeds to Mrs Hamilton with witnesses present. The property deeds will be reissued in the correct name of Mrs Ellen Hamilton of Louisburgh.'

'And we are changing the name of Northville to Huntley Vale, Mr Stone,' Bridget told him.

'You are? Very good.' Mr Stone wrote some notes, then wrote on an official document which he then gave to Mr Huntley to sign. 'This is a document to say you have signed over the deeds to Mrs Hamilton and so on. I shall send a letter to the land registry with the new information.'

Patrick and Mr Huntley signed where they needed to, and Bridget watched on with mounting satisfaction.

Mr Stone placed the papers to one side before selecting a letter. 'This letter from Mrs Hamilton has also instructed me to give Mr Huntley a fee of two hundred pounds in acknowledgement of his generosity of time and conducting business on behalf of Mrs Hamilton.'

'There was no need for a fee.' Mr Huntley frowned. 'That is most generous and unnecessary.'

'Nevertheless, they are my client's instructions.' Mr Stone handed over the money.

'Purchase yourself a horse, Mr Huntley, and name it after Mama,' Bridget joked.

'I feel luncheon is on me then?' Huntley's wry smile appeared. 'Mr Stone will you join us?'

'I'm afraid I cannot. I have a meeting in twenty-five minutes, but thank you for the offer.'

Taking their leave of Mr Stone, they walked down to the post office where Bridget posted letters before entering Mandelson's Hotel to dine.

'Mama is going to be so happy. To be rid of Mr Roache is a blessing,' Bridget said, unfolding her napkin. 'We must let it be known that Northville is no longer that but now has a new name.'

'To Huntley Vale!' Patrick raised his glass to toast.

They joined him in the toast just as Mrs Barnstaple walked past.

'Bridget, Patrick!' She hurried over to their table, which had the men quickly standing in respect. 'I was just this morning deciding that I should send a letter to you.'

'How are you, Mrs Barnstaple?' Bridget smiled at the older woman who had become a dear friend of Mama's a few years ago.

'Well enough, and to see you in town is a gift indeed.'

Bridget made the introduction to Mr Huntley.

'Please join us,' Mr Huntley invited.

The four of them sat and the maid took their orders.

Mrs Barnstaple lowered her head to murmur. 'The business with Mr Roache...'

'All done,' Bridget murmured. 'He has no idea we bought Northville, which as of today will be known as Huntley Vale, in honour of Mr Huntley.'

'How splendid. Your mother will be extremely pleased.'

'You must come out to us,' Bridget invited. 'Stay a few nights, if you please to?'

'I will, dear Bridget, I will.' Mrs Barnstaple nodded happily. 'I always enjoy visiting when your mother is in residence. We go on such pretty walks by the creek. I am terribly lonely in my cottage with no family to keep me company.'

When the meal was completed, Patrick excused himself to visit the cobblers to have a pair of boots mended and Mr Huntley settled the bill.

'He is a fine man.' Mrs Barnstaple indicated the departing Mr Huntley. 'I don't see him being a bachelor for long, not with good looks and charm. You must have noticed his attributes?'

Bridget fiddled with her teaspoon on the saucer. 'I have.'

'Lock him in quick then, Bridget dear.'

'It's not so simple, is it? Such a decision can never be taken lightly.'

The older woman chuckled. 'Listen to me, I might be old, but I have eyes and ears and let me tell you the man couldn't take his eyes from you all through the meal. If you want proof he admires you, then I've just given it to you.'

'We've known each other only a short time. Mere weeks.'

'But you like him?'

Her cheeks grew hot. 'I do.'

'And your dear mother trusts him, obviously, and Austin, too, since he was the one to befriend him and invite him to Emmerson Park from what Ellen told me in a letter.'

'Yes, the family has accepted him as a good friend. He has been invaluable to us in this Roache business.'

'Is there any other man who has your affection?'

'No, not at all.'

Mrs Barnstaple sat back in her chair. 'To be honest, even if you had, any other man would pale in comparison to Mr Huntley. It's like comparing wheat to chaff!'

Bridget laughed. 'Oh, Mrs Barnstaple, you are a delight.'

Back at the buggy, the three of them waited for Patrick to join them.

'Will you return to Louisburgh with us, Mr Huntley?' Bridget asked, hoping he'd agree.

He took a moment to reply. 'I would like that enormously, but I have decided to travel south to Yass and investigate possible properties. The bank manager this morning mentioned some land for sale which he was dealing with. He also mentioned that a large farm has come up for sale at Collector.'

'Then you must explore what is on offer.' Bridget tried not to sound disappointed.

'But on my return, I shall visit you at Louisburgh, if that is agreeable to you?' His earnest gaze held her still.

She smiled warmly, flattered. 'I shall look forward to it.'

Mrs Barnstaple kissed Bridget's cheek. 'Now I shall come to you on Monday, shall I? And stay until the following Saturday, so I am home on Sunday for church. Is that suitable to you?'

'I'll send the buggy for you.'

'Excellent.' Mrs Barnstaple shook hands with Mr Huntley. 'Let us hope we meet again soon, Mr Huntley. Goodbye.'

When Patrick joined them, Mr Huntley took Bridget's gloved hand and kissed it. 'Until my return, Miss Kittrick.'

'Travel safe, Mr Huntley.' A smile played on her lips in reply.

Driving home, Bridget hummed a small tune, looking out at the ranges.

'You seem happy.'

'I'm always happy!'

Patrick stared straight ahead.

'What is it?' Bridget asked, noticing his expression.

'Nothing.'

'Liar.' She frowned at him. 'Tell me.'

'Would you consider returning to Berrima with me?'

'What? No.' She shook her head. 'There is much to do here.'

'I don't want you on your own. This place is too isolated. There are hazards, dangers. You are a young woman alone. I don't like the thought of it.'

'Brother, I have half a dozen men and servants surrounding me. I am perfectly safe.'

'You shouldn't be on your own, not out here.' He swept one arm out to encompass the vast land nestled between the ranges. 'If you stayed in Goulburn with Mrs Barnstaple, I'd feel better.'

'How am I to oversee Louisburgh and Huntley Vale from Goulburn? You're being ridiculous.'

'But—'

'I'll be fine. Go back and find your land, since it's all you're wanting to do.'

'Roache's place will need a great deal of sorting. What of the men there? They must be dismissed, for I doubt any of them is trustworthy. How will you handle them?'

'I have Mr Denby to help me. He is our overseer and that is his job to take on those responsibilities. Also, Mr Pegg will be joining us in a few days.'

'Mr Denby is a good man.' Patrick looked worried. 'But men like to see a boss. Someone in charge, the owner of the property preferably. Everyone in this region knows of Mammy, for she is always here, being part of the land, talking to the workers, hiring and firing as needed. Seeing to their living needs, and so on.'

'And I will simply replace Mama.'

'It's not so easy.'

'Why?'

He shrugged. 'Mammy is married. She is older and has power and knowledge and respect.'

Bridget folded her arms crossly. 'And I don't.'

'No. Roache's men will see you as the spoilt daughter of the house. One who doesn't have any authority.'

'But I do have authority and I will show them I am in charge.'

'They won't take any notice of you, Bridget. It's the truth. I should stay. I can't leave you out here to face it all alone.'

'And what of your land you want to buy?' She shook her head. 'If you don't act soon, it might be gone. Go and purchase the land so its secure and then come back here for a few weeks with Aunt Riona. I'm completely capable of taking care of myself and both properties until then.'

'It's a tall task.'

'And one I am quite capable of achieving. Mrs Barnstaple will be here on Monday for the week and if you send Aunt Riona down here after that, and you know she will come if you ask because she adores you so, then I shan't be alone, and you have a few weeks to do as you please.'

'Are you sure?'

'Completely.'

'And what of Huntley Vale? Have you any idea what you want to achieve?'

'Oh yes, and I'll go over my plans with you when we get home, but first we have to ask poor Mrs Webber if she wants to travel with you to Berrima and start a new life with Aunt Riona's help.'

'If she does, then we'll leave in the morning.' Patrick nodded seriously, but Bridget could also sense his relief.

'Mr Huntley said he'd call after he's travelled south. He might stay a few days while Mrs Barnstaple is here.'

'He has become a valued friend to our family.'

'Mama did well to pay him a fee for his services. I could see it meant a lot to him.' Bridget glanced over the landscape. A mob of kangaroos were grouped in the shade under several trees. Overhead came the shriek of white cockatoos who contrasted sharply against the vibrant blue of the sky. Covering the gentle rising hills were herds of brown cattle.

'Though we know nothing of his past,' Patrick said.

'His father was an officer in one of the Highland regiments. His parents settled in Hobart.'

'And that's all we know,' Patrick mused.

'What else do we need to know? He is a gentleman. Austin has done business with him and trusts him.'

'What is his fortune?'

Bridget stared at him. 'Is that important?'

'It might be if you are interested in him as a potential husband.'

'I never said a word about that!' She flared, her cheeks flaming.

'You didn't have to. I know you better than anyone, remember? You watch him whenever he's in the room, and Mr Huntley watches you. There is some sort of connection there, I sense it.'

Bridget smoothed her skirts, her mind tumbling that Patrick was aware of an attraction between her and Mr Huntley. It was something she could barely make sense of herself.

'I'm not saying he's a wrong choice, Brid,' Patrick muttered. 'I'm just saying we don't know much about him.'

'Except that he is trustworthy, and he is a man who hardly knew us, yet he helped Mama enormously. We've spent days in his company and not once has he said or done anything to give us reason to think unkindly of him.'

'I shall write to Austin and ask him for more information of Mr Huntley.'

Laughing, Bridget elbowed her brother in the side. 'There has been no mention of Mr Huntley and I having any kind of agreement between us.'

'But you'd like there to be?'

'Perhaps...' She twisted away to stare again over the dry grassy plains as they rode up a small hill. 'He may not feel the same.'

'Trust me, the way that man looks at you, he is interested.'

Blushing, Bridget hid a smile and hoped to God Patrick was right.

Chapter Seven

With Mr Denby by her side, Bridget rode Ace over the fields between Louisburgh and Huntley Vale, checking the water levels of the creeks that filtered through the lands like veins.

'We could do with some rain before winter, miss,' Mr Denby said as they slowed to inspect a creek which ran at the base of the Cookbundoon Ranges to the east. 'This bank has eroded.' Mr Denby dismounted to get a closer look. 'Trees need to be planted along the bank. Their roots will stop the erosion. We don't want flooding.'

'Then order trees, Mr Denby.' Bridget took note of the bank's disturbance by the cattle going down it to drink.

'Very good, miss. There are some shallow banks further down, if we get the men to dig and dam a few spots along the way, the cattle can drink in those spots, but the higher banks need protecting to channel the water through the fields to prevent wide scale flooding when the heavy rains come.'

'Sounds like a good plan,' Bridget agreed as they rode on. 'The stock on Huntley Vale are in poor condition. Would it be better to move them onto Louisburgh land to fatten them up over winter?' She wiped the dust from her face.

'Yes, in theory that sounds sensible, but we must be careful of over stocking. My thoughts were to put the newly acquired stock up in the ranges on the Louisburgh side while we plough and reseed the fields around Huntley Vale.'

'But that will take some time for the grass to grow, especially with winter coming in a few months.'

Mr Denby, an affable and intelligent man, one who'd had the complete trust of the family, rubbed his chin. 'If we start now, by spring the fields will have new growth and by the end of summer the stock can be returned to it.'

'And what of the crown land to the north. Shall we continue to graze the herds there as Mr Roache has done?'

'We should inspect it first. We have no idea if the grass has been eaten to dust already.'

Bridget nudged Ace along the bank. 'What of hiring some land to graze the flocks and put the beef herds into the ranges?'

'It's more expense, miss. Something your mother was loathed to do.'

'Yes, but Mama wasn't aware of the overgrazing state of Roache's land.'

'My advice, miss, is to sort through the old Northville stock and sell off the unsuitable beasts cheaply, then have the remaining cattle put up into the ranges closer to Louisburgh to graze over winter.'

'And the sheep?'

'If the crown land in the north is still suitable, put the flock on it while we plough and reseed.'

'And if the crown land has been eaten to dust?'

'Then we rent land until our own is ready for use.'

'Very well.'

They rode on ahead, checking the erosion of the banks and the water levels.

'We are on Huntley Vale land now, miss,' Mr Denby warned. 'Mr Roache may not yet have vacated.'

'It's been three days. He should have gone by now.'

'The men say he's still there.' Mr Denby sighed heavily. 'He's stripping the place of everything he can and filling carts and it's not all personal things, but farm equipment that was in the sale.'

'How dare he!' Bridget spurred Ace into a canter. 'That man's time is up.'

She rode over the hill, filled with a burning anger at the spitefulness of the wretched beast who'd been a thorn in her mama's side for years.

The scattered buildings of Huntley Vale were in various states of disrepair. Shingles were missing from the roof of several outbuildings and a door swung useless off one hinge on the barn. Around the house, a modest dwelling that lacked character, various wagons and carts were piled with crates and boxes, furniture and other household goods.

As she slowed Ace, Roache came out of the house with two other men, laughing. Behind them, a maid with a black eye lugged a heavy portmanteau towards a cart.

'What are you doing here?' Roache sneered at Bridget, marching closer.

'Why are you still here? You had two days to leave. That time was up yesterday.' Bridget wished she could barge Ace straight over the horrible man.

'What I do has nothing to do with you! Get away from here.'

Bridget turned to spy a plough on the wagon, plus other tools. 'That farming equipment belongs to this property. It was part of the sale.' She had read the contract several times. 'You are stealing.'

'Listen, you little witch, I'll not have you laying down the law to me like your bitch of a mother thought she could do.'

'My mother had to! You have no idea how to be a respectable neighbour. You broke fences down so your stock could graze on our land, you dammed the creek beds to stop the water from reaching our property, you didn't maintain the condition of your animals so disease spread to your neighbours, and so much more. Someone had to teach you how to be a farmer!'

Roache grew red in the face and his fists clenched. 'And your whore of a mother is that person? A bog-dwelling Irish witch?'

His friends laughed.

Bridget wished she had a stock whip to lash across his smarmy face.

Rocking on his heels, Roache preened in front of his companions. 'Well, you'll be pleased to know that as of today I am gone, and you will have a new neighbour. I wonder how long it will be before your mother makes an enemy of him? Where is she, anyway? I've not seen her for weeks.'

She didn't want to tell him anything but couldn't help herself. 'That is because she is travelling to England, but before she left, she gave very clear instructions about what to do with this property.'

Roache scowled. 'What are you talking about?'

'Mama bought this property. It's hers to do with as she wishes, and she wants me to have it. Therefore, you are looking at the new owner.' Pride made her sit up even straighter in the saddle.

Roache's thin lips curled back in a snarl. '*Mr Huntley* bought this property.'

'With Mama's money. He promptly signed it over to her,' she taunted.

'That can't be right.' Roache glanced at his two friends as if seeking their input. 'I would have known!'

'But you didn't.'

'It was a private auction!'

'But word gets around, Mr Roache. You were not careful enough.'

'This is illegal! That witch won't have my land! I refuse to let her have it!'

'It is all signed and lodged with solicitors, and you've been paid.' Bridget leaned forward in the saddle. 'Now get off *my* property.'

'You slut!' Roache reached for her, pulling her out of the saddle.

Bridget screamed with anger and alarm as she fell to the ground with a thump. The air was knocked from her lungs for a moment.

'Miss Kittrick!' Mr Denby lunged his horse forward into the back of Roache, sending him sprawling, then he quickly dismounted and helped Bridget to stand. 'Are you hurt?'

She spun to Roache, rage blinded her. 'You filthy scum! I'll see you in jail for assault.'

Roache charged back to her, his hands poised to go around her throat. 'I'll kill you, you Irish whore!'

Mr Denby pulled out his pistol and cocked it. 'Touch her and I'll shoot you dead.'

Eyes wide, Roache took a step back. 'Calm down, fool, before you kill someone.'

'Not so brave now, are you?' Shaken, Bridget glared at him, her elbow and side throbbing from where she had landed on them. 'Now get on your horse and get off my land.'

'You thieving Irish! I would never have willingly sold to your family. Not ever!'

'You have the money. The deal is done. Now go!'

'I have belongings inside.' Spittle sprayed from his lips such was his anger.

'They'll be sent to the post office. You can collect them there.' She straightened her hat, ignoring the aching in her side. 'And don't even think of taking those carts and wagons.'

'I have a right to my own furniture!'

She turned and pointed to the man on the seat of the first wagon. 'You! Don't you dare move that wagon or you'll be arrested for stealing.'

Mr Denby who still had his gun pointed at Roache, took a step. 'Get on your horse, Mr Roache.'

Roache stood his ground, his expression full of loathing. 'I will not leave without my possessions.'

'Take that bag and go.' Bridget pointed to the portmanteau that the maid still held like a frozen statue.

'You'll pay for this!' Roache argued as he snatched the bag from the maid and threw it to his companion who stumbled as he caught it. 'Tie that to your horse.'

'Do not ever return, Mr Roache,' Bridget told him as he mounted.

'Come back here to this cesspit? Not likely. You and your pox-riddled mother are welcome to it.' He nudged his horse closer to Bridget. 'But take heed, Miss Kittrick, you don't make a fool of me and get away with it.' Danger lurked in his small eyes.

'Goodbye, Mr Roache.' She turned away from him and marched into the house.

Inside she waited until she heard the sound of hooves pounding the dirt and then let out a shuddering breath. She brushed the dust off her skirt, ashamed of being dragged off Ace like a common thief.

'Miss Kittrick?' Mr Denby asked in the doorway. 'Are you badly hurt?'

She summoned a smile from somewhere. Inside her stomach churned and her heart raced. 'I'm fine, really.'

'Your hands are bleeding.'

She raised them up to look. Beads of blood spotted her shaking palms. 'It's nothing. Shall we begin?'

Mr Denby beckoned the frightened maid. 'Is there tea?'

'Aye, sir, but not much and no tea service, just the old pottery ware us servants use.'

'That'll do. Make a brew, lass,' he instructed kindly.

Bridget walked the length of the room on legs that weren't so steady and peered out the window to see the dust rise in a cloud behind the departing riders. Roache had gone. She hoped to God it would be the last time she saw him.

Gathering her remaining dignity, she turned to Mr Denby. 'Let us begin.'

'The stock?'

'No, gather the staff left behind. Let us see what we are dealing with.'

'Right you are, miss.' He hesitated at the door. 'Do you want to rest a bit? We can do this later.'

'No. We'll do it now. Thank you.' Once he'd gone, she glanced around, hating the bare mean little room and its history of debauchery, of Roache's violence to the women in his employ. The room only had two small windows, the walls whitewashed, the floor uneven wooden boards and a fireplace that smoked for it had blackened the front of the chimney. The bedroom at the back was just as bare and horrible with cobwebs in the corners and a dirty window covered by a thin piece of material. This wasn't a home. Roache had used it as a whorehouse, a place to drink and host wild parties. She hated the house. She would tear it down.

Walking outside, she sucked in a breath of fresh air, squinting against the bright sunlight.

'Some of the men have gone, miss, but the others are coming.' Mr Denby stood by her side.

'I'll have no one stay here who isn't decent. I don't care how knowledgeable they are of stock.'

'Absolutely.'

The maid brought a cup of black tea in a thick brown cup. Bridget nodded her thanks and sipped at it.

'I put sugar in it, miss.' The maid bobbed her knee, her hair falling over the black eye she sported.

'What is your name?'

'Littlewood, miss.'

'Your first name?'

'Minnie.'

'How old are you?'

'About fourteen, miss. I don't rightly know for sure. I was at the orphanage until I was twelve and they sent me to work out here. That was two summers ago.'

'Do you wish to stay here to work, Minnie?'

'Aye, miss, especially if that man is gone.'

'Roache won't be returning. This is my property now. You are a kitchen maid?'

'I did all sorts, miss. Kitchen, house and laundry.' She shrugged, looking older than her years.

'How many other women are there?'

'Just one more. The others have run off. No one stays here long.'

'Why didn't you run away?'

'Because me brother is a cripple and I have to look after him. He came from the orphanage last winter. He's twelve.'

'Where is he?'

'He lives up in the ranges.'

'What does he do up there?'

'He hides from Mr Roache who said he was a useless dog and would shoot him if he ever saw him again.'

Bridget swallowed back a sharp retort. 'Well, Minnie, go and find your brother and bring him back here. He is welcome.'

'He, Ronnie, can mend saddles, miss.' The girl twisted her hands together in suppressed excitement. 'Ronnie's ever so good with leather work, but he doesn't talk. He doesn't like people. They used to hit him a lot at the orphanage and Mr Roache tied him up and his friends would throw stones at him for fun.'

'Nasty swine,' Mr Denby mumbled under his breath.

'If Ronnie is handy in mending, then we'll give him a job and he will be treated well here. I promise you.' Bridget smiled, happy that she could help this girl's brother. Roache was gone. She would show the whole estate she was the better master.

For the next five minutes workers arrived to stand in a group in front of Bridget. Most of the men were unkempt, dirty and wore sullen looks on their bearded faces. Ten men loitered around, none eager to hear what she had to say.

'Is this all of them?' she asked Mr Denby.

'There are a few more out with the stock.' He kept his eyes on the men. 'I don't like the look of any of them.'

Bridget took a box from by the door and brought it out to stand on. She straightened her shoulders and eyed each and every man. 'I am Miss Bridget Kittrick from Louisburgh. You know of our property and of the high standards set at Louisburgh. My family have now bought this estate.'

Mumbles and murmurs drifted around the men.

She waited for it quieten. 'My intention is to let the lot of you go. I have no time for men who are lazy and unmanageable.'

'Hey, hang on there, miss!'

'What? No way!'

'You can't sack us!'

'Who said we're lazy?'

The complaints rose as the men protested and grumbled.

Bridget held up her hand. 'You *are* lazy. Look around you. The state of the buildings is deplorable. You are all dirty and smell. When did any of you last wash? The animals are in poor condition, the grass overgrazed and nothing but dust. A stockman of any honour would not wish to work on such a poorly run estate as this. Therefore, I can only assume you are all lazy and have no morals or work ethic. Am I right?'

A round of murmurs rose again.

'If I were to keep any of you, how would I trust that you would work hard for my family?'

'If we were paid right, we would!' one voice rang out.

Bridget looked at the man who'd spoken, a short, thin man. 'You are underpaid?'

'Aye. Roache paid us mostly in beer or rum, which doesn't help us when we need new boots or a hat.' The man spat on the ground.

Bridget glanced at Mr Denby. 'Your thoughts.'

'A fortnight's trial,' he said quietly. 'Get rid of the drink. It does nothing but cause fights. Have the same rule here as at Louisburgh.'

Nodding, she turned back to the men. 'You may all have a fortnight's trial. If you do not satisfy me, or Mr Denby, then you will be let go. There are to be new rules in place. No alcohol on the premises. If you want to drink, you do so in your own time in town.'

'That's not possible to walk into town and back in one night,' one man said.

'Then I suggest you limit your intake to the days you have leave. This rule applies to the men at Louisburgh. They have no problem with it. If you stay, you'll receive a proper wage for a proper day's work. And believe me, there is a lot of work to do here. All the outbuildings will be repaired and, in some instances, they will be torn down and replaced. Improvements, better living and working conditions will be implemented here just as they have at Louisburgh. My mother understands what it's like to be treated unfairly. She respects her workers and sees them as people, not slaves. If you wish to be a part of this sheep station and have a home and work, then you have to earn it.' She took a deep breath. 'No one has to stay. The decision is yours.

But if you do remain here, let it be known that there is no drinking, no fighting, no stealing and respectful behaviour to all is the only behaviour acceptable.' She gazed at the men, seeing some bow their heads and not meet her eyes, while others nodded.

'Those that wish to stay come speak to Mr Denby so he can write down your details. Those who wish to leave, go and get your belongings. A cart will drive you into Goulburn. Oh, and one more thing. Northville is no more. From this moment onwards this property is to be known as Huntley Vale.' She stepped off the box a little shaky. She'd never had to speak to a workers' group such as that before. She wished Patrick or Mr Huntley were here for support. Then she chastised herself for being weak. She'd told Patrick she could handle this situation and so she must, but the confrontation with Roache had shaken her, she had to admit.

'Well done, miss,' Mr Denby said proudly. 'Your mother would have said exactly the same.'

Relieved, she nodded and walked over to where the wagon and cart drivers sat on their seats. The first wagon was full of furniture. 'Good afternoon.'

'Miss.' The driver tipped his hat.

'Are you hired from town or one of Mr Roache's men?'

'Hired from town, miss.'

'Then, please take this wagon load of furniture to the post office store. Have them label it all as Mr Roache's goods. Send your bill to him. He's likely residing at Mandelson's Goulburn Hotel.'

'Right you are, miss.' The driver flipped the reins and with a lurch the horses and wagon set off.

She strode to the next wagon full of farming goods but before she spoke the driver grinned. 'You want all this returned to the barns?'

'I do, thank you.'

'Very good, miss. Oh, and I'm hired, too.'

'Then you've had a wasted journey, I'm afraid.'

'Nah, the show was worth it, miss.' He grinned and slapped the reins.

At the cart full of Roache's personal belongings she stared up at the sour looking man on the seat. 'You are?'

'I'm Mr Roache's man.' He spat tobacco down at her feet. 'I'm takin' his things to him, and I won't be back. I ain't workin' for no soddin' woman.'

She stiffened at the insult. 'That is your prerogative. Good day.' She moved to turn away when she abruptly spun back. 'But that is *my* horse and cart.'

He frowned at her underneath his low hat. 'So?'

'So, you aren't taking it anywhere. Get down.'

'Mr Roache needs his things.'

'And he'll get them, but my own man will take them and return with my horse and cart.'

The old man grumbled as he got down. 'Damn bitch. Yer'll get what's comin' to yer.'

Outraged by the constant vulgarity she'd endured, Bridget stepped up to him. 'Swear once more, old man, and I'll have you tied to a tree for the night!'

'I've suffered worse in my time,' the old man answered back.

'Then you will be used to walking, too. Get off my land.'

He frowned. 'I can't go in the cart?'

'No, *amazingly* I'm not inclined to offer a lift to someone who speaks so rudely to me. Now, go!' Bridget strode away. 'Mr Denby have a man drive the cart into town, please. If there's no one you can trust, I'll do it myself.'

'I'll do it.' A man, taller than the others, came forward. He eyed Bridget nervously. 'I can drive, miss.'

'You are?'

'Peter McVitty, miss.'

'Very good, Mr McVitty. Mr Denby will give you instructions.'

Mr Denby closed the notebook he'd been writing in and followed her to the horses. 'Five men are staying, seven are leaving. The ones going are no loss to us, for they did nothing but talk of drinking. Besides, this place has more men than it needs. We can do without them.'

'Have them go with the cart.' Bridget patted Ace's nose, her back to the men and their hard stares. She rested her forehead against Ace's neck and closed her eyes. She'd never been spoken to so crudely in her life as she had been today.

Mr Denby joined her. 'That was the hardest part, miss, and you've done it.'

She smiled gratefully. 'Thank you, Mr Denby. I could not do it without you.'

'I'm your mother's man, miss. She has given me a home and work and taken care of my family. There is nothing I wouldn't do for her or her family.'

She nodded, knowing he spoke the truth. 'What shall we do next?'

'Let us inspect the buildings and speak to those that are staying. They better than anyone can tell us what needs improving.'

'Agreed.' She straightened, finding more energy. 'Mr Silas Pegg will be here soon. He will be a good overseer. A man with a wife and hopefully children in the future. This property needs to ring with childish squeals and laughter and rid it of its unsavoury past.'

Mr Denby gazed around. 'A touch of paint will see the house right, too.'

'Oh no. That house will be demolished. We shall start building a new one further up that hill.' She pointed to a gentle rise in the land closer to the creek.

'A new house?' Surprised, Mr Denby nodded with approval.

Bridget kicked at the dusty path. 'And gardens.' She suddenly missed Emmerson Park and the soft evening light of the shadowy hills, the formal gardens tended to by a dedicated team, the colourful flowers, the scent of the roses and the long grassy slope down to the winding river. More than that she missed her mama and her wise counsel and gentle smile.

Would Mama be proud of her efforts today? She hoped so. Looking around the drab yard and dishevelled buildings, she knew she had to transform this property into something to be proud of and doing so would make the time pass quicker until Mama and the family returned.

Chapter Eight

In the small office at Louisburgh, Bridget added up the figures in the old Northville ledger once more while Mr Denby waited, drinking a cup of tea. 'It seems Mr Roache was running at a loss.'

Mr Denby replaced his empty cup and saucer on the tray. 'It doesn't surprise me.'

'Which is why he sold, obviously.'

'The man had no head for farming.'

'No...'

'We can rebuild the property, turn it into a place just as equal to Louisburgh. It'll take time, of course.'

'Yes. Last night I drew up some plans for the new house. I shall send them to a builder in Sydney that Mama has used before. As soon as the men's' quarters are complete, the old house is to be pulled down. I spoke to Mr Pegg about it yesterday.'

'Mr Pegg, although young, seems to be the right man for Huntley Vale. He's enthusiastic and eager. He also knows a great deal about caring for stock.'

'He and his wife are a nice couple and will be an asset to Huntley Vale. I'm ashamed they are living in a tent.'

'We'll have a hut built for them in no time at all.' Mr Denby grinned. 'The workers who stayed might be regretting it now. They are working from dawn to sunset.'

'They can always leave.' Bridget still didn't trust any of the men who remained.

'McVitty is a hard worker, kind too. He's taken young Ronnie under his wing. The boy can't speak but he's intelligent and works leather like a seasoned old man.'

Thinking of the poor crippled boy, Bridget smiled warmly. 'I like Ronnie. What a shame one of his legs is bent and withered.'

'He still gets about rather smartly.' Mr Denby stood. 'I'd best get back to it. Tomorrow we'll start sorting out the flocks.'

'The out stations haven't been inspected this week, have they?'

'No, I haven't made it to the far reaches of the property yet. I sent word for the flocks to be taken northeast to the base of the ranges. The beef herd, well in my opinion they need to be culled and started again.'

Bridget thought deeply about it. The beef herd was small and in poor condition. 'Sell at the next market?'

'You won't fetch a good price, miss.'

'No, but as it is, they are eating grass that could benefit better beasts.'

'Agreed.'

'Take them to market, Mr Denby.'

'Will do, miss. I'll have the herd driven to Goulburn tomorrow ready for the Wednesday market.'

Bridget closed the book as the sound of a horse and buggy came through the open window. 'That will be Mrs Barnstaple.' Bridget walked out of the room with him.

On the front verandah they parted ways, but Bridget's smile for Mrs Barnstaple froze in surprise as Mr Huntley helped the older woman from the buggy. A wave of pure happiness at seeing him flowed over her. 'Mr Huntley! I didn't expect you so soon.' She walked down the steps to greet them both. 'Welcome.'

'My dear, I met Mr Huntley in town this morning.' Mrs Barnstaple took her bag from the seat. 'He decided to ride with me to visit you.'

'You must stay with us, Mr Huntley, for as long as you wish to,' Bridget invited, shading her eyes from the sun.

'That's exactly what I said.' Mrs Barnstaple directed Ruth, the housemaid, to gather the rest of her bags.

'Thank you. I'd like that.' Mr Huntley's warm gaze rested on Bridget. 'I'm still riding Blaze.' He indicated to the horse. 'We've done a good many miles and he needs a rest.'

'You both must rest.' Bridget turned to Boswell, the groom who'd driven the buggy to Goulburn to collect Mrs Barnstaple. 'Boswell, will you see to Mr Huntley's horse, too, please? Give the saddlebags to Ruth.'

'Yes, miss.'

Mr Huntley pulled off his riding gloves as they entered the house. 'Comfort.' He sighed happily. 'Some of the inns I've stayed at weren't fit for dogs.'

'I shall go upstairs and wash off the road dust.' Mrs Barnstaple headed for the stairs.

'Una will be waiting for you,' Bridget told her before walking into the parlour with Mr Huntley. She was ridiculously happy that he had arrived.

'How have you been?' Mr Huntley asked, waiting for her to be seated.

'In good health and very busy, just as I like it.' She absorbed his movements as he sat in the leather chair by the unlit fireplace. She took in his every detail. The long legs clad in dark riding trousers. The straight cut of his brown riding jacket that stretched over his broad shoulders. His hair had grown a little, touching the white collar of his shirt. He was clean-shaven, and her gaze lingered on his mouth before rising to meet his eyes, which were staring at her intently.

'I'm glad to hear you are happy,' he said sincerely.

'Were you successful in buying some land?' Bridget asked him, not looking away. She wore only a day dress of sprigged cotton and wished she wore something more elegant in his presence. Her hair was rolled up and secured with plain wooden combs. If she knew he'd be arriving today, she'd have asked Una to curl it and set it with tortoise-shell combs and ribbons.

'No. Nothing was to my liking. The property at Collector was not well kept and lacked enough water.' Mr Huntley shrugged slightly. 'There will be other opportunities.'

'Indeed,' Mrs Barnstaple agreed, coming into the room. 'I shall keep an eye on the newspapers for you and should I hear anything in town, I will write to you immediately.'

'Thank you. That is kind.'

'So, what will you do now?' Bridget asked, dreading the idea of him leaving for good.

'I shall have to reconsider my options.'

'I hope we don't lose you to the north, Mr Huntley,' Mrs Barnstaple echoed Bridget's thoughts.

'Ideally, this Argyle County is better suited to cattle. I was hoping something might be available in the Berrima district, or Marulan.'

Bridget's heart leapt. 'Why, yes, I'm sure there is something worthwhile which is nearby. I shall write to Patrick and ask him, shall I? He is buying land in the Yarrawa area, east of Bong Bong. There might be something for you there, too?'

'Patrick did mention it to me before he left. It's worth investigating.'

Ruth brought in a tea tray with cake, bread and cheese.

'After we've refreshed ourselves, I might have a nap, Bridget dear,' Mrs Barnstaple said quietly. 'The day is hot for autumn, and it saps my energy after a journey.'

'Of course, take as long as you need.'

Mrs Barnstaple sipped her tea but over the rim of the cup she eyed Bridget. 'And while I nap perhaps you can give Mr Huntley a tour? There's a lovely walk by the creek, Mr Huntley.'

His wry smile fleetingly appeared. 'I shall look forward to exploring.'

Bridget caught his eye and smiled, ignoring the strange ways her body reacted to him. Her gaze dropped to his lips again, and she shivered slightly wondering how they would feel against hers. Did he want to kiss her? Her stomach fluttered in anticipation and hope.

'Bridget?'

'What? Sorry?' She was startled out of her imaginings.

'I said tomorrow we should go on a picnic?' Mrs Barnstaple grinned at her.

'Yes, yes, a wonderful idea.'

'How are you getting on with Huntley Vale?' he asked her, biting into a piece of cheese.

She dragged her eyes away from the action and focused on the teacup in her lap. This desire that gripped her needed to be controlled. She took a deep steadying breath. 'Well enough so far, but there is much to be done.'

'May I be of help while I'm here?'

The kindness of his offer softened her heart even more. He was a true friend after all he'd done already and yet he was still offering up his time. 'That would be most considerate, Mr Huntley. Poor Mr Denby is forever riding between the two properties to sort out one thing or another, but Mr Pegg will soon be settled at Huntley Vale.'

'Pegg will do well, I believe.'

'I agree. Tomorrow we are riding out to inspect the flock but also the cattle herd needs to be driven to market in the morning.'

'It's never dull on a working farm,' he said, sipping his tea.

'Another opinion on things would be valued if you have the time?' She wanted him to stay for as long as possible.

'I have time.'

'What of your own plans?' Mrs Barnstaple asked.

'A few days here will likely not alter my plans that much. I can put some advertisements in the newspapers about a suitable property.'

'That's settled then,' Mrs Barnstaple said cheerfully, taking another slice of cake. 'What a merry little party we shall be.'

That evening as the sun set in a brilliant orange and pink sky, Bridget strolled along the creek with Mr Huntley. They had spent the afternoon riding over to Huntley Vale, where Mr Denby showed them the work going on and then they inspected the cattle herd and agreed the beasts should be sold and a new improved herd bought. Mr Huntley had a keen eye for cattle, his knowledge clearly showing as he spoke of their health issues and breeding problems. Both she and Mr Denby had been impressed by his expertise.

Now, as they strolled, Bridget was extremely aware of his presence. With no one around it was just the two of them in the golden light with the trickle of water and the odd cry of a crow in the trees. For the first time in her life, she struggled to find something to say. No man had ever made her feel like this before and she was out of her depth. She rarely sought someone's good opinion and was used to family and friends taking her as she was, spirited, bold and forthright. Only now she wondered if that was what Mr Huntley wanted? It was suddenly vitally important that she didn't put him off. She enjoyed his company and the pull of attraction couldn't be ignored.

'You must be missing your family?' he asked, plucking a tall blade of brown grass and chewing on it.

'I do, very much.'

'Do you wish you had gone with them?'

'Sometimes, but not often. Maybe when I was being dragged off my horse by Mr Roache.' She shrugged, then realised what she had said.

'He did what?' Mr Huntley jerked around to stare at her. 'He manhandled you?'

'He was angry. We both were. He... I told him we owned his property, and he didn't take it well.' She'd told no one about the humiliating incident and had sworn Mr Denby to secrecy as well. The last thing she wanted was her brothers hunting the man down for revenge.

'Miss Kittrick, you shouldn't have done that.' Mr Huntley sighed with a shake of his head.

'We argued severely. We both lost our tempers. Granted, I could have handled it better, but I didn't expect him to pull me off my horse. Mr Denby drew his pistol.'

'You could have been seriously hurt. What if Mr Denby had shot him? He'd have gone to jail for that wretch.'

'I know, yes. I was foolish.'

'You should have let Roache go on his way never the wiser about who owned the land.'

Her teeth worried her bottom lip. She had shown him another side of her, the tempestuous side. Good Lord, would he run a mile now? At times, she was no lady. 'My temper can sometimes get the better of me.'

'So, it seems.'

'The horrid man riles me so much. I couldn't help myself.' She glanced at him, then because it wasn't her nature to be demure, she stopped and confronted him. 'I am not the quiet and shy type, unfortunately, Mr Huntley. I have too much of my mama in me. I won't back down when I'm faced with adversity.'

'Standing up for what you believe in isn't always a bad thing.' He gazed over to the ranges lost in his thoughts. 'But there can be repercussions.'

'I will always stand up for myself. Perhaps it is a failing, perhaps not.'

'We can't let the bad people of this world win, can we?' He turned his eyes on her. 'I do not condemn you for fighting for what is yours. Only, sometimes, the price we pay is too much.'

Her reply faltered at his words, which sounded painful and honest. 'Are you speaking from experience, Mr Huntley?' she asked quietly.

He pulled at another blade of grass and twirled it between his fingers. 'I've done things that I'm not proud of, Miss Kittrick.'

'Haven't we all?'

'Not to the extent that I lowered myself to. But my past is a subject I don't care to speak about.'

'Oh? I thought... I assumed you had a happy life in Hobart with your parents.'

'A happy life?' He chuckled without humour. 'How I wish that could be true.'

She sensed his withdrawal, saw the pain in his eyes. Something had happened to him, but she had no right to question him. Although intrigued, she had the good manners to not pursue it. 'The future is all that matters, Mr Huntley,' she forced brightness into her tone.

'I hope so, Miss Kittrick.' He gave her a small smile.

She interpreted it to mean something, a positive sign that maybe their future was linked.

They walked on heading into a strand of eucalyptus trees of young and old. A fallen trunk was a favourite seat whenever the family walked this far. The creek widened slightly into a shallow pool and sandstone rocks protruded out of the water causing miniature rapids to cascade.

Bridget sat down on the trunk. 'We should have a picnic here tomorrow.'

Mr Huntley bent and threw a small pebble into the water. 'What are your dreams, Miss Kittrick?'

Surprised by the question she considered it for a moment. 'A long life full of happiness.'

'And what clarifies as happiness to you?'

'Family, good health, enough money to not have to struggle through life, not that I am, Mama has seen to that... And also, the love of a kind man.'

'Children?'

'Yes, one day.' Children had never been her burning ambition. She just considered that they would be there once she was married. 'What do you wish for?'

'The same as you.' He bent and threw another pebble into the water and watched the ripples. 'Achievable goals would you say?'

'I'd like to think so, yes.' She watched him. He could be so serious at times, his expression unreadable. Was he hinting at anything between them?

'There is a rider.' Mr Huntley pointed to the track that led from the road to the house.

Raising her hand to shield the setting sun from her eyes, Bridget squinted to make out who it was. 'I can't tell who it is. Likely one of the stockmen.'

'Shall we return to the house?' Mr Huntley held out his hand to assist her up from the trunk.

The touch of their hands meeting sent a shiver along Bridget's skin. She gazed up at him and he stared at her. Very slowly he pulled her hand closer to him and she stepped forward, breath suspended. All she wanted was his kiss.

'Miss Kittrick...' he said her name on a sigh.

For her it was enough, and she reached up and placed her lips on his. He stilled for a moment, then gathered her into his arms and kissed her, holding her tightly.

It was a kiss Bridget had never experienced before. A kiss from a man who knew what he wanted but could control himself just enough not to be overwhelming. She gripped his shoulders, not caring she had made the first move, all she knew was this embrace felt right, the desire flooding her was natural and real. She wanted this man in every way and didn't care who knew it.

Eventually, they broke apart. Mr Huntley raised his eyebrows at her. 'I wasn't expecting that.'

'Were you disappointed?'

His smile told her everything she needed to know. 'Not at all. Just surprised. It's not every day a beautiful young lady kisses me.'

'It's not every day that I kiss a man,' she countered.

'I'm pleased to hear it. I'd hate not to be specially chosen.'

She laughed, happiness filling her whole being. Her smile wide, she headed for the house wanting to skip and run and twirl, but she did none of that. Instead, she called over her shoulder. 'Perhaps if you're lucky, Mr Huntley, I may kiss you again.'

His chuckle reached her as she walked away.

In the morning sun, Lincoln sat on Blaze watching Bridget ride ahead through the flock of sheep with Mr Denby. He couldn't take his eyes off her and that was becoming a problem. Since their kiss yesterday, he'd spent last evening with his mind in turmoil. Thankfully, Mrs Barnstaple kept the flow of talk constant, and his lapses of silence were not noticed.

What was he to do? His night had been sleepless. He lay tossing and turning, aching for a woman he couldn't have, tortured by a past he couldn't escape. A deep need to kiss Bridget, to be free to marry her and take her to his bed and make his own filled him until he was unable to think of anything else.

Before dawn he was up and walking along the creek bed, haunted and saddened that true happiness could never be his.

Bridget Kittrick was a wonderful woman, strong, independent, intelligent, from a good family. Loving and loyal. He knew all that about her, but she knew nothing of him. How could he tell her his shameful past? How could he have allowed his feelings for her to develop so fast? The truth was he had no control over how he felt about her, but he did have control over his actions.

He had to leave and not return. The idea he had to buy land in this county needed to be squashed once and for all. To stay within a day's ride of her would be too tempting. He had to settle much further afield. He could not deal with the look on her face if she ever found out the truth about him.

He'd been a fool to make friends with the family. Why had he allowed his business dealings with Austin to spill over into friendship? He should have remained aloof, kept it strictly business. It was safer to keep people at a distance. But Austin's winning charm and easy manner had slipped through his defences. For once he enjoyed having a friend who didn't judge him, didn't know his past. He'd left Hobart to escape the old life he had endured, but he should have been wiser and realised that the past followed a person forever.

And now he'd integrated himself into Austin's family and felt the warmth, the kindness from them. He'd witnessed the family love, the affection so freely bestowed to each other and he had wanted to be a part of it in a small way for just a short time.

Miserable at the thought of saying goodbye to the beautiful woman who had captured his heart, he sat on Blaze and gave himself the treat of just watching her as she spoke to the stockmen. Silas Pegg had arrived, the rider of the evening before, and he and Mr Denby were discussing the condition of the flock, while Bridget listened carefully.

He could play no part in the discussion for tomorrow he'd be gone and would never return, but he could feast his eyes on Bridget and wish the future could have been different.

She turned Ace around and headed back to him. 'Mr Huntley, we are riding further north, taking provisions to the outstation for the stockman there and to check that flock.'

'Very well.' He clicked his tongue for Blaze to walk on.

'You are quiet this morning,' she said as they rode.

'I didn't sleep much last night.'

'Nor did I.' She gave him a shy look which was so unlike her to be coy.

He looked away. Bridget would expect him to propose to her. God, he wanted to. She was *the* woman for him. He adored everything about her, even her temper and her boldness. She was refreshing, captivating and he loved her. Loved her too much to allow her to be tainted by his murky past or for her to look at him in contempt, which she would do once she knew what he'd done. No, he couldn't ever see that. It would wound him to the bone.

What a mess he'd made of it all.

He halted Blaze, took a deep breath and faced her when she stopped Ace to glance at him. 'Actually, Miss Kittrick, I shall return to Louisburgh for my belongings and then ride for Goulburn.'

She jerked in the saddle, shock widened her blue eyes. 'You're leaving? Now? Today?'

'It is best. I have much business to contend with. It is time I got on with it.' He flinched at the distraught expression on her face. 'You have much to occupy you here without an extra guest to be concerned about.'

'But you are welcome to stay...' Confusion filled her eyes.

Lincoln cursed inwardly, feeling like the biggest cad. 'Your hospitality has been a highlight of my time here, Miss Kittrick. Thank you.'

'Will you come back?' she whispered.

'Of course,' he lied. 'Once I have settled on a property.'

She nodded, the light gone from her glorious blue eyes. 'Perhaps you can write to me and tell me how you fare?'

'I shall.' He had no intentions of writing, of prolonging the pain.

'Call at Emmerson Park if you're travelling north. Aunt Riona will be so pleased, and Patrick might know of some land available where he is looking to purchase that might benefit you, too.'

He heard the desperation in her voice and steeled himself not to change his mind and stay, for her. 'I wish you all the luck with everything you do, Miss Kittrick. I'm sure you will achieve great things at Huntley Vale.'

It took a moment for her to answer. 'Thank you, Mr Huntley. Safe travels.'

He waved to Mr Denby and Silas and looked at Bridget one last time, before putting Blaze into a trot and then a canter, widening the distance between him and Bridget. His head and heart were at odds, but there was nothing he could do about it.

Chapter Nine

Bridget couldn't concentrate as she rode with Mr Denby and Silas Pegg along the western boundary of Huntley Vale towards the north. She didn't understand Mr Huntley's sudden departure. Had she bored him with her constant talk of improvements? Was she not witty enough to entertain him? Last evening he'd been very quiet and again this morning. Did he find her dull? True, she had changed slightly since coming to Louisburgh. The Bridget he met at Emmerson Park had been fun and gay, laughing and dancing at her birthday party and then playing about with her brothers and sisters, enjoying picnics and making one of the party on tours that Austin took him and Miss Norton on. At Emmerson Park she had no responsibilities and could simply enjoy herself and do whatever entertained her.

Yet, once at Louisburgh, duties became hers. She was accountable for the safe keeping of not only her mama's favourite property, but the acquisition of Huntley Vale and the problems it contained landed on her shoulders too.

Had Mr Huntley felt he was wasting his time here when he had his own home to purchase? Was she not enough to keep his attention? Obviously, she mustn't have been. Disappointment rose sharply. Foolishly, she imagined Lincoln Huntley felt the same attraction as she did. He'd kissed her as passionately as she kissed him. Had she imagined that?

'Miss Kittrick.' Mr Denby came alongside her as they came over the rise of a hill. He pointed east to the plume of smoke rising into the sky. 'That's coming from Huntley Vale.'

Fire was the one danger that terrified everyone in the country for it could spread far and fast in minutes. The country was dry from summer and bush fires could consume hundreds of acres in a short time, decimating grazing areas and animals alike.

They spurred the horses down the slope and cantered over the fields towards Huntley Vale. Closer, they saw one of the barns was alight and stockmen were hurriedly throwing buckets of water onto it.

Mr Denby quickly gave orders to empty the adjoining tack room. Bridget dismounted and helped fill buckets of water from the troughs.

'Thankfully, there is no wind, miss,' Silas said, taking a bucket from her and throwing it onto the flames. 'But we'll run out of water soon.'

The heat intense, they rushed to contain the flames on one side of the barn.

'Get a rope tied around that beam,' Mr Denby instructed. 'We need to pull the barn down before the flames reach the tack room.'

Men ran to do as he bid while Bridget and the little maid, Minnie, ran with buckets to the water barrel near the house.

A loud crash filled the air as the barn was brought down. Flames rose briefly and smoke billowed up into the sky.

'More water!' Silas shouted. Stockmen were using blankets to whack at the flames to put them out. Buckets of water were being brought from the creek now, a hundred yards away.

It took another ten minutes to get the fire under control until only embers flared intermittently. The men worked hard to scrape a clearing around the barn to stop any flareups.

Minnie brought out a jug of lemon cordial and poured cups of it for everyone.

'Well, that was unexpected,' Mr Denby said, gulping down his drink, his face soot-stained.

Bridget stared at the smoking ruin of the barn. 'I'm just thankful that the fire didn't spread.'

'If it had been windy, it would have been very dangerous. The grass is so dry.'

'We are very lucky to have contained it. Losing a barn is a small sacrifice.'

'It gives pause for how we want to place the new buildings.'

'With large spaces between them, Mr Denby,' Bridget said. 'And we need more water barrels placed around the yard.'

He brought out his pocket notebook to write in and Bridget noticed he was bleeding. 'Mr Denby, you have a wound.' She stood to examine his hand.

'It is nothing but a scratch.'

'And one that can turn bad if not cared for. Minnie!' Bridget called the maid over. 'Take care of Mr Denby's hand. It needs cleaning properly.'

'I can do it, miss,' Mr Denby protested.

'Let Minnie attend to it. She can clean it better than you can with one hand. Minnie, have a honey poultice put on it and bandaged well.' Bridget gazed at the men resting, their faces streaked with black soot and sweat. Around them were the debris of the barn and also the produce they'd managed to drag out before the flame grew too fierce. She walked around the crates of vegetables and the sacks of grain. 'Mr Pegg, when the men have rested, we need to store everything we saved from the barn.'

'Where, miss?'

'Make room in the house. I know the men are sleeping in there at the moment, but the food is important, too.'

She walked to the men, and those sitting on the dirt quickly stood and took off their hats. 'You have all done well. Thank you.'

An older stockman pointed with his hat to the smouldering ruin. 'If you don't mind me saying, miss, we should continue to add some water to those embers. We don't want the fire to restart.'

Bridget looked at the blackened beams where red embers winked in the sun. 'I agree. What is your name?'

'Bill Blackburn, miss.'

'Can I leave that in your capable hands, Mr Blackburn?'

'Aye, miss, aye.' He nodded respectfully and slapped on his hat. 'Right, men, you heard Miss Kittrick, let's get to it.'

Bridget entered the house through the open back door and into a room which was used as a kitchen and scullery combined. Minnie was bandaging Mr Denby's hand. 'How is it?'

'It's a decent size cut and a minor burn next to it, miss,' Minnie answered before Mr Denby could. 'It'll need regular checking for infection.'

'You should be taken into Goulburn, Mr Denby, and visit a doctor.'

'There's no need, miss. It's fine. I'll keep an eye on it.'

'And so will the doctor. You are too valuable to me, Mr Denby. I cannot have anything happen to you.'

'There's too much to be done for me to go to Goulburn.'

'I can manage. We have the cattle being driven into town as we speak. You can stay overnight and attend the market tomorrow. It'll save you riding there before dawn in the morning.'

'And what of the flock inspection?'

'I can ride with Mr Pegg to the north outstations to assess the flock there. I want you taken care of, Mr Denby, please. It will put my mind at rest. Now ride back to Louisburgh and have someone take you in the cart.'

'It's not necessary, miss.' Mr Denby winced as he moved his hand.

'No arguments. I need you well, Mr Denby.' She smiled. 'Now, please go home and have someone take you to Goulburn and please tell Mrs Barnstaple I'll be a few hours yet, not that she'll mind, she said she wanted to paint by the creek when I left her this morning.'

Bridget washed her hands and face and lightly sponged down the skirts of her burgundy riding habit to make herself tidy after fighting the fire. She called for Silas and the two of them were soon riding over the wide flat fields towards the furthest boundary, which jutted out to the east between a gap in the ranges. If they travelled further north, they would eventually come to the small town of Taralga, but instead they guided the horses right and headed for the base of the high wooded ranges.

As she rode, Bridget tried not to think of Mr Huntley and his abrupt departure, but of course her mind refused to obey, and her thoughts drifted to him. She felt since their kiss he had withdrawn from her. Was he ashamed to have compromised her reputation? If so, he needn't have worried for no one saw them. Or did he believe that now he was honour bound to propose to her? That he might consider he now had an obligation to marry her? Not from one kiss, surely? He must know she'd not hold him to such a declaration from only a kiss? She wasn't that type of girl.

She rode on, her mind in a whirl. The temperature dropped a little as the land rose and they steered the horses over higher hills. Thick forest grew at the base of the ranges, before spreading out sparsely across the undulating plains, which in winter were often covered with snow. From the top of another treeless hill, the view of the distant mountains and the shallow valleys that dipped and curved, shaping the ancient land was breath-taking.

The outstation, a small little hut on wheels where the shepherd slept at night, came into view at the edge of a steep slope. The ranges were closer now, towering above them, the dark-green tree foliage covering the hillsides right to the very tops. In between the trees, sheep could be seen grazing up the slopes, cream dots against the green.

'I can't see the fellow,' Silas said, reining in near the hut and dismounting. 'Cooeee!' His loud call was the bushman's signal.

Birds fluttered from branches, the sheep raised their heads to stare dolefully at them.

'His fire is nothing but embers,' Bridget said, dismounting to peek inside the hut, which was no longer than six foot and the same wide. A coat hung from a nail and several blankets lay on the thin straw mattress. A tin whistle sat on the grey pillow and beside that was a candle and a bar of soap. By the fire were cooking utensils and a stump to sit on.

'Coooeee!' Silas called again, picking up the leg hobbles for a horse. 'The man can't be far away, the flock is right here.'

'Perhaps he is answering the call of nature?' She took out a folded map and scanned it. 'There is a creek nearby.' She scoured the surroundings. 'Over there where the two slopes dip.'

'He must have heard me call.' Silas frowned.

The sound of hoofbeats drifted to them, then a crash as a horseman thundered down the incline through the trees, scattering sheep as he went.

A gunshot sounded, scaring the horses.

'What the hell?' Silas reached for his horse's reins to settle him.

Alarmed, Bridget grabbed Ace's bridle.

The horseman headed straight for them but kept looking behind him and then Bridget saw them. Four riders chasing him.

'Miss!' Silas dragged his horse closer to her. 'Get up, quickly.'

'Bushrangers?' Bridget, her thoughts scattered, quickly mounted Ace just as the lone rider reached them.

'They're after me!' he shouted, galloping past them.

Turning in the saddle, Bridget stared at the four riders and her blood ran cold when she recognised Roache. 'What is he doing here?'

'Just go, miss!' Silas shouted, trying to mount his horse which was spinning in circles, wild-eyed.

Curiosity overcame her fear as the men drew close enough for her to see the surprise on Roache's face. He slowed his horse and stared at her, a pistol in his hands. In fact, all the men had pistols.

Outraged, Bridget gripped the reins. 'What do you think you are doing?'

'Well, this is an unexpected surprise.'

'Why are you after my stockman?'

'I wanted him to answer a few questions, but he spooked and rode off. Idiot.' Roache wheeled his horse around her, grinning like a fool. 'I didn't reckon I'd see you until tonight.'

'Tonight?' Her mouth went dry.

'Yes, when me and the lads raze Louisburgh to the ground. As we hoped to raze Northville earlier today, but you managed to put that fire out.'

Her blood ran cold. 'You started the fire?'

'We did! We planned to burn everything your bitch of a mother owns.' He laughed like a lunatic. 'Starting with Northville, and then all of Louisburgh. But now, perhaps, I have a better prize. I have you. A beloved daughter your mother will never see again.'

Fear gripped her stomach, but such was her hatred of the man she was reckless. 'I'll shoot you dead if you try to harm me or my property.'

Roache laughed again and turned to the men behind him. 'See what I mean? I told you she was a witch, just like her mother. She has no fear.'

'She needs a good horse-whipping.' A thin man with a straggly beard leered at her.

'Now, Sap, you might have an idea there.' Roache roared with laughter.

'Mr Pegg, ride for the constables,' Bridget ordered, frightened.

'Miss, let us go together. Come on, away from them.' Silas nudged his horse alongside Ace. 'We need to go,' he whispered.

'You're not going anywhere.' Roache pointed his gun at Silas. 'You're coming with us. Mickey, get a rope.'

'You are trespassing,' Bridget said coolly, 'amongst other things, such as threatening arson. The police will have you in a cell by nightfall.' She sounded braver than she felt.

The man called Sap inched his horse nearer to Roache. 'We could have some fun with this one, what do you say, Mr Roache?'

'God, no.' Roache shuddered dramatically. 'I couldn't bear to touch Irish scum.'

'I bet she's a virgin,' Sap replied, eyeing Bridget as though she was a tasty steak he needed to devour.

A shiver shook her. The danger had escalated. As she nodded to Silas for them to go, Roache raised his pistol straight at her.

'You will stay here.' He prodded his horse up to Ace and grabbed his bridle, the gun pointed to her face.

'Leave her alone!' Silas demanded.

Roache nodded to Sap who drew his pistol and shot at Silas. The blast made Bridget scream and the horses jib and stomp. In horror she watched Silas fall to the ground with a thud.

'What have you done!' Bridget yelled at Roache, trying to dismount, but Roache grabbed her arm. She tried jerking her arm free, but he held on tight, pinching her flesh. 'I'll see you hang, you piece of filth! You've shot an innocent man.' Her mind reeled at what she'd witnessed.

'Stay in the saddle, scum.' Roache waved the pistol to the other men. 'You, Sap, and you, Mickey, take this bloody wench away. I never want to see her again.'

'Can we have her before we kill her?' Sap grinned.

Roache stroked his chin. 'No, on second thoughts keep her pure and take her to Donovan. I owe him a debt, she will be the payment. No doubt he's in need of a woman out there in the mountains miles from civilisation.'

'Aww, Donovan, the Boss? His camp is days away,' Sap whined.

Roache sneered at him. 'Do as I say, or I'll shoot you now. Remember, I own you!'

'What do we do when we've given her to the Boss?' Mickey asked, a younger man with thick black curly hair sprouting beneath his wide-brimmed hat.

'I don't bloody care,' Roache snapped.

'If we do this, are we free from our debts to you?' Mickey sounded hopeful.

'Yes, yes.' Roache waved him away. 'Deliver her to Donovan and you're free from any debt you owe me. Donovan might award you handsomely, too, being given such a woman.'

'Who is Donovan?' Bridget asked, trembling. Maybe she could reason with him more than Roache.

'You'll soon find out.' Roache gave Ace's reins to Sap.

'Let me go, Roache!' Not for the first time, Bridget wished she had a gun. 'You cannot do this! If I go missing, the entire district will come searching for me and that will lead to you.'

'After tonight they won't find me.' Roache gave her a taunting grin. 'A part of me wants to keep you with me so I can see your pain when you watch everything burn, but the other part of me just wants you gone. You're like a splinter needing to be removed.'

'We can talk about this!' Bridget pleaded. 'Is it money you want?'

Roache's laugh sounded eerie. 'I will take your money and whatever valuables you have in the house before I burn it.'

'I have a guest, servants, they are innocent.'

'What do I care? Once Louisburgh is burning, I shall leave this blighted country and never return.'

'Please, let me go. I'll tell no one.'

'And how will you explain him?' He nodded at Silas on the ground.

'I'll say it was an accident.'

'I don't trust you,' Roache sneered. 'No, this way is much better. You'll be gone and no one will find you. It'll be payback to your mother and her constant harping she's done to me over the years.'

'Listen, please, we can sort this out!' she pleaded, close to tears.

'Take her! I can't stand the sight of her.' Roache glared at Sap. 'And if Donovan doesn't want her, kill her.' He rode away, heading for Huntley Vale's homestead.

'Roache!' she screamed.

Sap took rope from his saddlebag and leaned closer to Bridget to tie her wrists together.

'No!' She jerked to spur Ace away, but Sap gripped the reins tightly. Ace dodged and skipped sideways.

'Get the bridle on the other side, Mickey,' Sap growled.

Mickey walked his horse in front of Ace, blocking his path and reached over to grab his bridle.

'Let me go!' Bridget struggled as Sap tied her wrists until a stinging slap across her face stilled her. Pain bit into her cheeks, stunning her.

Sap gripped her chin cruelly. 'Now listen here, bitch. We've three days ride ahead of us and I'm not putting up with your behaviour, understood? Be sensible or I will ravage your body and then kill you and leave you in the bush for wild dogs to eat you.'

Shaking, Bridget couldn't speak. A fear so deep rendered her mute.

'Tie one of her feet to the stirrups, Mickey, and gag her.'

Mickey, ever obedient grabbed a rope from his saddlebag and tied it around her right ankle to her stirrup.

Sap then tied another rope to Ace's bridle and knotted it to his saddle. 'Let's go.'

A dirty handkerchief was placed in her mouth and tied at the back of her head under her straw hat. She heaved at the rancid smell of the handkerchief, eyes watering. She felt unable to breathe and mumbled her words to Sap, needing air, but he ignored her and clicked his heels to his horse.

Ace tossed his head, not used to being tethered to a horse in front. She couldn't even soothe him and so sat still, trying to stay calm. Her mind in turmoil, she held onto the reins, knowing she couldn't escape right now but she would at the first opportunity.

They rode past the shepherd's hut, and she prayed the man would return and see Silas and go for help. Once into the trees they climbed upwards, the flock moving out of their way as the horses picked a path through the forest covering the side of the ranges.

Bridget took deep breaths to calm her fraught nerves. She needed to think. To plan. Having ridden in the bush since she was a child, she'd been taught by Mr Thwaite, the overseer at Emmerson Park, and Douglas, the head groom, about how to identify her surroundings in case she became lost. Smothering her fear for a moment, she gazed around as they climbed higher. The view through the trees was hampered by the thick canopies, which also blocked out the sun. But they were riding up to the top of the ranges, at least for now.

A flash of something caught her eye as Ace veered around a tree trunk. Bridget searched through the tall grassy undergrowth and the eucalyptus trees, then she saw it. A face peeking low down behind a trunk.

She raised her tied hands, but the face withdrew. Was it a child? No, it couldn't be. Her mind was playing tricks on her. Was she to go insane from shock?

She twisted slightly to look back, not wanting to draw attention from Mickey who rode behind, but he was busy rolling tobacco, his head down. Again, came the face, from another tree trunk. In surprise, she watched Ronnie use his brawny arms and one good leg to propel himself across the grass from tree to tree. Minnie's brother!

The boy stopped and hid. Bridget desperately wanted to yell, to jump off Ace, but she was tied to the stirrup. The boy peeped out once more, gave her a salute and then disappeared.

Bridget searched the trees for him until they reached the top and then they were above the tree canopies. The view was breathtakingly beautiful and any other time she'd have stopped to take it in. For as far as the eye could see there was nothing but blue-grey bushland, distant mountains and shadowy hills. To the west, high hills rolled on only broken by the odd clearing of farmland. Sap kept going, not caring of the view, and started the steep descent on the other side. She held onto the saddle as Ace carefully picked his way down, one wrong step and they could tumble to their deaths. She and Ace moved as one, in tune to each other. A brilliant horsewoman, Bridget let her body go languid enough to ease the tension from her muscles, helping Ace take his time to pick his way down between the trees and boulders. However, as much as she tried, she couldn't stop the tears dripping over her lashes. Each step took her away from home and towards an unknown horror.

Chapter Ten

The longed-for rain that farmers worshipped by the end of a hot dry summer softly dripped through the trees to splash on Bridget as she rode behind Sap. The evening was drawing in, the warmth of the day's sunshine had been replaced by scudding grey clouds that she could see through the tree canopy. They'd been riding for hours, keeping within the thick bushland covering the ranges. The rugged terrain barely changed, just constant trees, scrub and mountains. They had only stopped once, to put on coats, luckily Bridget had her waterproof cloak rolled up behind her saddle, and Mickey had wrapped it over her shoulders but refused to untie her. Her straw hat was ruined, the brim sodden and drooping down to her shoulders.

In the crevice of a steep mountain incline, huge boulders jutted out of the earth at an angle, forming a natural weather break. Above them the trees swayed gently in the misty rain, blotting out light and casting a grey dismal gloom below.

Sap held up his hand to stop them and dismounted. 'We'll camp here for tonight. Mickey, find some dry wood.' He untied Bridget's ankle and roughly pulled her off Ace. 'Don't try anything foolish,' he warned harshly, pushing her away.

Stiff from riding, Bridget, her wrists still tied, took Ace's reins and guided him to the side of the largest rock to shelter from the rain. Night would fall soon, and she had neither food nor water for him.

'There's a small creek,' Mickey told them as he returned with sticks and small pieces of wood. 'It's about fifty yards away.'

'Make the fire here. I'll go and take the horses to drink and fetch some water in the billy-can for tea.' Sap took his and Mickey's horses and, reluctantly, Ace.

Standing alone, shivering in the dampness, Bridget watched Mickey gather the driest leaves he could find and strike the flint against them. 'I can help.'

'No.' Mickey performed his task until finally got enough flame to ignite the leaves and bits of twigs. By the time Sap returned with the horses a good fire was burning near the wall of the rock. Mickey put the water to boil in the billy-can and added tea leaves to it. Then he set about making a rough damper bread to cook in the embers.

'Damper is all we have. I wasn't prepared to make this journey today,' Sap whined. 'Bloody Roache.'

'We're lucky I have flour, salt and water with me,' Mickey said with a sense of achievement. 'I'm always prepared, I am.'

'If you were always prepared, then you should have carried more than just that!' Sap jeered. 'We've days ahead and no shops to stop at.'

'At least it's something,' Mickey snapped. 'What have you brought to eat?'

'Nothing! Like I said! Idiot.'

'Do you want me bread or not?' Mickey fumed, placing the ball of dough into the fire's ashes to cook.

Sick of them bickering and even the sight of them, Bridget crouched down and leant against the rock wall, eyes closed. She would not cry again. She'd not give them the satisfaction. However, a surge of anguish flooded over her. She was at their mercy. Two strangers, criminals. In a mad rush of blood to the head they could easily kill her, or rape and beat her, leave her for dead in the wilderness.

Was anyone at home aware she was gone? Mrs Barnstaple must be worried by now. Had they found Silas? She fought back a moan of sadness at that nice young man being killed. Was she to be next?

She had to escape. She twisted her wrists, trying to slacken the rope around them, but that only caused chaffing and pain. Sap had tied Ace to a tree twenty yards from where she sat, only she doubted she could make a run for him and mount him with wrists tied before Sap or Mickey caught her.

'Miss,' Mickey spoke.

Bridget immediately stood, back against the wall. She didn't trust them to be so near.

'Damper?' He held out a quarter of the ball of cooked dough.

'Thank you.' Bridget took it from him, the black burnt outer crust was hot and sooty. She cracked the ball open to reveal fluffy bread inside. It smelled delicious. She tried to eat it slowly, to savour it, for who knew when she'd next eat. She kept her gaze on Ace, who had enough rope length for him to nuzzle at the clumps of grass at his feet. Poor boy, he'd be hungry.

Mickey handed her a cup of tea, black, milk-less and sugarless, but it was warm. She held the cup in her gloved hands, watching the two men. One small and thin, Sap, and the other larger with wide shoulders, Mickey. Both men wore untidy beards, dirty clothes, sweat-stained hats and pistols in their trousers. Both were dangerous.

'I need to relieve myself,' she murmured to Mickey.

'Aye.' He walked with her to the edge of the trees.

'I can't do it with my hands tied.'

He gave her a sour look as he untied her wrists. 'Don't run. Sap will hunt you down and shoot you.' He turned slightly away.

Bridget rubbed her wrists from the rope marks, eyeing the surrounding bush. Could she run?

'Hurry up.'

She wouldn't leave Ace behind and knew she'd not make it to him before Mickey grabbed her or Sap shot her. Defeated momentarily, she turned her back on Mickey and relieved her bladder.

Back at the fire, Mickey retied her wrists.

The angle of the rock above her gave her some respite from the soft rain, but as darkness descended, it grew colder. She crept closer to the heat of the fire, warily watching the two men roll out the blankets. She didn't have a blanket, but she wasn't going to need it, anyway. The minute Sap and Mickey were asleep, she'd flee. Ace was still saddled and waited just on the other side of the fire. If she could quietly ease him away into the trees, she might then mount and ride away. They'd been heading north all afternoon, so if she headed east and left the ranges, she'd come to a settlement soon enough.

Suddenly, Sap took off his jacket and unhooked his braces. He turned and grabbed her wrist.

She yelped in fright. 'What are you doing?'

'Playing it safe.'

Panic rose in Bridget. Was he to rape her?

Sap threaded the end of one of his braces through her tied wrists and the other end around his own wrist. 'Just in case you had any idea to run, missy.' He jerked her to the ground next to him, nearly catching the wide skirts of her riding habit in the fire.

Scared, Bridget fought to remain calm even though anger built in her chest. Hatred, too. She pulled at the braces, desperate to be free.

'Give it up,' Sap growled, tugging her back closer to him. 'Don't try anything stupid.'

Lying awkwardly as far away from Sap as the braces allowed, she cursed him soundly under her breath. Tied to him as she was, she'd not be able to escape. Anger and frustration battled in her chest until she felt fit to scream. Only, screaming wouldn't help her.

She lay staring into the dying flames, cold and frightened. She wanted her mother, desperately. How would Mama have coped? She'd be sensible, use her brain and make a plan. That's what she would do, too. Be patient, be clever. The right time to escape would come.

Miserable, she closed her eyes. She thought of those at Louisburgh who'd be so worried. Had Roache burned it to the ground? Had messages been sent to Aunt Riona, Patrick and Austin? Were the troopers out searching for her already? Had Minnie's brother told them what he'd seen? He was a mute, but surely he could convey to his sister enough to get the message through?

As tiredness overcame her, her thoughts drifted to Lincoln Huntley. He didn't even know she was missing. Would he care? She thought of their kiss, how lovely it was, how much she enjoyed it and wanted to do it again and again. Then he had abruptly left as though it meant nothing. Why?

A rough push on her shoulder woke her. She jerked in awareness as Sap untied the braces joining their wrists, his leering face close to hers. 'Morning!'

Bridget turned her head away from his foul breath. Somehow, she'd managed to nap fitfully during the night. She needed to be sharp and alert.

A grey light filtered through the trees, but a light rain still fell, quietening the birds usual dawn chorus. The unique smell of eucalyptus and damp undergrowth filled the air.

Mickey squatted by the fire, stoking the embers to make more damper and tea. He didn't look at her or talk.

'I'll take the horses to the creek for a drink, then after we've eaten, we're off.' Sap walked away to see to the horses.

'I'm just going to relieve myself,' Bridget told Mickey. 'I'll not run.'

He rose and untied her wrists. 'You'll not get far without a horse in this country, anyway.' He shrugged and turned away, coughing.

She'd not leave Ace and so had no choice but to return to the fire after her nature call. Mickey gave her the tea to make while he mixed the damper, though the fire smouldered with wet wood.

'What made you become a criminal?' she asked him, adding tea leaves to the creek water in the billycan.

'Who says I am?'

'You must be to partake in kidnapping me.'

He concentrated on the dough. 'I was an orphan lad. I fled the orphanage in Sydney and worked about the country here and there as a labourer, but could never make enough money for a decent life.'

'And living like this is decent?'

'No, but I'm my own man. I don't spend every day at the beck and call of a master or a damn overseer with a whip in his hand.'

'You obeyed Roache. Is he your master?'

'I owe him money. I'm repaying a debt. He doesn't own me.' He was becoming defensive.

She didn't want to rile him and kept her voice soft. 'Do you have a trade?'

'No.'

'Can you read and write?'

'No.'

Bridget nestled the billycan on the glowing embers to boil the tea. Smoke billowed into her face, stinging her eyes. 'If you learnt to read and write, you might find a better job.'

'Oh aye, sounds simple enough.' He chuckled mockingly.

'If you help me to return home, I'll keep you on as a stockman. I'll teach you how to read and write, too.'

For a moment a flash of surprise and longing filled his expression before he bent his head. 'If I helped you, we'd both be dead.'

'Sap couldn't kill us both if you were to jump him. I'd help you,' she said with more confidence than she felt.

Mickey pinned her with his incredulous stare. 'We'd have to kill him, or he'd come after us. The man has killed before and likely will do again.'

'There's a warrant for his arrest?' She thought the worst of him was being a horse thief perhaps, not a murderer.

'Aye. He's Francis Bean, bushranger, known as The Sap because he's as thin as a sapling and can disappear into the bush like mist.'

A shiver tingled down her spine. She'd heard of Francis Bean, a horse thief and killer. He'd shot the driver of a mail coach.

'Listen, I don't want to see you dead,' Mickey continued, watching the damper struggling to cook. 'Just stay calm and maybe when we reach Donovan, he'll have a plan.'

'But what kind of plan? And who is this Donovan?'

At that moment, Sap came through the trees leading the three horses. 'Is that food ready? We've got to get going.' He faltered for a moment staring at Bridget. 'For Christ's sake, tie her wrists!'

Reluctantly, Mickey retied her wrists together. 'She ain't escaping. She doesn't know where we are.'

'And let's keep it that way,' Sap thundered. 'I ain't doing all this for nothin'.'

Bridget put on her sodden straw hat and kept her gaze down. She knew they were in the mountains that separated the outlying Sydney settlement to the east and the wide plains in the west. If she escaped, she may possibly make it to a farm without a problem.

However, her confidence plummeted as they mounted and set off through the dripping trees once more. Sap kept them in the thick bush, giving her no chance to see anything that she could identify or use as a marker.

After an hour, Sap checked his compass and satisfied, he led them north-west, or at least that is what Bridget thought. Without the sun, it was harder to maintain direction.

'Where does this Donovan live?' she asked Mickey as they rode along a sparsely timbered mountain top.

'In the mountains.'

'Which mountains?'

Sap twisted in the saddle to glare at her. 'Stop asking questions, or I'll gag you.'

As they crested a sharp ridge, Bridget stared at the vista before her. Again, as far as she could see in the murky light, tree-covered mountains stretched before her. There was no sign of human settlement, just mountains and steep gorges.

A wave of disappointment and despair flooded her. Not a single farm in view.

Sap kept them going, a slow descent to the bottom of the next gorge, where a creek flowed and plunged over rocks. They climbed again and reached the top of another elevation.

Finally, Sap stopped his horse. 'We'll camp in the bottom of the next ravine.'

Bridget was tired and very hungry. The rugged terrain was hard going for the horses. Mickey and Sap's horses were starting to blow, even Ace, a superior beast and well cared for was hanging his head.

'We should rest the horses more,' she spoke to Sap's back, but didn't receive a reply.

The wind picked up and the clouds scudded over, creating a fog that blotted out the landscape. Bridget shivered in her clothes, which were damp and filthy. She felt wretched and knew she looked it, too. How was she to endure another night sleeping in the open in foul weather, watched and snarled at? The depressing thought made her want to scream. But no one would hear her. No one would rescue her.

~elle~

Lincoln sat at a table in the Goulburn Hotel. He'd packed his bag yesterday and had been ready to leave on the first coach this morning, but the coach to Berrima had broken an axle and so he wouldn't be leaving until tomorrow. He'd left Blaze at Louisburgh after his abrupt departure of Bridget at Huntley Vale. Mrs Barnstaple's confusion at his sudden leaving caused much conversation as he gathered his belongings and asked to be driven by cart to Goulburn.

The old woman had waved him off, not fully happy with his excuses of why he was going. She told him to wait until Bridget returned but he'd refused. He had nothing to say to Bridget, or anyone, really. His life, his past, meant he'd forever be a loner. What he'd done wasn't accepted in decent society. He'd been a fool to imagine he could erase it all by moving elsewhere.

No, he must go further north, into the wilderness and seek out an existence there where polite society didn't venture. Where his past didn't matter because no one would live close enough to wonder about him.

A young man entered the taproom and leant on the bar. 'Beer, maid, if you please?' He placed coins onto the counter for the barmaid. 'I've a right thirst.'

'What have you been doing to create such a thirst?' she asked pleasantly.

'I've had to ride like the wind from Louisburgh for a doctor and the police troopers.' The man swiped a hand over his face in tiredness.

Lincoln jerked to his feet. 'What did you say?'

The young man turned sideways and eyed him. 'What's it to you?'

'I'm a friend of the Kittricks. I was at Louisburgh yesterday.'

'Oh, well, you must have left before all the drama then.'

'Which was?' Lincoln prompted.

'A stockman was found, shot. He was left lying on the ground on the property to the north of Louisburgh, Huntley Vale it's now called.' The fellow took his tankard of beer and gulped at it before wiping his mouth. 'Miss Kittrick didn't return last night either.'

The words shattered Lincoln. 'She didn't return?'

'No, something has happened to her for sure. The old lady guest is in a state. Screaming at us all to search for her. Riders have been sent to Berrima to Miss Kittrick's family, and her brother in Sydney.'

Lincoln grabbed his hat. 'I need a horse!'

'I've brought a spare for the doctor, but he's gone in his buggy. I just needed a drink and then I'm going back.'

Taking the tankard from the man's hand, Lincoln glared at him. 'You can drink later, lad. Let's go.'

Riding faster than he had for a long time, Lincoln pushed the horse as much as he could to make it to Louisburgh in record time. He flung himself from the sweat-lathered horse and raced up the stairs and inside the house.

Mrs Barnstaple sat at a desk, writing. 'Mr Huntley! Oh, I am so pleased to see you. Have you heard?'

'Yes.' He wiped the dust from his face. 'I rode back with the doctor and the stockman, who has taken the doctor straight to Huntley Vale. What news is there of Miss Kittrick?'

'None!' Tears slipped down her wrinkled cheeks and fogged up her glasses. 'I cannot believe it. Bridget has been taken. A young cripple boy saw her tied to her horse and being taken into the mountains. Bushrangers must have her!'

Lincoln's chest tightened in fear. 'Has a search party been formed?'

'Yes, Mr Denby has men out there now from here and Huntley Vale, and the troopers came, but what could I tell them? I know nothing. I haven't seen her since breakfast yesterday morning. She's been out all night with villains!'

'I left her...' Shame and guilt filled him. Why hadn't he waited until she was safely back at the house?

'A stockman was with her, Silas Pegg. He's been shot.'

'Silas!' Lincoln couldn't believe it. 'He's dead?'

'Near enough, yes. They didn't find him until this morning.' She dabbed at her eyes. 'Last night I wrote letters to Patrick and Riona and had a groom ride fast during the night to deliver them. My dear friend Ellen is on the high seas clueless to what has befallen her daughter. I feel responsible.'

'How can you be? Miss Kittrick was checking the stock, something she'd do whether you were here or not.'

'I should have acted sooner. When she wasn't back by nightfall, I should have sent for the police, but I waited, thinking she might be staying at Huntley Vale a bit longer. Then, when it was past ten o'clock and no message, I began to worry. Word reached me that Mr Pegg hadn't returned to Huntley Vale either. Without Mr Denby—'

'Denby? Where was he?'

'He rode to Goulburn for treatment to a burn on his hand and a nasty cut. He was to stay overnight to attend the market this morning, but he rode back at once on receiving my note and arrived in the wee hours.' Mrs Barnstaple wiped her eyes. 'I pray to God she is not hurt or worse...'

Her words spurred Lincoln into action. 'We need more men out searching for her.'

'When I wrote to Patrick, I mentioned for him to bring men from Emmerson Park and anyone else he can find.'

At that moment, a trooper knocked on the open door.

'Oh, Senior Constable Sullivan.' Mrs Barnstaple rose from the chair. 'This is a good friend, Mr Lincoln Huntley.'

'Any news?' Lincoln asked.

'No, sir. I'm heading back to Goulburn to alert the other police stations in this area and higher authorities. I'll send a telegram to the Police Superintendent in Sydney.'

'We need trackers,' Lincoln spoke of the aboriginal men who the police used to track criminals or lost people in the wild bushland.

'There's a black stockman, Old Sammy, who has already helped us. We know there was a party of possibly four men who confronted Miss Kittrick and Silas Pegg. Two rode off south, and three horses rode east up the ranges, Miss Kittrick being the third rider, according to young Ronnie. I have men scouring the ranges now.'

'Have there been sightings of bushrangers in the area?' Mrs Barnstaple asked.

'Not recently in Goulburn, but we are always on alert for the villains seem to be loitering behind every tree and bush. There was a hold up last week on the road to Braidwood. Good citizens robbed.'

'Then we have no time to waste!' Lincoln was eager for the trooper to be gone on his way.

'Yes, indeed. I shall return with more men. We have to move fast as they have a good start on us.'

Lincoln looked to Mrs Barnstaple as the senior constable left the room. 'I need a horse. I shall search myself.'

'You'll not wait for Patrick and Riona?'

'No, Patrick can follow. I doubt he'll not be here before nightfall.'

'Go fetch a horse from the stables if there are any left and I'll organise some food for you to take.'

Hurrying over to the stables he heard the thundering sounds of hooves and carriage wheels. He stopped in surprise as Patrick's horse skidded to a halt, behind him the Hamilton carriage rolled into view, and beyond that several men on horseback. The horses were spent, foaming, the men covered in dust.

'Is she found?' Patrick panted, dismounting.

'No. I'm heading out now.' Lincoln shook his hand. 'You made good time.'

'We left as soon as the rider arrived this morning. We've ridden hard. The horses need a rest.'

'There's not many left here.'

'We need Old Sammy.'

'He's already found tracks. I believe he's out with Mr Denby.' Lincoln bowed his head at Bridget's aunt as she descended from the carriage. 'Miss O'Mara.'

'Mr Huntley. Any news?'

'Only that tracks have been found leading up into the mountains where young Ronnie saw them go.'

'Bushrangers?'

'Very likely.'

Riona put a gloved hand to her mouth, staring wordlessly to Patrick.

'We'll find her, Aunt.' Patrick's lips thinned in determination. 'We sent a servant to telegraph Austin. He will bring more men from Sydney, but he'll be a couple of days.'

'And what state will she be in when you do find her, if they haven't already murdered her?' Riona's paleness made Lincoln worry she'd faint at his feet. His mind shied away with the thoughts of what lawless men could do to a beautiful woman. He could not and would not entertain any images of their possible deeds towards Bridget. 'We must hurry.'

'This horse is thrashed.' Patrick gave the reins to a stable boy. 'What horses are left?'

The boy pointed to the field by the creek. 'Mrs Hamilton's mare, Sugar, and Mr Hamilton's new horse, Merlin, and there's the horse Mr Huntley came on.'

'Fetch them,' Patrick ordered. The boy dragged Patrick's horse into the stables and then ran out again to the field.

'Riona!' Mrs Barnstaple hobbled out of the kitchen door, carrying a heavy canvas bag full of supplies.

'Mrs Barnstaple.' Riona embraced her. 'I can't believe it, so I can't.'

At that moment, a man turned the corner of the stables, looking dishevelled wearing a long waterproof coat, a battered hat and a ragged beard. He looked to be in his fifties, but it was hard to tell. His eyes were watchful, his body tense.

'Who the hell are you?' Patrick demanded.

'Patterson. Eddie Patterson. A friend of your mother and Miss Bridget.' The man stood ten yards from them.

'I've never heard of you,' Patrick challenged.

Riona stepped forward. 'I have. You are the man who found Bridget when she was taken by her uncle, Colm Kittrick, when she was six.'

'That's correct, madam.'

Patrick stared at his aunt. 'This man?'

'I'll tell you the story later, but Mr Patterson is trustworthy. Your mammy has been allowing Mr Patterson to camp in the ranges whenever he passes through this way. We owe him a great debt.'

Patterson adjusted his hat as though embarrassed. 'I've heard about Miss Bridget being missing. I've come to help. I know the bush well. I've spent the last twenty years living in it. I want to find Miss Bridget.'

'More the better,' Lincoln said, another curious piece of Bridget's past entering his mind. She had been taken by her uncle as a child?

Patrick nodded. 'We're losing time. Do you have a horse?'

'No. It died last year.' Patterson shrugged.

'You'll have one of ours. Let's get saddled up.' Patrick kissed his aunt. 'As soon as we find her, I'll send word to you somehow.'

Aunt Riona unwrapped her dove-grey knitted shawl from around her shoulders. 'When you find her wrap her in this. It'll be like I'm there.' Riona kissed his cheek again. 'Find her alive, Patrick, for I can't bear to write your mammy...'

He nodded and turned away.

Lincoln, watching the tender scene, felt a tug at his heart. Such love in this family amazed him. His mother had cared for him in a secret kind of way, only out of sight of his father. Any signs of affection were not encouraged in his family home. He thrust the past memories from his mind and saddled up as Patrick's men did the same.

All he had to do was concentrate on finding Bridget. He blamed himself for leaving her, another man there when those bastards turned up might have made a difference. If he hadn't had left, she could be at home right now. A muscle in his jaw twitched. Just another thing he had messed up. It was the story of his life.

Chapter Eleven

For a second night, Bridget sat hugging her knees on the wet ground, shivering with cold and hunger. Her riding habit was filthy and damp under her waterproof cloak. She kept her ruined hat on simply to try and keep the worst of the rain off her face.

The drizzle, which had misted about them all day, had turned into a proper downfall in the late afternoon. The rain had fallen fast enough to pierce the tree canopies above and drench them. Another day without sun totally disorientated her. All she knew was that they were still in mountainous country, and even for March the autumn weather was colder than normal at this elevation.

'I'm bloody starvin',' Sap complained as he and Mickey tried to get a fire started, but wet wood refused to light.

'A cup of tea would go down a treat.' Mickey continued to strike the flint at the wood and leaves.

'We need to unsaddle and rub the horses down,' Bridget told them, feeling sorry for Ace. Constant riding in harsh terrain and lack of decent food was showing in the way he held his head down.

'They've been watered,' Sap muttered. 'They are eating the grass.'

'It's not enough! That grass is not good feeding.' Bridget ungainly got to her feet. 'I want my wrists untied so I can take his saddle off. He'll get sores.'

'She's right, Sap,' Mickey added. 'The horses are wet, the saddles will rub.'

'Shut up!' Sap marched around to Bridget. 'Not another word from you!'

Furious, she glared at him. 'You might not care for your horse, but I care for mine!'

The stinging slap across her cheek stunned her for a moment. The pain ricocheted across her face. Her eyes watered.

'Sap, none of that!' Mickey stood.

'You can shut up too. I'm sick of the sight of the pair of you.' Sap swore under his breath.

Despite the utter shock of being slapped and her throbbing cheek, Bridget walked over to Ace and awkwardly started to unbuckle his saddle girth.

'I said no!' Sap knocked her away. 'They stay saddled.'

'Why?' she shouted, full of hatred.

'Because we might have to make a run for it at any time.'

'Out here?' She laughed in his face. 'There is no one for miles.'

'You don't know that. Anyone can be hiding in the trees. Go and sit down.'

She faced him, loathing him. 'I'm taking Ace's saddle off and rubbing him down with bunches of leaves.'

'I said sit!' He struck her face again, snapping her head back on her neck.

Stars burst before her watering eyes, pain bit deep, her cheek burning. Incensed, she lunged for him, her nails on his face, scratching, wanting to hurt him as he'd hurt her. She screamed at him, filled with rage at what he'd done by taking her.

'Get off!' Sap fought her, grabbing her arms.

Bridget fought like someone possessed of the devil. She took all her frustration out on him, wanting him to pay for her fear.

'You bloody bitch!' Sap howled as her nails ripped his face. He pushed her so hard she was flung backwards landing on her back with such force the wind was knocked from her lungs.

Stunned, she lay for a moment staring up at the branches feeling the rain splatter her face.

'Enough!' Mickey came to her side.

'What are you helping her for?' Sap snarled. 'The witch has taken off skin.' His hands were dotted in blood where he'd put them to his face. 'I'll kill the bitch!' Sap advanced on Bridget, drawing his pistol.

'No!' Mickey leaped forward. 'You're not killing her! We take her to Donovan.'

Sap hovered over her, gun pointed at her head.

Bridget couldn't breathe. She froze. She stared at the barrel of the gun, her mind went blank waiting for the bullet.

'No, Sap!' Mickey yelled.

Sap twisted around. The gun blast jolted Bridget, exploding the air, deafening her.

'What have you done! You stupid fool!' Mickey hollered, his arms out wide.

Heart thudding in her chest, Bridget stared up at Sap, but he wasn't looking at her as he lowered his gun, which pointed the other way.

Dazed, confusion making her mind fuzzy, she glanced down her body. No blood. No pain. She'd not been shot, had she? The gloominess of the bleak evening made it hard to see.

Then Mickey looked at her, his eyes full of apology. Good God had he been shot?

Bridget scrambled up onto her knees in the mud, staring at Mickey.

'She can walk from now on,' Sap declared and stormed away into the dark trees.

Bridget frowned at Mickey. 'Are you hurt?'

He shook his head and looked towards the horses. Slowly, Bridget got to her feet, but already in the corner of her eye was the prone shape of a horse on the ground. Ace.

She swayed, light-headed. Mickey caught her to him, but she thrust him away. *Ace.*

Stumbling, moaning, she fell to her knees beside her darling horse. Sap had shot him in the chest. Ace's big brown eyes rolled, he snorted as she cradled his head to her. 'Oh, my boy, my dearest sweet boy.'

She sobbed into his neck. The hurt so intense she wanted to die from it. Her beloved horse. The one her mother had bought her after her first horse, Princess, died ten years ago. Ace had been everything. He gave her freedom, he gave her love, they had been a team for ten years. She cried heartbrokenly.

'Miss, he's suffering,' Mickey said quietly, crouching down beside her.

'Leave me alone!' she raged at him, blinded by tears and fury.

'You don't want him to suffer, do you?'

'Suffer? Suffer!' She railed at him. 'He didn't deserve any of this!' she screamed, her voice echoing through the rain-drenched bushland.

'Let me put him out of his misery, miss.'

Bridget hugged Ace's neck tighter, willing him to live, but knowing it was impossible. Blood seeped out of the hole in his chest. Bridget couldn't fix him. Heart-wrenching sobs broke from her until she fought for breath. She wanted to shriek and yell and thrash about such was the anguish. Her darling Ace.

'Miss, move aside.'

'No!'

'He's hurting, miss. Let me do it.' Mickey gently pulled her up.

Shock vibrated through her body, numbing her mind. She heard the cock of the pistol in the stillness of the evening.

Another blast.

Bridget reeled and everything dimmed to black.

When she woke, she found her head resting on a saddle, the leather smell strong in her nose. Over her cloak lay Ace's dark grey saddle cloth. Bridget remained still as a wave of anguish swept over her again. Her mind wouldn't accept Ace was dead.

In front of her, a small pitiful fire spluttered in the darkness, the billycan pushed close to the little embers to boil, a useless task on such a small fire.

'You're awake,' Mickey said, though she could barely see him in the shadows. 'I'm trying to make tea. I found some dry sticks and leaves under a log, but the rest is too wet to make a decent fire.'

She didn't answer him. She had no words, no thoughts except hate towards Sap, but she was too tired to do anything about that now. Tomorrow though, tomorrow she would create a plan to kill him.

—⁓ℓℓ⁓—

Lincoln sat on his horse and looked at the fast-flowing creek. The rain pummelled them relentlessly. For three days they had ridden through varying downfalls from torrential to soft drizzle and mist. The result was the creeks and rivers that they passed through were becoming more dangerous as the water rose and flowed faster. The mountains were treacherous. He'd ridden in the mountains of Tasmania before, but never looking for someone, never needing to be watchful of men with guns. These rugged peaks and steep gorges took no prisoners. They had lost two men already, one had fallen off his horse when it shied at something in the grass. The man had broken his leg, which meant another man had to take him back to the nearest farm for aid.

Each night they had camped in some miserable spot, trying to keep out of the rain. No fires would start and so they drank water and ate hard oat biscuits. Patrick kept silent, brooding. The harsh weather and difficult terrain made for slow going. Distances usually made in a few hours on the flat, took a full day as they slowly picked their way up the mountainsides and carefully descended below into narrow gorges. There were no well-used roads or stock trails to ease their way. Instead, they weaved around trees and giant boulders, picked their way through dense undergrowth or down slippery stony cliffs with the fear of the horse stumbling beneath you the whole time and sending you over the edge to your death.

He didn't stop thinking of Bridget. Old Sammy followed the tracks he believed were hers and the two men that held her captive. The black tracker had said little, just continued to study the ground and point. Patrick trusted him completely, but they knew they were losing time. Creeks had risen sharply overnight and took longer to find safe places to forge them.

Now, as the rain trickled off his hat and ran down over his waterproof coat, he watched Old Sammy shake his head and speak with Eddie Patterson and Patrick.

'No good, Boss,' he told Patrick.

'Surely, it's not that high we can't cross?' Patrick argued.

'Water swirl.' Sammy pointed to the gushing water that crashed and foamed over rocks. 'Trap you under.'

'We'll have to find somewhere to cross.' Patterson looked down the rushing water. 'Further to the east, perhaps?'

'The tracks are here.' Sammy knelt, peering at the faint outlines of hooves in the mud. 'They crossed here.' He stood and pointed to the other side of the creek where the land angled sharply upwards into the eucalyptus trees.

'We'll cross further down and then return and come back up on the other side,' Patrick decided. He glanced at Lincoln. 'You agree?'

'I do.' Lincoln flexed his cramped fingers from holding the reins too long.

Suddenly there came a rumble, thin and whiney at first, then the noise grew louder sounding like the engine of a steam train, thunderous and threatening.

The men, alert, struggled to calm their horses as the animals sensed danger and jibbed and stomped.

'What is it?' Patrick yelled over the roar.

Then Old Sammy looked up at the opposite side of the mountain and pointed.

'Bloody hell!' Patterson swore.

Lincoln stared up in awe for a moment. The bushland parted and split, swallowed up by the landslide that devoured trees and rocks as it journeyed down the mountain. As deafening as thunder, it destroyed everything in its path at lightning speed.

'Go!' Patrick shouted above the roar.

Fleeing, Lincoln urged his horse back the way they'd come, racing through the undergrowth and back up the slope to higher ground, while behind him the landslide hit the water with loud splashes.

On a small plateau halfway up the mountain, Lincoln wheeled his horse to a halt and stared in amazement. On the opposite side, a large ugly scar tore through the vegetation from top to bottom.

'Christ almighty,' one of the men muttered behind him.

'Is everyone accounted for?' Patrick asked, twisting in the saddle to check the men.

'Where's Old Sammy?' Patterson asked, looking through the trees.

'Sammy!' Patrick shouted through cupped hands.

'He might be further down.' Lincoln clicked his heels to send his horse back down the slope.

'Likely up a tree,' one of the men joked.

Lincoln rode beside Patrick back to the creek which had now altered course. The landslide had pushed into the water, sending it gushing over the bank to create a new channel between boulders.

One of the men dismounted and walked closer to a fallen tree. 'Over here.'

Lincoln noticed the red of Old Sammy's shirt through the bushes.

'Is he hurt?' Patrick flung himself from the saddle.

The other man, called Fletcher, shook his head sadly. 'Dead, Mr Kittrick. Though there's not a mark on him.'

Lincoln dismounted and joined Patrick, Patterson and Fletcher by the side of the old black tracker. 'Had his heart given out?'

'Looks that way.' Patrick checked the body but there was no blood or sign of injury.'

'He was old,' Fletcher said. 'At least three scores and ten from what we could make out with his stories. A good age for any man, black or white.'

Patrick strode away, swearing loudly. 'Not only have we lost Old Sammy, a good man and our tracker, but without him we'll never find Bridget!'

'Can we hire another tracker?' Lincoln went to him, putting a hand on his shoulder. 'We can't give up.'

'I'm not giving up,' Patrick snapped, then sighed heavily. 'We didn't need this, Lincoln.'

'No.'

'We'll have to bury Old Sammy here. He has no family to mourn him, but he'd want some kind of traditional ceremony. Sammy deserves that.'

Lincoln frowned. 'How can we do it? Do you know what to do?'

'No. I sense fire is involved somehow.' Patrick beckoned Patterson over.

'We burn him?' Lincoln didn't like the sound of that.

Wiping the rain off his face, Patrick shook his head, sending a spray of water from his hat brim. 'No. Besides, there isn't enough dry wood for a funeral pyre. We'll bury him. I've a small shovel on my saddle. We'll make camp in the trees over there.' Patrick hung his head. 'If only we'd been able to make it over the creek, we could have seen the tracks and known which way they headed.'

'If we'd made it over the creek, we could have been swallowed up in the landslide and all been killed.' Lincoln gave him a pat on the back as the rain fell heavier than before. 'We need help. More men covering a wider area.'

'That will take time, too much time.' Patrick turned to Patterson. 'Could you find the tracks?'

'I doubt it. I'm not as good as the black trackers. I just know how to survive in the bush.' Patterson waved towards the landslide. 'That will have erased all tracks.'

Frustrated, Patrick threw his hands up. 'We have no tracker, possibly no tracks left to follow anyway now the landslide has torn through the bush, what in hell's name are we to do? Every minute we stand here is another minute Bridget is further away from us.'

'What do you suggest?' Lincoln argued. 'That we turn back, leave Bridget to her fate?'

'Of course not! But look around us. We've been travelling through mountains for three days and the only way forward has gone. If we cross the creek, there is no way we'll be able to find the tracks without Old Sammy, especially not is this bloody weather.'

Lincoln took a second to calm down. 'Listen, we need to get out of these mountains and find some kind of settlement or farm. We're running low on provisions. If we can restock, send a letter to your aunt for any news, contact some local police see what they know...' Lincoln was clutching at straws. The ordeal had grown so large, so uncompromising he wondered how they'd ever find Bridget. Yet, he wouldn't give up, not now, not ever.

Patterson rubbed his beard. 'We should head west. That last ridge we topped this morning I saw a stretch of land in the west. It might be the start of some grazing or farming land. From memory Bathurst should only be a day's ride from the base of the mountain range.'

'Then in the morning we make for Bathurst,' Lincoln agreed, looking at Patrick. 'Yes?'

'Yes.' Patrick peered at him through the rain. 'She'll be all right, won't she?'

Lincoln swallowed back a glib retort. They both knew the danger Bridget was in. 'Your sister is a tenacious woman, and clever. She won't let them win.'

'Like our Mammy.' Patrick seemed to take comfort from that.

Patterson let out a long breath. 'Ellen Kittrick is the toughest woman I've ever known. Her eldest daughter is just like her.'

Gazing over at the devastation the landslide caused, Lincoln shuddered whether it be from the rain trickling off his hat or the monumental task before them to find Bridget, and with each passing day, he felt she was becoming further out of reach.

'Stay strong, my girl,' he whispered. 'Stay strong.'

Chapter Twelve

Holding her filthy skirts up, Bridget stepped over a fallen trunk, the ground slippery beneath her mud-covered boots. Surrounding her, thick rainforest rose like green damp walls. At intervals she spied the broken sky above her, a flash of blue between puffy white clouds. The sun didn't reach far into this forest, which had changed from the blue-grey of the eucalyptus trees and scratchy dry undergrowth, to ancient old trees so tall she couldn't see the top of them. Beneath these moss-covered giants were soft bright green ferns with large fronds like umbrellas. The forest floor was soft and spongy with leaf decay, and everything smelt of damp.

However, the beauty of the rainforest was lost to Bridget. Since the shooting of Ace yesterday, a cold band of steel had encircled her heart, covering up any kind of tenderness. Leaving Ace this morning had been such a wrench, her hatred of Sap multiplying. Tonight, while he slept, she'd steal his pistol and shoot him dead. That's all she thought of as she took one step and then another for hours.

They were at the bottom of a long valley, the rainforest scenery all they could see. Small black kangaroos had stiffened in surprise at seeing them force their way through the trackless route to where the elusive Donovan lived. Bird calls, some sweet, others eerie, kept them company. One bird had a call like the sound of a whip being cracked. She'd heard that call in the bush around Emmerson Park when she'd been riding, it was familiar, comforting. She liked it even more because Sap found it irritating.

Hunger gripped her stomach. Days without proper food and water made her a little clumsy as she walked behind Sap who led his horse, as did Mickey behind her. Thankfully, Mickey had argued for her wrists to be untied. She couldn't outrun him or Sap, so what was the point of her being tied.

Little did they know that she would escape as soon as she could. Without Ace, and the worry of him falling and breaking a leg, she could now freely run and hide from them. She knew to follow any water course, as eventually it would lead her to a farm, people.

Abruptly, Sap stopped, and checked his compass. 'Not much further, thank God,' he muttered.

Alarmed, Bridget quickened her steps. 'What do you mean?'

'Donovan's hide out.'

'We'll reach him today?' She panicked, expecting to camp out another night. The rain which had finally stopped that morning had slowed them up considerably, but not enough it seemed. How was she to take Sap's pistol if they weren't camping tonight?

They walked for another few hundred yards before Sap stopped and untied his checked handkerchief from around his neck. Before she was aware, Sap grabbed Bridget and yanked her to him. He wrapped the handkerchief over her eyes. 'We can't be too careful. Donovan will hate that we've brought a stranger to his hideout. We have to lessen the risk of her remembering how we got here.'

Bridget gagged on the smell of the handkerchief's stale sweat. Blinded, she whimpered, stumbling as Sap dragged her alongside him. It felt like hours but was only a few minutes. The blindness of not seeing heightened her other senses. She heard more, the jingle of the harness, the call of the birds, a snap of a twig. The moist air caressed her face, the scent of wet earth of the forest floor sharp in her nose.

Eventually, Sap stopped and took the blindfold off her head. 'The track is too narrow to walk abreast. Follow behind me.'

Bridget blinked, raising her head to stare up at the soaring rainforest towering above her. They stood in dim light amongst the thick tree roots covered by green moss and lighter-coloured lichens. Large tree ferns dominated the landscape with small bird's nest ferns underneath them.

'Through here.' Sap turned at a marked tree, but the mark looked natural, a score in the bark could have been made by anything.

She followed him and his horse through a narrow split in a large rock face jutting out from the mountain and then they descended a short incline to walk beside a pretty creek that trickled over moss-covered rocks. The rainforest grew thicker here, the large ferns touching her face before she swept them aside. Ancient trees stretched majestically to the sky, so high Bridget couldn't see the top of them.

Suddenly, there was a gap, perhaps twenty yards wide where the sun pierced through the canopy and Bridget gasped in surprise as she saw why. Trees had been felled to allow the light into a space where vegetables grew. Neat rows of cabbages, onions, carrots and the last of a potato crop were cultivated. A crudely constructed water barrel stood at the end of the garden where a kookaburra was perched on the rim.

Craning her neck past the horse's rump in front, Bridget spotted a rough-looking cabin tucked into the side of another rock face. Next to it in a lean-to a horse snickered to the new arrivals.

'Donovan!' Sap shouted shattering the quiet, making the horses toss their heads and birds to flutter from the branches above.

Sap grabbed Bridget's arm and dragged her to him. 'Donovan!'

'No need to shout.' A man emerged from the shadows of the graceful ferns beside the cabin.

Bridget's eyes widened as the man, Donovan, walked forward. He wore no hat, his dark blond hair thick and the colour of wet sand contrasted against the backdrop of dark green. Clean-shaven, his face was as handsome as Bridget had ever seen and it took the breath from her.

'Who is this?' he barked, scowling, ruining his attractive features.

'A gift.' Sap pushed her forward so hard she tripped on her damp skirts and fell to her knees.

'Ease up!' Donovan dropped to kneel next to her and helped her to stand.

Close, Donovan radiated a hidden strength and Bridget saw intelligence in his green eyes. Still, he couldn't be trusted, none of them could. She ripped her elbow out of his grasp. 'Do not touch me!'

Donovan's hard gaze turned on Sap. 'Who is she and why is she here? The answer better be good.'

Stunned to hear he had a soft cultured Irish accent, Bridget gaped at him.

Sap strutted over to the water barrel and scooped up a handful of water to drink. 'She's from Roache. He wanted her out of his hair. She's a present in lieu of the money he owes you. I've brought her here as a mark of respect to you.'

'I do not want a woman.' Donovan stood straight and rigid. 'Is this some kind of joke?'

Sap shrugged. 'Roache said you'd want her. She's a lady, educated, not some backstreet whore. Roache thought you might be lonely in your mountain lair. Besides, there's probably a reward out for her by now. So, you could make some coin once you're done with her.'

'Are you insane?' Donovan's voice lowered to a growl. 'Do you honestly think I want the troopers sniffing around here, you great eejit!'

'They will never find you. You've been here two years and they've not hunted you down.'

'Surprising as that is since you tend to believe you can come here whenever you want and bring along God knows who with you!'

'Only a handful of people know where you live.'

'And I want it to stay that way.' Donovan's jaw clenched.

'I can post a letter for you, saying you've found her and want a reward.' Sap sniggered.

'No. You're to take her to the nearest farm and release her. Then I suggest you ride a long way away.'

'Oh, I intend on getting away from here, but I need money.' Sap eyed Donovan with a mixture of distrust and respect.

Donovan's eyebrows rose. 'And I'm to give you some, am I?'

Sap shrugged, but his stony stare spoke for him.

'How did I end up with you?' Donovan lamented.

'Because I saved your life,' he boasted.

Sighing, Donovan put his hands on his hips as though ready to argue and then thought better of it. 'Rest your horses tonight but I want you all gone by morning.'

Sap grabbed his horse's reins. 'I ain't taking her with me. She's yours. I hate the bitch!' He led his horse over to the narrow creek running through the clearing and allowed it to drink, Mickey did the same with his horse.

Standing a few feet from Donovan, Bridget needed to focus on a plan to kill Sap and then to escape, but first she raised her chin and stared at Donovan who watched her keenly.

'Your name?' he asked.

'Bridget Kittrick.'

'Irish?'

'County Mayo.'

He inclined his head in acknowledgement. 'Dublin myself. Why did they take you? Did they hold up your carriage and you refused to give them your valuables?'

'Roache was our neighbour. We bought his property. He didn't like that. He had me taken.' Her words were clipped, hard. She wouldn't converse with this villain any more than she had to.

'I have nothing to do with Roache's activities. The man owes me money that is all. A lot of money.'

'And I am to repay his debt?' she jeered. 'I can assure you, Mr...' She flustered at not knowing his full name. Was Donovan his first or last name? 'I can assure you that I am a poor substitute for money or gold. My family will seek revenge for my kidnap and every man involved will swing from a rope.'

His green eyes narrowed. 'My neck will be safe, Miss Kittrick.'

'I highly doubt that. Roache has made a big mistake taking me. All his associates will be implicated, too. Sap, Mickey and you.'

'Not me.'

'You will let me go?' she asked hopefully.

He shrugged. 'Perhaps.' A small smile played about his lips. 'But not yet.'

Her stomach swooped in reply. What did he mean?

'You must be hungry?' He waved towards the cabin. 'Come in and eat.'

Her stomach rumbled at the mention of food so she couldn't argue that she wasn't. Reluctantly, she followed him inside and was astonished by the tidiness of the cabin, and the homeliness of it.

On the right of the door a crude timber bed heaped with animal skin blankets sat beneath a simple wooden shelf that held shaving equipment and books. The back wall was the rock face the cabin had been built around but at the bottom of it was another roughly made wooden bench. On the left wall the fireplace dominated. The chimney was constructed of stones as was the hearth. A small fire burned, cooking the food that hung suspended over it in a black iron pot. The delicious smell made her stomach rumble again.

At the edge of the embers a black kettle sat, and she noticed beside the fireplace there were wooden crates that held plates, bowls and some food such as bags of flour and tea, a sack of potatoes, a string of onions, loose turnips and a small jar of salt.

In the middle of the cabin was a roughly made table surrounded by a few tree stumps that Bridget assumed where stools to sit on. She moved aside as Sap and Mickey entered the cabin. She eyed Sap with distaste, not trusting him.

'Are your boots clean?' Donovan asked them. 'This is my home.'

Sap swore and returned outside to wipe his boots, while Mickey nodded and sat on a stool.

'Miss Kittrick?' Donovan indicated she should also sit, but she remained standing.

'You've done some improvements since I last was here,' Sap said, returning to sit beside Mickey.

Donovan dished out stew into small tin bowls. 'I refuse to live like a vagabond. Through trial and error, I've learnt enough skills to make the place more comfortable.' He handed a bowl and spoon to Bridget. 'I'm no cook, but my kangaroo stew is good.'

She took it and stayed standing near the door. Carefully watching each of the men, she ate a spoonful of the stew, enjoying the taste. She needed the food for energy to run when the time was right.

Donovan brought her tea in a tin cup. 'Forgive me, I have no milk or sugar.'

Their eyes locked, but she looked away first, not wanting to comment or indulge in small talk as though she was at some social gathering. She was here against her will and despised them all. She was also desperately frightened, but she refused to show it.

Returning to the fireplace, Donovan added another log to the flames. 'I'd rather you'd brought me a new coat for winter or newspapers than a kidnapped lady.'

Sap slurped his tea. 'It was Roache's idea not mine, but I owe him and so I did as he asked to wipe my debt.'

Donovan ate with a frown. 'Why would he assume I'd want her?'

'Obviously, he wasn't thinking,' Sap declared, burping. 'Roache was just taken by surprise when we rode down to steal the flock and there she was with her stockman.'

'You were going to steal our flock!' Hatred rose again in Bridget.

Chuckling, Sap helped himself to more stew. 'We were going to burn down Louisburgh as well. Perhaps Roache succeeded? Or perhaps kidnapping you was enough? He is eaten up with hatred for your family.'

A whimper escaped Bridget before she could stop it. Louisburgh burnt to the ground... Mama would be devastated. What of Mrs Barnstaple who was at the house, Una, the maids...

Distressed, angry, Bridget threw her bowl at Sap, hitting him on the shoulder, splattering his coat with the remaining stew from the bowl.

'You bloody bitch!' Sap yelled, lunging for her. 'I've had enough of you by God!' His fist smashed into her face.

Blinded by pain, her head ringing, Bridget fell back against the door, banging her head. She slid to the ground, stunned.

'Enough!' Donovan immediately knelt by Bridget as Mickey wrapped his arms around Sap and held him back.

'Touch her again and I'll shoot you,' Donovan said coldly to Sap.

'She deserves a good thrashing and more!' Sap sneered, pushing Mickey away from him. 'Let me take her down a peg or two. I'll teach her a lesson she won't forget.'

'In the lean-to is a tent. Go and put it up. You and Mickey will be sleeping out there tonight.' Donovan glared up at him where he knelt beside Bridget.

'Not in here?' Sap scowled.

'You can't be trusted. Miss Kittrick will have my bed and I'll sleep on the floor. By morning I want you both gone.'

'And what will you do with that witch?'

'You don't need to worry about that.'

'If you want me gone, I'll need money. We've nothing,' Sap whined.

'I'll give you money.' Donovan jerked his head towards the door. 'Out.'

Grumbling, Sap and Mickey walked outside.

Donovan closed the door and faced her. 'You'll be safe, I promise. It's not in my nature to show a woman any disrespect.'

'Will you take me home?' she murmured, holding her nose as it bled.

'I can't, not yet. Troopers will be crawling everywhere looking for you. I can't risk it.' He grabbed the bucket by the fire and taking a cloth dipped it in the water and brought it back to her.

'You're a wanted man?' Of course, he was, she didn't know why she asked.

He nodded and turned away. 'I'll fetch some buckets of water for you to wash. I have soap and a towel.'

When he'd gone, Bridget sighed deeply. She fought the tears that wanted to spill. In no way would she show weakness in front of those men. A tiredness so deep flowed over her, making her movements slow and heavy as she stood and dabbed at the blood around her nose.

She stepped to the fireplace and picked up the bowl she'd thrown at Sap, wishing it had hit him harder, or better yet, she'd shot him. Still, she had the night to kill him. She just had to find a pistol. Donovan would have one or more, surely. She'd shoot Sap while he slept and then run. Unless they tied her up. Her mind was working quickly, which was difficult when her nose throbbed, and her head ached. She needed to convince Donovan that she wasn't capable of escaping and hope he'd let his defences down.

Donovan returned with two buckets of water and a tin basin. 'I usually wash outside. The light is better for shaving,' he told her. 'There's soap on that shelf. In the trunk at the end of my bed is a clean towel and my clothes. Would you care to wear them while your dress is washed and dried?'

She stared at him. 'Your clothes?'

'Yes. A shirt, some trousers. No one will see you wear them out here.' He poured the kettle into the basin and placed it on the table. 'I thought it might make you feel better to wear something clean.'

She was sorely tempted. Gazing down at her filthy dress and touching her ratted hair that had escaped her ruined straw hat, she knew she must look a fright.

'Anyway, I'll leave you to it. No one will come in. I promise. I'll stand right outside the door.'

She waited until he'd gone before going to the trunk and, kneeling, she lifted the lid. Inside were neatly folded clothes and a towel which she took out. Then impulsively she eased the clothes aside to search for a pistol. At the bottom she found what she was looking for. Checking it, she saw it was loaded. Her pulse quickened. She replaced the pistol and the clothes and closed the lid. She was about to stand when she noticed something under the bed. Bending down she peered into the gloom and noticed a rifle.

Voices outside had her quickly grabbing the soap and the towel and returning to the fire to wash. Taking a chance that Donovan wouldn't allow anyone inside, she unbuttoned her bodice and peeled off the filthy garment. The hat she threw into the fire, for it was beyond salvaging. As the flames engulfed it, she quickly washed her face, arms and neck. She drew out all the remaining pins that held her hair up and shaking it loose decided to wash her hair, too. Dunking her head in the cold water of the first bucket, she rubbed the soap thoroughly into her long black hair, scrubbing it clean from days of riding, lying in the dirt and living rough by a smoky campfire.

Washing her hair was a chore that Una performed for her, and the drying of it and brushing it. Tears threatened as she thought of home, her family. Would she ever see them again?

Taking a deep breath to calm herself, she squeezed the water from her hair and roughly dried the ends with the towel in front of the fire. Her riding skirt was disgustingly grubby. She glanced at the trunk. Trousers?

She hesitated. In the past she had often joked at wearing trousers while riding for the freedom and ease, but she'd never thought to actually do it. However, now, out here in the wilderness with no one to see her but three men she hated, what did it matter?

Hurriedly, before she could change her mind, Bridget untied her boots and pulled them off before she unfastened her skirts and let them fall to the hard-packed dirt floor. She retrieved the trousers from the trunk, her fingers fumbling as she tugged the unfamiliar attire on and buttoned them. Then she plucked a white shirt from the trunk and donned it over her chemise and corset, before pulling a short light-weight jacket of good quality from the trunk and putting that on too. Decently covered, she sat on the stool. The effort of washing and dressing had tired her out even more. She eyed the bed, longing to sleep, but she had to be on her guard at all times.

Instead, she refilled the kettle with water and placed it on the flames. It felt weird to be wearing trousers, to not have the coverage of voluminous skirts seemed indecent, yet also rather liberating. She stretched her legs wide, amazed at the freedom. She could stand close to the hearth without fear of catching fire.

A gentle knock on the door spun her around. 'Yes?'

'Miss Kittrick, are you finished?' Donovan called.

She paused, not wanting to be in his company or anyone's. Days of being constantly watched was wearing thin on her nerves.

'Miss Kittrick?'

'I am.' She stood by the fire as he came in.

He paused on seeing her dressed in trousers and smiled. 'How do they feel?'

'Ridiculous.'

'Would you like me to wash your clothes for you?' He waved to the riding habit and petticoats piled on the floor.

'I can do it.' She scooped them up in her arms, grabbed the soap and walked past him. Outside, the canvas tent drew her gaze. Mickey was hammering the last stake into the ground securing a rope.

Ignoring him, Bridget strode to the edge of the creek. She knelt and sank her clothes into the water by her feet. The scrap of soap she held wouldn't do much to clean the multitude of mud stains, but she'd do her best. As she scrubbed, she noticed Donovan gathering some carrots from the garden while Sap hovered around him, talking quietly. Every now and then Sap would look in her direction and she'd freeze, wondering what he spoke about. Was she safe as Donovan said, or was it all an act? Would they kill her and bury her body in the forest? No one would ever know.

A chill ran over her skin. She glanced at Donovan who was shaking his head at Sap. Did she stand a chance with him? He seemed less menacing, more refined. He'd stopped Sap from hitting her again, or worse. Donovan had been kind, allowing her to wash, to wear his clothes. Yet, he was still a wanted man, a criminal in hiding. She could trust no one.

Standing, she squeezed the water out of her bodice and walked to a tree near the lean-to where she hung it over a branch to dry. Donovan's horse was a beauty, its chestnut coat gleaming. He nudged his head at her, wanting attention. Could she steal him and ride away during the night? She might not know the surroundings, but the horse would. Somehow, she had to escape.

Her thoughts whirled as she continued her washing. The heaviness of her wet riding skirt surprised her. She had a newfound respect for the women who worked in the laundry at Emmerson Park and had to deal with all her family's clothes and bedding. If her sisters could see her now how they would be both horrified and amused. A pang of love, of missing them, stilled her. She missed her family so much her chest hurt. The twins, their cheeky smiles and mischief, and her mama... No. she couldn't think of them now, that would be her undoing. She had to stay strong, alert, and survive.

'Can I help you?' Mickey asked as she struggled to hang the long thick skirt over the branch.

She nodded and stood back, allowing him to organise the weight of it on the branch so it would dry quicker.

'We're going in the morning,' Mickey whispered. 'I just wanted to say that I'm sorry for all that's happened. I never wanted to be a part of it.'

'But you were. You could have helped me escape.'

'Sap wouldn't have been happy if I'd done that.'

Bridget glared at him. 'Well, you remember that when you're swinging from a rope. My family will not rest until you all are.'

'They won't find us. We're going to Queensland, no one will find us up there.'

She leaned in close. 'Maybe the black fellows will and spear you through the heart. I've heard there are some vicious tribes up there. One way or another you'll both get what's coming to you.' She stomped away, annoyed. Did he deem an apology would make everything better?

As darkness closed in spreading deep shadows across the rainforest valley, Bridget sat before the fire while Donovan cooked potatoes and carrots. Sap and Mickey were in the tent where they would eat and sleep, leaving Bridget and Donovan alone in the cabin.

Since finishing her washing, she'd stayed in the cabin by the fire, planning her escape. Donovan had come in and out, preparing the evening meal, fetching water and wood. He'd left her in peace, giving only the odd smile when their eyes met. For some reason she didn't feel overly scared with Donovan, not like with Sap or Roache. The aura of respectability that cloaked Donovan even in this remote wilderness removed the dangerous threat somewhat. She wasn't sure why it did, for she also sensed a strong-willed man beneath the civility, a man who was wanted by the police. What had he done?

'Here you are. It's nothing fancy.'

She jumped when he spoke.

Donovan handed her the bowl of food. 'I won't hurt you, Miss Kittrick.'

'Words mean nothing to me. I am here against my will. Actions are what counts, not words.'

'Understandable. However, believe me when I say you'll come to no harm while here.'

She lifted her chin in defiance. 'As your prisoner.'

'As my guest,' he muttered.

'A guest can leave when they please,' she muttered, not wanting to push her luck as so far, he'd not bound her wrists together, for which she was thankful for they were bruised and chafed.

She ate in silence, eating the bland food of boiled potatoes and carrots, hoping the men would fall asleep soon so she could carry out her plan.

However, it was another two hours before Donovan offered her his bed, the rickety wooden cot. He took some of the animal skins, mainly kangaroo, off it to use some for himself, but left her with the thin grey pillow and an equally thin grey blanket and a kangaroo skin.

Bridget wrapped her cloak over the top as the night temperature had dropped. She didn't have the layers of material from her normal clothes to keep her warm, just the trousers. She lay listening to the logs shift in the fireplace, to the stomp of Donovan's horse in the lean-to on the other side of the timber wall.

Of the man himself, he lay on the floor facing the fire and so she waited for him to fall asleep, fighting the yawns that refused to stop. She was so dreadfully tired.

She woke with a start, disoriented. She cursed herself for falling asleep. Hours must have gone by as the fire was mere winking embers in the darkness. She lay for a moment, listening. No sound. The eery quiet and the darkness made her nervous as she quietly pulled back the covers. The cot squeaked as she climbed from it. She paused, her eyes focusing on Donovan's form on the other side of the table.

Carefully she wrapped her cloak about her shoulders and slipped on her boots, not bothering to button them. She crept to the trunk, easing the lid, wincing at the creak of the leather hinges. With no windows, the corner of the cabin was in near blackness, but she knew the pistol lay at the bottom of the trunk. Her hand clasped the cold metal tip of it. She swallowed and slowly drew it out, keeping her fingers away from the trigger.

Fortunately, the cabin door opened silently, and the coolness of the night air woke her fully. An eerie cry came from the rainforest, some kind of animal. One of the horses tossed its head. A streak of delicate moonlight cut between the trees lighting up the open ground of the vegetable garden. No movement came from the tent, but she heard a soft snore as she silently crossed the grass.

Breathing became difficult. She reached the tent, her hand gripping the pistol. She had to remain calm. Yet her mind fought for sanity. To kill a man, even as one as evil as Sap was not as easy as she thought. *Think of Ace.*

She opened the tent flap, the dimness inside showing two sleeping forms. Mickey was a larger built man, so she focused on the shadowy shape of the thinnest body. Slowly she raised the pistol.

A hand grabbed it from her and yanked it away as another hand clasped over her mouth stifling her scream.

Abruptly, Bridget was pulled from the tent, dragged across the opening and back to the cabin.

Donovan let her go and she ran to the rock wall, breathing heavy. Frustration and anger coiled inside her.

'You'll thank me for stopping you,' he said quietly, crouching and adding sticks to the fire's embers.

'No, I won't!' She wanted to yell and scream.

'You aren't a killer.'

'He deserves to die!'

'Most likely, but you don't want to be the one to pull the trigger.' He kept feeding the fire, not looking at her.

Incensed, Bridget marched over to him. 'You do not tell me what to do, understand?' Tears filled her eyes. 'I have to do this. That vile wretch killed my horse and my stockman!'

Donovan stood and faced her. 'Sap will meet his unfortunate end soon enough, don't worry about that. Do not burden yourself with a guilty conscience for taking another man's life. It will haunt you for the rest of *your* life.'

'Are you speaking from experience?' she spat at him.

'No. I haven't killed a man, but I have been kept in a cell with those who have. I've been chained to men who have killed in self-defence or accidentally and they were never the same again.'

She stared at him. 'You were a convict?'

He nodded and sat on a stool to attend the glowing fire. 'Twelve years ago, I arrived in Van Diemen's Land, now called Tasmania.'

Bridget shivered at the mention of Tasmania and fleetingly the image of Lincoln Huntley entered her head, but she had no time for Mr Huntley now.

'I found out later that our ship was one of the last to take convicts to that island. The town's people were decidedly unfriendly to our arrival. They had petitioned to stop convict transport.'

'What crime did you commit?' Why she needed to know she didn't understand, but it mattered.

'Political. I kept getting into trouble with the law over my political speeches I made in public concerning the British rule in Ireland. I followed in my father's footsteps, he'd already died in prison for his rallying to arms against the British.' Donovan bowed his head. 'So, my name was already on the lips of the police, especially in Dublin. After three short stints in prison the judge had enough of me when I appeared before the courts a fourth time. You see, they thought a well-educated young man from a good family should know better, perhaps learn from my father's mistakes and stop being a nuisance. But I used my knowledge, my contacts, my family's name to further the fight for freedom from British rule. So, they sentenced me to exile. Fourteen years in the colony of Australia.'

'That seems rather harsh for a political prisoner,' she murmured.

'I would agree with you.' He chuckled without humour. 'Once arriving in Hobart, I lasted two years working on government schemes, constructing roads, bridges and buildings. Being educated I was given the tasks of getting jobs done, but that also meant working to time constraints and when my fellow convicts slackened off, I had to be the one who gave out the punishments or ordered for them to be done.'

Bridget stood and listened without comment.

'Witnessing men being flogged because they were too weak to work is the stuff of nightmares, Miss Kittrick,' he said softly. 'An old man died in my arms from the shock of fifty lashes on his frail body which had been reduced to torn bloodied flesh... One day I simply refused to do it any more and absconded with Sap and a few others.' He suddenly walked away to the cot as if the memories were too tough to deal with.

Bridget stared into the flames, conflicted by Donovan's honesty and his past. 'Have you hurt people since you've been on the run?'

'No. I've only hurt people's pride as I held them up and stripped them of all their valuables. I'm not proud of it.' His tone hardened. 'But I had to survive. I was robbed of my life in Dublin, so I rob to stay alive here.'

He moved to the door, but glanced over his shoulder at her, his expression unreadable. 'I need to fetch more wood. Oh, and the rifle and pistol under the bed aren't loaded.' He shut the door after him.

A wave of exhaustion swept over Bridget. She was alone and could easily run from the cabin, but how far would she get before fatigue claimed her or Donovan found her?

Wearily, she climbed into the cot and pulled the coverings over her and faced the wall in utter despair.

Chapter Thirteen

When she woke, sunlight flooded through the open cabin door. She climbed from the cot, her head sluggish after a deep sleep. Her hair hung about her shoulders, needing a brush and to be put up, but that was the least of her problems as she stood at the door. Sap and Mickey held their horses' reins while talking to Donovan. She couldn't hear what was being said, but Sap caught her eye and glared at her for a moment. She shivered at the hatred in his look, especially when he touched the scabs on his face where her nails had raked him.

She felt no remorse. If Donovan hadn't stopped her last night, the man could be dead.

Bridget watched them lead their horses through the narrow gap in the immense trees and the large ferns. Relief that they were leaving mixed with annoyance because she wouldn't be able to kill Sap now, but her revulsion for him was buried in her heart for life.

The sound of a whip cracking came from the trees. That particular bird call that Sap detested. Bridget sucked in a deep breath as the whip crack echoed around the gorge. Sap was gone.

Donovan collected a bucket from the tent and realised she stood watching.

'Good morning.' His handsome smile appeared naturally. 'I didn't doubt you would want to say goodbye to them.'

'No. Why didn't you send me with them?'

'Is that what you want?'

'Of course not!'

'I didn't think so. Murder would have been done by one of you for sure. I didn't want to risk it.'

'So, I'm to stay with you?'

'It seems that way, yes.'

'For how long?'

'I don't know, Miss Kittrick. I'm working it out as I go along.'

'If you take me to the nearest farm or village, I'll tell no one about you. I promise.'

'Maybe.' He took the bucket to the creek and filled it.

Maybe. What did that mean? And now she was alone with him. Just her and a man in the middle of nowhere. She felt both terrified and safe at the same time and wondered at it. Why didn't Donovan instil such loathing in her as the others had done?

'I need to hunt for fresh meat. I've given those two the last of what I had.' He returned from the creek and stepped past her into the cabin. 'Are you hungry? The kettle is warm to make some tea and I made damper earlier.'

Bridget made herself some tea and broke off a sizeable chunk of the bread.

He busied himself loading his rifle while she ate. 'Did you wish to accompany me?'

'Do you not trust me to stay here by myself?'

'I trust you. Beside what can you do? If you run, you'll be lost within hours. You might steal what little food I have and survive for a few days, but these mountains are dangerous, full of deep gorges. Without a fire at night, you'll freeze now summer is over. One wrong turn, a stumble and you could fall to your death, or you could starve before anyone found you. Your choice.'

'You don't frighten me. I can look after myself.'

'Out here, really?' He grinned as though Bridget amused him.

'People are out searching for me. My brothers Patrick and Austin won't rest until I am found. They'll have several black trackers with them. We employ them at Louisburgh as stockmen,' she lied. They had one, Old Sammy, and he was becoming frail.

'Where is Louisburgh?'

'Near Goulburn.'

Donovan jerked. 'Goulburn?'

'Yes. You know of the town?' She knew he did for he'd reacted as such. 'Our other home is in Berrima.'

'Other home? You have more than one.' He was disturbed by the information.

'Indeed,' she crowed. 'We have many properties. My family is wealthy. They will put a price on your head, or they can reward you for my release. Perhaps you should ponder about which one you should take. *Your choice,*' she repeated the words he'd just spoken to her.

He took a bag from a nail in the wall and filled it with the rest of the damper and a water canteen. 'Tomorrow I must go for supplies.'

'Where?'

'Wherever I can find them without creating suspicion.'

'But if you have lived here for two years, surely you have been forgotten about?'

'I hope I have but one can never be too careful.' He grabbed the pistol and loaded it as well. 'Are you coming?'

'Yes. Give me a minute.' She walked outside into the thick forest to relieve herself and realised the density of the rainforest started immediately beyond the cabin. The clearing Donovan had made was the only open space in any direction. The valley walls rose high above her head, steep and in places sheer rock. Escaping could cost her life, but what was the alternative?

Donovan was taking his horse from the lean-to when she joined him. The horse, standing in a streak of sunshine, looked magnificent.

'He is beautiful,' she murmured, patting the horse's velvety nose.

'I agree. This is Zeus.' Donovan led him past the cabin into a tunnel of wide leaf ferns. Sunlight didn't penetrate down as far here but Bridget noticed signs of Donovan's occupation. Chopped wood was stacked under a small structure made of branches and fern leaves to keep the weather from it. There was also evidence of a working area. A half-completed rope made out of thin strips of vine hung from a tree branch, a kangaroo skin was stretched to dry out.

They left the cabin behind and ventured up a steep incline which took all her concentration for the ground beneath her boots was slippery and spongy with leaf matter.

'I've found a few different species of kangaroo, the common one is small and black living amongst the outcrops of rock nearly at the top of the mountain peaks. They are dwellers of the ranges more than their grey cousins,' Donovan told her.

She didn't know why he was making conversation. She had no wish to talk to him about anything other than him letting her go. Still, she replied, hoping to win him over, so he'd release her. 'The grey kangaroos like the open grasslands. We have a great number at Louisburgh and Huntley Vale.'

'Huntley Vale?' he asked, winding through the eucalyptus trees, climbing higher.

'It's the property we bought from Roache. It adjoins Louisburgh. Mama wanted to annexe it.'

'Your mama?' He sounded surprised.

'She is a shrewd businesswoman.'

He gave her a flash of a grin over his shoulder. 'She sounds interesting. Like her daughter.'

Bridget didn't like the way her stomach swooped at his handsome grin. She couldn't be dropping her guard. The man was keeping her here against her will. They weren't friends, she had to remember that.

'How did you get involved with Roache?' she asked, for Donovan and Roache were nothing alike in any way.

'I met Roache a few years ago through Sap. He hid us for a while at Northville.'

'Ah, so that's why your face changed when I mentioned Louisburgh and Goulburn before. You've been in that area.'

'Yes.'

'And Roache borrowed money from you?'

'Yes.' Donovan stopped and turned to her. 'He was in deep debt. I had just pulled off a successful... robbery. Roache begged me to lend him some of the money and in return he'd keep silent about me.'

'Does it not bother you that you rob hard-working people?'

'But I don't rob hard-working people.'

'Then who do you take money from?'

'The church.'

That surprised her. 'The church?'

A hard look came into his eyes. 'The church, all religions, rob people every day. They suppress people when they should be caring for them. They ask for money from people who would give their last penny to be saved, yet the church has more land and wealth than anyone else. They expect devotion, yet turn a blind eye to corruption under their own roof.'

'You sound very bitter.'

'I have a right to be.' He stared away. 'I was brought up a Catholic, but I wasn't even a man before I saw the way the church ruined lives instead of healing them.' His green eyes were lost to memories. 'My sister found herself pregnant, raped by a group of drunk young lads. Our church blamed her, banished her, shunned her in front of everyone, made an example of her at Mass.'

'That's terrible.'

'My sister killed herself from the shame. Even then... even then the church blamed her, she'd committed a sin by taking her own life. The church didn't give us solace, didn't give my sister a grave on holy ground. No, they did none of that and the devastation caused my mother to lose her mind. Father had her committed into an asylum for he was too busy fighting for freedom from the British to care for my poor mother.' Donovan sucked in a breath. 'So, you see between the British Rule and the Catholic Church I grew up a very disillusioned and angry young man. Was it any surprise I ended up in chains?'

He walked away, quickly putting distance between them, preventing any more questions, shutting himself down to further conversation.

Sensitive to such sadness, Bridget said no more.

They kept trudging far above the rainforest below, the landscape gradually changed to more of the scrubby bushland she was used to. The tall, majestic trees covered in moss and vines were replaced by straggly eucalyptus bent out of shape by the strong winds that howled over the peaks.

Although the sun shone, the higher they climbed the cooler it became, but the energy it took to trek the uneven ground made Bridget sweat, though she was grateful for the trousers and the ease in which walking was done in them. They were a revelation.

At the top, Donovan paused and took a drink from the canteen and offered it to Bridget. As she drank, she gazed about her. Nothing but grey-green mountains as far as she could see in each direction. If she ran, she'd be lost for days, weeks. How were her brothers going to find here out here? Hopelessness filled her.

Donovan watched her, his gaze tender as if to say, I told you so.

Ultimately, they started down the sharp descent on the other side, slowly walking between large outcrops of rocks and big boulders that dotted the terrain. It was easy to lose balance on the uneven ground. Rocks were a trip hazard as was the slippery silky tuffs of grass. At one point there was a sheer drop off the edge of a cliff.

'Go slowly,' Donovan warned, inching his way past a large tree only a few yards from the edge. He coaxed Zeus carefully along.

Concentrating, Bridget stayed well away from the cliff side until they reached a wider grassy area that levelled off for twenty yards or so.

Here, Donovan paused, eyes searching. 'I'll leave you with Zeus. He can't get down there. I'll creep down further. I might be gone a while.'

She nodded, not really caring. She sat on a large rock, holding the reins while Zeus cropped at the grass and Donovan disappeared from sight into the trees below.

Although tempted to climb on Zeus's back, she knew to do so would be fraught with danger. The sides of the mountain were too steep to ride without care. There could be no headlong rush to flee. As much as she wanted to, she'd not risk danger to the beautiful horse or her own neck.

A gunshot startled her. Zeus threw his head and a flock of white cockatoos screeched from the trees in the gorge. Bridget patted Zeus's neck. 'Everything is fine, boy.'

A while later, Donovan broke through the trees and lumbered up the incline dragging a kangaroo. Bridget held Zeus so Donovan could place the dead animal on his back.

'One shot.' Bridget couldn't help but admire the hunter. She'd been on a kangaroo hunt many times and knew the difficulty of shooting the animal when it was at full pelt, bounding away.

'Years of practice. I have to make each shot count. I don't have an infinite supply of bullets.' He roped the kangaroo securely.

'We have so many kangaroos at home. They are a menace. We attend many hunts and host our own just to keep the numbers down to a manageable level, but it is near impossible.'

'For me the meat is part of my life. I get tired of eating it, but I have no alternative.'

'I bet you'd enjoy a nice roast beef or lamb dinner. Our cook, Moira, at Emmerson Park, cooks the best roast beef I've ever tasted.' Why was she talking to him like a friend?

'I've not had a decent roast beef meal since leaving Dublin...' A dullness came into his green eyes.

'Can you not give yourself up and serve the rest of your time? Then one day you'd be free.' Why did she care?

'I am free, Miss Kittrick. Look around you, there are no bars or chains constraining me.'

She frowned. 'As I see it living here is another form of prison. You're not free, not really.'

'I'm as free as I'll ever be. I'm away from the flogging, from being in chains. I'll not go back to that, thank you.'

'And be alone for the rest of your life?'

'I don't mind my own company.'

'But look at what you're missing out on, being married, having children, having friends, eating fine meals, drinking fine wine, attending shows, dinner parties.'

'That was my previous life. It no longer exists.'

'It could again.'

'As a convicted felon?' He scowled with a huff. 'You are so naïve, Miss Kittrick.' Without another word, Donovan took the reins and led them back to the cabin.

While Donovan skinned and gutted the animal, Bridget checked her drying clothes, before wandering over to the rows of vegetables. Zeus cropped at the grass near the trickling creek and the birds twittered and flew from the branches. The scene was rather idyllic if circumstances had been different.

Donovan came from behind the cabin to wash his bloodied hands in the creek. 'I've used the last of my salt to brine some of the meat, the rest I'll roast for us to eat. It should last us a couple of days.'

She nodded and walked back to him. 'You will get supplies tomorrow?'

'Yes.' He stood and shook the water off his hands.

'Can I come with you?'

'No.'

'Will you not let me go?' she pleaded.

'I can't, not until Sap and Mickey are well clear.'

'Why?'

'I promised Sap he could have a few days head start.'

'I won't tell the police. I'll keep all your names out of it.'

'Sorry, no.'

'But in a few days, you'll let me go?'

'Yes.' He gazed at her, his green eyes soft, questioning.

Inside she leapt for joy. She was going home soon.

He gently touched her arm. 'Until then, perhaps you can simply relax and enjoy being here? I will never hurt you. I swear that on my life.'

A shiver prickled over her skin as he smiled warmly. He was genuine, she sensed it. For some reason, she couldn't take her gaze from him. There was something charismatic about Donovan. Born and raised as a gentleman's son, an educated rebel, a man with his own code of honour. There was a mysterious manner about him which fascinated her. Anywhere else, under different circumstances, she'd have wanted to get to know him better.

In many ways, he reminded her of Lincoln Huntley...

And as with Mr Huntley, she could not deny there was a spark of attraction between them.

He left her to collect some wood and she stood staring down at the flowing water.

What was the matter with her? She find her captor attractive? How could she converse so easily with him as though they were acquaintances? Why didn't she hold him in contempt as she did with Sap and Mickey?

Scattered clouds blotted out the sun casting the clearing in shade. Bridget went into the cabin to find Donovan building up a good fire ready to roast the meat on a crude iron spit.

'It won't take long to cook,' Donovan told her. 'Did you want to make some tea while we wait? I'll see to the vegetables.'

'You're very domesticated.' She placed the kettle on the embers at the side of the fire.

'Just because I live in the forest doesn't mean I have to forgo all civilisation. I like comfort.'

'But you must get lonely, bored with the solitude?'

'Sometimes. When I do, I venture into the nearest village. A few times I have travelled to the nearest town just to hear people talk, to buy a newspaper to read the current news.'

'That is a risk.'

'It is, which is why I don't do it often.' He chuckled. 'Twice a year I venture to a large town where I can easily mingle with the populace. I wear a large hat pulled low.' He indicated to a large black hat on a nail near the door. 'I act normal and buy my supplies and people take no notice of me. I don't visit a public house or draw attention to myself. So far, I've been successful.'

'There is a man I know... Patterson...' Bridget passed Donovan a tin cup of tea. 'He is a wanted man. He saved me once and as a thank you Mama allows him to stay on our land when he passes through. There is a hollowed-out tree trunk in a certain spot in the ranges on our property. In the trunk, Mama places a blanket, a coat, a knife, flint, jars of jam, some money... that kind of thing. Items to keep him going until he next passes through.'

'Your mama sounds an extraordinary woman.'

'She is and as her daughter I have learned from her.' She sipped her tea, not taking her eyes from him. 'So, you see, we are not the type of people to run to the police. I wouldn't tell a soul about you.'

He sighed heavily. 'I believe you.'

'Then you will let me go home in a few days as promised?'

Donovan added another log to the fire that sent sparks up the chimney. 'I won't break my promise to you, Miss Kittrick.'

She nodded, trusting him.

'I'll leave early in the morning before sunrise. Can you keep a fire going while I'm gone?'

'Yes.'

'I should be back after dark.' His expression was unreadable as he looked at her. 'I hope you are still here when I return.'

'As tempting as it is to run, I know I won't make it far before nightfall and I'll get lost.'

'There are no tracks to follow up here. You saw today how steep and dangerous it could be if you're not careful. The nights are drawing cooler now its autumn, especially out here in the mountains. Being without fire or shelter can make you ill and you could die of exposure.'

'I understand all that, of course I do. I may be many things but stupid isn't one of them.'

'You are far from stupid. Any other woman would have fainted a dozen times by now or spent the entire time crying and sobbing or simply gone mad with fear. But not you, Miss Kittrick. I admire that strength of character. To other men like Roache and Sap they want to break that strength, control it, force you to be biddable.'

'Not you though?'

He shook his head. 'I did curse Roache for sending you to me. I don't know what he was playing at, some kind of game I wasn't aware of, but I'm glad you're here. You have brought distraction into my simple life. How can I be angry at that?'

She stared at him, hearing his loneliness, seeing the slump of his shoulders, but only for a moment, then he straightened his back and raised his head. The look he gave her was honest, open and then he smiled slowly, warmly.

Before she contemplate what to say or understand her reaction to him, he strode outside.

Chapter Fourteen

Light drizzly rain kept Bridget in the cabin most of the following day. Donovan had left before she woke so she made a cup of tea and ate damper from the day before. The cabin was low on supplies, but she had roasted meat from the evening meal to eat during the day.

The cooler weather and the rain quietened the usual noise of the rainforest. Instead of numerous bird calls, the only sound was the water dripping from the cabin roof and the croak of a frog near the creek.

When a shower had passed, she quickly went out to wash the plates and bowls from the evening meal and refill the buckets with clean water. Needing to keep busy, Bridget hung her riding habit near to the fire to dry the last remaining dampness from it. Then she used a handmade broom made from leafy branches tied together to sweep the dirt floor. She shook out the blanket and the skins and laid them on the bed. After that she brought in an armful of logs.

Seeing the lean-to needed mucking out, she did that too, using a broken handled shovel. Although she'd been brought up with grooms caring for her horses, she knew how to look after them, too, and a dirty stall was not healthy for a horse.

When the next rain shower sent her indoors, she sat in front of the fire wondering what to do next. Impulsively, she knelt in front of Donovan's trunk and opened it. His neatly folded clothes were on top but other things were underneath, things she'd overlooked when searching for the pistol.

She drew out a dark wooden box. Inside were many pieces of jewellery, necklaces of pearls, gold rings, diamond bracelets, ruby brooches. She lifted the items out one by one, amazed at the beauty of them, yet also knowing they were stolen goods.

Bridget closed the lid and replaced the box in the trunk. Her eye caught a leather satchel, she opened it. Inside was a wad of bank notes worth hundreds of pounds. She glanced over her shoulder at the door, fully expecting to be caught holding stolen money.

At the bottom of the trunk, she noticed a small piece of narrow cloth in a loop. She tugged at it and the bottom of the trunk popped up to reveal a false floor. Underneath were small bags, dozens of them. Amazed, Bridget lifted one small bag and teased the string loose to peep inside. Glittering gold dust and small gold nuggets winked at her in the light.

The trunk held a small fortune. Carefully, she replaced all the items back into position and closed the lid. Donovan was a rich man, yet he lived like a hermit in the middle of the wilderness. He would be hanged if caught with such a bounty. Yet, if cleverly arranged, he could use that money to escape the country and start a new life somewhere else. Why hadn't he done that?

She sat back at the fire and made some tea to give herself something to do. Then, with her riding habit finally dry, she stripped off and washed herself with warm water and the last of Donovan's soap. She felt instantly feminine again once she donned her proper clothes. She combed her hair with Donovan's comb and plaited it, tying the end with a piece of string.

The sound of a horse snorting made her jump. She hurried to the door, surprised Donovan had returned so soon. Only, she froze on seeing the stranger on horseback by the tent. The rain eased and the man dismounted.

'Good day to you, missus.'

'Good day.' She tried to remain calm. No one came here Donovan said.

'I'm pleased to have stumbled across you for I'm fair lost.' The man walked closer. His dishevelled and dirty appearance gave her a jolt of alarm.

'You must be. We don't receive many callers out here.'

'May I have a drink, missus?'

'Of course.' She hurried inside and poured him a cup of water. The quicker she got it the quicker he would leave. When she turned the man was standing in the doorway. Bridget stiffened, suddenly afraid. 'There you are.' She handed the cup to him, forcing a smile to her frozen face.

'Can I trouble you for some food?' The man spoke through a thick black beard, his soddened hat pulled low. 'And maybe stand before the fire to dry off a bit?'

Bridget nodded and fetched him a plate of roast kangaroo strips. Her skin prickled at his nearness.

'Nice little place you have here,' the man said, staring around as he chewed the meat. 'Where's your husband?'

She thought quickly. 'He's just gone for some wood. He'll be back shortly.'

'Has he?' The man frowned, his tone showing he didn't believe her. He nodded to the bed. 'A single cot for a married couple?'

Swallowing back her fear, Bridget stepped backwards towards the crates at the side of the fireplace. Donovan left a loaded pistol there, just in case he needed it.

'You're here alone, aren't you?'

'No, Donovan will return shortly.' She was inches from the pistol.

The man's eyes narrowed as they raked over her. 'Something's not right here. You're dressed in fancy clothes. No wife, living in a cabin, wears what you're wearing.'

Fear caught in her throat. 'My husband—'

'You don't have a husband. You're wearing a fancy riding outfit and there's no wedding band on your finger and this cabin has a single cot.' He laughed a harsh dry sound. 'I don't know what's going on here but something's not right.' He looked around. 'I might I'll stay awhile.'

'No, you should leave. *Now.*' Bridget faced him, his smarmy smile reminded her of Roache, another man who thought he could do as he pleased.

'Nah.' The man stuffed the rest of the meat into his mouth, chewing loudly. 'I reckon you're here alone.'

'I'm not.'

'Have you run from a wealthy husband? Is that it? Or an overbearing father?' He grinned, revealing half-chewed food and several black teeth. 'Do you have any whisky?'

'No.' She inched further to where the pistol lay in the crate. 'I want you to leave.'

The man suddenly jerked forward and grabbed her by the arms. 'I'm staying, missy! And I just might sample what's under those skirts.'

She fought him. Jerking and twisting to be free of his grip, but his strength far out matched hers and he laughed at her struggles.

'Come on, you'll enjoy it,' he gasped in her ear, trying to manoeuvre her to the table.

Bridget screamed. She fought harder, kicking and yelling. She smacked him in the ear, desperate to get away. Her skirts hindered her kicks.

'Jesus, you little slut!' The man slapped her across the face.

Stunned, Bridget cried out in pain and fury.

'Now behave and let me have my way. I'll be quick, it's been a long time.' As the man pushed her over the table, Bridget twisted sideways and fell to the floor.

'It's the floor, is it?' He laughed, desperately trying to unbutton his trousers.

Screaming, Bridget crawled away, kicking out at him but her long skirts limited the damage. Terrified, she reached the fireplace just as he grabbed her ankles. Her fingers stretched for a piece of wood, but he jerked her backwards towards him.

'Come here!' he panted.

Crying in fear, she kicked again and lunged away. On hands and knees, she scuttled for the crates, frantic to get the pistol. Her fingers found the frying pan and threw it at his head.

'God damn it, you whore.' He rubbed his forehead where the handle of the pan had hit him. 'You're going to pay for this. I'll bloody do you in when I'm finished with you!' The man leapt for her, knocking Bridget into the side of the fireplace. She banged her head and fell forward, toppling the crates down around her. Pain throbbed in her temple, making her dizzy for a second or two until she saw him come at her again.

Breathless, panicking he would kill her, she crawled to reach the pistol where it had fallen amongst the few remaining vegetables. Grasping the handle of it, she quickly cocked it, turned and fired.

The blast burst through her ears. Her head rang with noise. A puff of smoke blinded her momentarily. She blinked rapidly, her heart twisting in fear. She wouldn't have time to reload the pistol...

Smoke haze drifted around the room. Bridget couldn't swallow, her mouth too dry. The man didn't move. He lay slumped on his face, blood slowly spread across the dirt floor.

Breathing heavily, she backed away to the wall and pulled herself up, not taking her eyes off the body in the middle of the room. Wildly scanning the floor, she found a knife and picked it up. Holding it out in front of her, she moved towards the door and opened it fully to lighten the room more. The man remained still.

Scared for her life, Bridget ran around to the side of the cabin where Donovan chopped wood and grabbed the axe. Armed with it and the knife she crept back to the cabin, her hands shaking so badly she nearly dropped both weapons.

Inside the body hadn't moved.

Had she killed him or was he waiting until she was close enough to spring upon her again?

A whip crack sound came from the bird in the trees. A normal sound, but nothing would ever be normal again. A light rain began to fall once more, but Bridget stayed standing in the clearing watching the cabin door, waiting for the man to come after her.

＊

Lincoln sat on the verandah of a farmhouse they'd stopped at two hours before during a heavy rainstorm. The farm was located on a wide flat plain on the western side of the mountains and thankfully the family, Mr and Mrs Loveday, who lived there were kind enough to let them stay the night. Mr Loveday had even agreed for his teenage son to ride immediately to Bathurst, the largest town in the district, to find out any news for them.

Austin, having arrived the day before, came around the side of the house and up the steps to sit next to Lincoln. 'The men are feeding the horses. I've given Patrick money to pay Mrs Loveday for their hospitality. I spoke with Mr Loveday and his labourer about joining us in the search.'

'And have they agreed?'

'Well, we have use of Mr Loveday's labourer for a few days and his son when he returns from Bathurst.'

'Wouldn't it be better for Loveday's man, and his son, to ride to other outlying farms and enquire about any sightings?' Lincoln sipped the tea that Mrs Loveday had brought out to him along with a piece of apple pie.

Austin sighed. 'Yes, of course. That's a sensible plan. I'm not thinking straight.'

Lincoln glanced at his friend who seemed to have aged ten years in a week. Since he made the mad dash from Sydney to join Patrick and Lincoln and the stockmen in the search for Bridget, Lincoln wondered if any of them had slept for more than a few hours. Which was why he sat on the verandah now, exhausted and aching from long days in the saddle.

Patrick joined them and fell onto a chair with a groan. He'd not shaven and sported a dark auburn beard. 'I've told the men we are to set off at dawn.'

'Are you confident in the young tracker we've hired?' Austin asked Patrick about the black tracker they'd hired from a property they'd passed that morning.

'We won't know until we try. The police don't seem to be having much luck.'

'There are too few of them to cover such a vast distance.' Austin rubbed a hand over his tired eyes. 'We have to hope Bridget is still in the mountains but there is every chance those bastards might have taken her to the coast by now, even into Sydney. They could be on a ship to somewhere.'

'In Sydney Bridget would easily be seen, surely?' Lincoln spoke quietly. For days they'd discussed all the possibilities of where the scoundrels had taken Bridget. The only thing they hadn't voiced was whether she still lived or not.

'We need to find Roache,' Patrick muttered. 'I'll beat the truth out of him.'

'The bastard is long gone.' Austin leaned forward and hung his head. 'I wish to God Mama had never got involved with that criminal.'

'No one could have known this would happen,' Lincoln said, filled with his own guilt for leaving Bridget alone with only Silas Pegg to protect her.

All three men stood as Mrs Loveday, a small petite woman, came out carrying a large tray of bowls filled with mutton stew and plates of bread and butter.

Lincoln took the tray from her. 'Thank you, Mrs Loveday.'

'I'm sorry I've nothing more to give you, gentlemen.'

'This is plenty and we're much obliged.' Austin smiled.

'The three of you are welcome to sleep by the fire inside. My husband and I have a bedroom to the back of the house, so you won't disturb us. I'll leave you some blankets.'

'Thank you, Mrs Loveday,' Patrick said, passing the bowls out.

'I understand you'll be gone early...' From her apron pocket, Mrs Loveday brought a handkerchief wrapped parcel. 'Give this to your sister when you find her. It's nothing much, just a handkerchief, a ribbon and a comb. She might want to tidy herself...'

Emotion clogged Lincoln's throat.

Austin sniffed. 'That is most kind of you, Mrs Loveday. Bridget will be grateful, I'm certain.'

She smiled and nodded and re-entered into the house.

In quiet reflection, they sat and ate the tasty stew, each lost to their own thoughts.

Lincoln simply wanted to find Bridget and tell her he was sorry he had left her. He'd been selfish, concerned only by his feelings, such feelings he wished he didn't harbour for her. Bridget, beautiful and spirited, was in his mind, his heart and his very soul and the idea terrified him. He wanted her as a man wanted a woman but more than that he wanted to share his life with her, care for her, love her. Yet he couldn't. To do so he'd have to reveal his past and he knew she'd turn away and never look at him again if he did.

In the dusky twilight, a horseman galloped along the track leading to the farm. Lincoln stood as did Austin and Patrick. No one rode that fast unless they had something important to tell. In the dim light they couldn't see who it was.

'Please let it be good news,' Patrick murmured.

Tensing, Lincoln waited with the brothers as the rider drew close enough for them to see it was Mr Loveday's son, Jimmy.

Austin hurried down the stairs to greet him. 'News?'

'Aye.' Jimmy dismounted in a hurry. 'There's been sightings of the bushrangers Sap and Mickey Nolan. They've been spotted at an inn on the outskirts of Bathurst this morning.'

'Sap? The bushranger the police said is the likely man responsible?' Austin repeated. 'Are you sure?'

'Aye. The Sap and Mickey Nolan are the names the police mentioned.'

Austin glanced at Patrick and Lincoln. 'Thank God Silas Pegg was able to remember their names and tell us before we left.'

'Was a woman with them?' Lincoln asked Jimmy, hopefully.

'Were the bushrangers captured?' Patrick asked from the top of the steps.

'No, they both got away.' Jimmy took off his cap and ruffled his hair. 'But apparently the police sergeant questioned the public who were at the same bar as the bushrangers and witnesses said that Sap was very drunk, and he mentioned to one of customers that he'd never travel with a woman again.'

Austin swore violently. 'So, they've definitely been in the area around Bathurst, not in the mountains between here and Sydney as we thought?'

'The police don't know for sure.' Jimmy shrugged. 'Sap and Nolan have scarpered. Someone got word to them that the troopers had found out they were in Bathurst.' Jimmy took a deep breath. 'The sergeant says if they capture those two villains then they'll know where your sister is.'

Austin went up onto the verandah to Patrick and Lincoln. 'What do you reckon? Should we search for Sap and this Mickey Nolan fellow or go into the mountains?'

'The mountains are vast, Austin,' Patrick said, his brow furrowed. 'If they have gone to Bathurst where would Bridget be if not with them? Perhaps they have her hidden somewhere near Bathurst? In a barn somewhere, or in the bush?'

Austin nodded. 'Lincoln?'

He thought for a moment. 'We could split up. Half the men go to Bathurst and the other half go back into the mountains with the tracker.'

Patrick scratched his ear. 'But why would she be in the mountains? Sap and Nolan will have her with them somewhere. She is valuable since we told the police that we'll pay a reward. Notices have gone up in all the towns.'

'I've paid plenty of money for the news to be spread,' Austin added, looking concerned. 'I doubt Sap and Nolan would simply let her go.'

'How would they claim the reward though?' Lincoln asked. 'To do so would be putting themselves in danger of getting caught.'

Austin rubbed his chin where short stubble grew. 'Unless they demanded someone else to make the claim and then share the reward money with them? These thieves have contacts everywhere. They band together, we know that from all the gangs that have terrorised the colony for decades.'

Jimmy patted his horse's neck. 'The police have sent a tracker and a few troopers out in the direction of where they were last seen.'

'We should be with them, helping,' Patrick said. 'Sap will know where Bridget is.'

'Ride through the night?' Lincoln asked, still wondering if Sap and Nolan had Bridget with them or had they left her behind somewhere or worse...

Patrick nodded. 'The horses have been fed, they are in good condition. Let's ride to Bathurst tonight and talk to the police. If we stay here, we'll lose too much time.'

'Agreed.' Austin turned to Jimmy. 'Can you show us the way?'

'Aye,' the youth replied. 'I'll take my dad's horse though. It's fresher.'

Lincoln glanced towards the high mountains in the east, which in the deepening darkness were just a black outline against a navy sky. He hoped to God Bridget wasn't in there, alone, suffering or worse…

Chapter Fifteen

Donovan led Zeus through the large ferns that covered the gap between the rocks to the hideout. He held the lamp up high careful not to trip on unseen hazards or for Zeus not to stumble and become lame. The horse meant everything to him. He was the only company he could rely on, his partner in working about the clearing, hunting and shopping expeditions such as today.

The moon peaked through the trees, giving a silvery light to the drenched clearing as they broke through the dripping ferns. Zeus whinnied, knowing he was home.

Exhausted, wet and hungry Donovan grinned at him. 'Yes, boy, you can rest soon enough.' Immediately after he'd spoken, he sensed something was wrong. No light came from the cabin. He paused and slowly drew out his pistol. Fear gripped his guts. Bridget. Had she gone? Was she hurt?

Then he saw a figure by the creek and a horse on the other side of the tent. The lantern threw just enough light for him to make out Bridget and his breathing resumed unsteadily. 'Miss Kittrick?'

She didn't move just continued to stare at the dark cabin.

'Miss Kittrick?' He left Zeus and stepped closer to her. 'Bridget? Are you hurt?' When she didn't answer him, he walked to her side and gently touched her shoulder.

She jerked around, lifting the axe up to ward him off.

'It's me, Donovan!' He backed away just as the rain started again.

Bridget lowered the axe, swaying.

'Come inside.'

'No...' She stared at the open door. 'No...'

'Tell me what's happened,' he said gently. 'You're safe now with me.'

Shaking her head, she closed her eyes and then opened them sluggishly, as though drunk or fatigued.

'What's in the cabin, sweet girl,' he crooned, edging closer again. Was it a snake that's frightened her?

'*He's* in there,' her voice broke.

Donovan stiffened and his head snapped around to stare at the cabin. 'Someone is inside?'

Moaning, Bridget looked ready to collapse.

He thought quickly. 'Sit down. Right here. Sit. That's it,' he whispered, lowering her to the grass. Not knowing who was in the cabin and if he'd been seen yet sent his senses into a spin.

'Now stay here.' He knelt down, his hand on her shoulder. 'If anything happens to me, you ride Zeus as far away as you can, understand? Let him have his way, Zeus knows the mountains better than you.'

She didn't reply. A trickle of sweat ran down his back. He stood and crept to the edge of the creek, wanting to sneak around to the door from the side. He cocked his pistol which sounded loud in the stillness of the misty night.

His blood pumping, he made it to the door and listened. No noise. Taking a deep breath, Donovan leapt inside, the pistol pointing into the dimness. The fire was nothing but winking ashes, giving off minimal light, however, with the moon shining between the clouds it was enough for Donovan to see the man lying on the floor, the table tipped over, the crates upended. Was the man asleep? Drunk?

Taking advantage of it, Donovan returned outside and grabbed the lantern. Bridget hadn't moved. Once inside the cabin, he placed the lantern on a nail by the door, his eyes not leaving the man on the floor, the pistol aimed. 'You! Get up!'

No answer.

Heart banging like an unsecured gate on a windy day, he stalked the man until he was able to nudge him with his boot. No movement, not even a grunt. The man was a huge beast, wide shoulders and easily over six foot.

With the pistol pointing at him, Donovan managed to roll the shoulders over with one hand. The figure flopped over onto his back. Donovan reeled in shock. The man had no face. A gunshot wound had destroyed it.

The contents of Donovan's stomach churned. He looked away. Bridget had killed him. Had the man attacked her? Probably. A beautiful woman alone in the bush, of course the fiend would have tried it on. The fool paid the ultimate price.

Donovan rubbed his face with his free hand. Bridget could have died. He could have returned to find her raped and killed. He shivered, his gut churning. She had shot the intruder. Was it any wonder she was out there in the rain looking like death?

He rightened the table, left his pistol on it and then began the heavy task of dragging the big man out of the cabin. Dead weight was a struggle to manoeuvre and pull along, especially after he'd been trekking through the mountains since before daylight and was tired.

Finally, he got the man into the large ferns by the side of the cabin. Tomorrow, he'd bury him, but for now he had to take care of Bridget.

Returning to the cabin, he found some water in the bottom of a bucket and poured it over the blood that had soaked into the hard dirt, then covered it with fallen leaves. He hauled the table over to conceal it until the morning when he'd deal with it properly. Placing the three stools around the table it wouldn't resemble the scene Bridget had witnessed. He straightened the crates and gathered all that had spilt until the place was tidy again.

He stepped out into the drizzling rain to Bridget. 'He's gone. You're safe.'

'Gone?' She stared up at him.

He reached out to her and was pleased when she grasped his fingers. 'The man is dead. I've taken him out of the cabin.'

'I killed him,' she said dully, shivering.

'Yes, but you had no choice. He would have done the same to you, sweetheart.' He led her inside and sat her on a stool. 'I'll bring Zeus into the lean-to and then make some tea.'

She remained silent, staring down at her hands folded in her lap.

Donovan worked quickly. He unsaddled the bags of goods he'd bought, more items than he'd ever purchased before, but madly he'd been thinking of Bridget as he shopped and wanted to spoil her. He must be losing his mind for sure.

Giving Zeus fresh water, a couple of carrots and a few handfuls of oats he'd just bought for him, Donovan was satisfied Zeus would be content.

Somehow, he didn't think Bridget would be so easy to settle. He gathered twists of dried grass he had stored and some kindling and lit the fire, instantly making the cabin more cheerful. He glanced at Bridget as he left the cabin for more fresh water. She looked pale and detached, shaking in the wet riding habit she wore. He swore under his breath. She was still in shock. Something like this, killing a man, being attacked, could send her insane. He had to tread carefully.

With the kettle warming and the fire burning well, he carried in the bags of goods he'd bought. 'Miss Kittrick, come by the fire. You need to get warm.'

She stayed where she was, mute and unresponsive.

Swearing again, Donovan knelt down in front of her. 'Miss Kittrick, Bridget. You need to get warm.'

The eyes she turned to him were a dull grey not the vibrant blue that had taken his breath away when he first saw her. 'Listen, lovely girl. You've got to get out of those wet clothes. Understand? I don't want you becoming ill.'

He dragged the cot over to the fire and then helped her to stand. 'Let's take these things off you and you can wrap the blanket around you.' When she didn't move, he started to undo the buttons. Too many times he'd dreamed of undressing her since the moment Sap thrust her into his life, but his ideas of seduction were far from his mind as he shed her wet bodice and skirts – clothes she'd been drying for two days. She stood by the fire in her chemise, corset and shift, her black hair hanging bedraggled down her back.

'Come closer to the fire, that's it.' He wrapped the blanket around her slim frame, wishing he could kiss away her pain. Instead, he busied himself making some tea. 'I was very daring and rode into Bathurst to do some shopping. I don't normally venture into a town but sometimes being one person amongst many helps to be unseen. Anyway, I bought us a fruit cake. I thought you might like it.' He cut her a slice and placed it on a plate. 'Eat it.'

She sat staring at the flames not responding to him.

He wished he knew how to break through her shock. Again, he knelt before her and lifted the tin cup to her lips. 'Drink it, sweetheart.'

She did as he bid, sipping gently at the warm tea.

'That's my girl.' He smiled, his heart melting at the sorry state she was in. 'Everything will be better in the morning.' He didn't know why he said that because it wouldn't be, not really. She would have to live the rest of her life knowing she'd shot and killed a man. That the blackguard deserved it wouldn't help, not at first, maybe not ever.

He drew her hands around the cup to give her some warmth and encouraged her to keep sipping while he built up the fire and hung her clothes on the nails by the door. He found fresh clothes from his trunk and changed out of his own damp clothes.

Although she hadn't eaten, she drank all the tea, and he'd eased her down sideways on the cot and covered her with the skins. 'Sleep now.'

Her eyes closed and he relaxed slightly where he sat on a stool beside the cot. He'd watch over her tonight and keep the fire built up. The rain lashed down outside cocooning them in the cabin. Donovan placed a piece of thick wood across the door which acted as his bolt and returned to the fire.

That a stranger had found his hideout alarmed him. After being on the run for years, hiding in old barns, sleeping rough in ditches or under bridges, he'd found this place by chance and decided to remain, to make it a home. The small gorge was so isolated, so well hidden, he believed he could live the rest of his life here.

For two years he'd been safe in the knowledge that only a couple of people knew where he was, Sap and Mickey. And although that dead fellow out there might have simply stumbled across the clearing by accident, it still sent his pulse racing to imagine that others might do so, too. Was the world beginning to crowd in on him? Was it time to move on?

How much longer could he hide out here in his special place, his home? And what was he to do about Bridget?

A voice called out to her. Mama?

Bridget couldn't see a face at first then slowly the shadows parted. A black figure grew closer, its eyes glowing red like fire embers. The smell of foul breath filled her nose. Hands with long talons clawed at her. She screamed. No one listened. She couldn't breathe! She had to run. Her legs wouldn't work. There was no air. She gasped, crying. She had to flee, but she was trapped. How could she escape? The black demon would devour her...

'Bridget!'

Shaken roughly, Bridget gulped for air. The room swirled in circles and then steadied. Donovan's face came into view. She panted, pulling at the blanket around her.

'You're fine, my girl. I'm here. You're safe,' Donovan crooned.

Freeing herself from the cot, she ran outside into the pale sunshine. The cabin, Zeus cropping at the grass, the trickling creek, the high sides of the gorge and the thick rainforest coating it all came into focus. Wearing only her shift, she stepped down to the creek bank and knelt on the moss-covered stones. The cold water she splashed over her face revived her.

A blanket was draped over her shoulders. Bridget looked up at Donovan. 'How long have I been asleep?'

'About twelve hours.' He shrugged and crouched down beside her. 'You needed it.'

She stared unseeing at the flowing water. 'I had a bad dream.'

'Yes.'

'But it's not a dream, is it?' Her breath quickened again as memories of the attack flashed through her mind. She started to shake. 'I have killed a man.'

'It was him or you.'

'I committed murder...' Saying the words out loud seemed ridiculous. How could she have done such a thing? She was Bridget Kittrick, a respectable girl from a respectable family. Yet, she'd taken another's life.

'Listen to me.' Donovan touched her shoulder. 'You had no choice. He'd have killed you, you know that, don't you? He would have raped you and then killed you and probably shot me as I came through the ferns.'

She shuddered. The enormity of what had happened still seemed unreal. 'I killed a man,' she repeated, not believing it but also knowing it was true.

'What you did was in self-defence.'

Bridget wrapped her arms about her body and rocked. 'Dear God in heaven!'

'You mustn't blame yourself.'

'I had wanted to kill Sap,' she moaned. 'I vowed I would. But I had no real notion about doing such a thing, of how I'd feel afterwards. I was angry, hurt.' Her throat tightened. 'But this... I didn't know that man... A stranger... I gave him water, food...'

'It wasn't your fault but his,' Donovan said determinedly.

'It doesn't matter,' she whispered. 'I should have tried harder. Talked to him, won him round, been pleasant.'

'Some men simply take, Bridget. He would have been one of those men, believe me. If he'd been a nice man, you would never have been frightened enough to pull that trigger.'

She closed her eyes. Haunted. People like her didn't shoot people. A sob rose threatening to choke her. What would her mama think? And Papa? Austin, Patrick, the twins, her sisters? They would all hate her, be disgusted by her disgrace. Ashamed of her actions. Aunt Riona would quote the Bible to her, *Thy shall not kill...*

How she missed them. An ache spread in her chest, deep and lancing, biting into her until she groaned with the agony of it. She wanted her mama.

'Bridie, come into the cabin.' Donovan helped her to her feet. 'It's going to rain again.'

'I don't care,' she murmured, as if *that* mattered.

'I do. I don't want you getting ill.' Donovan sat her at the table on the stool closest to the fire. 'I've been cooking.'

Her stomach rumbled. She couldn't remember when she last ate, but the act of eating, of moving, of thinking seemed insurmountable. She simply wanted to curl up and die.

'I bought you a few things.' Donovan took from a canvas bag a hairbrush and two ribbons of emerald green. He placed them on the table and then took out a white blouse and a coffee-coloured skirt. 'The woman in town said you can adjust the skirt easily enough by moving the buttons, so I bought some thread and needles. I know I have some darning to do so they'll come in useful.'

She gazed at the offering. Simple clothes for a simple woman like a farmer's wife or... a woman in hiding in the forest.

She turned away and stared at the flames. 'You called me Bridie,' she said dully. 'That was my grandmother's name.'

'It suits you.'

'No, it doesn't.'

'I'm sorry.' Donovan moved to the pot simmering on the hook over the flames. 'I've made a good stew. And damper. There's fruit cake and I bought a bottle of plum cordial.'

Bridget smelled the stew wafting from the pot and the wisp of smoke from the fire. Outside a light rain fell and the damp from the rainforest also became a smell. This was her life now. All these humble smells, tastes and belongings. The thought whirled in her head until it tumbled out of her mouth. 'I can never go back.'

Donovan paused in dishing out bowls of stew. 'Yes, you can. I will take you to the edge of town. Tomorrow.'

'No. I cannot return to that life. My life, my old life, is gone.'

'That's not true.' Donovan sat beside her and pushed a bowl closer to her. 'You *can* go back to your life, your family.'

'I'm a murderer.'

'No one will ever know. I'll not be telling a soul and you don't have to either.'

She frowned, her head aching with a throbbing headache. 'You believe I can just pick up my life as I left it?'

'No, that's not possible. Of course, you'll feel different. It has changed you. You've been through so much, but don't allow this difficult time to alter everything. A strong woman such as yourself can overcome all this and continue and be even stronger for it.'

'How easy you make it sound.'

'I'm not saying it'll be easy, but it's doable.'

'You haven't done it. You hide yourself away in this rainforest.'

'My life isn't yours.'

'But it will have to be.' She stirred the spoon in the stew. 'I cannot live with my family and not tell the truth of what happened here. I'll be an embarrassment. They will be horrified.'

'Perhaps, but it sounds as though your mother is a formidable woman. Would she be so very upset that her courageous daughter fought for her life and survived?'

'Mama would understand and accept it, but I have more to be concerned about than only Mama. My brothers and sisters. The scandal would severely ruin their chances of good marriages and I won't be responsible for their unhappiness.'

'Eat. You need to build your strength.'

For a while they ate in silence, the only sound was the logs shifting in the fire and the drip of rain outside.

However, Bridget's mind wouldn't rest. 'Where is he?'

'I buried him this morning.'

'Nearby?' She shivered at the thought.

'I tied him to Zeus, and he dragged him a good distance away from here.'

Her stomach churned the stew she'd just eaten.

'Listen to me,' he took her hand, 'I know it's overwhelming, but you will get through it. In time the memory will fade enough for you to live your life normally.'

'I find that very hard to believe.' She liked the comfort of his hand on hers. A simple touch could do so much, offer so much solace.

'You will return to your home, your family and you will live a happy life.'

'How can you be sure of any of that? Look where we are, what has happened. It's a bad dream come true.'

'Trust me.' His earnest green eyes held hers.

'I cannot go back,' she whispered. The very thought of telling her family what had happened made her want to vomit.

Donovan nodded. 'Let's take it day by day, shall we?' He gave her a long look, stood and placed his bowl in the water bucket, before donning a waterproof coat. 'I'll leave you to get dressed. I need to cut some wood.'

She glanced around the cabin, not wanting to stay there by herself. 'I can help.'

He shook his head. 'Stay in here where it's dry. Get dressed.'

Forcing herself to move, she cleared the table. Washing the bowls in the bucket, Bridget tried not to think about anything but the task she was doing. The future was too bleak and scary to contemplate. She would take each day as it comes as Donovan suggested.

She glanced around the cabin, frightened by any sudden noise. This was her home now. Emotion clogged her throat. To survive each day, she had to block out her family. She refused to embroil their lives in scandal more than she had. They would assume her dead, which was better than the alternative, that their daughter and sister was a murderer.

Chapter Sixteen

Lincoln crept low through a scratchy scrub of bushland on the outskirts of Bathurst. Beside him Patrick did the same, pistols at the ready. Ahead police troopers were stationed around a farmer's small house, hiding behind anything that was large enough to cover their bodies. Inside the house, holding up the poor farmer's family were Sap and Mickey.

'We can't get too much closer,' Patrick warned. 'We don't want them to see us.'

'The bush is thinning out.' Lincoln crouched down behind a scrubby thin tree and watched the house.

The reports of Sap and Mickey being seen around the district in various places hindered them for weeks. False reports sent them on wild chases into unknown bushland where they wasted days searching only to nearly find themselves lost.

The police worked hard to find the criminals, but often other business kept them from following all leads and so Patrick and Lincoln took on the responsibility to hunt the bandits down, while Austin spoke with town officials and reporters of all the newspapers. Austin offered a five thousand pound reward for Bridget's safe return, but this caused more problems than it solved. Austin was kept busy with the police in dealing with the false claims from unscrupulous people. Patterson helped initially, but he was weary of being too close to the police. He was a wanted man and needed to stay hidden. Patrick told him to return to Louisburgh in case any news had reached there about Bridget.

Now, as the cool May day sent a chill down his back, Lincoln wondered if capturing Sap would end with him telling them where Bridget was. There'd been no sightings of her, which worried him. Patrick flatly refused to consider her as dead. Lincoln understood Patrick's determination to believe his sister lived, but if Sap and Mickey didn't tell them where she was, how were they to ever find her?

A yell snapped Lincoln's attention back to the scene. Beside him Patrick froze. Lincoln tensed as troopers spoke to the inhabitants inside the house. Someone was yelling back, and a single shot fired through a window at the police.

'I can't hear,' Patrick murmured. 'We have to get closer.'

'Let the troopers do their job, Patrick,' Lincoln counselled. Over the days and weeks of searching for Bridget he and Patrick had become as close as brothers. Together they'd lived rough, camping out in all weathers, going hungry and thirsty between towns, sleeping curled up under trees in downpours, talking quietly of strategies and of the woman they both loved.

A warm feeling encircled Lincoln's heart when he thought of Bridget. She'd captured his interest from the very first day when he saw her at her birthday party back in February. It seemed a lifetime ago since those enjoyable days when he'd gone riding with Austin and Miss Norton around Berrima, or enjoyed dinner at Emmerson Park seated opposite Bridget. He remembered them falling down the cliff side at Fitzroy Falls, laughing with her at the relief they hadn't been hurt. How bold she was, seemingly fearless. Was she summoning that courage now? Was she in that farmhouse worried for her life or somewhere else?

'Come out with your hands above your heads!' called the senior sergeant.

'Drop your weapons or we'll kill the lot of them,' came the reply from a window.

'Why is it taking so long?' Patrick fumed. 'They should just run in there and take the bastards.'

'There's a woman and child in the house,' Lincoln soothed. 'It's frustrating I know, but they must have a plan.'

'You think so?' Patrick's sarcastic tone matched his expression. 'Those troopers don't seem to have a clue.'

'A shoot out with bushrangers isn't something that they do every day, I wouldn't have thought.'

Patrick stared ahead. 'Bridget could be in that house.'

'I know, which is why this whole thing has to be done properly.' Lincoln frowned at the troopers, some of which were creeping closer to the house. 'Come on, they're moving up.'

'Look, who are they?' Patrick pointed to a cart of men who'd just pulled up some distance behind them.

'Reporters for the newspapers.'

'Bloody hell. That's all we need.'

Step by step, on full alert, Lincoln and Patrick crept to the edge of the scrub.

'If we run over to that water barrel,' Patrick said, pointing to a barrel standing beside a wooden log shed, 'we can both fit behind there.'

Lincoln nodded.

'Right, go,' Patrick whispered.

Lincoln sprinted for the log shed, he'd been fast as a boy, and the danger of being shot at leant wings to his feet. He fell in a heap behind the shed with Patrick nearly landing on top of him.

They hardly had time to catch their breaths when a hail of shots rang out of the house. The police returned fire. Screams came from inside the house. Smoke from the many pistols firing created a fog. The troopers moved forwards. More shots rang out. A constable fell, shot in the leg. He yelled in agony.

'Come on!' Lincoln rose, unable to keep out of it. If Bridget was in there, he wanted those filthy scum captured and her free. He jogged forward, his newly bought pistol pointed in front of him. A bullet pinged the dirt at his feet. He knelt behind a fence post, aware of nothing but the door of the house.

A flash of fire came from a window. A trooper fell at the steps of the verandah. The senior sergeant gave a signal then crashed through the door. More shots echoed, filling the air with an unnatural sound.

Without thought, Lincoln rushed into the dim interior of the house, searching for Bridget. A bullet whizzed past his head and splintered into the wood behind him.

Beside him, Patrick turned and fired, but the shooter was already down. Two troopers ran at the figure, while the other shooter was slumped against a wall in the corner. A baby cried, the mother too, hiding behind a bed, the farmer cradling them both.

Lincoln couldn't see Bridget.

'Are you the bushranger Sap?' the senior sergeant asked, kneeling by the man with blood seeping from his chest.

'Aye. I'm The Sap. Best bushranger you've ever seen,' he boasted, blood trickling from his mouth into his beard.

'I doubt that,' the sergeant scoffed.

Patrick lunged for Sap. 'Where is my sister, you bastard!'

'Hey! Hey!' The sergeant pushed Patrick away. 'Calm down.'

Sap grinned, blood staining his teeth. 'The hot-blooded Bridget?'

Lincoln had to hold Patrick back from punching the man, even though he wanted to do the exact same thing.

'She was a looker...' Sap slurred. More blood dribbled out of his mouth. Panic entered his eyes. 'I'm done for, matey.'

'Where is she!' Patrick yelled, trying to get free of Lincoln's hold. 'Don't you dare die. I want to see you hang!'

'Nice piece of flesh she was.' Sap laughed, then choked.

'Where is Miss Kittrick?' The sergeant pulled him up by his shirt. 'Answer me!'

'Dead.'

The room went still.

Lincoln blinked. Had he heard correctly?

'No...' Patrick moaned. 'You lie!'

Sap's eyes rolled, then he focused on Patrick. 'Tasty she was... a fighter...'

'Where is she? Tell me she's not dead!' Patrick flung himself out of Lincoln's hold and fell to the floor beside Sap. He grabbed the man's throat. 'Where is she?'

'Gone. Hated that bitch...' Sap's eyes closed, and he slumped into death.

Stunned, Lincoln ran across the room to the other bushranger.

'He's dead, too,' the trooper said without emotion. 'Good riddance.'

'He said nothing?' Lincoln asked.

'One word. Donovan.' The trooper shrugged. 'God knows what that means.'

The quietness of the small house hurt Lincoln's ears, even the baby had stopped crying. Lincoln strode outside to lean on the verandah post, needing air. Bridget dead. The words throbbed in his brain. That beautiful face now white in death. Her infectious laugh silenced.

Something bumped into him. Patrick. Like a drunken sailor Patrick weaved over the grass to fall onto his knees and vomit.

Shattered, Lincoln didn't know how to comfort the man. Words were inadequate.

Reporters swarmed the scene. An illustrator set up his easel and stool and sat to draw the farmhouse.

'What news?' a fellow asked him, pencil at the ready.

'We need witness statements,' another said, writing on his piece of paper.

'Go away. All of you, just go away.' Lincoln pushed past them. He slowly walked over to where they'd tied their horses and brought them back to Patrick. Without speaking, Lincoln hauled him to his feet and handed him the reins. As the reporters spoke to the police, Lincoln and Patrick mounted and rode back towards Bathurst.

The hour it took them to ride to Bathurst passed without a word spoken. Lincoln knew of loss, of the pain that it brings all too well. He still mourned his mother, the only person he had ever loved.

He'd been a fool to let his feelings grow for Bridget. How many times had he told himself he didn't deserve to be part of a family? Yet, he'd foolishly allowed Bridget to crept beneath his armour and steal his heart.

Well, look where that had got him. Once more he suffered. Never again.

In town, they dismounted at the stables behind the coaching inn and hurried through to the bar where Lincoln ordered straight shots of brandy for them both. 'Has the Sydney coach arrived?' he asked the barman.

'It's due any time.'

Lincoln nodded his thanks and glared at the brandy shot. He'd not touched alcohol since he was a foolish youth... He swore he never would. Needing to keep a clear head, he passed the shot to Patrick who gulped it down with his own.

'Bad day?' the barman asked, pouring two more shots.

'Not great.' Lincoln gave the glasses to Patrick. 'Do you want anything to eat?'

Patrick shook his head and gulped the brandies down one after the other. 'How do we organise a funeral without a body?' He looked as white as a sheet.

'Coach is coming.' The barman cocked his head to one side. 'I can hear the bugle.'

'How do I tell him?' Patrick murmured.

'We'll do it together.' Lincoln stood straight, prepared for the task while Patrick leant over the bar, looking like death himself.

Austin entered, carrying a small case. He raised his hand at Lincoln and joined them. 'What a journey. The coach got bogged in mud coming over the mountains. We all had to get out and help push it clear.' He glanced down at his muddied boots. 'Anyway, what's been happening? I've spoken with a reporter from the *Sydney Morning Herald*. He said the editor will run a feature on Bridget's kidnap in Friday's edition with the reward clearly stated.'

'Tell them not to bother,' Patrick said, lifting his hand to the barman for another shot.

Austin's handsome face scowled. 'What?'

'Let us sit down at a table.' Lincoln turned to the barman. 'May we have use of your snug for a few minutes?'

'Aye, it's free at the minute.'

Lincoln grabbed Patrick's arm and led him to the small room opposite to the bar.

'What's happened?' Austin asked as soon as he shut the door on the noise of the inn.

'She's dead.' Patrick burst into tears.

The colour drained from Austin's face. 'Who said so?' he spoke harshly.

'The man who killed her. Sap.' Patrick covered his face with his hands, his shoulders heaving.

Austin stared at Lincoln his mouth opening and then closing as though he couldn't manage any words.

Lincoln sighed deeply. 'There was a shoot-out. Sap and his offsider were killed. As he lay dying Sap told us that he'd killed Bridget.'

Austin staggered. Lincoln rushed to keep him upright and then lowered him into a chair beside his brother. Patrick cried silent tears, head bowed.

'I can't believe it,' Austin whispered. 'Our darling sister…'

Patrick threw his hat onto the table. 'We don't even know where her body is. She could be anywhere…'

'Do we know when he did it?' Austin's voice was tight, straining to keep control.

Shaking his head, Lincoln sighed desperately sad. He didn't know how he was keeping himself together when he too wanted to howl his pain like Patrick. 'No. She's been gone for weeks so it could have happened anytime and anywhere.'

'Animals would have got to her if they didn't bury her,' Patrick croaked and dashed from the room.

'Do the police have any idea where she might be?'

'I don't know. We left straight away. Reporters were everywhere. I wanted to get Patrick away from there. We needed to tell you before you heard it from reporters coming back into town.'

'Thank you.' Austin rested his head in his hands. 'I can't believe it. I was certain we'd find her.'

'You'll need to speak with the police.'

'Yes, and then we should go home to Berrima. My aunt…' Austin swallowed, 'This will destroy my family.'

'I want to keep searching,' Lincoln surprised himself with his words.

'Searching?' Austin stared at him. 'For Bridget's body?'

'Yes.'

'It's a near impossible task.'

'I have the time. I have no family, no demands on my time, no responsibilities as you and Patrick do.' He shrugged, not understanding his need to continue, but knowing he must. 'I can't rest until she is found.'

'Where will you start?'

'I'll search from here back towards the mountains.' The plan was vague, and he'd need to buy equipment, but something in him knew this was what he had to do. He couldn't walk away without knowing where she was.

'You have been the very best of friends, Lincoln.' Austin stood and shook his hand. 'I don't know what I'd have done without you these last months.'

'Take Patrick home, see to your aunt. I'll keep in touch.' Lincoln left the room and walked outside.

He sucked in great gulps of air. The muscle in his jaw twitched. In the far distance the blue haze of the great mountains that divided the Bathurst plains and the Sydney settlement cut the skyline. Instinct told him Bridget was there, whether alive or dead, she was there. All he had to do was find her.

Chapter Seventeen

Although the air in the gorge chilled her, Bridget sat in a shaft of sunlight by the creek washing the bowls and plates. Mundane chores were all she focused on now. She lived each minute without thought to the past or the future.

In the two weeks since the attack, she had stayed close to the cabin. While Donovan hunted, skinned his kills and chopped wood, Bridget would cook and clean, hoe the vegetable garden and brush Zeus. She kept her distance from Donovan. Every day he said he'd take her to the nearest farm so she could make her way back to her family, and every day she rejected the offer.

There was no going back.

So, she kept busy, made herself useful, doing what she could so he wouldn't find an excuse to take her away and leave her somewhere. After dinner each night, she'd go to bed early, her back turned against the room and not move until morning when Donovan would rise and go outside and not return for hours. She hated being left behind. Bird calls and the trickling creek were the only sounds to keep her company. All her life she'd been surrounded by family, by the noise several people create, talking, laughing, singing, humming, the twins whistling, her sisters' gossip and chatter, Moira's blasphemies and so much more had been the background noise to her days. Now all she had was the sharp call of whip bird and the other birds' choruses, the odd snicker from Zeus and the rhythmic chop of Donovan cutting up wood.

She rose and carried the bucket of washed bowls and plates into the cabin and put them away. She swept the dirt floor with a broom made from branches. The cabin was neat and tidy. Nothing out of place. She glanced at her riding habit hanging on a hook. She'd not worn it since Donovan bought her the blouse and skirt she wore. The riding habit reminded her of home, of riding Ace, of her kidnap, of shooting a man dead.

The past.

Impulsively, she grabbed the habit and balled it up and threw it on the fire. The material singed, smoked and then flamed. Without emotion she watched the last remnants of her old life shrivel and die. No more. No more would she wallow in what had happened to her. The choice to stay was made. As much as she missed her family, she had made the right decision to not go back to them. They could not be burdened with her sins.

Feeling better suddenly, she lifted her chin and took a deep breath. Today she would begin again.

Leaving the cabin, she walked around the side into the trees and ferns to where Donovan chopped wood. He'd been doing it for a long time. He'd taken his shirt off and wore only his dun-coloured trousers. A long thin tree, the trunk grey with age, lay on the ground and Donovan was cutting off the branches and then stripping those branches of smaller ones until he had clean logs.

Part hidden by the ferns, Bridget admired the muscles rippling in his shoulders and back. His tanned forearms lifted the axe high and brought it down cleanly. Sweat made his skin glisten, darkened his blond hair.

Desire surged through her hot and needy. Donovan was her future just as much as this hideaway cabin. She didn't have to be alone.

Another decision made, she stepped forward into his line of sight.

His small smile seemed wary as though he wasn't sure if he should smile at her at all. 'Come to help?' he joked softly, his green eyes warm, kind.

Bridget walked up to him and took his face in her hands and kissed him. Donovan jerked back. 'Hey now.'

She ignored him and kissed him again, pushing her body closer to his, lowering her hands to his shoulders, feeling the muscles tense beneath her fingertips.

'Bridie...' he breathed against her mouth. 'Don't start this.'

'I want you.'

'Sweet girl, I'm not the one for you.'

'You're the only one for me.' She meant every word. They were in this together. Two lonely, displaced people thrust together through events neither of them expected.

'You'll regret this.' He put his hands on her waist and pushed her away a little. 'Don't sacrifice yourself to me. I'm not worthy.'

'I'm to spend the rest of my life with you here in this rainforest.'

'You don't know that. One day you'll realise you want more than this.' He swept his arms out to encompass the cabin. 'Staying with me will ruin your life.'

'It's already ruined.' She unbuttoned her blouse, desperately needing him in a way she'd never known before. 'Let me be your woman.'

'You're better than that.'

'You were once a gentleman, and I was once a gentlewoman. We are equal.' She dropped the blouse to the floor and then her skirt until she stood in her corset and chemise. Her heart hammered in her chest.

'You'll regret all of this,' he murmured, but desire darkened his green eyes to emerald.

'I'll prove you wrong.' She stood inches from him and trailed her finger-tips down his chest. She smiled when he sucked in a breath. 'I'm yours.'

'Mine?' He smirked as her fingers closed around the buttons on his trousers.

'Until the day you die,' she whispered against his lips.

In one swift move he scooped her up into his arms and carried her into the cabin and laid her on the cot. He undressed and stood before her. 'Are you sure?'

She nodded unable to take her eyes from him. A burning need curled in the pit of her stomach. 'Do you not want me?'

'I've wanted you since the moment you walked into the clearing filthy and drenched, covered in mud.' Donovan moved slowly, leisurely stripping off the rest of her clothes until she too lay naked.

Carefully, the cot creaking under their combined weight, Donovan gathered her in his arms and kissed her deeply, his tongue exploring her mouth before he rained kisses along her neck and chest. His hands cupped her breasts, and he teased her nipples with his lips until she thought she might faint from it.

'Are you sure?' he whispered, kissing down her stomach to the private part of her where he nuzzled and stroked.

She gripped his hair in response half mad with yearning.

He came back to kiss her again, intently and demandingly. Bridget arched up against him, seeking the fulfilment she knew he could give her. Lying between her legs, he paid attention to her breasts again before once more kissing her. Then entered her and stilled.

Bridget grasped his shoulders, breath suspended.

Donovan started to move, gently, steadily, building up her pleasure as he intensified his kisses.

'You're mine now, my girl...' he whispered, thrusting deeper.

Her body accepted him wholly, gratefully. She felt herself rising, spiralling upwards, reaching for something and then suddenly her body burst with sensations that made her cry out. She held him close as Donovan also moaned, his eyes closed.

In awe she watched his handsome face as he took a breath and opened his eyes to smile at her. 'I didn't hurt you?'

'Hurt me?' She frowned. 'How could any of that hurt? It was wonderful.'

Donovan chuckled and rolled to the side. 'Apparently it can, for a woman's first time.'

'Oh.' Bridget wondered about the act and couldn't stop grinning. She felt alive. Free. She now knew the experience of being with a man. No more guessing what it was like to lay with a man, being envious of married women having all the knowledge, no more wondering what it all meant. Now she had done it. And liked it.

Donovan cupped her cheek. 'If you're staying, I need to make a bigger bed. I'm sick of sleeping on the floor.'

She raised herself up onto her elbow, her long black hair falling like a curtain. 'I'll help you.' She kissed him boldly, brushing her breast against his chest as desire for him flared once again. 'But not just yet.'

He laughed as she kissed him.

In the days and weeks that followed, Bridget grew to be more content in her own world – a world that only existed within the gorge.

She spent the daylight hours working alongside Donovan and at night loving him with a growing confidence and abandonment.

The temperature dropped as winter advanced. The June weather grew colder, frost sprinkled the tops of the peaks. The vegetables didn't grow as well or as quickly, and Donovan spent more time out hunting. Only now, Bridget went with him. With no calendar or clock to keep track of time, she lived hour by hour, eating when she was hungry, sleeping when she was tired and working when jobs needed doing. She helped Donovan build a bigger, stronger bed, in which they made love for hours, careless to anything other than their own needs.

Bridget found she couldn't keep her hands off him. Day and night she wanted his body as much as she wanted food or air. It was as though instinct was telling her to take each precious day as something special for no one knew what tomorrow would bring.

'You know I should go into town. We're running low on everything,' Donovan said one cool winter's morning as they lay in bed.

Bridget's heart twisted in fear. 'No. You can't leave me alone.'

'Bridie, girl, I must get supplies.' His fingers gripped hers. 'Winter is already making its presence felt. It snows up here. We can't be caught without food.'

'Then I'm coming with you.'

The light died in his eyes, and he yanked back the blanket and got out of bed. 'Please yourself.'

Annoyed, she scowled at him. 'What does that mean?'

'Nothing. I mean nothing.' He pulled on his shirt.

She jumped out of bed, naked and furious. 'Yes, it does. Talk to me.'

He reached for his trousers, but she slapped them away.

'What is it?' she demanded.

Donovan sighed. 'If you come into town... Well, you might see what you've been missing and want to go home.' He looked away. 'I wouldn't blame you.'

All her anger melted away. 'Are you saying you'd miss me if I left?'

'Of course, I bloody would, woman. What kind of question is that?' he snapped, getting dressed.

'Do not worry. I've made my choice. I'm staying here. I cannot go home. I have committed murder and slept with a man who isn't my husband.' For a moment humiliation filled her, but only for a moment, then she lifted her chin stubbornly. 'I choose to be here with you.'

'We can never be married in a church. I can't risk it, even after all this time.' Donovan pulled on his boots.

'I never asked you to marry me.' She hated to see him quiet and thoughtful, especially now when she'd experienced him happy, laughing, teasing and playful.

'You are sacrificing too much, Bridie.'

'I have all that I need here with you.' She stepped closer to him and kissed him tenderly.

Donovan kissed her back hungrily as if to stamp his mark on her. Bridget raked her nails down his back, eager for him. They fell onto the bed in a desperate need for each other. Her fingers unbuttoned his trousers to free him and he entered her quickly. She bit into his shoulder, wrapping her legs around him to take all of him.

'I can't have you leave me now,' he murmured against her mouth.

She stared into his eyes. 'I won't.'

—ele—

Lincoln rode through the scrub and entered the trees at the bottom of a deep valley. A small creek ran alongside him, and he reined Blaze to a halt and his pack horse trailing behind also stopped. He allowed them to drink while he refilled his canteen from the rushing water.

He stood and stretched. Hours in the saddle made him ache, and he felt every one of his thirty-four years. Two days ago, he'd spent his birthday on the side of a mountain in gale force winds, cold and tired, contemplating his life. Still, something drove him on to keep searching for Bridget, alive or dead. As winter shortened the days and the temperature dropped, he was losing confidence of finding evidence of Bridget's whereabouts.

At every farm he passed he asked questions if anyone had seen Bridget. He made enquiries at any small village he rode into, but the responses were the same. No sightings of a beautiful young woman named Bridget Kittrick with black hair and steel-blue eyes.

Regularly, he wrote to Austin, but sending no news to the distraught family felt worse than no note at all. Austin told him to quit. It had been months since Bridget was taken from Louisburgh, they had run out of hope. But Lincoln hadn't. He couldn't understand why he continued. Only, walking away seemed wrong, as though he was letting Bridget down by giving up. Her brothers believed her to be dead, and she might be, yet Lincoln couldn't accept it until he saw her body.

So, he continued to search even as the cold June weather chilled him. Yesterday, he'd left the small town of Oberon after stocking up on supplies and travelled south towards the mountains. He believed the answer to Bridget's whereabouts was in the mountains, but they were so vast that it could take him years to search every part of it. Some of the deep gorges were impossible to descend into and he shied away from any thoughts of Bridget being flung to the bottom of one of them.

A pair of black cockatoos screeched above his head. He watched them fly over the trees and then up the side of the cliff high above him. How he wished he could fly and soar above to see everything below.

Instead, he took Blaze's reins and walked beside the creek, heading further into the valley. Less daylight meant he had to camp earlier. Finding a suitable spot could take time. He had brought a small tent with him, a warm blanket, food, cooking equipment and a compass, all of which were packed on the spare horse. In the inside pocket of his long coat, he carried a pistol, just in case. Bushrangers were notorious in the country and a pistol, and a rifle were a necessity, but he could also hunt with them if he ran short of food.

After an hour of walking east along the valley floor, he found a wide grassy spot that circled out from the creek and stopped to make camp. The sun had set beyond the peaks, throwing long shadows. A mob of small kangaroos raised their heads to stare at him. The mothers with young in their pouches bounded away, but some of the others stayed and watched him.

Unsaddling the horses was a routine he barely thought about now such was the habit. He started a fire and as it burned, he erected his small tent and laid out his bedding inside

Seated by the fire on a large rock he'd found by the creek, he made damper and set the billycan on the flames to boil the tea. This rough life didn't bother him. Although many thought him a gentleman, he'd not always been living a comfortable life. As a boy he'd spent most of his time working on surrounding farms learning skills he'd never need as the son of an innkeeper. He didn't have many happy childhood memories, but those he did were of fishing in the rivers around Hobart, of camping out in the bush and sleeping under the stars, precious times away from the inn, away from his father.

A sudden gunshot made him jump, spilling the boiling tea he was about to pour into his cup. He rose, grabbing his pistol as he did so. All around him, on either side of the creek, the dense trees created a barrier, like a walled fortress. His pulse raced. His eyes scanned the landscape, trying to pick out any movement in the shadows of the bush.

'Cooee!' the call came in a long drawn-out sound.

Lincoln mumbled a curse. Someone was close. Would he be friend or foe?

'Huntley!' the call echoed around the valley.

Lincoln frowned. Had he heard correctly? Did someone shout Huntley or Cooee, the known bush call that the Aboriginals and white folk used when lost in the bush.

Was someone lost? Lincoln walked up the slope a little way. Cupping his hands around his mouth, he let out the call. 'Cooee!' The yell bounced around the trees eerily.

'Cooee!' the reply came swiftly.

Lincoln ran back down to the camp and took the rifle from the tent to have both weapons to hand. The stranger calling could be a bushranger ready to rob him. Standing close to the horses, with the creek at his back and the fire in front, Lincoln waited for what seemed an eternity until he finally heard the jingle of harness and the snicker of a horse coming from the trees.

He tensed, senses alert.

'Huntley!' A figure walked between the trees leading a horse.

Confused that they knew his name, Lincoln tightened the grip on his weapons.

'Huntley. It's me, Patrick.'

Lincoln sagged in relief. 'Bloody hell!'

Patrick smiled that slow smile of his and pushed his hat to the back of his head to show his face. 'I did give warning.'

'Yes, but still a man doesn't expect visitors out here unless they are of a dubious kind.' Lincoln chuckled, putting his guns away before both men slapped the other on the back. 'What are you doing out here?'

Patrick sat on the grass by the fire. 'I couldn't rest at home. I tried to get on with my life. I travelled out to Burrawang and bought some land, but my heart wasn't in it. I kept thinking of you out here searching, of Bridget... I knew I had to come and help you.' Patrick threw a stick onto the flames. 'It seemed wrong that you were looking for her by yourself when you're not even related, yet her two brothers have given up.'

'I care for your sister,' Lincoln admitted. 'More than I wanted to care for any woman.'

Patrick nodded. 'I thought so. I've seen the way you watch her when she's nearby. Bridget looked at you the same way.'

Lincoln smiled sadly, the notion warming his heart. 'I like to believe she did, too.'

'I know my sister and she felt something towards you.'

Taking a deep breath, Lincoln put the billycan back on the flames. 'And I left her at Huntley Vale... I was a coward regarding my own feelings for her. If I'd stayed, she may never have been taken.'

'Perhaps, but the whole episode could still have happened, and you'd have been shot like Silas Pegg, worse killed.' Patrick stood and returned to his horse to unpack his things and gave Lincoln his tin cup to fill. 'We'll search for her together for as long as it takes.'

'Have you told Austin?' Lincoln poured out cups of black tea for them both.

'Yes. I sent him a letter with Aunt Riona. She was travelling to Sydney to stay with Austin for a while. Emmerson Park is too lonely for her and her grief.'

'Have letters been sent to your mother?'

Patrick cradled the tin cup in his hands. 'No. Austin decided the news is too shocking and to wait until the family return to Sydney.'

'Ignorance is bliss,' Lincoln murmured, blowing on the hot brew.

'Exactly.' Patrick sipped his tea. 'Mama will be devastated. It's better we tell her face to face than by a letter.'

'Let's hope we have more to tell her by the time she returns next year.'

Patrick scowled as the fire smoke blew into his face. 'You still sense Bridget is alive, don't you?'

'We have no proof either way, but my gut tells me that she may live.'

'Lost? Out here? For all this time?' Patrick shook his head. 'My sister is clever. She would have found a way to reach a farm and get help by now.'

They were silent with their thoughts for a time until Lincoln began to cook the damper.

'I'll set up my tent.' Patrick rose with a sigh.

'Do you like fig jam? A farmer's wife sold me a jar that she'd made.'

'I eat anything but seaweed,' Patrick replied. 'I had enough of that as a poor child in Ireland.'

Lincoln grinned to lighten the mood. 'We're a long way from the sea, so I believe you're safe from that.'

'We're a long way from anywhere,' Patrick grunted.

Concentrating on the damper, Lincoln understood the younger man's misery. He hadn't expected to be living rough in the bush with winter approaching. By now he'd hoped to have bought a nice property and be setting up a home for himself and breeding his Angus cattle. Instead, he was on some wild hunt for a woman he'd only known a few short months but who had managed to make him feel again after years of numbness.

Chapter Eighteen

Bridget opened her eyes and shivered. Her breath came out in a cloud of vapour. The freezing air in the cabin permeated beneath the blanket and skins despite the fire blazing.

Donovan had lit a lantern on the table to dispel the predawn gloom and as he opened the door and entered, a wave of more cold air whispered over to her. 'Morning.' He rubbed his hands together. 'Zeus is saddled. We need to go.'

She didn't like the idea of getting up and dressing in the cold or walking the miles through the forest to reach the edge of the mountains and the beginning of the open plains. However, they needed supplies, and she wouldn't be left behind. Climbing out of bed, she hurried to the fire and grabbing her clothes from a stool, quickly dressed.

Donovan knelt before his trunk and opened it. 'I've been thinking.'

'Oh?' she asked, tying up her hair into a neat roll.

'I'm going to bury this money. I don't want to take it all with us in case we get robbed on the road, and to leave it here for someone to find is a risk not worth taking.' He pulled out the false bottom and picked up the small bags of gold. 'When I was at the top of the peak yesterday, I saw a column of smoke to the south.'

She caught the worried look in his eyes. 'How far away?'

'Some miles yet, but people could be encroaching on the mountains all the time, especially loggers and gold seekers. I don't know how much longer we'll stay undiscovered.'

She shivered again, not from cold but from the thought of the man who'd entered the cabin and attacked her. How many more men like that would come? 'Perhaps it's time to consider moving on?'

'It's crossed my mind.' Donovan raked down the fire until it was just smoke and embers.

'We could head north to Queensland.' She sipped some of the tea Donovan had left for her and chewed on a piece of dried kangaroo meat.

'We'd have to go somewhere remote. Change our names.'

'The blacks are wilder up there.'

'And the weather not as kind I've heard. Hotter and dryer than here, especially out west.'

Bridget donned her cloak. 'We'd manage.'

Donovan collected the bags of money. 'I'll just bury these under the fern behind the log store, then we'll go.' He paused to raise his eyebrows at her. 'Are you sure you want to come? We'll be walking for six hours or so.'

'I don't want to stay here by myself.' She thought of the man who attacked her and couldn't risk enduring that again. Her fingers shook as she tied the cloak's top buttons.

Donovan touched her cheek softly. 'I understand. At the edge of the mountains is a farm. I've been there before. They are good people. I can leave you with them and ride Zeus into Oberon. It'll be faster if I can ride him rather than us walk the entire way.'

'We should have kept the other horse.' She spoke of the horse the man who attacked her owned. Donovan had released it into the mountains a mile or so from the clearing.

'No. That horse might be recognised. We don't know who that man was. If he was known and his horse recognised people would start asking questions as to why we had it. Setting it free was the only option.'

'This farm, where you stop and buy things. They will also ask too many questions,' she fretted. Could she keep up the pretence of being a normal common woman and not someone who'd been kidnapped and a murderer?

'They've never done before when I've been there to buy food from them. The farmer, Beecroft, is a quiet man, and his wife offers me a drink, sells me a few jars of preserves, eggs and then leaves me alone on the front step to have a quick chat to her husband. I don't linger.'

Bridget didn't want to be parted from Donovan and left alone with strangers. 'Let us wait and see how I feel when we reach the farm.'

They set off as the night sky turned from navy to pewter. The stars in the clear sky twinkled and the bird's dawn chorus accompanied them as they guided Zeus across the clearing and into the tunnel of ferns and tall moss-covered trees. The smell of damp and rotting vegetation was strong as the sun rarely reached the bottom of this gloomy cut into the mountain.

Emerging from the fern tunnel, Donovan led them west out of the gorge. 'Take note of this path,' Donovan instructed to Bridget. 'Each third tree has a knife cut under its lowest branch, see?'

Bridget peered at every third tree as they trudged upwards over the first incline. 'Yes, I see.'

'If you ever have to follow them, they will take you over this ridge. Always head west and you'll eventually come to the grass plains and farms.'

At the top, Donovan stopped and pointed between the trees as the sun broke on the horizon behind them. 'Keep the morning sun at your back and if it's afternoon, keep the sun in your eyes.'

She nodded and then started down the side into the next steep valley. Bridget paid attention to her surroundings as she always had done since a child learning to ride in the bush around Emmerson Park with Douglas the groom.

As the sun climbed higher, Bridget's feet started to ache from walking the rough terrain. For so many weeks she'd stayed close to the cabin only going on short walks with Donovan to hunt or to gather wood. Blisters formed on her heels before they'd even left the mountains. She knew she was slowing him down and cursed at herself.

When they finally cleared the last of the eucalyptus trees hugging the mountains, she paused for breath and took a drink from the canteen. Spread out before her, the wide grassy fields opened up the country for miles. It felt strange to be in such openness after being sheltered by sheer cliffs and tall trees for so long.

'The farm is about a mile away, beyond that clump of trees in the distance. His house is on the other side. They are his sheep.' He pointed to a small flock nearby.

Exhausted by hours of walking, she simply nodded and followed him, wincing with each step.

'I'll stay at the farm if the wife is home,' Bridget told Donovan as the small wooden house came into sight.

'Good idea. I'll be quicker riding. What name will you give?'

'What do they know you as?'

'Don Smith.'

'Then I'll be... Ellen Smith, your wife.' Saying her mama's first name was difficult and she quickly pushed away the image of her mother, her family and buried the ache of missing them.

Donovan smiled. 'Sounds good.'

As they approached the house, a dog barked from where it was chained to a peg near a shed.

A woman came out onto the verandah wiping her hands on her white apron. 'Mr Smith.'

'Good day to you, Mrs Beecroft.' Donovan shook her hand. 'This is my wife, Ellen.'

'Good day, Mrs Smith.' Mrs Beecroft shook Bridget's hand with a warm smile. 'I didn't realise you were married,' she said to Donovan.

'I was wondering if I could leave my wife with you, Mrs Beecroft, while I travel into Oberon for supplies?'

'Aye, of course. I don't often have company out here. Come inside.' She held open the door.

'I'll go then.' Donovan took Bridget's hand and kissed her cheek. 'I'll be as quick as I can.'

'Have you got the list?'

He winked. 'I have.'

Bridget waited for him to mount Zeus and ride away before she returned inside.

The front door led straight into a sitting room and beyond that, through another open door, Bridget could see a kitchen area. Another door to the right showed a bedroom.

'My husband has gone to town today, too. It's market day and we had pigs to sell.' Mrs Beecroft walked towards the kitchen. 'Please, sit down. I'll make some tea.'

'Thank you.' Bridget sat in the chair by the cheery fire and glanced around. Although sparsely furnished, the walls were decorated with many simple and unframed paintings of landscapes. A thick woollen blanket hung over the back of a chair, and another was in the process of being knitted.

Mrs Beecroft brought in a tea tray. 'As I said, I didn't know Mr Smith was married. He's never mentioned it in the few times he's been here to buy goods from us. You should have come before and made friends.'

'We are only recently married, and you know there is always things to do in the house,' she lied.

'How have you taken to living in the mountains? I take it that's where you live as we know all the neighbouring farms.'

Bridget accepted the teacup with a slight tremble. They knew Donovan lived in the mountains. She didn't know what to say, but she had to throw the woman off the scent before Bridget said something she'd later regret. 'We actually move about a lot,' she murmured.

'Ah, is your husband a fossicker?'

'Yes. Ten years ago, he was in the goldfields near Ballarat. He can't shake the urge to dig for gold.' The lies rolled off her tongue so easily she half believed them.

'It's like a poison some say. Once you start mining, you can't stop.' Mrs Beecroft cut a generous portion of a sponge cake. 'I'm glad my Harold never thought to go fossicking. Farming is what we know and what we'll do until we die. Though there's many who go searching for gold and gems in the mountains around here and there have been some finds lately. Recently, we've had more strangers than ever passing the farm.'

Bridget didn't like the sound of that. Men entering the mountains gave more chance of the cabin being found. 'I hope you don't mind that I have called unannounced?' Bridget bit into the cake and her mouth watered at the sweet taste. It'd been far too long since she tasted anything with sugar in it.

'No, I don't mind at all. It's nice to have female company.' Mrs Beecroft had taken off her apron and wore a dull grey skirt with a matching bodice. Her brown hair had a streak of grey along the left temple. 'I only speak to women when I venture into Oberon, but I couldn't face it today, I've had stomach cramps all night.'

'You are ill?' Bridget asked, alarmed.

'Just the usual women's curse. It hits me bad each month.'

'Oh...' Not knowing what to say, Bridget ate more cake.

'I wouldn't mind so much if I had a dozen children to take care of, but the pains each month remind me that my womb is empty...' Mrs Beecroft's sad expression lasted only a moment before she smiled at Bridget. 'Do you have children, Mrs Smith?'

'No.' The thought had never entered Bridget's mind, but now that it had she felt the blood drain from her face. Good God that could be a possibility!

'I'm sure they will come in time. Though I've said that to myself now for twelve years.' The other woman shrugged as though she didn't believe it either and gave herself a little shake. 'You didn't fancy going to Oberon with your husband?'

'No, walking all morning has given me blisters on my heels. Don... my husband said I should stay here with you as he'll be quicker on horseback. He said you were kind to him in the past.'

'Bless him.' Mrs Beecroft smiled warmly. 'He always pays me well for whatever he buys from me. That little extra coin allows me to treat myself.' She reached over to the half-finished woollen blanket. 'Last time I was able to purchase enough wool to make a blanket for our bed. Winters can be so cold.'

'You're very talented.' Bridget admired the navy wool blanket. 'Do you paint as well?' She pointed to the landscapes.

'Yes. I taught myself. It gives me something to do. Takes my mind off things... My husband can be away from the house for hours in the fields and when my work is done, I like to paint.' She stood and took one from a nail on the wall. 'My husband thinks it a folly, but he indulges me. I have all this scenery the minute I look out of a window or walk out of the door. He doesn't understand why I want to paint it, too.'

'You have an eye for it.' Bridget sipped her tea, trying to relax.

'I'd like you to have this one.' Mrs Beecroft gave the painting she held to Bridget.

'Oh, I couldn't possibly.'

'I insist. I have more than I need.'

'You could sell them.'

'Perhaps I will sell some of them, but this one I want you to have. If you move away, you'll always have that painting to remind you of this area.'

Bridget took the painting from her. The canvas was stretched over a thin homemade frame the size of a large book. The scene was a winter painting of the mountains covered in snow with trees etched with white and a moody grey sky. It was rather nice, and Bridget smiled her thanks to the woman. 'It is beautiful.'

Mrs Beecroft preened at the praise. 'I'm glad you like it. I painted that last year when it snowed for a few days. I feel we might get snow again this year. It's become colder earlier than last year.'

'Thank you. I'll treasure this.'

'I hope you don't think me rude, but I need to be in the kitchen. I've bread rising and a meat and potato pie to finish making.'

'Then let me help you?'

'I couldn't do that.'

'Please? In return for your hospitality. I can wash vegetables or whatever you need doing. I'm not a great cook. In fact, I'm not even a *good* cook, but I can wash things.'

Laughing, Mrs Beecroft led the way into the kitchen and passed Bridget her spare apron. 'If you could chop those carrots, that would be perfect.'

As Bridget set to work, Mrs Beecroft spoke of her neighbours, of one in particular whose cows kept breaking through fences and eating her cabbages.

'I've told them a dozen times to make the fences stronger, but they are useless,' Mrs Beecroft said, kneading the bread dough. 'One day I shall just keep the blessed animals here and they can join our herd.'

'Neighbours can be a trial for sure,' Bridget muttered, thinking of Roache.

'Still, mostly we are happy here. We've had some trouble with bushrangers but not as much as the areas near Bathurst. Did you hear recently about the shoot-out north of Bathurst?'

'No.' Bridget kept chopping, enjoying having someone different to chat with.

'Bold they were. Taunting the police, holding up a poor farm. The woman had a baby with her. The horror of it. Imagine, your own home used in a shoot-out.' Mrs Beecroft shook her head, kneading rhythmically.

'It would be terrifying,' Bridget agreed, shivering at her own memories of bushrangers.

'The villains were shot dead by the police, thank goodness. I can't remember their names. One was Nap or Map, no Sap! That's it.' Mrs Beecroft chuckled. 'What kind of name is that, I ask you?'

Shocked, Bridget dared not look up. She gripped the knife and tried to catch her breath. 'Sap?'

'Aye. Silly isn't it, what those bushrangers call themselves? Anyway, he was shot, killed and his offsider, too.'

'They are dead?' Bridget slowly gathered up the chopped carrots and dropped them into the pot, stunned, but knowing she couldn't show it.

'Both of them shot. The one named Sap spoke to the police. Said he'd killed the woman he'd kidnapped. Imagine that?' Mrs Beecroft shook her head in amazement. 'Poor woman.'

'He said that?' Bridget sat on a chair by the table, her legs wobbly.

'The two of them were wanted for the kidnap of a young lady from down south somewhere, near Goulburn, I think. It's been all over the newspapers. A reward was offered for the lady's return by her brothers. Five thousand pounds. Incredible sum. Not that it will do any good now. Everyone believes her to be dead.' Mrs Beecroft divided the rounded dough into two tins and sprinkled flour on top. 'Such a disgrace. We are not safe in our beds with these criminals roaming the country. The police need to do more.' Mrs Beecroft placed the tins in the oven.

Bridget bowed her head, tears blinded her. Austin and Patrick. She missed them so much she nearly moaned at the agony of it. They thought her to be dead. They would be so upset and Aunt Riona, too.

'I'll just collect the eggs. I shan't be a minute.'

While alone in the kitchen, Bridget sniffed back her tears and took some deep breaths. She could not let Mrs Beecroft suspect anything was amiss. But her heart thumped. Her family thought her killed by Sap. How they must be suffering.

The whole episode seemed so long ago. She'd become used to living in the cabin, of not thinking about her family, for her own sanity. However, Mrs Beecroft's mention of it brought the whole event into a different perspective. Austin and Patrick searching for her, offering a reward, speaking to newspaper reporters, police investigating, a shoot-out.

Yet here she was in some woman's kitchen chopping carrots. If it wasn't so tragic, she would have laughed. Her throat clogged with emotion. The whole disastrous event was a living nightmare.

Donovan returned three hours later with Zeus packed with full bags and even a small crate with two hens in it was tied on his back. 'Rested?' he asked Bridget when she came rushing out to meet him.

'Can we go?' she whispered, nearly crying in relief.

'Let me thank Mrs Beecroft.' He stepped up onto the verandah. 'Good to see you again, Mrs Beecroft, and thank you for taking care of my wife.'

'It was a pleasure, Mr Smith. We've had a lovely time. Mrs Smith helped me in the kitchen.'

Bridget pulled herself together and climbed the steps to shake Mrs Beecroft's hand. 'I hope I can visit again soon,' another lie fell from her lips.

'That would be grand, Mrs Smith.' Mrs Beecroft smiled broadly, giving her the painting that she'd left on the table.

'What's that?' Donovan asked.

'Mrs Beecroft has given me one of her paintings.' Bridget showed it to him, but with her back to Mrs Beecroft she gave him a desperate look to hurry up.

'It's delightful.' Donovan forced a smile. 'Goodbye, Mrs Beecroft.' He returned to Zeus and gathered his reins.

'Goodbye, Mrs Beecroft, and thank you again.' Bridget waved.

'I was as quick as I could be,' Donovan murmured as they walked away. 'The market was on, and the town was busier than I expected but it helped to keep me hidden in plain sight, so to speak.'

'Did you hear anything?' Ignoring the pain of her blisters Bridget walked fast to clear the farm.

Donovan frowned and pushed his hat back a bit now he didn't have to hide his face. 'About what?'

'Sap and Mickey have been in a shoot-out. They were killed!'

'Christ!' Surprise widened Donovan's eyes.

'Did you not hear about it in Oberon?'

'No. I didn't speak to anyone but shop keepers, and they were so busy I was served without a fuss or comment. I've bought two newspapers for us to read later, but I heard and saw nothing about a shoot-out.'

'Sap told the police that he killed me.'

'Killed you?' Donovan's step faltered. 'Why would he say that?'

'I don't know.' She was as confused as him.

'It makes no sense for him to say that unless he wanted notoriety in death.' Donovan swore under his breath. 'Knowing Sap that's the likely reason. He'd want to go down in history with everyone talking about him.'

'My brothers have been searching. They put up a reward but now they assume I'm dead,' her words came out in a rush, choked with emotion.

Donovan remained silent until they reached the start of the thick bush-land. He stopped. 'Do you want to go home?'

'There's something else...'

'What?'

'Mrs Beecroft made me think of it.'

'Think of what?'

'That... we... there might be a baby...'

Once more Donovan swore. He took Bridget's hand. 'Yes, it's a possibility. We share a bed.' His green eyes bored into hers. 'So, my question remains. Do you want to go home?'

Chapter Nineteen

The whip bird cracked his call from deep within the gorge, the sound echoing through the tall ferns and filtering up through the eucalyptus canopy. Bridget gathered small sticks for kindling, the crate nearly full. She'd wandered beyond the clearing, the winter sunshine highlighting small spots of undergrowth where the trees parted. The crisp mountain air chilled her face and hands.

She glanced at her fingernails, broken and dirty, callused from working without gloves. The skirt she wore had stains from cooking and the hem would never come clean after constantly trailing in dirt. No one would recognise her as a daughter of a wealthy family now. She'd likely pass by her brothers and they not recognise their sister with her lank hair barely brushed, hatless, gloveless, reduced to wearing plain clothes of poor quality.

As much as she wanted to dwell on her situation, it did no good to ponder on what might have been. The fates had decreed that her life must take this turn, this path. To ponder on her past, her family, only brought heartache and pain. Let them think her dead. It was better than the alternative. To be seen as a wanton woman living in sin with a convict, and as a person who'd killed... No, it was better her family mourn for her death and leave them with happier memories.

'Bridget!' Donovan's call drifted to her.

'Coming.' She picked up the crate and headed back to the cabin, pushing away her unhappy thoughts.

Donovan secured his rifle on the saddle and slipped the reins over Zeus's head. 'I'm away to hunt.'

'I'll come with you.' She placed the crate of sticks by the door.

He gave her a wry smile. 'And what of your heels?'

'I'll bandage them.'

'You can ride until we have a beast to throw over Zeus's back.'

'If you successfully shoot one this time,' she teased.

'Yesterday's miss wasn't my fault, the breeze shifted. That kangaroo smelt us.'

'What nonsense you do talk. Your aim was off.'

Donovan grabbed her to him and tickled her waist. 'Oh, and you can do better, can you?'

'Probably!' She grinned, slipping her arms around his neck, but her smile froze as suddenly, crashing through ferns covering the narrow cut came several horsemen.

In one quick movement, Donovan noticed her face, spun and pulled out his rifle and aimed it at them.

Fear clenched Bridget's stomach against her spine. Roache's smarmy face came out of the shadows and into the sunlight in all its evilness. She recoiled as though struck, her hands flailing for Donovan.

'Get behind me,' he murmured, not taking his eyes off Roache.

Unable to move, Bridget stood rooted to the spot, air trapped in her lungs like she was under water.

'Well, well...' Roache smirked. 'What do we have here?' He dismounted as did the four men with him. 'You seem to have welcomed my gift, Donovan? Are you pleased with me?'

'What are you doing here?' Donovan asked, the rifle still pointed.

'To simply stay a night or two.'

'How did you find me?'

'Sap gave me directions. True, it still took me two days to find you. The clues are well hidden, but I was determined.'

'Why?'

'Will you put that rifle down, man?' Roache scowled. 'Are we not friends?'

'No.'

Roache stiffened. 'You have accepted my gift of this slut, surely we are square now?'

'I never wanted a woman.'

'Every man wants a woman, especially out here alone.' Roache looked around him. 'You've done well with this place.'

'You should go,' Donovan's warning came from between clenched teeth.

'Did you hear about Sap and Mickey?'

'I did.'

Roache scratched his whiskery chin. 'Listen, let us be at peace with each other. I know I owe you money and I will repay you.'

'I care less about the money. You have come to my secret hideaway, bringing four others with you. Are you as stupid as you look? Do you suppose I would thank you for not only landing a kidnapped woman on me but for leading others to my hideout?'

'They won't say anything to anyone. They are wanted men, too. Who are they going to tell?'

'For a price they could tell the police, or when drunk tell a fine story to all in a bar.' Donovan swore. 'Get going, Roache and don't ever return.'

'Now don't be too hasty, man. For God's sake we are all in this together. My men are trustworthy.'

'Huh, I highly doubt it.'

Roache glared at Bridget. 'Tell you what. Give this witch to me and I'll claim the reward for her. We'll split the money. What do you say?'

'How could you possibly do that?'

'I'll send her with one of my men. He can claim the money and bring it back to us.' Roache nodded. 'We can be thousands richer in a few days.'

'That's why you've come...' Donovan grunted. 'You want Bridget and the reward for her.'

'We both can share the reward.' Roache's eyes narrowed. 'You must be finished with her by now?'

Donovan's expression tightened. 'Bridget stays with me.'

'Are you mad? There's five thousand pounds offered. We can be rid of this wretched country and sail anywhere we want to and start again.'

Donovan watched him. 'You've spent all your money again, haven't you? The money you received from the sale of your farm.'

Roache rubbed the back of his neck. 'I had debts to pay.'

'And you gambled the rest. You never learn, Roache.' Donovan reached out for Bridget, and she grabbed his hand and stepped closer to him. 'Bridget stays with me.'

Chuckling, Roache shook his head. 'Fallen for her, have you? Does she perform well for you? She's hot-headed so I imagine she would be good in bed.'

'Get off with you.' Donovan's grip tightened on the rifle. 'Now.'

'Are you willing to kill us all for her?' Roache asked incredulously.

'If that's what it takes.'

Roache turned to his men, and all four pulled out pistols and aimed them at Donovan. 'Think this through. You'll have one shot at me, but you will die afterwards and if she's still alive, the men will take her in turns. Want to take that risk?'

'You're not taking Bridget,' Donovan replied.

'I need the money.'

'Find another way. Now go.'

Roache hunched his shoulders. 'I think not.' He turned to his men and as one they dismounted and surrounded Donovan and Bridget. 'Shall we have a meal? Can the witch cook?'

'I'm telling you for the final time, Roache,' Donovan warned.

Suddenly a man on the left moved swiftly hitting Donovan over the head with the end of his pistol.

Bridget screamed as he collapsed to the ground unconscious. She fell to her knees beside him. 'Donovan. Wake up.' Her hands trembled as she cupped his face, then shook his shoulders. 'Dear God. Wake up.'

'Feed us, bitch.' Roache grabbed her by the hair and dragged her towards the cabin.

Pain tore through her scalp, making her eyes water. She screamed and fought to be free. Her head felt on fire such was the agony as he dragged her inside.

Roache flung her towards the fireplace. 'Cook! We're starving.'

The men followed them inside and sat on the stools around the small table. Each one seemed as desperate as the other, all dirty, unshaven and stinking.

Shaking, Bridget got to her feet, her knees wobbly, her heart racing.

'Feed us!' Roache demanded, lying on the bed.

She turned from him, mind whirling. The aching in her head blurred her vision. Donovan was outside. She needed to get to him.

'Do you have ale?' one man asked, scratching his long black beard.

She ignored him and picked up a frying pan. They had some cured ham slices that Donovan had bought in Oberon, but no eggs and the hens hadn't laid. To feed five men would take so much of their supplies.

'I said do you have ale?' Suddenly the man was right beside her, his body touching hers.

'No!' She fought to breathe and stepped aside.

'Then make tea,' Roache demanded, climbing off the bed to rummage through Donovan's trunk. He turned out clothes and books, scattering them across the floor.

The sight of the mess, of Donovan's clean folded shirts just flung over the dirt switched something in Bridget's mind. An intense rage burned through her pain and fear. She lunged forward. 'Get away from his things!' She brought down the frying pan on Roache's head sending him sideways onto the floor.

The men jumped up and grabbed at her arms, but she swung the frying pan as a weapon, her thoughts demonic. She would kill them all. 'Leave us alone!' Her black hair flew about her head as she swung for them. She kicked at Roache where he lay moaning.

'She's mad this one!' said one of the younger men.

'Gone crazy from living out here,' another agreed as they watched her warily.

'We'll have to knock her out to get her into town and claim the reward.'

'She'll need to be tied, wrists and legs,' another stated.

Brandishing the frying pan, Bridget edged closer to the door, but just as she sensed freedom, a hand caught her ankle. Roache.

She whacked him again, but he defended the hit by throwing his arm up. He wrenched her leg out from under her and she fell on her back, hard, knocking the wind from her lungs.

'That'll teach you!' Roache jeered. He scrambled up over her and slapped her face, before giving her a second backhanded slap.

Bridget screamed. Stars burst before her eyes. Pain bit deep into her face. She fought wildly, crying, screeching, clawing at Roache's body.

'She's bloody insane!'

'I ain't going near her, that's for sure. I like my women to be soft and yielding, not hissing like a wet cat,' another grumbled, turning away.

At that moment a shot rang out.

Bridget jerked sidewards as Roache slumped over her. His weight crushed her chest. She cried out, heaving him off her. She scrambled across the dirt floor away from him as blood flowed like a silent red river from his chest.

Donovan stood in the doorway, the rifle pointed at the men. 'Who is next?' His voice was steel cold.

One man pulled out his pistol and Donovan shot him. The tall man with the black beard drew his pistol and fired and then the next man did the same.

Smoke filled the cabin as gunfire shattered the air like fireworks. Bridget huddled in the corner, her arms over her head, trying to make herself as small as possible while the men fought it out.

Eventually, silence reigned.

She raised her head, ears ringing, eyes adjusting to the grey-white smoke. Someone dashed past her, then another, running outside, but she didn't care because by the door Donovan lay bleeding from a wound in his stomach and another one in his shoulder.

Clambering over Roache, she rushed to Donovan's side. 'Oh God! No!'

'I'm done for...' His words were slurred. He gazed about at the three men lying on the floor. 'Couldn't get them all...'

'Quiet now.' Bridget hurried to the fireplace and grabbed a bucket of water and a cloth. 'We need to stem the bleeding.' She clamped the cloth to the hole in his stomach and pressed on it.

Donovan winced and groaned. 'No use.'

'There's every use, silly.' She brushed tears from her eyes with her forearm. 'We'll get you cleaned up and bandaged.'

'Bandages won't fix this, sweetheart.'

'I'll nurse you.' She avoided looking into his eyes.

'Bridie...' He sucked in a ragged breath. 'Look at me...'

Slowly she raised her eyes to his, noting the pasty colour of his skin. She swallowed back a sob. The dark green of his eyes locked with hers, sending her silent messages his lips couldn't utter. She saw his fear, his pain, his acceptance.

'Kiss me...' he whispered.

She did, gently, reverently.

'I'm glad you came into my life...'

'Me, too.'

'Be happy, for me...'

Bridget held him tightly to her as the last breath left his body. For a long time she sat holding him until cramp spasmed in her leg and she carefully released Donovan and stood up to stretch out her painful calf muscles.

Bewildered, horrified, she tried to think what to do. Four bodies lay in the cabin. The place that had become a home was now tainted in blood and death. But then, hadn't it been since she killed the man who attacked her?

Fighting back a whimper, she washed her bloodied hands in the bucket of water. Her mind wouldn't work.

She stared out the door at the clearing. The setting sun cast long shadows across the creek. Winter darkness came early to the gorge where daylight only briefly shone during the midday hours.

Instinctively knowing she couldn't stay here tonight, she left the cabin and found Zeus grazing with the other three horses. However, to ride away would mean leaving Donovan to rot, exposed to animals...

Tears slipped over her lashes as she collected a spade and drifted closer to the creek. Mindless, she began to dig. The soft ground yielded well under the spade and before long she had a shallow grave two-foot deep.

She lit a lantern and placed it by the grave then returned inside and taking Donovan by the shoulders, she dragged him across the grass, stopping now and then to get a better hold until she carefully placed him into the grave.

Bridget knelt and crossed his arms over his chest. He looked young and peaceful. She kissed his lips for the final time. 'Rest at peace now. Go and be with your sister.' She'd not forgotten his story about his sister and hoped that now they would be together.

From the trunk, she took his books and laid them over him and also placed a clean shirt over his face and other personal effects into the grave. Then she shovelled the dirt over him until a neat mound rose. Collecting large rocks from the creek she covered the dirt as full darkness cloaked the gorge.

For a long moment she stood beside the grave, adjusting one or two rocks, her mind blank, her heart closed to emotion.

Taking the lantern, she dug behind the log store and recovered the buried bags of gold and placed them in the saddlebags, then she added the rest of the money from the trunk. Lastly, she took the ribbon Donovan had bought her and tied it around her hair.

She caught the other three horses and tied their reins to a long rope on Zeus's saddle. She entered the cabin one last time and took a water canteen and a thick chunk of damper and the painting Mrs Beecroft gave her.

At the door she turned and threw the lantern against the wall and watched as it smashed. Flames reared up from the spilt oil, flashing light and heat. The fire spread quickly.

Bridget walked to the grave and placed a hand on the top rock in farewell. Moonlight broke out between clouds but the cabin was rapidly being eaten by fire and so she had enough light to see by as she mounted Zeus and rode out through the ferns.

———*ele*———

Lincoln sniffed the air. 'I smell burning.'

Patrick turned from where he knelt by the campfire and did the same. 'Bushfire?'

'Damn, I hope not.' A shiver of dread tingled down Lincoln's spine. 'We've nowhere to hide if a bushfire races through here. We're stuck between two gorges.'

'Can you hear it?'

Lincoln listened hard but only heard the sounds of the night, frogs in the water, crickets chirping, a rustle in the undergrowth, the snigger of one of the horses and jingle of harness.

'We should take it in turns to stay awake tonight,' Patrick said, standing staring out to the black silhouettes of the peaks. 'I'll go first. You turn in. We've had a long day of riding.'

'You're just as tired as I am,' Lincoln protested.

'Aye, but I'm younger than you,' Patrick joked.

'Good point.' Lincoln climbed into the small tent and covered himself with the blanket. He kept his coat on for the winter night temperatures in the mountains often dropped to zero or below. His body ached from difficult days of trekking up and down gorges, crossing creeks and cresting high summits. They saw nothing of human presence. Sometimes, in the distance, they saw a plume of smoke from a campfire, or heard a shot from a hunter's rifle, but they saw no evidence of human life in the rough terrain.

Settling down, trying to find a comfortable spot on the hard ground, he thought of Bridget, as always. Was she close by? Was she with anyone? Were they hurting her? Was the plume of smoke they saw her campfire? Mindless questions swirled in his brain giving him a headache. He needed a drink. Cursing, he left the tent.

'Can't sleep?' Patrick asked, poking the fire.

'Sleep and I aren't bed partners at the moment.' He threw another log on the flames, suddenly cold. The smell of bushfire was stronger than before. 'Are you concerned about the smell of smoke?'

Patrick nodded. 'I might walk up to the top of the peak and see what's happening.'

'In the dark? That's dangerous.' Lincoln didn't like the sound of that at all.

'We need to ascertain how close it is.'

'Agreed but what we don't need is you falling down a cliff in the darkness.'

Patrick glanced around. 'I've been watching for any embers floating down, but so far nothing. There's no wind either.'

'At least we have the creek should it suddenly come upon on us.' Lincoln glanced at the water shimmering in the moonlight. It wasn't deep but it would be enough to save them if fire roared through the gorge.

'At dawn we should climb to the next ridge and assess the situation.' Patrick brought his blanket out and wrapped it about him. 'I doubt we'll get much sleep tonight now.'

'I'll make some tea.' Lincoln needed something to do.

'Tea.' Patrick chuckled. 'Something stronger is called for, really.'

'You know I don't drink.'

'Yes, and neither do I have anything, so it doesn't matter, anyway. Can I ask why you don't drink?'

Lincoln thought whether to tell him the truth or not. The silence stretched for a long moment. He never spoke of his past or his family. 'My father...' He hated mentioning the man's name. 'He was a drunk.' Images of his raging father flashed in the darkness. Lincoln flinched as a raised fist loomed in the shadows before him, the screams...

'Hey steady on!' Patrick took the billycan out of Lincoln's hands. 'You nearly scalded yourself then!'

Back in the present, Lincoln shook off the memories, not realising how close he'd been to pouring boiling hot water over himself. Not that it would be the first time boiling liquid had touched his skin...

'You all right, mate?' Patrick asked, setting the billycan on the edge of the flames.

'Sorry about that.' Lincoln stood and walked away into the trees making Patrick assume he needed to relieve himself when he actually just needed a minute to calm down. The muscle in his jaw twitched violently, which always happened when he thought of his past and when the memories came back to haunt him.

By the time the dawn's rays breached the peaks and began to lift the gloom, Patrick and Lincoln were saddled and the fire doused, and the pack horse loaded. They had spent an uncomfortable night dozing by the fire, talking little, but on alert for floating embers. The smell of smoke diminished before dawn easing their anxiety that they'd be swept into an inferno.

Riding up the incline, weaving between trees, Lincoln followed behind Patrick. His breath plumed a vapour in the wintry morning air, but he was warm enough under his coat and gloves kept his fingers warm.

The higher they climbed, the lighter it became. The sun streaked the sky with strips of pink and orange. Birds became more vocal. A kookaburra's laugh rang out loud and clear, its throaty warble loud in the quiet. They spotted small black wallabies jumping between outcrops of rock and a fat furry wombat lumbered slowly towards a round hole in the ground, which he promptly disappeared into.

Rounding a large rock, they glimpsed a view of blue-washed mountains and shadowed valleys. Patrick reined in and scanned the horizon. 'There!' He pointed to a plume of dusty smoke in the next gorge to the north.

'It doesn't look a large fire,' Lincoln murmured.

'Perhaps it's been contained.' Patrick tapped his heels into his horse's flanks to walk on. 'I think we should go there and see who is about.'

Lincoln nudged Blaze onwards across the top of the peak and then steadily down the sharp incline back into the thick of the trees covering the slope. Neither man spoke as they held on and concentrated on getting their horses safely down the side of the mountain. In parts they had to dismount and lead them by rein as the grade became too steep to ride. The rough ground gave them difficulties as numerous times large outcrops of rock blocked their path down and they would have to scramble sideways to pick another way to descend.

An hour later, they reached the bottom of a narrow ravine between two steep cliffs. A tiny stream of water gurgled between round ponds in the sandstone riverbed. The horses drank deeply, while Lincoln and Patrick also took long swigs of water from their canteens.

'We should be close.' Patrick refilled his water canteen from a tiny waterfall at his feet. 'I need to pee.' Patrick headed off into the trees.

Lincoln stretched and took his hat off to run a hand through his hair. What he wouldn't give for a hot bath right now to ease his aching muscles and a good meal, a nice roasted chicken and afterwards fresh strawberries and cream. His stomach rumbled at the thought.

The snap of a twig had him turning to stare through the trees behind him. Shadows thrown by the steepness of the valley created pockets of deep shade at the base of the mountain, but he saw movement. 'Patrick,' he warned low and urgent, taking his pistol from his inner coat pocket.

Patrick rushed to his side, also pistol in hand. 'Come out and show yourself!' he shouted into the trees.

Two black cockatoos screeched above their heads, but Lincoln kept his eyes on the trees. He clearly saw a horse. 'One rider?' he whispered to Patrick.

'We are armed and ready to shoot!' Patrick called again. 'Show yourself!'

The horse walked forward out of the shadows.

Lincoln tensed, pistol aimed. Were they to be ambushed? He dared not look around in case he saw men and rifles pointed at his head.

Suddenly the horse stopped, and a figure came out from behind it, walking dazed, shoulders bowed. A woman. She stared at them through ragged long black hair.

'Bridget?' Patrick barely breathed the word.

Lincoln blinked. No. It couldn't be. Not the thin, scruffy figure before him.

'Bridget?' Patrick's tone was more of a plea.

The woman fell to her knees in the grass.

Both Patrick and Lincoln sprang to action and raced to her. Lincoln caught her as she fainted.

'Bridget!' Patrick cried, tenderly pushing her hair back from her face where Lincoln cradled her against his chest.

'I've got you,' Lincoln murmured, holding her tightly. 'You're safe.' His heart exploded with happiness and also worry for this woman hardly resembled the feisty beautiful woman he'd fallen in love with months ago.

Bridget's eyelids fluttered and she gave a soft moan, before slumping unconscious in his arms.

Patrick tapped her cheek gently. 'Sister. It's me, Patrick. Wake up.'

'She must be exhausted,' Lincoln said. 'Build a fire. She needs some tea, food, warmth. She's cold to the touch.'

'I'll do it now.' Patrick quickly unpacked their belongings and brought over both his and Lincoln's blankets and wrapped them over her. Then he set about collecting sticks and leaves for the fire. 'Why doesn't she have a coat?' Then he shook his head. 'What a stupid thing to say! My sister is alive, that's all that matters.'

Lincoln didn't have the answer as he rubbed her arms to bring some warmth to them. 'To be out at night in these low temperatures...'

'She needs a doctor.' Patrick worked quickly, striking a flint that was more precious than gold in the bush.

'I agree, but she needs warming first, or will never survive the journey to the nearest town.' He looked up at the towering cliffs hemming them in. 'We might have to camp here tonight, just to revive her, get her warm and strong enough to ride out in the morning.'

Patrick nurtured the fire into a blaze before glancing at his sister. 'She's skin and bone. I wish she'd wake up.'

'She will when she's ready.' Lincoln enjoyed having the comfort of her in his arms, but knew he couldn't hold her all night. Besides, when she did wake up would she want to be found in his embrace?

'Why did that Sap fellow say he'd killed her? I *believed* him. We wasted so many days thinking Bridget was dead...' Patrick's face twisted in torment. 'It's a good thing he's dead, or I'd happily swing for killing him myself.'

'None of that need concern us now. We have to get her well.' Lincoln's throat tightened with emotion as he stared down into her beautiful pale face.

'I need to tell Austin and Aunt Riona. Thank God we didn't write the news to Mammy.' Patrick dashed away a tear. 'I can't believe it. After all this time... she survived.'

'She's a strong woman is your sister.'

Patrick nodded and stared at Bridget before glancing at Lincoln. 'You never gave up though, did you?'

Lincoln shrugged. 'I just had a hunch.'

'You love her very much.' It was a statement not a question.

'I do.' Lincoln took a deep breath. 'But she may not feel the same, not after all she's been through.' Not wanting to dwell on the unknown future, Lincoln gently laid her down on the grass. 'I'll erect my tent. She can sleep in there.' For a moment he gazed down at her, then reluctantly went to unpack his tent.

While Patrick made tea and damper, Lincoln created a bed inside the tent, then with Patrick's help they carefully lifted her into it and tucked the blankets around her.

'Let's hope we don't have rain, or I'll be drenched tonight,' Patrick murmured, trying to joke.

'You? Bridget is in my tent.'

'And you'll sleep in my tent tonight. It's the least I can do for the man who saved my sister.'

'I haven't done anything that you haven't.'

'If you had not continued searching, then I wouldn't have joined you. We wouldn't be here now and have Bridget with us. Our family can never repay you for what you have done.'

'I don't need repayment. Bridget alive is all the thanks I need,' Lincoln said with a thankful heart. He found it hard to believe that she'd walked straight to them.

Patrick continued cooking. Lincoln led the horses to the creek for them to drink, before hobbling them on the only patch of grass in the gorge.

For hours they sat by the fire, waiting for Bridget to wake, but she slept on. The sun slipped behind the mountains casting darkness across the camp and still she slept. As the stars winked in the black sky above them, Patrick and Lincoln ate a little and drank tea, listening for any murmur from within the tent. They left the end of the tent open so they could see any movement within, but Bridget didn't stir.

'What do you suppose happened to her?' Patrick asked, the shadows of the flames dancing on his face.

The thought played on Lincoln's mind as well. 'We should be prepared for the worst.'

'Rape?'

Wincing at the word, Lincoln nodded. He felt sick at the thought, but he had to be sensible about the possibility of it happening. 'She was with rough men, criminals. Men without honour.'

'Bastards all of them.' Patrick threw a stick into the embers.

'Bridget will take some time to heal in both mind and body. Maybe she never will.'

'God, I hope she does recover. I've missed her terribly.' Patrick sighed deeply.

Lincoln rubbed his eyes, exhaustion creeping up on him. 'She will always be haunted by what's happened to her. She'll need her family.' How would *he* fit into such a future? Her abduction could put her off men for life. He had to steel himself for her rejection. However, it was only what he deserved. He ran from her and his feelings like a coward. Perhaps his father had been right all along? He was worthless.

A fierce look came into Patrick's eyes. 'Roache started all this. Austin and I will make him pay.'

Lincoln wasn't interested in revenge. His one thought and motivation had been to find Bridget. What came next, he didn't know. He'd have to wait and take whatever happens.

Chapter Twenty

The shrill call of a magpie in the branches of a nearby tree woke Bridget. She lay for a moment disorientated. It took a minute for her to realise she was in a tent. Whose tent?

Her whole body ached, and she winced when she moved. A dull thud pounded in her head, and she was dreadfully thirsty. She sat up and froze. Through the open tent flap she saw a tall man standing outside, near the edge of the stream. Voices drifted to her. Her heart twisted in fear.

Where was she?

The last thing she remembered was burying Donovan in a grave she had dug. Pain gripped her chest. He was dead.

The voices came closer. Bridget's mind raced. She needed to escape. She looked around for a weapon but there was nothing in the narrow tent. At least she was dressed. Had these men found her somewhere? Had they assaulted her while she was senseless? Although instinct was to run, she barely had the energy to sit upright. Had she gone from one capture to another?

'Will you fetch more wood, Lincoln?' the voice was outside of the tent. 'I'll make a fresh brew.'

Bridget's chest tightened. She knew that voice... and Lincoln? There weren't many men of that name.

Forcing herself to leave the warmth of the blankets, she crawled to the edge of the tent and peeked out. Disappearing into the trees was the tall man, but near the campfire squatted another. Even with his scruffy beard she recognised Patrick. She wanted to cry out, to sob, but her mouth remained closed her eyes dry. Instead, she wanted to hide. She wasn't the Bridget they knew.

Patrick looked up and straight at her. His eyes widened and he smiled the biggest smile. 'Bridget, darling!' his Irish accent had faded slightly over the last ten years, but in times of upset or excitement they all reverted back to their native accent.

He ran to her and gathered her in his arms. ''Tis good to see you awake, sister, so it is. I've been out of my mind with worry.' He kissed her cheek and hugged her to him.

For a moment she relished the embrace, the joy of being with her beloved brother.

'How are you feeling, Brid?' Patrick leaned back to peer at her.

'Fine,' she lied. She was beaten, broken, hollow. 'How did you find me?' she asked.

'You found us. You just walked out of the trees and collapsed into Lincoln's arms. It's a miracle, and no mistake.' Patrick stood and helped her out carefully. 'Will you come by the fire? Have some tea?' He turned, cupping his hands around his mouth. 'Lincoln!'

Bridget frowned at his shout. Her nerves were shattered, her senses edgy as though her mind and body didn't know how to work together.

Patrick led her to a large log near the fire and she sat on it, wincing in the bright sunlight.

She glanced at Lincoln as he came through the trees, sticks and small branches in his arms. He walked slowly to her, his face unreadable.

He knelt and placed the wood by the fire and dusted his hands before turning to her fully, his smile gentle as was the look in his eyes. 'I'm so happy you're safe.'

She gazed at the man who before her kidnap she'd wanted to marry. Lincoln looked a little older, thinner. He wore riding clothes that needed washing and could do with a shave. Yet, there was a quiet strength to him that called to her broken spirit. And his eyes, those cornflower-blue eyes reached into her soul. What would they find there?

'Lincoln never stopped searching for you,' Patrick told her. 'Even when we were told Sap had killed you, Lincoln never accepted it and continued to search.'

Bridget digested the information slowly. This man had looked for her. Why? They had no understanding between them. If she remembered correctly, he had left in a hurry and without explanation.

'Will you have some tea?' Patrick asked, adding more wood to the fire and placing the billycan on the embers. 'I've made damper too and we have a bit of jam left.'

Bridget, aware of Patrick's fussing and Lincoln's silent presence, felt overwhelmed.

Patrick set out a cup for her. 'After we've eaten, we can pack up and head out. There's still a good few hours of daylight left. We might make a farm or a village before dark.'

The sudden idea of being in a town with people frightened her senseless. 'No!'

Patrick jumped at her abrupt bark. 'What?'

'Sorry.' Her breathing grew short. 'I-I don't... I...'

Lincoln leaned forward. 'You don't have to do anything you don't want to do.'

She stared into his eyes, fighting the urge to flee.

'Bridget?' Patrick asked, uncertain.

'Perhaps your sister needs a little bit of time.' Lincoln moved back on the log. 'There isn't any rush to leave.'

'But we have to get her back. Austin and Aunt Riona need to know she's alive.' Patrick took off his hat and knelt beside Bridget. 'You want to go home, don't you?'

In truth, she didn't. So much had happened. She felt lost and alone and so very different to the person she used to be. She'd changed when everyone else had stayed the same. 'I'm not ready, Patrick,' she whispered.

Disappointment clouded his face. 'But we need to go home.'

'Yes, but...' She couldn't put into words her emotions. For months she'd been sheltered in the mountains, living rough within the folds of the valleys and gorges, hidden by the majestic tree ferns and the towering eucalyptus. To face people, to answer questions, to confront the world again after all that had happened... No, she wasn't ready.

'I have an idea,' Lincoln spoke quietly, gazing at Bridget. 'Would you feel better to enter a town again if you were well rested and dressed in new clothes?'

'What do you mean?' Patrick scowled.

'I mean if one of us was to go to the nearest town and buy Bridget new clothes, a hat, gloves, that sort of thing, she might be more at ease being among people. We should stay camped here for a few more days and let her rest.'

'It's time she went home.' Patrick looked at Bridget. 'Surely you want to return to Emmerson Park and see everyone? They've all been out of their minds with worry. They believe you're dead.'

'Then send a telegram to Austin in Sydney,' Lincoln said. 'Have him prepare everyone. The newspapers will hound her—'

'Newspapers?' Bridget baulked. 'I don't want to talk to newspaper reporters.' The desire to flee was becoming harder to resist.

'You won't,' Lincoln soothed. 'If Patrick gets word to Austin, then Austin can speak to the newspapers and give them a comment to diffuse the excitement of your survival.'

'They will ask so many questions.' Bridget panicked.

'We all have questions, Bridget,' Patrick said, passing her a tin cup of tea. 'How did you survive? What happened to you while you were away?'

She stared down into the steaming black tea not wanting to answer, to discuss her time with Donovan. It was too painful.

Patrick broke apart some damper and passed that to her. 'Did Sap take Ace?'

She jerked at the mention of her beloved horse. For weeks she'd taught herself not to think of Ace, and the ache of his death.

'Bridget?' Patrick persisted.

'Sap shot Ace.' Her words were clipped, cold. The familiar hatred for Sap rose in her chest.

'Jesus wept!' Patrick fumed.

'That must have been terribly difficult for you,' Lincoln said, his gaze tender.

'I vowed to kill Sap...' She raised her head to stare straight ahead. 'I'm glad he's dead for I wouldn't have rested until he was.'

'You know he's dead?' Patrick frowned in confusion.

'I heard.'

'And the others? The men who took you. Was it just Sap and his offsider, Mickey?'

Bridget glared at her brother. 'Roache started it all. He ordered Sap to take me away.'

'Roache will swing for this.'

'He won't. He's dead, too,' she said matter-of-factly as though talking about the weather.

'Dead?' both men said in unison, shocked.

Visions of Roache hitting her, of the gunfight, the acrid smell of smoke and blood replayed in her mind until she suddenly strode away from the fire and stood by the small stream.

She wrapped her arms about her, shivering, grieving for Donovan. She didn't want to reflect on Roache or anything. If only it was possible to close off her mind like turning down a wick in a lamp.

Bridget stiffened when someone came behind her, then to her side.

Patrick placed his arm around her shoulders and for a second, she wanted to resist the touch, She didn't want comfort but also, she did. Very much. She relaxed and laid her head on his shoulder.

'I forgot to give you this.' On her shoulders Patrick placed Aunt Riona's shawl.

Bridget rubbed her face against the material. She smelt the delicate perfume her aunt wore. Tears burned behind her eyes. The shawl was like having her aunt's arms around her.

'Also this.' He handed her a handkerchief, a comb and a ribbon. 'A farmer's wife gave it to me to give to you when we found you.'

'That's kind,' she whispered. Her hair was too dirty to comb it.

'Lincoln and I have been talking. I've decided that I'm going to ride to Oberon or Bathurst, whichever has the next coach to Sydney. It might be best to speak to Austin and Aunt Riona in person rather than send a telegram.'

Bridget nodded.

'Between the three of us we'll speak with the newspapers and the police.'

'Thank you.'

'I'll buy you some new clothes and things you might need. Aunt Riona will help. Then I'll return to you, and we'll go home, to Emmerson Park, hopefully without a fuss being created.'

'I like that plan.'

'Lincoln believes you'll want to stay here, but I reason that you should go and stay in an inn somewhere. It'll be more comfortable than sleeping in a tent.'

She straightened and glanced at him. 'I'm perfectly fine to stay here. I'm not ready to face anyone yet.'

'But to stay with Lincoln, a single man...' Patrick reddened.

Eyebrows raised, she snorted. 'Gracious, Patrick. I've spent months with strange men. My reputation is in ruins even though I didn't ask to be kidnapped, but people will talk and speculate on what I endured anyway so what does it really matter if I'm left alone with Lincoln, a man I know and trust, a family friend?' How could she ever tell Patrick about Donovan?

'Yes, forgive me. I was being ridiculous.'

'Exactly. There is no need to protect my reputation any more as my brother. All that is lost.'

'You mean...' His cheeks flushed. 'Did they...'

'I refuse to talk about it to you.' She walked away, feeling as old as time, far older than Patrick.

Soon after, Patrick walked his horse out of the gorge, telling them he'd be back as quickly as possible.

Lincoln made a comment about hunting for fresh meat. 'I saw crayfish in the creek. I'll try and catch some for us.'

Alone, Bridget sat by the fire as the sun lowered behind the mountains casting an orange and pink glow across the sky. Further down the bank, Lincoln squatted under a low tree branch. She sat on the ground, against the log and rested her head back and closed her tired eyes.

Suddenly, the image of Donovan was behind her eyelids, his cheeky smile, the desire in his eyes. A lump of emotion lodged somewhere in her throat. She missed his presence, but she was also terribly relieved to be free. Free of what she didn't know, perhaps just the sense that she wouldn't be hiding from her family any more, that she was no longer causing them grief.

Soft footsteps made her open her eyes.

Lincoln knelt before the fire, his smile was a little self-conscious. 'I didn't think I'd catch one.' He held up a large crayfish, it's tail flapping madly. 'He's a beast.'

She couldn't remember the last time she had fresh crayfish. It seemed forever ago.

'You must be hungry.' Lincoln plunged the crayfish in the billycan's boiling water.

It was fully dark by the time they'd finished eating the delicious fresh crayfish. A meal they ate in silence. A meal that Bridget picked at, her stomach in knots.

Bridget felt awkward. Once she had been beautifully dressed in the latest styles from London, her hair washed and styled. She'd laughed and been carefree, ready to have fun. That had been the person Lincoln knew, the person she had wanted him to see. Now, she sat by a campfire dirty, smelling of smoke, her hair lank and in tatters, her plain clothes stained. She had committed murder, slept with a man not her husband and been violently attacked. She had set fire to the cabin where dead bodies lay, destroying the evidence of a gunfight. Finally, she'd buried a sweet and complicated convict with her bare hands and then taken his stolen hoard of gold.

Who was she now?

Not the old innocent Bridget Kittrick and definitely not someone new worth admiring.

A sob rose in her, then another. Her heart raced. She felt afraid, lost.

'Bridget?' Lincoln's tender voice made her back away from the fire.

'I cannot...' She fought for air.

Lincoln was by her side in an instant. 'Bridget! It's all right. You're fine. No one will hurt you. You're safe.'

'I'm not! I'm nothing!' She pushed away his hands that held her arms and took a few steps back as though ready to run. Oh, how she wanted to run and never stop.

'That's not true.' Lincoln remained calm.

'You *know* nothing,' she said scathingly.

'Then tell me.'

'No.' Horrified, she backed further away.

'I will not judge you. I have no right.'

'Everyone will judge me, that's why I must never speak of it.'

Lincoln turned and poured out two tin cups of tea. 'Come,' he soothed, indicating for her to return near the fire.

The night was bitter, with a clear black sky full of stars. He took a blanket from the tent and gently wrapped it over her shoulders as she sat down on the log. He passed her the tea and taking his own sat on the same log as her but not too close.

His tenderness brought a lump to her throat. 'Why are you so kind to me? Why did you keep searching?'

'Because I would like us to be friends.'

'You don't want to be a friend to someone like me. I'm not the person I once was.'

'No, you aren't, but that doesn't mean I will reject the person you have become.'

Abruptly, his sympathy irritated her causing an anger to build. 'What do you care about the person I am now? You are nobody to me. A friend of my family, my brother's friend, not mine,' she declared harshly.

He watched her. 'I can be.'

'I don't *want* you as a *friend*!' Her voice rose even higher. 'You know nothing about me, what I have endured, what I have done!'

'Then tell me.'

'Tell you?' she yelled, furious. 'Shall I tell you how I was taken and so frightened that I wanted to die? Shall I tell you how I had to ride away from my home with my hands tied thinking at any moment Sap would rape me and leave me for dead? Or how he shot Ace right in front of me?' Her voice broke but the rage bursting from her needed an outlet. 'I'll tell you how I was taken to live with a man who was wanted by the police. Do you want to know of my fear and anger then?' she cried, tears rolling over her lashes. 'Do you want to hear that the man Sap took me to cared for me? Was kind? But one day while he was away from the cabin another man came. Shall I tell you how I had to survive by my wits to stop from being killed?' She sobbed, trying to get the words out. 'That man attacked me, wanted to rape and kill me, but I fought back. I... fought... and fought... and I *killed* him!' Bridget howled like a wounded animal, releasing all the pain inside.

Lincoln moved to hold her, but she reared back.

'Stay away!' she sobbed. 'I don't need your embraces.'

'Tell me what you do need then,' he said softly, sadly.

'I want all this to go away,' she cried. 'I don't want to be the person who was assaulted, the person who has killed a man, the person who slept in another man's bed!' she yelled at Lincoln as though he was to blame. Hurt and angry, she just wanted it all to go away.

'I don't want to be the person who set a cabin on fire to burn the bodies inside. I don't want to be the person who buried my lover with my bare hands. There, are you satisfied? Now you have it all!' she flung at him, sobbing.

For a long time, Lincoln remained quiet, letting her cry. Eventually, he added more wood to the fire and the movement brought her head up. She wiped her eyes with the edge of the blanket. She was worn out, confused with grief.

'I'm sorry,' she whispered, her throat sore from yelling, her eyes swollen from weeping.

'You have nothing to apologise for, not one thing. All that has happened to you was not your fault.'

'That's not true. I made decisions.'

'Because of circumstances, yes?'

Drained, she shrugged, not having the energy to argue with him.

'You survived,' he said, admiration in his eyes. 'You went through hell and came through the other side. Be proud of yourself.'

'How can I be proud when I have done things that will make me a pariah in society?'

'No one ever need find out. You make the choice as to who you tell, and what you tell. No one will ever hear it from me, I promise you that.'

She didn't know what to say.

Sighing, Lincoln stared into the flames. 'You have been honest with me so may I tell you something honest in return?'

Weary, feeling so low she would happily die, she nodded, not really caring about anything he had to say.

'The day of your kidnap I left you without any explanation,' he began.

Bridget frowned, not wanting to remember that awful day.

'The reason why I left you was because I was becoming overly drawn to you.' He paused. 'That's an understatement.' He scoffed at his own words. 'I had fallen in love with you.'

Shocked by the admission, Bridget stared at him. Lincoln had developed feelings for her? She had been correct that there'd been something between them, it wasn't just all in her head. 'You felt that for me?'

'Yes.' Lincoln continued to focus on the flames. 'I didn't want to be in love with you, far from it. I had vowed to never marry just as I had vowed to never drink alcohol. But it was far easier to never drink than it was to not want you. From the first day I met you at your birthday party, you intrigued me, you awakened my senses that had been dormant. I am a man with a man's needs. There are... women who provide a service for those needs as you are fully aware of, I'm sure. I thought that would be enough. I didn't need a wife, I didn't deserve one, or a family. Knowing that, I put all those natural desires from my head and thought I could live my life with the choices I made. Until I met you. Suddenly I wanted all those things I vowed to reject, a family, love. I wanted them with you.'

His honesty shocked Bridget. She paid attention to his words that for a blessed moment blotted out her own pain.

'I left without warning that day because all these feelings I had concerning you alarmed me. I needed to sort myself out, to extract myself from the situation because I couldn't have you.'

'Why?' she blurted the word out before she was even aware of it.

'Because of my past.' He finally raised his head and looked at her. 'I am not the honourable man you believe me to be. I have done things which will haunt me to my grave.'

'Me, too,' she whispered.

'Yes, I thought so. I can see it in your eyes. It's the same look I see in the mirror.' He sipped his tea, once more staring at the fire and then took a deep breath. 'I killed my father.'

Bridget took a moment to consider the statement. Those four words sounded of pure torment. She knew that torment. The last vestige of compassion in her heart went out to him.

'My father was a drunk,' Lincoln stated. 'All my life I'd been witness to, and on the receiving end of, his drunkenness. He was a tall man, over six foot, like me, with a wide chest, powerful arms. He did boxing as a pastime, had done since he was a young man before he joined the army. He was the youngest of four brothers, so he had to learn how to fight and win from an early age. That's what he told me once, when he was sober. There would be periods of him being sober, usually after he'd beaten my mother senseless, and he was sorry. Then he'd be the perfect father and husband. It never lasted, of course. I spent my childhood hiding from his fists and watching my mother being beaten black and blue. She was such a tiny little thing, skin and bone. I lost count of how many babies she lost from his punches.'

Bridget winced at the anguish in his voice.

'As I grew older, I tried to protect my mother from him. When Father retired from the army and bought an inn, his drinking became worse. He was always fighting, any excuse had him taking off his apron and walking around the bar to smash a customer in the face. He prided himself on running a respectable inn, where no trouble occurred. No one had the nerve to start a scrap in our inn for they knew my father would finish any fight that started.'

Lincoln added another log to the fire and watched the embers spark into the cold air. 'Protecting my mother became my primary concern. Despite his advancing age, my father was a fit man. A blow from his fist could knock down any man so you can imagine what he did to my mother. The older I got, the more involved I became, much to my mother's concern. She'd always tell me to leave the room when Father started at her, but it was impossible to leave her. I was growing as tall as him, but never as strong. I hated seeing him drinking all day, knowing at night my mother or I would have to face the consequences.'

'Mother would always make excuses for him, try to please him in every way. Not that it did any good. He'd still hit her for any small thing, and she'd have to hide herself away until the bruises faded.'

'It sounds horrendous,' Bridget murmured, sensing he needed to unburden himself as she had just done.

'One day a few years ago,' Lincoln continued, 'my father lost a bet and was drunk. He came upstairs where our living quarters were and took out his frustration on my mother. I'd been away working...' He shook his head. 'As much as I hated living there, I couldn't leave my mother to face my father alone. I'd return every Saturday and be with her until Monday morning. As a man, my father had stopped hitting me for he knew he'd get back as good as he got, so I tried to shield my mother from him when I could.'

Taking another sip of tea, Lincoln ran his hands through his hair. 'I came home one Saturday to screaming. I ran upstairs and found my father beating Mother. She was in such a mess, her face battered. I lost my temper and flung myself at him to drag him off her, but he wouldn't let her go. He was trying to kill her. He said he wanted to kill her. His rage was ugly, and I knew my mother would die. I grabbed the iron poker near the fireplace and struck him with it, more than once. Saving my mother was all I cared about, but also, deep inside me I wanted revenge on all the times he'd hurt me, on all the times he made Mother cry and bleed...'

Bridget wanted to comfort him but couldn't. She wasn't ready to cross the gap between them.

'I hit him too many times on the head. He fell to the ground dead.' Lincoln's voice was a flat tone. 'My mother, barely alive herself, pleaded with me to run, to go away. She said she'd take the blame, that she would confess because she knew she'd not survive. She said I wasn't going to hang for killing that hateful bastard. I didn't want to leave her. I wanted to fetch a doctor, but she wouldn't let me until I promised to tell the doctor that she had killed my father.'

Swiftly Lincoln stood and paced a few yards around the campfire, agitated. 'Mother said if I loved her then I would do that last thing for her. She didn't want to die knowing I would swing for killing a man who had tortured us both for so long.'

'Your mother sounds like a brave woman.'

Lincoln nodded. 'She was. And yet, I let her take the blame for killing him. I fetched the doctor and the constable and Mother lasted long enough to tell them she killed him in self-defence before she died of her injuries in my arms.' Lincoln rubbed his hands over his face as though to wash the memories from his mind.

Sympathy rose in her chest for him and the pain he'd been harbouring for years. 'It was what your mother wanted and, as your mother, she was protecting you from wasting your life by confessing. It was the one thing she could do for you after years of abuse.'

He squatted down and poked a stick at the fire. 'That doesn't make it easier to live with. I killed my father and everyone in Tasmania believes my mother did it. What kind of man does that make me?'

The anguish on his face was hard for Bridget to see. 'It makes you a man who loved his mother and bowed to her wishes, so she'd die in peace, knowing she'd saved her son. Let her have that.'

'The newspapers had a great time reporting on all the drama. The whole town understood my father was a man to be wary of and felt sorry for my mother, but they never believed it would end as it did, and I had to face them all, hear their condolences. Live a lie. I had murdered him.'

'Is that why you left Tasmania?'

Lincoln returned to sit on the log. 'Yes. I sold the inn. I needed to get away, but I've found that the memories remain in your head with the pain and the guilt. Which is why I vowed to never drink alcohol so I wouldn't end up a drunk like my father.'

'But why not to marry?'

'In case I ever lost my temper and hit my wife or children as my father did.'

'Do you lose your temper often?'

It took a minute for him to answer, as if considering the question for the first time. 'Rarely at all.'

'Then you are nothing like your father.'

'Perhaps not, but the fear of turning into him has kept me from living my life fully.'

'Then maybe it's time you started living without the past controlling your decisions?'

Lincoln took a ragged breath. 'I believe it is something we both should do.'

A wave of tiredness flowed over Bridget. 'I need to lie down.' She left him and climbed into the tent. Pulling the blanket over her she shivered with cold. Her mind played over the scene by the fire. So much had been said, revealed.

Lincoln had loved her before the kidnap. Did he still feel the same now he knew the truth about her? She couldn't blame him if he didn't.

Chapter Twenty-One

The freezing cold woke Bridget early the following morning. As she left the tent, she was shocked to see the campsite covered with a light dusting of snow.

Wrapping the blanket about her like a cape, she walked into the trees to relieve herself. Grey clouds blanketed the sky and the icy conditions had quietened the wildlife.

There was no sign of Lincoln by the campfire, so she set about bringing the embers back to life by adding twigs to get enough heat to boil the billycan. She built a huge fire to stave off the cold, warming herself as she made the tea.

Her thoughts wandered to the night before, of Lincoln's honesty and her own outpouring of emotions. Amazingly, she felt better for the outburst, stronger, as though she'd gone through some sort of cleansing like the natives did at their special ceremonies.

For so long she had kept her feelings in tight control, not daring to think about what was happening to her, what she had done and what she had endured to survive. Perhaps the explosion of emotion would help heal her enough to face the future. She hoped so. Her family would not understand what she had gone through for she didn't imagine she'd ever repeat everything again so truthfully as she had done last night to Lincoln. The entire episode was over, and her family deserved for her to try and cope the best she could and be the Bridget they thought her to be.

She didn't know if that was possible, but for them, she'd have to give it her best.

Lincoln arrived back at camp, his rifle slung over his arm. 'I sense every animal is hiding out of this weather.'

'I couldn't blame them,' she replied.

She thought she'd be awkward with him after the confessions and feelings of last night, but thankfully she didn't, and Lincoln didn't act out of character either. All the veneer of politeness had been stripped back, revealing their true selves and they had weathered it and come through the other side. There was nothing to hide now, no pretence, and there was a great sense of relief in that. In a companiable silence they simply attended to making some sort of breakfast with what they had left in supplies.

'I hadn't been expecting it to snow,' Lincoln said, returning to the fireside after moving the horses into the trees where there was more grass for them to eat. 'We don't have enough food or shelter to weather such conditions and the horses need better feed.'

'What do you suggest?'

'We should try and make it to Oberon.'

'Patrick won't know where we are.'

'He will. Before we left, he said if we do leave here then to head for Oberon. He'll check there before coming back into the mountains.'

She nodded. It was sensible. As much as she didn't want to be with people, the icy conditions were not suitable for camping without warm clothes and proper tents and cots.

Packing up, Lincoln paused to give her a tentative smile. 'You don't have to talk to anyone. I'll find you a room somewhere and you can stay there without being disturbed.'

'You are very kind.'

'Last night I told you about my sordid past and you listened with sympathy. After all you've been through you had the grace to let me unburden myself to you. That means more to me than anything in the world.'

She rose from the log and crossed the space between them. Taking his hand, she looked into his eyes. 'You did the same for me.'

He lifted her hand and kissed the back of it. 'I expect nothing from you, Bridget, but know, when the time comes, if you ever need me, then I'll be by your side for as long as you want me to be.'

Tears brimmed in her eyes at his sincerity. 'Thank you.'

With a nod he turned away.

They began the task of dismantling the camp, talking little as they packed the horses and doused the fire. With a last look, Bridget led Zeus from the campsite and up the slope. The frigid air caught her breath as they walked higher, the snow dusting her boots. For hours they trudged up and down the mountains, heading west until they made it out and onto the farming plains.

They rode until the sun began to set, and still were miles from Oberon.

'We need to find shelter,' Lincoln said as a bitter wind sprang up carrying with it sleet.

'Where shall we go?'

'There's a farmhouse over there.' He pointed to a wooden shack on the left, half hidden by trees.

Bridget urged Zeus towards it, frozen to the bone.

An old man with a long grey beard opened the door to them, his eyes widened in surprise. 'Good God, are you both mad to be out in this? Come away in.'

'The horses?' Lincoln said, stepping inside.

'There's a barn out the back, nothing much, but you can put them in there.' The old man took his coat off a peg on the wall. 'I'll come with you. I've some hay you can give them. I'm Albert, by the way, Albert Pennywise.' He shook Lincoln's hand.

'Pleased to meet you, Mr Pennywise. I'm Lincoln Huntley and this is Miss Bridget Kittrick. We are to meet Miss Kittrick's brother in Oberon, but the weather has beaten us today.'

'Indeed, it has. Only a fool would be out in it.' Albert chuckled. 'Miss, take a seat by the fire. I've a stew on the simmer and stewed pears for afterwards. Make yourself at home.'

Left in the ramshackle house, Bridget stepped to the fire while gazing about. The large room was stuffed with furniture and all manner of things, but despite that it was clean, if cluttered. The fireplace held a cooking pot on a swinging hook and beside that a small oven had been bricked into the chimney.

A table held a lamp that helped to light the room in a golden glow and at the far end, divided by a curtain, she spied a double bed. Another door in the side wall led somewhere, probably outside, but Bridget remained by the fire to thaw out her chilled body.

A few minutes later the old man returned, all smiles, and took off his coat. 'By it's nippy out there for sure. Mr Huntley is seeing to the horses. I've stacked more wood by the door for the night. It's started to snow again.' He limped over to the fire and Bridget realised he had a wooden leg.

'Thank you so much for helping us.'

'You're very welcome, lass.' He stirred the stew. 'Good job I made plenty.'

'We'll compensate you for the food and board,' she quickly assured him.

'Nay, your company is payment enough. It gets mighty lonely out here. I'm thinking of moving to Bathurst where my son has a shop. His wife, a dear sweet woman, worries about me being out here.'

'Sounds like you have a lovely family.'

'I do. Four grandsons, all grown now and spread far and wide, but they return home at Christmas. I should be closer to them all, really. The company would be nice.'

'Then I think you should,' Bridget encouraged. She had a deep longing for her mama. She missed her so much it was like a physical ache.

'I'll heat the warming pan and stick it in my bed for you.'

'Oh no! I couldn't take your bed.'

'And I might not be born a gentleman, but I was raised with manners and no woman will sleep on a hard chair or the floor while I sleep in a comfy bed, my wife would turn in her grave for sure. There are clean pillowslips that you can put on. My wife always had a clean pile ready.' He smiled warmly. 'I can see you've not had it easy, lass.'

Bridget stiffened.

'Now, don't be alarmed, but I've figured out who you are. I spend all my spare time reading every newspaper printed. What else is a man to do at night sitting by the fire alone?' He pointed to a large stack of newspapers beside a trunk in the corner of the room. 'As soon as I heard your name, I remembered reading about your kidnap. The reporters have made a drama of it, but it was also stated in the newspapers that the bushranger Sap killed you?' His wrinkled face looked confused.

'I heard he'd told the police that, too. I don't understand why.'

'But you were found.'

'My brother and Mr Huntley kept searching for me.' She didn't mention that Lincoln had refused to give up on finding her. The sudden thought of that made her heart leap. He had wanted to find her no matter what. That told her the kind of man he was.

'Well, I'm glad you're safe now, lass.'

'My brother has gone to Sydney to inform our oldest brother, and the police. I didn't want to be around people, but the weather became worse...'

Albert nodded sagely, setting out three bowls from a cupboard. 'You did right to seek shelter. You didn't want to survive being kidnapped only to die of cold.'

Lincoln entered, bringing in with him a blast of chilly air. He glanced at Bridget, and she smiled to reassure him she was fine.

'Mr Pennywise knows about me. He reads the newspapers and recognised my name.' Bridget sat at the table, trying not to worry that soon everyone would know Sap didn't kill her. She would become a sensation in the newspapers, gossip fodder. A shiver ran down her back.

'Oh.' Lincoln scowled.

'I'll not be telling a soul,' Albert promised. 'Miss Kittrick can stay here as long as she needs to.'

'That might be better?' Lincoln looked at Bridget. 'I can stay in Oberon until Patrick returns. It'll keep you away from people.'

Under the table, Bridget clenched her hands together. She didn't want to stay alone with the old man, as kind as he was. 'I'd rather come with you,' she murmured to Lincoln. The truth was she suddenly didn't want Lincoln out of her sight. He was the only one she trusted. He knew the truth.

'Beef, potatoes and turnips,' Albert said, ladling out the thick stew. 'I travelled to town yesterday and bought stewed pears from a widow, a friend of mine. You'll not taste better pears this side of the mountains. I call on her once a week to buy from her and have a cup of tea.'

'It smells delicious.' Bridget took a spoonful, and the savoury taste was pure nectar after eating simple basic food for months.

Lincoln caught her eye. 'I'll not leave you,' he whispered as Albert attended to the fire.

Relieved, she relaxed and ate the meal and listened to Albert talk of local village people in Oberon.

The following morning, they woke to a white world. Snow dusted every surface, but the sky was a bright blue and the sun shone, sparkling the ice crystals. Albert set about making porridge with milk from his own cow, a treat Bridget again had not tasted for months, as well as having milk in her tea and a spoonful of sugar.

The thing she wanted most was a bath. Never again would she take for granted having Una wash her hair with scented soap and then brush it dry. Bridget felt grubby. No doubt she looked it. Her clothes were beyond washing now and needed burning, especially her petticoats and shift. But dirt was ingrained into her skin, under her nails. However, the most unexpected event was her monthly curse starting. She wasn't with child. The information gave both relief and sadness. Thankfully, Albert gave her the opportunity to wash, and she sorted herself out with folded napkins she found in a drawer. There would be no baby to shame her further.

Lincoln and Albert entered the house after checking on the horses.

'We need to ride into Oberon village when you're ready,' Lincoln said, holding his hands out to the flames. 'I don't expect Patrick today, but he could arrive tomorrow. He said he'd be as fast as possible, just give the news to Austin and then return immediately. Including travelling, he might be in the village tomorrow. Albert says there is a stagecoach three times a week from Oberon to Bathurst that meets up with the Sydney to Bathurst coach. I dare say Patrick will be on that coach tomorrow.'

'Then let us go. I'm sure there is an inn in Oberon to accommodate us?' Bridget asked Albert.

'There isn't much in the village, but there is an inn, where the coach stops. You'll get a room, no doubt.' At the end of the bed, Albert opened a trunk. 'It's freezing out there, Miss Kittrick. You need something warm over you.' He pulled out a long black coat and knitted gloves. 'These belonged to my wife. She'd want you to have them. She hated seeing anyone suffering, and you'll suffer riding today without these.' He gave them to her with a fond smile. 'My Mary would be pleased to see them being used.'

'Thank you.' Tears gathered behind her eyes at his kindness. 'I'll never forgot your generosity, Mr Pennywise.'

'Well, I like to hope that if my family were ever in need, someone would help them. It never hurts to help others, does it? That's what my Mary used to say.'

'I wish I had met your Mary.' Bridget clasped his hand.

Albert tapped her hand. 'Right, let's be getting you both sorted.'

Half an hour later, mounted and waving goodbye to Albert, Lincoln led the way from the farm towards the village of Oberon. The sun rose melting the thin layer of snow except where it was shaded by trees.

She kept glancing at Lincoln, wondering what was on his mind as the rode along.

He gave her a smile. 'What is it?'

She shrugged.

'Everything will be fine, I promise.'

Bridget rubbed Zeus's neck. 'Will it?'

'Look to the future.'

'I don't know how.' She thought of home, Emmerson Park, Louisburgh, Huntley Vale, all her plans she had for creating a village there. 'Do you know if Roache burnt down Louisburgh or Huntley Vale?'

'No, he didn't. He disappeared the same day you did.'

Relief made her light-headed. 'I am sorry about Silas Pegg.'

'Poor man.'

'I'm responsible for his death because of Roache.'

'Death?' Lincoln reined in Blaze to stop beside her. 'Pegg isn't dead.'

'He isn't?'

'No, he nearly died of his injuries but the last I heard was that he was recovering slowly but will survive.'

'All this time I thought him dead.' She couldn't believe it. 'I'm so grateful to hear he lives.'

'His injuries aren't your fault. That whole incident was down to Roache.' Lincoln rode on.

Bridget nudged Zeus on. 'So Pegg told everyone about my kidnap?'

'No, Ronnie did.'

She remembered seeing the boy hiding in the trees and her heart swelled with gratitude. She would make sure that boy was always cared for.

Warm in Aunt Riona's shawl, the long coat and gloves, Bridget found the few miles to the tiny village passed quickly as her mind absorbed the news that Pegg lived, and Louisburgh remained intact.

Soon, they rode along a wide dirt street.

'That looks to be the inn.' Lincoln pointed to a white squat building made from wattle and daub with a timber slat roof. Behind it stood several outbuildings of the same description housing horses and various carts. Along the street huts in square fenced gardens lined the road.

They dismounted in the yard as a woman wearing a white apron came out of the back of the inn with a bucket. Geese honked from a pen near the stables and chickens pecked around the yard.

'Needing a feed?' the woman asked, throwing the bucket of water over an empty garden bed.

'And two rooms if you have any?' Lincoln asked.

'I've one. Only a single.' The woman turned to a young boy peeking over the half door of the stable. 'Fred! Get over here and see to these horses.' She glanced back at Lincoln and Bridget. 'Just the one room as I said. If you're not fussy, sir,' she continued, staring at Lincoln, 'you can bed down in the barn. Plenty do.'

'Thank you. We'll take the room.'

'And the meal?'

'Yes.'

The woman sniffed and went back inside.

'Do we follow her?' Bridget asked.

Lincoln grinned. 'I suppose so. She isn't very welcoming, is she?'

A smile tugged at the corners of her mouth. 'We could ride on to Bathurst.'

'We could...' Lincoln's expression showed he was weighing up the option.

Abruptly, a thundering sound vibrated the air. Over the rise in the road came a carriage being pulled by four horses.

'Is that the Sydney coach?' Lincoln frowned. 'Albert said it was to be tomorrow.'

'It looks like a private carriage to me.' The loud rumble of the carriage wheels shattered the quietness of the yard. Bridget winced at the sound, at the prospect of mingling with others in the inn.

The driver hauled the horses to a stop, scattering squawking chickens. A man descended with his back to them and helped down a lady dressed in dark brown fringed with black, with a sloping hat decorated with small black feathers. Immediately the woman was out of place in the tiny rustic village.

Bridget gaped at the elegance of the outfit. Then the woman turned, and Bridget cried out in utter surprise. Aunt Riona.

She ran, crying to the woman who was like a second mother to her, nearly knocking her aunt off her feet as she threw herself at her.

'Gracious!' Aunt Riona gasped and stepped back, eyes wide until she realised who was before her. 'Bridget! Sweet Mary and her angels. It's you!'

Crying helplessly, Bridget sank into her aunt's arms.

'Oh, my darling, darling girl.' Aunt Riona held her so tight Bridget thought she'd stopped breathing and didn't even care.

'Let us look at her then.' Austin grabbed Bridget from his aunt and hugged her tightly. 'By God, you are truly alive,' he whispered, his voice thick with emotion.

Cradled by Austin and her aunt, Bridget sniffed and wiped her eyes, hardly daring to believe she was with them.

Patrick, the last to leave the carriage, gave her a wink. 'It was impossible to leave them behind,' he joked.

'As if I would stay in Sydney when my niece has been found?' Aunt Riona rebuked him but smiled too. Her eyes wet with tears, Aunt Riona clutched Bridget to her. 'We'll get you home, precious one.'

'There will be interviews with the police,' Austin said gently, his forehead creased with worry. 'In Bathurst. We will be with you the whole time.'

Cringing at the thought of police questions, Bridget looked at Lincoln who stood apart from them, allowing the family to be together. 'If I must talk to the police, then I will.'

'First, we get her to the hotel in Bathurst,' Aunt Riona declared. 'She is not going to face anyone until she has bathed and is dressed appropriately.'

'Am I that bad, Aunt?' Bridget asked self-consciously.

Aunt Riona cupped Bridget's cheek. 'Dear girl, you look like your mammy did when she fell in a bog on her way home one time back in Ireland. A pig smelled sweeter than she did, and you are exactly the same.'

Her brothers chuckled, but the mention of their mother made them all sad.

'I wish she was here,' Bridget murmured.

'I know, but I'm also glad she didn't have to live through what we have done.' Aunt Riona guided her to the carriage. 'Let us go.'

'Wait, Zeus, my horse.' She wouldn't be without Zeus. He was Donovan's.

'I'll bring the horses to Bathurst,' Lincoln spoke for the first time. 'I'll see you there tomorrow.'

Bridget stepped to him and took both his hands. For a long moment she stared into his eyes. She didn't want to leave him. 'You promise you'll be there?'

'I will. I ran from you once before, I'll not be doing it again.'

'Even after all that I have done?' she whispered. How could he bear to look at her after she'd slept with another man?

A tender look of love warmed his eyes, and he brought her hands up to kiss the back of them. 'Neither of us are without fault. You did what you did because it felt right at the time. I'll never judge you for that.'

'But—'

'No, buts.' His voice dropped to a whisper. 'I've never loved you more, trust me in that.'

'I do.' She squeezed his hands, fearful to let go. He'd been the one she'd revealed everything to, the one who listened, not criticised. Lincoln's strength, his quiet caring had given her the courage to go on.

In return, he had trusted her with his secrets, opened himself to her with honesty and vulnerability.

The shadow of Donovan hovered behind her, but no matter what the future brought, she knew Lincoln Huntley would be there and that was her greatest comfort.

Acknowledgments

Dear readers,

Thank you for choosing my book to read. I thoroughly enjoyed writing about Bridget's story. Since starting the first book, A Distant Horizon, about Bridget's mother, Ellen, I always sensed there would be a series. As books one and two formed and Bridget's character grew, I knew she'd have to have a book of her own. Further down the line, I'd like to write Austin and and Patrick's stories. I might write about all the children, we'll have to see.

Australian history is fascinating. The Victorian era was raw and unique with settlers struggling to tame the land against disease and wild weather conditions from droughts to floods. Bushrangers were, for a period, a challenge to the authorities. Most were ex-convicts, but some were free settlers who turned to crime, especially once the gold rush hit and there was more money and gold travelling the roads. Bushrangers were either seen as villains or heroes, depending on your perspective, but they were definitely written about in the newspapers of the day. Their every deed, robbery, escape or capture made headline news. For research, I read the book, Bushrangers

(Australia's Greatest Self-Made Heroes) by Evan McHugh. Fascinating stuff. I wanted to create my own version of bushranger villains and heroes in The Distant Legacy. I hope I've done that.

As always, I'd like to thank all my readers for their encouragement and their support. Receiving personal messages from readers via my website makes me so very happy, and those who say hi on Facebook, or who tell others that they've enjoyed one of my stories gives me a thrill every time. Also, a special thank you goes out to all those who leave reviews on Amazon. Thank you. Being an author is all I've ever wanted to do, so to live my dream is something I will never take for granted.

A huge thank you to my husband and family. They put up with me living in another century most of the time!

With love and gratefulness,

AnneMarie Brear

NSW Australia 2022

Also By

Kitty McKenzie's Land

Southern Sons

<u>The Slum Angel Series</u>

The Slum Angel

The Slum Angel Christmas

<u>Marsh Saga Series</u>

Millie

Christmas at the Chateau

Prue

Cece

Alice

<u>The Beaumont Series</u>

The Market Stall Girl

The Woman from Beaumont Farm

<u>The Distant Series</u>

A Distant Horizon

Beyond the Distant Hills

<u>Contemporary</u>

Long Distance Love

Hooked on You

About Author

AnneMarie was born in a small town in N.S.W. Australia, to English parents from Yorkshire, and is the youngest of five children. From an early age she loved reading, working her way through the Enid Blyton stories, before moving onto Catherine Cookson's novels as a teenager.

Living in England during the 1980s and more recently, AnneMarie developed a love of history from visiting grand old English houses and this grew into a fascination with what may have happened behind their walls over their long existence. Her enjoyment of visiting old country estates and castles when travelling and, her interest in genealogy and researching her family tree, has been put to good use, providing backgrounds and names for her historical novels which are mainly set in Yorkshire or Australia between Victorian times and WWII.

A long and winding road to publication led to her first novel being published in 2006. She has now published over thirty historical family saga novels, becoming an Amazon best seller and with her novel, The Slum Angel, winning a gold medal at the USA Reader's Favourite International

Awards. Two of her books have been nominated for the Romance Writer's Australia Ruby Award and the USA In'dtale Magazine Rone award and recently she has been nominated as a finalist for the UK RNA RONA Awards.

AnneMarie lives in the Southern Highlands of N.S.W. Australia.

You can learn about AnneMarie's books at her website and sign up for her quarterly newsletter. http://www.annemariebrear.com

http://www.facebook.com/annemariebrear

CPSIA information can be obtained
at www.ICGtesting.com
Printed in the USA
BVHW032355170123
656422BV00020B/67